PRAISE FOR
Gordon R. Dickson's
"DRAGON KNIGHT" adventures . . .

"Since the beginning of his career, Dickson
has been . . . providing readers with some of science
fiction's finest moments."   —*Omni*

"One of the long-lasting pros!"
—*Asimov's Science Fiction*

"One of the more underrated medievalists in
contemporary fantasy."   —*Chicago Sun-Times*

"Dickson writes adventure with a flair for the details
that bring a person or place to life."
—*Reader's Guide to Science Fiction*

"A major writer in the field."   —*Fantasy Review*

"Entertaining books that move at a fast pace, with action
and fighting as well as commentary on scientific
thinking."   —*SF Commentary*

. . . and "THE CHILDE CYCLE"—
Tales of the Dorsai

"The grandest saga in the history of science
fiction."   —*Ben Bova*

"Makes me want to stand up and cheer!"   —*Analog*

THE DRAGON, THE EARL, AND THE TROLL

GORDON R. DICKSON

ACE BOOKS, NEW YORK

This Ace Book contains the complete text of the original hardcover edition.

THE DRAGON, THE EARL, AND THE TROLL

An Ace Book / published by arrangement with
the author

PRINTING HISTORY
Ace hardcover edition / December 1994
Ace mass-market edition / January 1996

ISBN: 0-441-00282-X

ACE®
Ace Books are published by The Berkley Publishing Group,
200 Madison Avenue, New York, New York 10016.
ACE and the "A" design are trademarks
belonging to Charter Communications, Inc.

PRINTED IN THE UNITED STATES OF AMERICA

10 9 8 7 6 5 4 3 2 1

To Kirby McCauley,
with respect and gratitude

CHAPTER 1

The Hobgoblin had come out into the kitchen again.

"I can't understand it!" Jim said. "Fleas, lice, rats, hedgehogs looking for a warm place to sleep—but hobgoblins!"

"Calm down," said Angie.

"Why do we have to have hobgoblins?" demanded Jim.

All hobgoblins lived in chimneys. They were small, harmless, sometimes beneficial Naturals. You left out a bowl of milk—or whatever you had to share with them—every night.

The Hobgoblin would drink or eat that, and not bother anything else. But the Malencontri kitchen Hobgoblin apparently went on periodic binges. He did not drink anything, unless it was milk; but when on a binge he took one bite only out of everything else that was eatable in the kitchen—and after that the kitchen workers would not touch anything he might have touched, for some superstitious reason.

"Calm down—" said Angie . . .

"—Remember?" said Angie now. "And that was just the day before yesterday."

She nestled a little closer with her head in the hollow of Jim's shoulder as they stood together, the only people awake and on their feet along the wooden walkway just behind the top of the curtain wall—that later centuries would rush to call "the battlements" of a castle—of their home, *Malencontri*.

A December dawn, icy under a cloud-heavy sky, was just breaking. In its gray light they looked out on the trampled open space before the wall, to the thick surround of forest, some hundred yards away, from which a few pencil-thin ghosts of gray smoke were beginning to rise, back a small distance behind the first treetops.

Yesterday's blood had turned black on the snow and become indistinguishable from the blackness of the miry ground, where snow and bare earth had been ground together into equally black mud, under heavy boots and iron heels.

A little snow had fallen during the late afternoon of the attack, and had to a certain extent hidden the dark shapes that lay still on the ground—those of their attackers who had been left to the crows and other scavengers that would follow after Malencontri had been taken. As taken it would be, today.

Its defenders were too few, and now too exhausted. Along the walkway to the right and left of where Jim and Angie stood, worn-out archers, crossbowmen and men-at-arms—those still able to fight in spite of their wounds—had fallen asleep where they had stood to push back the attackers that tried to climb in from scaling ladders on the outside of the curtain wall.

Given sufficient defenders inside her walls, Malencontri could have held off an army, let alone this small force of two or three knights with perhaps a hundred and fifty trained men-at-arms and archers and a couple hundred ragtag and bobtail of the lower classes, armed with whatever they had been able to bring or acquire on their raid into this part of Somerset.

But Malencontri had had no warning—not even time enough to call in the people who belonged to it from the surrounding forest and fields that were part of the fief, who might have swelled their force to the point where the attackers would have no chance.

As it was, the attackers must clearly be in ignorance of the fact that Jim was in the castle. Otherwise they would never have had the courage to attack a fortification owned by any low-ranking magician—let alone one who had the notoriety that Jim had gained as the Dragon Knight.

"They'll be waking up now out there," murmured Angie.

"Yes," said Jim. He, too, had been watching the fingers of smoke from the remnants of the overnight fires of their attackers; watching for an increase in the smoke they sent up, as new fuel was added and some kind of food was cooked or warmed for those who would attack again today.

"At any rate," said Angie, squeezing Jim's waist with the arm she had around it, "this ends all hopes for the baby." She was silent a moment. "Was I really unbearable to you with all my worrying about her?"

"No," Jim said. He kissed her. "You've never been unbearable. You know that."

The baby, as it had come to be referred to, had been Angie's particular concern for the last year or so. She was only in her mid-twenties; but here, history was still in the Middle Ages, and all around her much younger women—girls even—were having children. She had been torn between her desire for a child and her feeling, which she shared with Jim, that it would be unfair to have it here.

Let alone bring it up in this medieval time, which was still in the equivalent of what had been the fourteenth century, in contrast to the twentieth-century version of Earth from which they had come.

So they had simply put off having children. Now, it was too late—which was probably just as well, given the fact that the attackers would kill everything living in the castle, once they had got inside.

"In fact," said Jim, "I should have found a way back for us before this."

"You did once, in the beginning," said Angie. "I talked you out of it."

"No, you didn't."

"Yes, I did."

They were both right, in a sense. For a brief time, after Jim had come here to rescue Angie from the Dark Powers that strove to upset the balance of Chance and History in this medieval version of Earth, Jim had possessed enough magical credit to send them both back to the twentieth century.

Angie had said then that she wanted to do what he wanted to do; and the truth was, he had wanted to stay. They both had—they still would have, if it had not been for the matter of the baby.

But then, neither of them had looked ahead to the fact that they would go on living, go on aging; and that a day like this day might dawn, in which it was practically certain that they both would die—hopefully before they could be captured; because if so they could only look forward to being crucified, impaled or tortured by those who would overrun and pillage their castle; as the attackers could hardly be stopped from doing before the sun set again.

In what the Middle Ages considered a "legal war," Jim and Angie and any children of theirs would have been held to ransom. But not in a raid like this, which was itself "illegal."

Jim looked again at the wisps of smoke. It was impossible to say whether they had started to thicken or darken at all; but the day was definitely brightening, and it could not be long now before those out there would be up and stirring. Some of Malencontri's men-at-arms had recognized some of those who were trying to get into the castle. They were retainers of Sir Peter Carley, a knight formerly in fief to the Earl of Somerset who had come to a parting of the ways with the Earl and now was in fief to the Earl of Oxford.

Since his violent parting with the Earl, Sir Peter had, in common fourteenth-century fashion, regarded all those in Somerset as legitimate prey; and he had used the recent march of a mob of peasants in revolt to London as an excuse to raid into the Somerset area—and it was this that had brought him to Malencontri.

"I hate to rouse them," said Angie, looking at the archers and men-at-arms that lay huddled against the inner stonework of the wall, curled up to conserve as much body heat as possible while they slept. "I don't know why most of them haven't simply frozen there, lying in the open like this."

"Some may," said Jim.

"Maybe it'll be easier on them, that way," said Angie. "I can't believe that none of our messengers got through. We had so many friends . . ."

Indeed, they had many friends. It was one of the things that caused them to be attached to this fourteenth century, in spite of its hobgoblins, hedgehogs, rats, fleas, lice . . . Naturals, magicians, sorcerers, Dark Powers—and everything else that made life here either interesting or perilous.

In fact, some of those they knew were almost more than good friends—incredibly loyal, trustworthy, back-you-up-and-come-to-your-rescue-at-any-time-without-question sort of friends. The mysterious thing was that none of these had come to help them this time.

It was true, Jim thought, that the messengers to these friends for help had been sent out, literally, within minutes after their attackers had been discovered less than half a mile from the castle. It was possible that all the messengers had been captured by those now trying to take Malencontri; and at this moment they were all very dead. But some should have got through.

True, both Dafydd ap Hywel and Giles o'the Wold were far enough off so that they might have not heard from the messenger and been able to get back here, in the two days since the attackers had first arrived.

But Sir Brian Neville-Smythe's castle—Castle Smythe—was less than a fifteen-minute gallop from Malencontri; and Malvern Castle, the fortress of which the Lady Geronde Isabel de Chaney was Chatelaine—she to whom Sir Brian was betrothed—was not an impossible distance off. Sir Brian should have come, and Geronde have sent fighting men to their rescue, if messengers had been able to reach them safely. But no assistance from either one had shown up.

Most curious of all was the nonappearance of Aargh the English wolf, who invariably knew everything that was happening in the land for miles around. Aargh might have been expected to show up on his own initiative; certainly he would have done so if he had known what was going on. He had come to join them in their beleaguered castle, earlier this same year, running literally over the backs of hundreds of closely packed sea serpents to do so, and needing to be hauled up from the moat with his teeth clenched in a rope dropped from the curtain wall to him.

For that matter, the failure of Carolinus to show up was also mysterious. True, Jim had foolishly overspent his magic reserve— this time in what even Angie would consider a good cause (but Carolinus would not)—helping to get the harvest in, this fall, and the castle prepared for winter.

But none of them had appeared.

"Most likely, the messengers didn't get through," said Jim, avoiding the fact that Angie would know as well as he that neither Aargh nor Carolinus should have needed to be summoned. They should have known when Malencontri was under attack; and then both would have come out of friendship—though neither of them would admit to such a weakness; and Carolinus additionally would have appeared out of a sense of responsibility to his apprentice in magic, which Jim happened to be.

"It doesn't matter," murmured Angie into Jim's chest.

"GREETINGS!" boomed an enormous voice.

Jim and Angie looked up, startled, to see a giant—a real giant, thirty feet if he was an inch—approaching the curtain wall from the woods with twenty-foot strides.

CHAPTER 2

"**R**rrnlf!" said Angie.

It was indeed the sea devil, whom they had met earlier in the year when the sea serpents had attempted an invasion of England in collaboration with the French. The most unlikely of rescuers—if he was indeed that.

Jim's gaze flew to the smoke streams above the treetops. Rrrnlf was advancing from an area of the surrounding trees not at all far from where the smoke streamers had been ascending. Now, Jim saw they were still there, but they were certainly no thicker or darker—implying the fires underneath them had not been refueled—and in fact if anything they were more thin and ghostlike than ever, as if those same fires were dying out.

Jim looked quickly back at the sea devil. Rrrnlf was almost to the curtain wall now and seeming to loom above them already.

Rrrnlf was not only a Natural, but one of the largest inhabitants of this world's oceans; though he also was apparently quite comfortable not only in fresh water but in the open air as he was now. However, aside from his thirty feet of height, his body had a strange construction.

Essentially, he was wedge-shaped, the point of the wedge being downward. He literally tapered from the top of his head to the soles of his feet. His head was large even for the rest of him. His shoulders were somewhat smaller than they should have been, according to human proportions, but only a little. However,

below those shoulders not only did his body taper toward the waist, but his arms narrowed down toward his hands—though not excessively, for his hands were as large as the shovel ends of a derrick. But from his waist he continued tapering down to feet that were only several times as large as Jim's. It was remarkable how those relatively tiny feet bore the weight of the rest of him about so briskly and without complaint. But of course, like all Naturals, there was a touch of innate magic in him; though, again like all Naturals, he had no real control over it.

He had reached the wall now. He put one massive hand on the top of it and vaulted over its twenty-foot height, landing on his feet in the courtyard. The wall shook, waking up all the sleepers along it, while the impact of his massive weight on the packed earth of the courtyard probably produced enough sound to wake up most of the rest of those exhaustedly slumbering inside the castle buildings.

"*Thu ne grete—*" he began, slipping into the Anglo-Saxon speech of a thousand years before. He checked. "I mean—you didn't say greetings to me!" he accused, looking down on them, with a reproachful frown from his heavy-boned, blue-eyed face, some dozen feet above them as they stood on the walkway.

"Greetings!" said Jim and Angie hastily and simultaneously.

Rrrnlf's visage cleared. It became a rather simple, friendly face, with nothing really terrifying about it except its size.

"My mother always told me this was the season for greetings amongst you wee folk," he rumbled, "or have I lost track of time and customs changed since I was here last?"

"No, Rrrnlf," said Angie, "you were here only five months or so ago."

"So I was!" said Rrrnlf. "I didn't think it had been too long. I've just had time to find some gifts for you. My mother—did I ever tell you about my mother?"

"Yes," said Jim, "you did."

"I had a beautiful mother," said Rrrnlf almost dreamily, paying no attention at all to what Jim had said. "She was beautiful. I can't remember exactly how she looked; but I remember she was beautiful. She took care of me for the first four or five hundred years while I was growing up. There never was a mother like that. Anyway, she told me lots of things; and one of them was that around this time of the year when the deep-sea currents change, you wee people greet each other and some of you give others gifts. Because you helped me so

much in getting back my Lady, I wanted to be sure I gave you gifts this year. I had some trouble finding them, but I've got some."

Rrrnlf's Lady, Jim had discovered earlier, had been the demountable figurehead of a ship, like the dragon figureheads that the Vikings took down from their long ships when putting in to land; because the land trolls were supposed to feel themselves challenged if the dragon heads were brought into their territory. But in this case, it had been a wooden carving from a sunken ship, intended to represent the ninth wave.

The folk saying was that "the ninth wave always came farthest up the beach," and the Norse people had called the ninth wave Jarnsaxa—'*the Iron Sword*'.

Jarnsaxa had been the daughter of Aegir, the Norse sea god, and Ran, the giantess. Those two had been the parents of all nine daughters who were the nine waves. Last and greatest of these was Jarnsaxa; and Rrrnlf had claimed that—wild as it sounded— he and the actual Jarnsaxa had been lovers. But he had lost her, when Aegir and Ran left with the other Norse gods and giants, taking their daughters with them.

So he had valued the figurehead very highly. But it had been stolen from him as part of the events leading to the attack of the sea serpents on England.

Jim had managed to rouse Carolinus—one of only three AAA+ magicians in this world—from a deep depression just in time to defeat the giant, deep-sea squid who was the mastermind behind the serpents; and so regain the figurehead for Rrrnlf.

"So, here they are, now," said Rrrnlf, dipping a massive hand into the pouch that hung from what looked like a small cable around his relatively narrow waist, tied over the skin—or whatever it was—he wore, wrapped caveman-fashion, around him and hanging from one shoulder, to end in a sort of kiltlike lower edge just above his knees.

The hand enclosed and hid what he first brought up, and he extended that massive fist toward Angie, who unconsciously took half a step backward from it.

"Here you are!" said Rrrnlf, apparently not noticing the fact that Angie had recoiled. "This is for you, wee Lady. Hold out your hands."

Angie held out both hands cupped together, and very carefully Rrrnlf gradually opened his enormous fist, shook it a little—and

something that seemed to be an assortment of tied-together small objects, glinting red in the clouded early daylight, dropped into Angie's hands, half filling them.

Angie gasped.

Jim stared.

What Angie held appeared to be some sort of necklace, with several strands all connected to a single strand that possibly was meant to tie or fasten behind the neck. Ornamenting each strand were what seemed to be—but what it was hard to believe could be, large as they were—enormous rubies. They had not been cut and faceted, as twentieth-century cut gems would have been; but they had been polished, and they shone with beautiful warmth against the gray day and the background of wintry trees, stone, snow and trampled earth.

"—And for you, wee mage," said Rrrnlf.

Jim got his own hands cupped out in front of him just in time to receive a box, about ten inches long by eight wide and four deep, beautifully carved and colored; with figures on its top and all sides, of what looked more like writing in Sanskrit than anything else.

The box was extraordinarily light. Because Rrrnlf seemed to be expecting him to do so, Jim made an attempt to lift the lid. It came up easily.

The box was empty. Clean, white-brown wood, beautifully fitted, enclosed a space with absolutely nothing in it except a space smelling faintly but pleasantly of a scent like cedar.

Jim put a large smile on his face and opened his mouth to thank Rrrnlf. But Angie, who had now recovered from her shock on seeing her own gift, was ahead of him.

"Rrrnlf!" she said. "They're enormous! Where did you find them?"

"Oh, on the sea bottom, somewhere. Some wreck of an old ship . . ."

Rrrnlf peered down at the rubies still cupped in Angie's two hands.

"Enormous? No, no. You're being kind, wee Lady, like you usually do. But I'll find something else for you, to help make your gift equal with the one I gave the wee mage. I promise. By the way, how do you like his present? That did take some getting, I can tell you! It's a box to keep his magic in."

"Oh—it is?" said Jim. "I mean—of course it is! Just what I've needed. I couldn't believe that I'd actually gotten something like that. I've just been looking at it, having trouble believing it's real!"

He caught Angie's eye.

"Yes," said Angie, "yes, indeed. Jim will never forget this present, Rrrnlf. I can promise you that!"

"Oh, well . . ." Rrrnlf almost simpered.

"Oh, well," he said, again. "It's nothing, really. But it'll do for a gift for now, anyway. But I really promise you, wee Lady, that I'll make up your gift into something more worthy just as soon as I can."

"You needn't, Rrrnlf," said Angie very sincerely. It occurred to Jim belatedly that Angie almost undoubtedly did not realize that what she held might not be real rubies, but spinels. The Black Prince's ruby, back in the fourteenth century of their own world, had been a spinel; and no one had known the difference then. Gems had not been cut in those days, and even an expert would have had trouble seeing the difference between the two shades of a real ruby and an isotropic spinel ruby. In this world and time, what Rrrnlf had just given Angie might as well be real rubies. The best thing for Jim to do would be to say nothing; and just be surprised along with Angie, if it was discovered later that the rubies were indeed spinels.

Trying to think of something more to say by way of thanks to Rrrnlf for the gift of the empty box, pretty as it was, Jim glanced out over the curtain wall and instantly noticed that the upward lines of smoke had faded almost to invisibility above the forest. The necessities of the present drove everything else out of his mind. He turned sharply on Rrrnlf.

"You came in from over that way," he said, pointing. "Tell me, did you see anything of other—er, wee men among the woods?"

"No," said Rrrnlf thoughtfully. "I wasn't paying too much attention, of course."

He brightened.

"I did see quite a flock of wee people further off, going away from here in that direction—all together and rather quickly."

He pointed off toward the east, at about a ninety-degree angle from the direction of his own approach to the castle.

Angie and Jim turned to each other instinctively and hugged each other in relief.

"They probably saw you coming and ran!" said Angie to the Sea Devil as soon as she came up for air. She and Jim separated.

"I wouldn't have hurt them," Rrrnlf protested. "I would have told them. I would have said, 'I'm Rrrnlf. I'm a Sea Devil. I'm your friend.' "

"Never mind, Rrrnlf," said Angie. "We're your friends; and so is everybody in the castle here. You've got lots of friends here."

"True—" said Rrrnlf, brightening.

"True? What's true?" demanded Carolinus, appearing suddenly on the walkway beside Jim.

"*Now* you get here!" said Angie, with no note of comfort in her voice at all.

"It's true that I've got lots of friends," Rrrnlf was telling the Master Magician. "But you probably knew that yourself, Mage."

The way Rrrnlf pronounced the word "Mage," speaking to Carolinus, was very definitely different from the way he pronounced it when referring to Jim as a "wee mage." Neither Rrrnlf nor anybody else ever referred to Carolinus as wee; although this had nothing to do with his physical size. In fact, he was a frail, white-bearded and rather skinny old man—if tall—in a red robe that could invariably stand washing. Angie happened to know that he had a number of such robes; but he also had a tendency to let the ones he had worn for some time simply pile up in a corner of his cottage by the Tinkling Water, until he thought of telling them magically to be clean again—so that he always looked as if the robe was something thrown away by a more prosperous magician.

"I've just been giving the wee mage and his wee Lady gifts because they helped me get my Lady back. You helped too, Mage. I'm sorry I don't have a gift for you. But look at what I gave the wee mage!"

Carolinus looked.

"A soothing box!" he said. He took the box from Jim, opened it, looked inside, sniffed, closed the lid and handed it back to Jim again. "You should be grateful, Jim."

There had been a dry note in Carolinus's voice, particularly in his last words. And he had called Jim "Jim"—which no one here in the fourteenth century, except Angie, ever did. He was otherwise always addressed as James, Sir James, the Dragon Knight, or "my Lord."

Jim would ordinarily have had no objection to being spoken to familiarly, except that there was something about the way Carolinus said it that made it almost a contemptuous form of address, as if he was speaking to a poorly trained dog. But

Carolinus, in addition to being one of only three AAA+ magicians in this world at the present moment (Jim was only a C–rated magician and Carolinus had openly expressed his doubt that Jim would ever go any farther), addressed everybody familiarly—commoners, kings, Naturals, fellow magicians or even the Accounting Office—which kept track of each magician's level of magical credit. Jim had once heard the Accounting Office make land, sea and sky tremble at once with the sound of an imperative order from its bass voice; but it was always polite to Carolinus.

Jim was resigned to the Master Magician's ways, now. Not so Angie, at this moment. Jim could see her stiffen with resentment. Right at the moment, Angie was not in a mood to have anyone speak contemptuously to Jim. Particularly Carolinus, who had not been here when needed.

"He can keep his magic in it," Rrrnlf was saying, beaming down at Carolinus.

"I don't need a Sea Devil to tell me that!" snapped Carolinus.

"No, Mage," said Rrrnlf contritely. "Of course not. I just—"

He was interrupted—which was something of a feat, considering the volume of his voice—by the raucous sound of a hunting horn. Or rather, the sound of a cow horn fitted with a nipple, so that what came out when it was blown was more like a musical tone and less like a raucous squawk.

They all turned and looked out over the curtain wall. A column of armed men was approaching from about the segment of woods that Rrrnlf had appeared from. At its head rode a figure in armor that was clearly Jim and Angie's very good friend Sir Brian Neville-Smythe; and riding beside him was a diminutive female figure, decorously wearing a tall, peaked hat, from which depended an equally decorous travel veil, to keep out the dust and other annoyances in the atmosphere while moving from place to place.

Someone who could be no one else than Brian's betrothed, Geronde Isabel de Chaney, who was indeed decorous—after her fashion. She was also Chatelaine of Malvern Castle and sole authority there, now that her father had been nearly three years gone to the Crusade.

"Hail, hail, the gang's all here!" muttered Angie.

Jim had not been wrong in what he had thought he had just seen and felt in her. She was in a dangerous mood, not only toward Carolinus, but against these friends to whom they had sent messengers for help and who were now appearing after Rrrnlf's fortuitous appearance had caused the attackers to run.

To put the icing on the cake of this particular situation, another familiar figure, four-legged, trotted out of the woods to join Sir Brian's group, moving along on the other side of the Lady Geronde from Sir Brian, and wagging his tail at her. It was Aargh, the English wolf.

"Carolinus!" exploded Angie. "What's the meaning of this? Don't try to tell me you aren't responsible for all this! Did you deliberately keep everyone from coming to help us?"

"Oh, Aargh did see how it was and came to me for help," said Carolinus. "There were too many of them attacking you for him to do much by himself. As it happened, I was gone to a special Emergency Meeting of magicians of A-rank and above. So, since Sir Brian lives closest to you, Aargh went looking for him; but found him and most of his men gone from his castle. The retainers that were left knew Aargh, however, and told him Brian had gone to pick up Geronde and her train at Malvern Castle; because the two of them were going to the Earl's Christmastide. So Aargh went after them, but they'd already left for that annual Christmas party at the Earl of Somerset's; and the wolf only caught up with them about the time I got to them as well."

"You got to them?" said Jim.

"That's right," said Carolinus. "I'd just come back from the Emergency Meeting—"

Carolinus broke off.

"Rrrnlf," he said, "don't you have some sea devilish things to do about now?"

"Why, yes!" boomed Rrrnlf, with a wide smile. "I was just going to go and find the wee Lady something more than that little reddish trinket I just gave her so that she'd have a present more equal to that I gave the wee mage."

"Well then," said Carolinus, "you'd better be about it, hadn't you?"

"Yes, Mage!" Rrrnlf turned, put one hand on the wall, vaulted it and strode off toward the forest as they watched.

Jim winced, looking at the wall, which had shuddered under Rrrnlf's weight like someone in pain. He looked back at Carolinus, who was glancing up and down the catwalk as if to make sure that no one else was within earshot.

"I've got to get him to stop that," he said.

"Now, now, pay attention!" said Carolinus. "As I say, I'd got to Brian and Geronde and Aargh; but the important matter was

I was just back from the Emergency Meeting, saw the situation at once in my scrying glass, and immediately magicked myself to where Sir Brian, Geronde and their escort were on their way to the Earl's Christmas Party. I told them, though, that I'd seen the Sea Devil on his way to Malencontri, and that Rrrnlf would get here before anyone else could—except me, of course—and before any further damage could be done; and he'd scare the attackers off, if nothing else. They'd have known that the castle was owned by Jim; and, seeing a giant coming toward it, they'd be sure that Jim had come back to it, too. Well, in a nutshell, I told Brian and Geronde to follow me back here; because you and Angie will be going with them to the Earl's."

Jim and Angie stared at him.

"We aren't going," said Jim.

"But you are," said Carolinus grimly. "Necessity requires it."

"Necessity—" began Jim; and he stopped himself just in time from saying what necessity could do with its needing him to take Angie and make a trip to one of the Earl's wild twelve days of celebration, piety, partying and dangerous physical violence going on under the name of healthy sport, all mixed together. A social situation that Jim did not believe Angie would like at all; and he knew he would not.

"The answer is NO," he said.

"Jim!" said Carolinus coldly. "Will you listen to me?"

Carolinus had a number of angry tones of voice. This was not one of them. This was coldly serious—enough so to send chills down Jim's back.

"Of course, I'll listen," Jim said.

"The Emergency Meeting I went to," Carolinus said slowly, "was called because a number of magicians around our world of sufficient rank had noticed indications that the Dark Powers would be attempting to change History at a particular Christian feast—specifically, at your Earl's Christmastide gathering a few days from now."

"But they can't do that, can they?" Angie asked. "It's a Christian Feast. The Dark Powers wouldn't have any power to interfere with anything there. Even if they did, aside from the Holy occasion, whatever clergy are around would have blessed the place and its environs and nothing belonging to the Dark Powers could even get close."

"Quite right," said Carolinus, "that's what makes this situation so serious. We can't imagine how they could have an effect under those conditions. But the indications are too numerous and too noticeable to be ignored."

"What sort of indications were they?" asked Jim.

"I won't try to explain them to you now," said Carolinus. "If you could see what's going on at World's End, for example—but, no point in going into details. For one thing you're nowhere near advanced enough in magic to understand the importance of much of what I could tell you. You'd have to be at least A-rank. But everything Angie just said is exactly true. In reason, there's no *direct* way in which the Dark Powers could have any effect on such an occasion. Take my word for it, they're simply acting as if they can—and that worries us."

"But if they can't—" began Angie.

"We don't even want them trying," said Carolinus grimly. "If they're thinking they can accomplish anything like that, it'll only be because they've come up with a plan to exert their influence in some way that none of the magicians in our world can conceive of. It wasn't my suggestion, but the assembled body voted overwhelmingly to have you go, with your otherworldly background, to see if you could notice anything one of us might miss. If you do, tell me. I'll be there, too."

They stared at him.

"You?" said Angie.

"Me!" said Carolinus. "Is there anything so remarkable in that? I'm an old friend of the Bishop of Bath and Wells, who'll be there. If anything difficult comes up, you can turn to me."

He surveyed them balefully.

"Now," he said, "Jim, that isn't asking too much of you, is it?"

Jim would have liked to have told him that simply asking him to be at the Earl's twelve days of Christmas under any circumstances was asking too much. Clearly, this was a case in which Jim, having accepted use of this world's magic for his own ends, could hardly turn around and refuse to give anything in return. But there were too many good reasons for their not going, though it would not be easy to tell Carolinus that.

Happily, Angie beat him to it.

"As Jim said," she told Carolinus. "The answer is NO."

Carolinus seemed to grow a foot. His eyes all but literally shot sparks.

"Very well!" he said. "See for yourself, then!"

Suddenly, the three of them were at World's End.

CHAPTER 3

It was unmistakenly World's End. There was no sign to that effect, nothing carved in a nearby rock, but it was simply impossible that it could be anyplace else.

In appearance it looked rather like a spur jutting out from a mountainside at high altitude. The mountain to which it possibly belonged, however, was completely hidden in mist, so that the visible rock made a sort of shelf with a hump on one side of it that reached up perhaps fifteen or twenty feet.

The spur narrowed down to a sharp point that seemed as if it would reach off to infinity, if only infinity would reveal itself behind the thick mist that also hid the mountain, and prevented them from seeing as well what kind of distance or void existed beyond the sharp end of the rock spur.

In the angle where level rock met the hump, some twenty feet or so back from the end of the spur, was an enormous nest, apparently made of some golden yellowish material like spun silk; and in this nest slumbered what at first glance seemed to be a peacock larger than an ostrich.

It was not, however, a peacock. For one thing, no peacock was ever so beautiful. Its fan of tail feathers covered the complete spread of the spectrum and had blendings of those colors that made Jim's head swim.

The peacock slumbered with a contented smile on its beak. Not so the oversized hourglass beside the nest. It was taller than Jim, and clearly built to allow a very large amount of sand to trickle very slowly indeed through a miniscule aperture between its upper and lower parts.

These parts consisted of two huge globes of glass with a narrow neck between them, all enclosed by a slim framework of some dark wood. Right now nearly all the sand seemed to be in the upper chamber of the hourglass, and only a few grains had so far trickled through into the lower chamber, which had a happy face drawn or painted on it—or, rather, a face that had been painted there originally as a happy face, but right now seemed anything but happy. Jim had to look twice, because it was upside-down, before he realized its mouth was turned down instead of up. In fact, it was a very unhappy happy face standing on its head.

"The Phoenix!" snapped Carolinus. "And its thousand-year hourglass!"

Jim and Angie stared at the nest and the hourglass, which were side by side against the rock.

"Why—" Jim began, but he was cut short by the hourglass when the mouth on the happy face suddenly spoke, interrupting him.

"Why, indeed?" it cried in a high-pitched, angry voice. "Do you have to ask that? I do my work, don't I? I'm patient, aren't I? I wait out my thousand years, don't I? Do I ask for overtime? Do I ask for time off? No! A myriad of Phoenixes, since this world was new; and I've had no trouble until this one came along. It had the nerve, the effrontery—"

The happy face began to sputter, and Carolinus held up a hand.

"There, there," he said in a soothing voice, "we completely understand."

"Well, I'm glad someone does!" said the hourglass, in a sudden startling bass. "Can you imagine, Jim and Angie—"

"How do you know our names?" asked Angie.

"Tut, tut!" said the hourglass impatiently.

"Tut, tut!" said Carolinus.

"But how *do* you know?" insisted Angie.

"I know everything!" said the hourglass back in its falsetto voice again. "Can you imagine? You see him sleeping there. His time's up! It's been up for nine days, thirteen hours, forty-six minutes and twelve seconds—and still he sleeps. It's not my fault. I woke him right on time when his thousand years were up. Who could imagine a Phoenix with such a small sense of duty, such a—"

It began to sputter again.

"There, there," said Carolinus.

"Well, it's unbearable, Mage, as you know," said the hourglass.

"It's not your fault," said Carolinus. "You woke him up. He got up, and from then on it was all his responsibility."

"But what about me?" cried the hourglass. "Here I am, counting off a second thousand years. Do you suppose the sluggard means to sleep another thousand years, while the world waits? It may be his mistake, but it's me they'll look to first. '*Why didn't you do something about it?*' they'll ask me!"

"No, they won't," said Carolinus. "Tell Jim and Angie about it, and see if they don't agree that it's not your fault and no one will blame you."

"Just picture it for yourself, JimnAngie," said the hourglass, back in its bass again and running their two names together in its emotion, so it sounded as if they were a single person. "I woke the Phoenix up—and he was hard to wake up. He always was a hard sleeper. I woke him up, he got up, staggered around a bit, searched in his nest, found flint and steel, tried to strike a spark, got a few sparks but couldn't get himself on fire, so that he could blaze across the heavens like a burning star—as he ought to, as a portent to the earth below that a new millennia was about to be started in the next thousand years. From now till the twenty-fourth century, you understand?"

Both Jim and Angie nodded.

"But the spark didn't catch, and, and—I don't know how to say this," said the hourglass, breaking into sobs, "but he actually threw the flint and steel down and I heard him say, 'Oh, to hell with it!' He staggered back to his nest and went right back to sleep!"

Drops of moisture emerged from the glass at the bottom where it joined with its framework, and rolled upward over the bulge of the lower half of the hourglass, in and around the narrow neck between the two parts and onto the swelling shape of the upper part.

"There, you see," sobbed the glass in falsetto, "even my tears are running the wrong way!"

"There, there," said Angie.

"And they'll blame *me*!" sobbed the hourglass.

"No they won't," said Jim and Angie together as one person.

The tears stopped rolling upward, and the face on the lower half of the hourglass ventured a tremulous smile.

"You really think so?" it asked.

"I'm sure of it!" said Angie. "Nobody would be that unfair!"

"The trouble is," said the face, in a calmer, middle-toned, more reasonable voice, "no one's helping me, down there. If some of them would just get busy and settle some of the troubles they've made for themselves, then the Phoenix would wake up again whether he liked it or not; and wouldn't be able to go back to sleep again. Do you suppose that might happen?"

"I'm sure of it!" said Angie firmly.

"I'm so relieved!" said the hourglass. It was actually smiling now, a true happy face. "I'll know the minute it does, because I'll turn right side up again, and the sand that's already dropped through will fly back up to the top of me where it belongs. Oh, I can't wait!"

"I think," said Carolinus in a voice that was almost ominous, "that perhaps we'd better stop talking, Angie and Jim. And leave. Farewell."

"Farewell," said the hourglass. "Farewell, JimnAngie."

They were suddenly back on the catwalk behind the curtain wall at Malencontri. The sun was up a little in the sky and it actually seemed somewhat warmer. Brian, Geronde and Aargh, with their entourage, were already beginning to approach the gate through the curtain wall.

"Well," said Carolinus to Jim, "there you have it. The Dark Powers are at work again and must be stopped. You have a job to do; and that job begins with your going to the Earl's party, you and Angie."

"That's right," said Jim bitterly. "Me against the Dark Powers again!"

"Yes!" said Angie. "It's not fair, Carolinus! You've said so yourself—sending a C-level magician to do something the strongest magicians in this world can't!"

"Of course it's not fair!" snapped Carolinus. "Whatever gave you the idea that this world would be fair? Was your world—the world you came from?"

Angie did not answer.

"Never mind," said Jim wearily. "I'll go, of course. Angie—"

There was a shout from outside the gates, almost mingled with the voices of the sentinels calling back that it was Sir Brian and the Lady Geronde outside wanting to get in. Angie was squeezing Jim's arm to let him know she was ready to go too, if he went.

"Let them in!" shouted Jim to the gateman. He turned back to Carolinus.

"What, specifically, am I supposed to watch for, then?" he said.

"We've no idea," said Carolinus. "The Dark Powers can't work directly; therefore they'll be working through other means or ways. You'll simply have to look for what shouldn't be. Look for anything that seems unreasonable, or that might be rooted in the aim of the Dark Powers to promote History over Chance, or vice versa. As I say, they'll be working at one remove, at least."

He paused a moment, fixing them each in turn with a sharp eye. "One more word. Because they'll be working that way, possibly even through people who don't know they're being used, you mustn't mention you suspect anything—to anyone. Not even to people as close as Sir Brian and Lady Geronde, here; because they may not know they're being used."

"And of course not Aargh," said Jim, with a touch of sarcasm in his voice in spite of himself.

"I doubt that Aargh will be anywhere near," said Carolinus. "He likes the idea of the Earl's feast as little as you do; and runs into considerably more danger, if he's seen by anyone there who doesn't know him. Your fellow guests—the knights in particular—will want to go hunting anything that moves; and Aargh would simply be taken as one more game item to be run down and killed."

Below them, Brian and Geronde with their retainers had passed through the now open main entrance in the curtain wall and Brian and Geronde themselves were just entering the doorway to the Great Hall.

"We should get down there," said Angie, looking at Brian and Geronde as they disappeared through the big double doors.

"Very well," said Carolinus. "But you understand, both of you—you too, Angie—no one must know that Jim is concerned with the problem I've just shown him?"

"No, no . . ." said Angie, still looking at the Great Hall.

"Very well," said Carolinus again, "we'll go."

He disappeared. Angie and Jim were just walking down the walkway toward the nearest ladder to the ground in the courtyard when Carolinus appeared on the catwalk again, looking cross.

"Why are you dallying around like this?" he snapped at Jim. "Use your magic, boy! Put it to good use, for once!"

The last statement was rather unfair, Jim thought. In his opinion he had always put his magic to good use. But, unfortunately, now he had to admit his poverty in that respect.

"I don't have any magic at the moment," he said to Carolinus.

Carolinus stared at him.

"You're out of magic?" said Carolinus. "Again?"

For once, he sounded more flabbergasted than outraged.

"Well, yes," said Jim. "You see, it was like this. I was home during harvest season; and what with getting Malencontri in state for winter and everything taken care of and making a few small changes in the castle—"

Carolinus closed his eyes and shook his head.

"Please," he said, "I don't want to hear the unlovely details. What baffles me is how you managed to run out of magic with an unlimited drawing account!"

"Unlimited?" echoed Jim.

Carolinus's eyes flew open.

"Unlimited is what I said!" he answered, in something more like his usual voice. "*Un-limited!* You remember how, after your tussle with those Hollow Men up on the Scottish border, I went to the Accounting Office and had things out with them? Got you promoted to C level; and got you a special drawing account because you're—well, in some ways, anyway—different from the ordinary apprentice magician? I can barely imagine you running through your C-level allowance—just barely, but I can. But also through an unlimited drawing account beyond that?"

"Was it unlimited?" said Jim.

"Of course!" said Carolinus. "I told you so."

"No, you didn't," said Jim. "You just said everything had been taken care of; and I heard your side of the conversation with the Accounting Office. I didn't hear you say anything about unlimited—just about my having an extra drawing account. But I've never known how to use it."

"Never known how to—" Carolinus interrupted himself, staring at Jim. "But any C-level magician knows how to handle an extra drawing account."

"But I wasn't a C-level magician, then," said Jim, beginning to get irritated in his turn. "Remember, I was only D level and you had them simply promote me to C even though I wasn't otherwise qualified?"

Carolinus glared at him, opened his mouth, closed it again and opened it once more.

"Accounting Office!" he exploded.

"Yes?" queried a deep bass voice out of thin air between them and about at a level with Jim's lower rib cage.

"You didn't tell him how to access his overdraft!" snarled Carolinus.

"No," said the bass voice.

"Why not?"

"I have no mechanism or procedure for taking into account the need for such explanations," said the Accounting Office.

"Why not?"

"I do not know. Perhaps such a contingency was not envisioned."

"Well, envision it now!" shouted Carolinus. "And tell him!"

"I cannot," said the Accounting Office. "He must be instructed in the method by someone of at least AAA magician class."

"You—" Carolinus checked. He turned to Jim and—in an almost gentle voice—said, "Jim, when you need some of the excess magic that I arranged for you, in case you were in an unusual position of having to have more because of your unusual history and situation, you call the Accounting Office and say, 'I want to activate my overdraft. So add the equivalent of a normal full supply of magic for a C-level magician to my account—or two times that amount—or five times—or five hundred times!' Whatever you need. Do you hear and understand me?"

"Yes . . ." said Jim.

"And you, Accounting Office," said Carolinus, still in that same gentle voice, "do *you* understand; and do *you* now have the procedure for replenishing Jim Eckert's account as directed when he asks you?"

"If I may suggest," said the Accounting Office voice, "five hundred times a C-level account is—"

"—Not that much more than he added to the world's supply of magic by his part in stopping the incursion of the Dark Powers from the Loathly Tower, when he first came among us!" snapped Carolinus. "I repeat, you've the mechanism now? And you'll deliver the magic as ordered?"

"Yes," said the Accounting Office. "It is merely a case now—"

But Jim was no longer listening. A decidedly unfair but very attractive thought had suddenly come to him. He had had no idea that the victory he had led at the Loathly Tower when he first came to this world to rescue Angie had been worth that much in generated new magic.

After that, Carolinus had told him he had enough magic to take the two of them back to their own twentieth-century world again. It occurred to him now that if he could make withdrawals from this overdraft of his—possibly in small chunks so as not to attract attention, but enough to build up sufficient credit in his regular account—he would be able to take them back now.

Angie would be able to have her child in the world in which she and Jim had both grown up. It would be anything but a good thing to do to Carolinus and all their friends in this world; but the possibility was now there and could not be ignored. It was in the back of his mind and he knew that it would continue to work on him.

He brought his mind back to the present moment.

"—Very well. Good day, then," Carolinus was saying icily. He turned once more back to Jim.

"Now," he said, "what are you standing there for? Call the Accounting Office and draw some extra magic."

"Accounting Office?" said Jim, a little hesitantly. He had never felt free to bandy words with the Accounting Office the way Carolinus did.

"Yes?" the bass voice responded.

"Could I have—say, two times the normal C-level supply of magic added to my account?"

"It is done."

"Thank you," said Jim. But the Accounting Office did not answer.

"Now that's settled, finally," said Carolinus, "the least you can do is use some of this magic you just got to move the three of us into your hall, so your struggling old Master doesn't have to do it for you. Do it now."

Jim did it now.

They all three appeared abruptly on the dais that held the high table. Brian and Geronde were already seated behind the table down at one end, drinking wine and eating some of the sweet cakes that the castle's kitchen had already started preparing for Christmas—it being only five days away now, and a good supply needing to be laid in.

Brian was a competent-looking knight with a square-boned, lean face with burning blue eyes over a large, hooked nose. His chin was jutting and generous. Jim happened to know that Brian was at least several years younger than he; but Brian, possibly because of his weathered face, and certain small scars about it, gave the clear impression of not only being half a dozen or more years older, but extremely experienced and able—an impression Jim would have given a great deal himself to project.

Geronde was shorter than Angie, possibly by a good four inches. But in addition to that, she was so fine-boned that she gave an impression almost of fragility. In fact, she looked like nothing so much as a life-sized, black-haired, very pretty doll— a classic case of deceptive packaging, in Jim's experience—with blue eyes that were startlingly similar to Brian's. She was wearing a traveling robe of autumn-leaf brown, tight-waisted and high-necked, with an ankle-length, very full skirt.

Altogether, thought Jim, she looked like something or someone who might break at a touch—except for the fact of a very ugly scar on her left cheek, put there by Sir Hugh de Bois de Malencontri, the former owner of the castle that Jim and Angie now inhabited. Sir Hugh, who had been more villain than knight, had got into Malvern Castle under false pretenses; subdued its fighting men; and informed Geronde that she was to marry him, so he would become Lord of Malvern as well.

Geronde had refused, whereupon he had slashed her left cheek and promised to slash her right cheek the next day if she was still holding out; and after that put out first her left eye, one day later, then her right eye on the day after that—and continue in this manner until she gave in.

Knowing Geronde as he did now, Jim knew that she would never have given in. His own first encounter with her had been when he had been in the body of the dragon in which his identity had inadvertently landed in this alternate fourteenth-century world. He had flown to the top of Malvern's keep, and the single man-at-arms on duty there had escaped down the stairs at full speed. But when Jim started down, he found Geronde coming at him with a boar spear. Wistfully, afterward, Geronde had told Jim of her high hopes of getting hold of her captor, Sir Hugh de Bois, someday again; and roasting him over a slow fire. She had meant it. Geronde, intensely loyal, and gentle by fourteenth-century standards, was not someone any reasonable person would want for an enemy.

But now both she and Brian had jumped to their feet on seeing Jim and Angie. Geronde and Angie embraced. Brian embraced Jim—heartily and painfully, since they were both wearing chain mail shirts under their jupons—each with his own coat of arms on it. He then kissed Jim on both cheeks.

Jim had finally gotten used to this frequent fourteenth-century kissing habit. He endured it with reasonable grace, even managing to make a stab at it himself when necessary. Happily, this time Brian was clean shaven, possibly because he was with Geronde.

"Great news, James!" cried Brian exuberantly. "Great news to hear that you will be with us all this Christmastide—and I have even more and other great news for you. Let us sit down, all of us, and talk. I've just been giving your John Steward and squire some words on how to prepare those who go with you to the Earl's and the others who will keep the castle here while you're gone."

For the first time Jim now also noticed John Steward, a tall, rectangular man in his mid-forties, rather proud of the fact that he had managed to keep most of his front teeth. With him was Theoluf, the hard-faced, dark-visaged, former chief of Jim's men-at-arms, now Jim's squire; they were standing just below the table at the end where Brian had been sitting.

"But you may go now, both of you," said Brian, turning to speak to the two of them. "Sir James or Lady Angela will give you their orders shortly. But for now we talk among ourselves. Sit, sit, all of us!"

The injunction was unnecessary for Carolinus. He had been seated from the moment he had appeared. However, Angie was still on her feet, and so was Geronde.

"I've got to go up to the solar," Angie was saying to Geronde. "Come along with me, Geronde. I need to talk to you."

They went off.

"Just as well," said Brian, looking after them. "Geronde knows whereof I would speak to you; and in any case I want to hear how you came to be besieged, and all else—as well as giving you the news I have to give. Great news, James—which, come to think of it, should possibly be spoken first."

Jim's spirits sank as he sat down on one of the padded and backed benches that the high table at Malencontri boasted—articles of furniture about as close to modern, comfortable chairs as Jim and Angie felt they could get away with in this particular time and place.

"Servitor, fill your Lord's wine glass!" snapped Brian. "By St. Ives! If you were a servant of mine you'd not dally so more than once, I can tell you that!"

The server, a young man with a wide mouth and a ready smile, was looking unusually sober, but was also already filling Jim's wine glass. In spite of the laggardness of which Brian had accused the man, Jim suspected he was not too impressed by the implied threat in Brian's voice. The server knew as well as Jim himself that this was just Brian's way of being protective toward Jim, whom he very often treated as knowing barely enough to come in out of the rain—under current medieval conditions.

"Well, now," said Brian, when the servitor had retired, following Theoluf and John Steward out. "Just you and I and Carolinus— where's Carolinus?"

Jim looked. Carolinus had disappeared.

"Something may have come up," said Jim diplomatically. Privately, he suspected Carolinus had never intended to stay in the first place.

"Drink! That's right, James. Get some good, stout wine in you! You'll be happy and astonished with what I have to tell you. I should have come and told you—implored you, even—to come with us in any case; even before Carolinus found us and said you were coming anyway. Could it be you heard about the Prince ahead of time?"

"The Prince?" said Jim. "No."

"Why, he will be at the Earl's Christmastide along with the rest of us. And John Chandos too, and many another worthy person who otherwise might not be there except in such a happy hap. Are you not astonished?"

Jim was. He made astonished noises, for Brian's benefit.

"And Giles de Mer will be there, as I possibly told you he wished to be!" went on Brian. "You remember I had promised him to break a lance with him by way of giving him a chance to learn perhaps a few tricks of lance-work. I was sad to hear earlier this year that there would probably not be a tournament, this Christmastide at the Earl's, because the Earl was—I heard privily—concerned about the expense of it."

"Oh?" said Jim. He had assumed that a tournament was a permanent part of the Earl's Christmas gatherings.

"Yes," said Brian. "The courtyard of his castle is too small for decent tilting, to say nothing of the tents and other necessaries at each end of the lists. Therefore it must be held without the walls— and one can hardly ask those from the lands beyond the castle, but bound to it, to work on feast days, to clear snow, or whatever else is needed to prepare the ground. If they do such labor, some reward has to be given to them, and this has proved somewhat rich in the past—they are almost all free men nowadays, you know, James."

"Yes," said Jim. His own tenants at Malencontri had not failed to remind him of that fact—obligingly and politely, but also both individually and collectively.

"But it seems," went on Brian, "that these same free men, like the true English breed they are, had been looking forward to the tournament as much as the guests. So they have offered to take care of the field out of sheer goodwill. Of course, they will still need in decency to be fed and given drink, and some other benefits, as well as a place before all the other common people who have come to glimpse the tournament."

"I see," said Jim. "But you say Giles will be there?"

"Yes!" said Brian. "I had a letter from him—well, actually a letter from his sister. Giles is no hand with a pen, perhaps you know. But I have his promise. It will be good to see him again!"

"Yes!" said Jim enthusiastically. He, too, liked Sir Giles de Mer, who had been associated with them in the business of rescuing England's Crown Prince from a AAA magician gone bad.

Giles was a silkie—which was to say he was a man upon the land, but turned into a seal once he was immersed in seawater. His family had some Natural genes, evidently; and Giles had looked, Jim remembered, like a harbor seal when he was in his animal, seagoing form.

Otherwise he was a fairly short, pugnacious young knight with a magnificent blond handlebar mustache, remarkable in a time when most knights were either clean shaven or had a neat, small mustache on the upper lip and something like an equally neat vandyke beard on the chin.

He was also a Northumbrian, living right on the northern border of England where it touched the independent kingdom of Scotland; and his dream was to do great things in a knightly way. When Giles had heard that Brian not only frequently took part in tournaments, but often won them, he had been understandably eager that Brian should teach him as much as he was able to learn about that sort of rough play. The fact was that, living where he did, he had never been able to take part in a tournament in his life. They were not common along the Border.

Brian was going on to talk about the other people who might be at the Earl's. John Chandos was coming, as part of the Prince's retinue. That retinue would be large, and consequently it was only polite for Brian and Geronde—and now it would only be polite for Jim, too—to hold down the number of retainers he would be taking with him. It required a nice balance between the number required, not only for show, but for protection going and coming. For the Earl would have more dependents of his guests to take care of than could easily be handled. They, too, would have to be fed and housed for the period of the twelve days of Christmas.

"—Since the Lady Angela and Geronde are not yet back," went on Brian, lowering his voice with a glance at the doorway through which the two he spoke of would be coming, "mayhap you would be interested in hearing of the trip to Glastonbury I took only a month and a half ago."

"Why, yes—" said Jim.

"Geronde was with me, but she was not aware of some of the small things that happened along the way," said Brian. "It chanced that at the first inn we stopped, the wife of the innkeeper was not unpleasing to the eye. Naturally, I paid little attention to her; and of course, Geronde was with me. So we went to our chamber and ate there. But, while Geronde went to sleep early, I found myself sleepless; and, rising, went back downstairs for a drop of wine and perhaps some company. There was another knight at the inn that eve . . ."

Sir Brian rambled on in a low voice; and it soon became apparent to Jim that what was developing was the fact that this other knight had also noticed that the innkeeper's wife was not unpleasing to look at; and that the situation was such that he had somehow gotten the idea—totally erroneous of course—that Sir Brian had also found her so.

" . . . I cannot imagine what might have given the fellow such an idea—" said Brian.

It was, of course, as Brian went on to point out, quite false.

After all, he was with Geronde, and could see no other woman when she was at hand. But clearly this other knight's idea was becoming more and more fixed in his mind; and things were developing toward the point where the two of them would clearly be stepping outside the inn for a quiet debate with their swords over this issue.

" . . . Language had been passed, you understand," Brian was saying, "that a gentleman could not overlook. Consequently, I had no choice but to be as ready for swordplay as he. Well, to make a long story short—"

But it was already too late to make a long story short. At that moment Angie and Geronde appeared through the entrance both Jim and Brian had been watching out of the corner of their eyes, came up to the table and joined them—both women wearing that slight look of secret self-satisfaction that usually signaled something accomplished and beyond the point where anyone else could undo it.

"Well, well!" Brian interrupted himself cheerfully, in a rather loud and hearty voice. "Glad indeed we are to see you, ladies! We have been dull and lonesome by ourselves, have we not, James?"

"Yes," said Jim. "Oh. Yes, indeed."

Brian tossed off the last of the wine in his glass and sat up straighter in his chair.

"Well, now," he said. "Here we sit, with matins long past and terce not too far distant. It will be mid-day before we know it unless we are moving. We must overnight in Edsley Priory if we are to reach the Earl's on the day of St. Thomas the Apostle. And if we are not there by then, I shudder to think what quarters may be left to house us. Let us to horse!"

Jim roused himself with a jerk. Terce was the canonical hour that corresponded to nine o'clock in the morning. Not necessarily early when you got up at dawn for matins, the first church service of the day—as theoretically they all had.

"That's right," he said. "I'm going to have to—"

"Everything is taken care of," said Angie.

"Indeed," put in Geronde, in her dainty voice, "Malencontri will be kept in good state while you are gone. The Lady Angela has a good staff of servants; and your escort will be a-horseback, already."

"But don't we have to pack?" Jim stared at Angie.

"All done," she said.

It had all been taken out of his hands, again. Well, there was no use protesting. His going to the Earl's was already in train.

"And you too will be able to break a lance with me, once we are there, James!" said Brian happily, as if this was the best Christmas present he could give his closest friend.

Jim managed a sickly smile.

CHAPTER 4

It turned out they were taking only fifteen of Malencontri's men-at-arms, as well as Theoluf, Jim's squire, who necessarily had to go with Jim on an occasion like this. That made sixteen armed retainers, plus three serving women, two of them for Geronde from Malvern and one for Angie; so that the total—together with the nine men-at-arms from Brian's castle and the twenty-five from Malvern—made up fifty-three extra mouths that the Earl would have to feed.

This would have been straining the Earl's hospitality if they had been the retinue of only a single guest. But altogether they were four such, and gentlefolk of substance, as well; this many followers could hardly have raised objections.

Jim had only the few minutes necessary to dress himself in proper clothing for the ride through the wintry day, together with the chain mail shirt and other light armor that he wore as Brian did for the trip. His best armor followed him on a sumpter horse under the control of one of the mounted men-at-arms.

It was not plate armor, for this was not in general usage here yet; and only the famous or well-to-do had it—men like Sir John Chandos and others around the King himself. But it was adequate to any demands that the twelve days of celebration should put upon it, except that Jim lacked one item for the tournament.

"But I can lend you a tilting helm!" Brian had said cheerfully as they were mounting up. "You can have my best helm, since the old one will do very well for me—and indeed I intended to take two because I foresaw I would need to lend one to Giles."

"You're too good to me," said Jim.

"James!" said Brian with real distress in his voice. "Never say that!"

Jim felt like a dirty dog.

The ride through the wintry day—happily it had stopped snowing—had been pleasant and almost invigorating at first. But by the time they had stopped to eat along the way at mid-day and pushed on through an afternoon in which the decline of the sun matched the decline of their spirits, they were looking forward eagerly to the walls and comforts of Edsley Priory.

"I would say," said Brian, as they stopped to breathe their horses after ascending a long slope through the tangled woods, "we're less than two miles from it, now. The fare they'll be able to afford us, James, will be lenten, indeed, because of course it is the fasting season, that ends with Christmas. But I doubt not that the Lady Angela has added some permissible, but more pleasant foods to our baggage; and I know Geronde has done so—why, what's amiss?"

He stood up in the stirrups, and Jim imitated him. The woods were thick enough ahead so that they could see no real distance into them. But their ears had picked up the sound of a horse galloping back toward them; and a moment later a mounted man-at-arms came into sight, one of the three that Sir Brian, whom experience with trouble had taught to take no chances, had sent ahead as a point-party.

"My Lords!" panted the man-at-arms—one of Brian's, whose name Jim could not remember at the moment—pulling his horse to a sliding stop before them. "We heard a noise off the road to our right; and Alfred, going to see what caused it, found at a little distance another path coming to meet with our road, and there a place where a party had been set upon and murdered. He came back to tell us, I went to see, and we heard again the noise that chilled our bones—the sound we had heard before, like the piping of a bird—but there was none alive there to make. Those dead were a gentleman of some age and a young lady, two common women and eight men-at-arms. All slain. All plundered."

Angie and Geronde, who had been riding close behind Jim and Brian, and talking animatedly up until this moment, now crowded their horses forward.

"Tell me about this noise again!" commanded Angie.

"As I said, m'Lady," replied the man-at-arms. "It was like the piping of a bird, but no living thing—"

"I want to see this!" said Angie.

She and Geronde pushed their horses past Jim and Brian and started down the road.

"Wait, damn it!" shouted Brian, putting his own horse in motion, with Jim half a second behind him. "I crave pardon, Ladies; but hold you where you are."

He and Jim had caught up with them now. The two women stopped; and Brian turned in his saddle to shout back commands to the squires and men-at-arms behind them. With a good dozen armed men, following and enclosing Angie and Geronde, Jim and Brian leading them all, they followed the man-at-arms who had brought the message up the road and into the woods; and so to the place he had been talking about.

There, one other of the men-at-arms in the point-party—who Jim now belatedly recognized as the Alfred who had just been mentioned—was sitting his horse, like a sentinel over the scene of destruction. Not only human bodies, but dead horses, were enclosed in a small open space of snowy ground surrounded by the trees.

"Have you heard it again—that noise?" called Angie, as soon as they broke into the open space.

The waiting man-at-arms turned to look at her.

"Thrice, m'Lady," he said. "It continued for a little time— as long as a man could with good intent begin the saying of his pater noster. I had got as far as 'pater nostros que est in caelis'—"

"When was the last time?"

"But a few moments past, m'Lady. But none lives here." Alfred cast a superstitious glance around the scene of destruction.

It was indeed a scene that would live in memory; but not, Jim thought, one that would be filed with those memories classed as happy.

The path on which the slain travelers had been riding was little more than a trail through the trees, marked more by the hoofprints of their horses than by any other evidence.

Just at this spot it opened out for about thirty yards of length and to a width that might be as much as half that at its widest; and this more or less egg-shaped space was surrounded by closely grown trees. The attackers would have been able to hide mere yards from those at whom they aimed their arrows.

"Everybody listen!" said Angie. "If it comes again we want to find out where it's coming from."

Her voice was tense. Jim's mind, however, was less on the mysterious noise than the scene itself. The black trunks and limbs of the leafless trees, the gray late-afternoon sky overhead and the dead white of the snow gave everything a look like some surrealistic painting.

Clearly, most of the party had been killed outright by the arrows sent from longbows at the extremely short range of the thick brush and trees immediately surrounding, for the shafts had passed with no trouble through the boiled leather jerkins the men-at-arms had worn, though these might have been expected to protect those inside them at more usual ranges.

There had been only eight of those men-at-arms—a small defensive party to go through woods as wild as these, on such a little-used trail at this time of year when outlaws in woods like this were starving; and sometimes less than human in their hunger and need. The dead had nearly all been killed instantly; and the two who had not had taken immediately mortal wounds. Probably they had also been knocked off their horses and unable to get back to their feet before their throats were cut.

In addition to the dead men-at-arms there were four other bodies. One was a tall, thin man in at least his mid-fifties, if not older. He wore plate armor under a jupon with a coat of arms blazoned upon it, but his valuable knightly sword was gone from its scabbard.

His steel cap had fallen off and his graying hair stirred slightly in the breeze coming even now through the trees. Below that hair, his face was oddly calm for a man killed so violently. He, also, had died immediately; for the shaft was through his upper chest in the center. He had an academic-looking face with a high forehead and peaceful blue eyes that now stared sightlessly at the darkening clouds overhead. Only he, and the dead woman next to him, were richly enough dressed to identify them as belonging to the gentry.

The dead woman had not died that easily. The arrow that had taken her had gone through her lower body only, and her throat had been cut after that. She did not lie on her back, as the older man did, and her anguish-twisted face showed her as being no older than her mid-twenties, although she lay on her side, with her face half-hidden in the barely three inches of snow that covered this spot in the thick woods.

Both her gray travel dress and the man's dark red over-robe had been cut and torn—obviously in a hasty search for whatever of special value the two might have been wearing or carrying. The bodies of the rest were undisturbed, except that the boots and weapons of the men-at-arms, like the dead knight's sword, were missing.

"I think they heard us coming, Sir Brian," Alfred was saying to Brian. "Whoever did this did not stay as they usually would to make closer search for anything other than food or valuables that they could snatch up and run off with. When we got to these bodies, they were still warm—even in this weather."

"Hush!" said Angie. "Everybody listen. If we hear that piping sound again, we want to be able to tell where it comes from!"

She urged her horse forward a few steps beyond where it had halted level with the horse ridden by Geronde.

"Can we be sure of that?" Jim asked. "Wouldn't the bodies stay warm for as much as fifteen or even twenty minutes? It's cold, but hardly that cold."

"The man is right," said a harsh voice somewhat below him. "They ran the moment they heard your men coming. Though I myself had heard them getting closer for some minutes. They were men in tattered clothes, and the whole matter took only a few minutes—then it was all over."

The wolf, as was his wont, had materialized out of nowhere. In the fading daylight, he bulked even larger than usual, so that he seemed virtually pony-sized among the horses—who at once all tried to shy away from him.

"You stood and watched?" snapped Geronde. "And did nothing?"

"I am an English wolf!" said Aargh. "What is it to me if you people kill or take from each other?"

He looked around at all of them; but then he went on in a slightly less grim tone. "But as it happened, Geronde," he said, "I was barely upon them before the action started. Though I had heard them speaking among themselves here and all their other noises, as well as the approach of the people they slew—let alone the approach of your own men."

"But when they went, you did nothing!" said Geronde.

"What difference would it have made?" said Aargh. "Would it have brought the dead back to life? Do not judge me by your own two-legged standard, Geronde!"

"I thought," said Geronde icily, "even a wolf would have more honor than that!"

"Honor is nothing to me," said Aargh. "I know all like you live and die by it; but to me it is nothing. Kill and be killed is the way things have always been; and as they always will be. I, too, will die some day—as these have died."

"Hush, I say!" said Angie in a loud but angry whisper. "Listen!"

She moved her horse forward a few more steps, until it was almost beside the closer of the two dead serving women who had been obviously accompanying the knight and the lady of rank with him. She did not glance at the body below her, which was of a somewhat stout, middle-aged woman in lower-class clothes, who had obviously also been killed instantly, with an arrow clear through her chest. A second serving woman lay some little distance off, huddled up, with an arrow driven through her from the back, so that she seemed as if she must have been hunched over on the ground when it was shot.

And then they all heard the sound.

It was a thin, small noise, but coming in a moment of silence between their own voices, it was clear enough. Only, it was not clear from where around them it was coming. It had that odd quality, which some sounds possess, of seeming to come from any direction surrounding.

"I do not like it," muttered Alfred.

But Angie was already off her horse and starting to run toward the second serving woman. She took the body by the shoulder and rolled it aside, turning it over on its back revealing the face of a girl no older than her mid-teens, but with large breasts swelling the front of her dress, even with the layers of clothes she had been wearing for this wintry travel through the woods.

Paying no attention to the dead girl, Angie snatched up what seemed to be a sort of bundle that had been hidden—almost protectively hidden—by the girl's body; and as she did, the piping sound came again, but more clearly, and was immediately identifiable as the cry of a baby.

"A babe!" cried Geronde; and, catching up the reins of Angie's animal, she led it forward the necessary few paces to where Angie stood, hugging what still looked very much like a bundle stiffened by a board at its back.

"Mount, Angela! You are in danger on the ground!"

"Not while I'm here," came the harsh voice of Aargh, who had kept pace with Angie, Geronde and the two horses. Geronde turned on him.

"You knew it was here all the time!" she said. "Why didn't you tell us?"

"I was waiting to see how long it would take you to find it for yourselves," said Aargh. His mouth was open in a silent lupine laugh. "But I would not have waited so long that the pup would die. Indeed, I would even have saved the girl who carried it, for that she tried to protect it with her body."

"Hand me the child, Angela!" said Geronde commandingly; for Angie was trying to climb on to her horse without letting go of the baby she held in her arms.

Reluctantly, Angie passed the baby up to Geronde, who held it until Angie swung into her saddle and immediately took the child back.

"Did you hear that?" said Angela. "She tried to protect her baby with her own life—and they killed her anyway!"

"She was a wet nurse, no more!" said Geronde, almost impatiently. "See, the child has been over-swaddled with a strip of the finest wool—wool as fine as that which clothes her dead parents behind us here. The wench was only a wet nurse. Look at her servant's clothes!"

But Angie was not listening. She was cuddling the infant in her arms, in spite of the awkwardness of the board at its back, to which it was swaddled. Surprisingly, for a child which had been dumped into the snow and left there—although it had fallen on its back, and the board behind it had kept it from direct contact with the white stuff—it was apparently making cheerful noises back to her through the small slit in the cloths that folded almost together over its face and hid its features completely. But after a few moments, the cheerful replies faded out and a little fretful crying began.

"It must be hungry!" said Angie.

"Well, there are no nurses among us!" said Geronde decisively. "But I have some fine sugar among the things I brought. We can mix that into a little water and twist the end of a cloth to make a teat the child can suck at."

"The water must be boiled!" said Angie swiftly.

"Boiled!" said Brian. "My Lady, we're in the midst of a wood with night coming on and Edsley Priory still some distance off. We can hardly make camp just to boil some water. There is snow enough around us that can be melted in a moment. But boiling it is another matter—"

"In truth, Brian is right, Angela," said Geronde.

"It must be boiled!" said Angie stubbornly. She looked at Jim.

"Yes!" gabbled Jim, instantly getting the message. "It must be boiled in this case, to—to keep the simulacra of these deaths from disenfranchising the child's future!"

There was no argument. The magician had spoken, and in words that were so completely impossible to understand that there could be no thought of arguing with them. Brian immediately set to ordering the necessary events.

"Alfred," he said, "gallop ahead, tell them to take one of my steel helms, put enough of snow in it for a cup of water—a cup only, Alfred, mark you—and set it to boiling over a fire. It must be boiling by the time we get there!"

Alfred thundered off through the trees.

"Four of you others," said Brian to the rest of the men-at-arms, "make a hurdle from the branches you can find here, and use it to drag the bodies of the dead knight and the lady back to where the rest wait for us. We will take those two to Edsley Priory for Christian burial. Let all those not needed for that come back with us, now."

He crossed himself and muttered a few words of what were obviously prayers, looking at the bodies in the snow. Geronde followed his example, and they turned their horses back toward the road. Jim and Angie with the extra men-at-arms followed. They moved their horses decorously at a walk, not so much for their own comfort, as because Angie refused to go any faster while she was carrying the baby, for fear of shaking it unnecessarily.

Once rejoined with their original party, they found the fire lit. The melted snow was taking the benefit of its flames, the helmet ingeniously propped up on the ends of two logs too thick to burn all the way through before the water was brought to a boil.

The water itself, of course, was not yet boiling. Nobody commented on this, however. In any case, the men were excluded at some distance—and happy to be so—while Angela, Geronde and their own three serving women fussed over the child in the process of getting some sustenance into it.

Some little time went by.

"Damme," said Brian; but in a low voice and only to Jim, whose horse was fidgeting beside Brian's horse as they sat a little apart from the men-at-arms. Brian sighed. His eyes met Jim's. "Oh, well!"

Just then, however, the infant's crying ceased; and shortly after that, the women rejoined them with a baby that they were informed was sleeping.

The rest of the ride in the fading daylight to Edsley Priory was a somewhat tense process. Angie was finally persuaded, mainly by Geronde, that a baby that had been carried on horseback as far as it obviously had been before its parents' death would be familiar with the motion of a trotting horse. Reluctantly she gave in. They all made better time; and the sun was still above the horizon when they came out of the trees into the open space surrounding the dark stone buildings of the priory—in fact a small stone castle in itself—to which they were admitted without delay as soon as Brian's and Jim's names and rank were announced to the gateman.

Jim was extremely happy to ride his horse through the gateway into the interior courtyard, and even happier to abandon the horse to one of the men and go through into the already rush-lit interior hallway of the priory. But it was almost as cold inside as it had been outside—except that here the icy breeze could not get at the marrow of his bones, the way it had seemed to be doing outside.

The men-at-arms had already been taken off to the stables, where a great deal of straw, and the clothes they had with them, should enable them to burrow in and make nests that would keep them from freezing during the night. If they could not, the priory would necessarily regret the fact, but it would be the will of God. The two squires—Jim's and Brian's—came into the priory itself, to be housed in a closet-sized room near the kitchen.

Jim and his companions encountered only a few fireplaces, with meager fires in them, as they were led through the building; but there was a good fire burning in the stone-walled room with one narrow, tapestry-covered window, which was made available to Angie and Jim.

Jim, however, found himself almost immediately banished from that warm place; it was immediately turned into a nursery populated by Angie, Geronde and the servant women only. There were all sorts of things to be done for the infant, particularly as it had come into their hands with no spare clothing, or anyone to nurse it.

Jim remembered vaguely that it had been ascertained back on his twentieth-century world that even otherwise childless women could produce milk for infants, if the proper stimuli were there. Angie, of course, would know about that. Meanwhile, it turned out—though he had no idea about how the message could have been passed so quickly—that the priory was already sending out to the surrounding lands it owned for a nursing mother to come in and feed the baby while it was in residence.

Jim himself was sent to join Brian in the cubicle—it could hardly be called a room—where he had been put. However it, too, did have a fireplace, and the room was small enough so that the fire was already making it comfortable.

Brian had made himself comfortable, Jim saw, with food and wine—which had probably been produced automatically by their hosts—that now sat on a small table. The wine was a bright, cheerful-looking red liquid, probably a vintage reserved for guests of quality. But the food consisted of a plate with several stock-fish—as dried herring were commonly called—which Jim could smell the moment he entered the room. For the moment at least, Brian was ignoring them. A lenten dish indeed.

"Drink up and sit down, James!" said Brian. He was sitting at his ease in a padded barrel chair with his legs outstretched, their lower extremities propped on part of his baggage so that the sodden soles of his riding boots—in appearance more like half-socks of leather, in their heelless fourteenth-century design, were toward the flames in the fireplace.

"No," he went on, "not from the pitcher. From the flask behind it. I brought some fine wine with me; and it would be a shame to waste it on just any chance guest at the Earl's who happened to visit my room there."

Jim immediately followed instructions. He sat down with a cup in the room's only other piece of furniture besides the bed, a similar barrel chair already placed before the fire. He pulled out a flask of Angie's boiled water from his own baggage, and added a polite dollop of it to the wine in his cup and drank gratefully.

The heat from the fireplace struck him comfortably in the face, warmed his hands and started to warm the rest of him; while the wine from Brian's flask did the same service for his throat and stomach. It was, indeed, a good wine, Jim recognized, remembering how he had only differentiated between wines on the basis of their color when he had first come to this world.

He sighed gratefully.

"Indeed," said Brian, "it is good to be warm and inside, is it not, James? Who would have thought you and the Lady Angela would arrive at the Earl's with a child in your Lady's arms? Children are not brought to a Christmastide like this until they are old enough to run around and find the jakes by themselves; and even then, not ordinarily. However . . ."

"Will we have much of a ride tomorrow to the Earl's?"

"Less than half a day," said Brian. "If I know anything, you'd best plan on sleeping here with me. The Lady Angela's chamber will be full of busy women the night long."

"You're probably right," said Jim. "I don't suppose there's any danger of running into trouble between here and there, now that Angie has this baby to take care of?"

"No, no," said Brian. "It is mostly open country. You may relax now, and enjoy the drink and provender. I have no forebodings about the morrow."

He stretched out the hand that was not holding his wine to the table which was just within arm's reach, picked up one of the dried herrings and began munching philosophically on it, gazing into the fire, washing down his bites with wine and obviously well contented with the moment.

Jim sat drinking the wine, with something less than his friend's contentment. He ignored the stock-fish, which smelled sickeningly and would taste worse. Brian had always been someone who took cheerfully whatever came, whether it be good or bad. Jim had never acquired that sort of self-discipline. Right at the moment his body might be here, but his mind was back in the room with Angie, the other women and the nameless child they had acquired.

In spite of their air of frantic overwork, all the women had seemed happy with the newest member of their party. It would be understatement to say that Angie was happy. She was considerably more than that. That, in fact, was what was keeping Jim from a contentment equal to Brian's.

Things were all very well for the present. But somewhere in the future Angie would have to give up the baby to someone else. Jim had no specific picture in his mind of what might result when that moment came; but his uncertain image was still an uneasy one.

He had forebodings.

CHAPTER 5

"Well, this is more like it," said Angie.

Jim agreed. Angie was referring to the two rooms they had been given at the Earl's—quarters that were far better than Jim had expected; but which they owed, evidently, to the fact that Jim was accepted as a Baron. That was a result of his own hasty lie in self-identification when he had first appeared in this world.

He had claimed to be Baron of Riveroak; Riveroak being the small town that had held the college at which he and Angie had been graduate students and assistant instructors.

Even that, he thought now, might not have entitled them to *two* rooms, if they had not had the baby in addition to Jim's title. Not that a baby by itself meant a great deal in this particular century, where an unthinkable percentage of them did not survive six months after birth—but a good story meant a great deal.

And this was just that—the whole, romantic story of coming upon the slaughtered party in the woods; and the fact that the dead man was now identified from Brian's report of the coat of arms he had been wearing, as Sir Ralph Falon, the dreamy—who else but a gentleman with only half his wits would travel with so small an escort—but wealthy and therefore powerful, Baron of Chene. They had brought his body and that of the lady with him, who had turned out to be his third, very young wife, on to Edsley Priory for burial. The fact that she also had been killed and of the whole party this child alone had survived—all this made a tale to make remarkable the season and the gathering. Particularly, all this, hard upon the anniversary of the birth of the Christ Child, gave Jim's party almost a Biblical aura.

All this gave the Earl the chance to act grandly and near-royally—an opportunity always appreciated in the upper ranks of society in medieval times. He had risen to the occasion by making a fuss over Jim, Angie and the child; and seeing they were supplied with the best of everything. Everything included these two rooms, which by medieval standards were large, clean, well furnished and even had tight shutters for the two fairly good-sized windows, for it was high in the main tower.

So, as things stood, Jim and Angie had what amounted to a small, private kingdom; one room of which could be given over completely to nursery purposes for the child and the wet nurse brought along from Edsley Priory—she being available because her own child had died—and the other room, which would be their combination bedroom-sitting room. Both rooms had adequate fireplaces and no shortage of fuel.

In addition to that, they had the comfort of knowing that, because of the child, no drunken guest of the Earl was likely to come hammering at their door sometime after midnight, with convivial inclinations born rather from alcohol than from any common sense. They were even to be allowed to post a guard at their door.

"Yes," said Jim, "it's much better than I expected."

For the moment they were alone in the outer room, with its door to the passageway outside firmly closed. The inner room had no door; but a heavy tapestry had been hung on the opening between it and the room Jim and Angie were now in. The voice of the baby being fretful did come through to them, as well as other housekeeping sounds; but one could not have everything.

"That mite," said Angie, sitting down in the barrel chair next to Jim's before the fire, and picking up the glass of wine that Jim had poured for her a good two hours before and she had barely tasted, "the Baron of Chene!"

"I'm not sure whether he's legally the Baron right away, or not," said Jim. " . . . It may be that he has to be identified legally in some way; or even that he has to come to a certain age before he can legally inherit the barony." He paused, then went on, "At any rate, for now, he's a ward of the King."

"The King!" echoed Angie, sitting up very straight.

"Yes," said Jim, not looking directly at her. He had deliberately thrown in this piece of information to start preparing her for the fact that the child might pass out of her hands almost without warning. "In any case where a landed couple of rank are both dead and a child lives, that child becomes a ward of the King. He can assign that wardship to anyone he wants."

"That drunken old man in London? He's just as likely to give young Robert to anyone!" The name of the baby had been discovered worked into his clothing with needle and thread.

"He isn't drunk all the time," said Jim soothingly. "Besides, something like such a rich wardship will probably be really decided not by him, but by the people of influence around him—like Sir John Chandos."

"And Sir John likes you," said Angie.

"Yes. I think he does," said Jim. "But he's only one voice. More to the point is the fact the King's got a generally good opinion of me, because the affair at the Loathly Tower added to his reputation."

He was speaking of the profusion of popular ballads which had celebrated Jim's rescue of Angie from the Dark Powers at the Loathly Tower—with the help of Brian, Aargh, the Welsh bowman Dafydd ap Hywel and Carolinus. The first balladeers to make up a song about it had invented a part in which Jim had gone to see the King first and asked his permission to attack the evil things in the Loathly Tower. Which permission, the King had then graciously given him. So that the general impression was that it had all been done on the King's initiative and command. The King had liked that.

"That's true," said Angie, relaxing a little. Seeing which, Jim decided to risk giving her a little more bad news.

"Actually, Sir Ralph Falon's sister is already here at the Earl's," he said.

Angie became rigid in her chair again. She put down her glass of wine, still without tasting it.

"Sister?"

"Yes, Lady Agatha Falon. A younger sister of Sir Ralph. They were the only two children of the previous Baron. In fact, I think she's a half-sister. She was born to the former Baron's second wife—the wife before Mary Briten—but she still has a claim on the estate—"

He tried to make the last of his message light in tone.

"Of course," he said, "once Sir Ralph had a new young wife,

and since a son of his is living, that rather cuts the sister out of the inheritance."

"Does it?" said Angie grimly.

"Yes," said Jim.

"Well, that's only right," said Angie. "Little Robert should get it all. After all, he's the one who'll have to raise a force from his barony and lead it to battle for the King, once he's grown up, while she's probably never done a thing in her life!"

Jim could not think of a woman he had met in this medieval world who had never done a thing in her life. They all seemed to be desperately active; as much as, if not more so, than the men. But his knowledge of Angie was enough to caution him against saying anything like that out loud right now. Besides, he still had one more bitter pill to pass on.

"It's natural she'd take an interest," said Jim. "Whoever gains the wardship of young Robert will be collecting and managing the income from the Chene estates until Robert comes of age. And the Chene estates—well, you've heard about them—a Duke wouldn't be unhappy with the income from them. I don't know what wild reason made the Baron come to the Earl's Christmastide, here, with only eight armed retainers—particularly through country like that."

"You mean," said Angie, ignoring the rest, "that this Agatha will be interested in the income from the Chene estates during the wardship—at least?"

"The way things are at this point in history," said Jim, "I can't imagine her not being interested."

Just at that moment there was a loud single knock on the door, followed by a pause and two rather timid little taps—as if the person knocking had suddenly remembered who was in the chambers to which he was asking admittance.

"Yes?" said Jim, raising his voice.

The door opened a crack and the lean, concerned face of Brian appeared.

"Jim—Angela!" he greeted them. "Jim, Carolinus asked me to step up and persuade you to come down and join the other guests in the upper chamber of the main hall. Everyone is there right now."

Jim got to his feet.

"Yes, I'd better," he said to Angie. "It's all right for you to spend most of your time up here, Angie. But I'll be expected to mix with the rest."

He went toward the door.

"Hmm," said Angie absently, getting up in her turn and going toward the inner room. She gave him a small wave of her hand and passed thoughtfully out of sight behind the tapestry veiling the entrance.

The upper chamber of the hall, when Jim and Brian reached it, was indeed crowded with gentlemen and ladies, other guests for this Christmastide gathering. All of them, like Jim, had gotten up at dawn for a necessary appearance at matins, the first church service of the day. After that, a good number of those Jim saw around him now would have probably done what Jim himself usually did, which was to slip back to their own rooms for some extra sleep. The coming midnight was the first hour of Christmas—the Vigil of Christmas—and he would have to put in an appearance at that, on top of making himself visible most of this day in public.

Earlier, after this day's morning service, a number of the heartier, more energetic male guests had gone out for a boar hunt, and spent a cold morning careening through the woods with hounds, finding no boars. In spite of that they would nearly all be, as Brian said, in the hall's upper chamber now; almost every one of those invited here—though not every knight and his lady in Somerset had been invited, of course. Sir Hubert, Jim's cantankerous, close neighbor, was among those missing. But there were enough guests here at the moment to considerably crowd a room made out of the upper part of the long hall belonging to the Earl.

It was, on a large scale, the fourteenth-century upper-class equivalent of a family, or rumpus, room. Along one wall was a table dormant; a table, that was, which was never taken down between meals, as most medieval tables were, but always stood furnished with food for the hungry elite. Like all respectable medieval tables, it was covered with a snowy white linen cloth.

On that cloth at the moment were a number of dishes that conformed to the letter of the rules for fasting in Advent (the days before Christmas); in other words—no meat, eggs or dairy foods such as butter or cream. But there were a number of fresh fish dishes, ingeniously grilled, fried, baked and otherwise cooked—most of them with sauces in which a cream made of pulverized almonds had substituted for the cow's cream and butter that would otherwise have made the sauces palatable.

There was, of course, no lack of wine, and there were such things as little pastry turnovers which avoided any of the forbidden foods, but contained tasty materials, probably often made with that same almond milk, rather than the usual milk or cream.

As a result, the gentlemen and ladies present could take up a glass of wine and something to munch on, while circulating, talking, or perhaps glancing out the one good-sized—and actually glazed—window at the common men of the Earl's estate. A number of these were amusing themselves (if they had been working, it would have been sinful) by clearing the tilting ground of the fresh snow that had fallen overnight. So it was possible for their betters to stand, talk, eat and watch them work—always a pleasant sight to those doing such observing.

Most of the other guests were people Jim had never met before. Carolinus, he saw, was busily in conversation with Sir John Chandos, and a large muscular, middle-aged man with straight, iron gray hair and a square face, perhaps in his late forties, and dressed in Benedictine black. He had been pointed out to Jim the day before as the Bishop of Bath and Wells. But he was a most unlikely-looking Bishop; giving the general appearance of someone who would rather be punching out sinners than comforting those who had repented.

Jim and Brian gravitated to the table, and Brian supplied himself with a full glass of wine and a handful of the small turnovers. Jim took another glass of wine but only three of the small pastries. The noonday feast would be starting soon. They moved away from the table to let other people have access to the food.

"You must not be tied down by this baby and Angela's care of him, James," Brian was beginning. "You—hah!"

Brian's glance had gone past Jim's face, out over Jim's shoulder to something or someone behind him. It had also changed expression; unfortunately, to one that Jim had seen on his friend's face a number of times before—invariably when Brian was about to go into battle.

Jim pivoted in time to see Brian marching over to confront a somewhat taller man of about his own age, and somewhat leaner, but in other ways not unlike him. This other was also a knight, for he wore a knight's sword belt—without sword, of course, as befitted a guest. His hair was black, his eyes hazel-colored, and he wore a definitely expensive, plum-colored cote-hardie over gray hose and neat black heelless dress shoes.

"Hah!" said Brian again, stopping a long step from the other man.

"Hah!" responded the other.

The two ejaculations rose over the general mumble and clutter of conversation in the room. The talk of other people died, and glances began to direct themselves to Brian and the other knight; for very clearly the two "hah!"s had not been mere greetings, but something decidedly more loaded with meaning.

"Sir Harimore!" snapped Brian. "I see you well?"

Sir Harimore had a small, carefully trimmed mustache on his upper lip. Outside of that, he was clean shaven. The mustache had little in the way of ends that could be twirled; but Sir Harimore reached up to twirl one of them now.

"Eminently well, Sir Brian," he snapped back. "And you, sir?"

"Thanks be to God I could not be in greater health!" said Brian.

"Hah!" said Sir Harimore, twirling his mustache.

"Hah!" replied Brian.

There was a moment of tense silence.

"I will see you then, here, in the days to come?" said Sir Harimore.

"Sir, you will!" said Brian.

"I shall look forward to it!"

"And I, also!"

With this last word, both Brian and Sir Harimore seemed to become aware that a complete silence had fallen on the gathering around them. They bowed to each other somewhat stiffly. Sir Harimore turned back to the two women and one man he had been talking to, and Brian returned to Jim. The general talk of the room welled up again around them.

"Who was that?" asked Jim, in a low voice under the cover of the general noise of the room.

"Sir Harimore Kilinsworth!" said Brian. His blue eyes were still looking as fierce as Jim had ever seen them.

This information told Jim nothing.

"I don't know him," said Jim. "Who is he? What—"

He could not think of how to phrase politely the question he wanted to ask, which was why the very sight of the man had immediately set Sir Brian off in a way Jim had seldom seen him react before. Brian took a gulp from his glass, as abruptly as if he had intended to snap the lip of the glass off in his teeth.

"What I mean, is . . ." Jim was beginning awkwardly, when Brian broke in.

"Sir Harimore Kilinsworth," said Brian, "an excellent swordsman. I have seldom seen the like. He is as well with other small

arms too; but he handles the lance in a way most praiseworthy . . .
I cannot bear the fellow!"

"You can't?" said Jim. "But why? What's wrong with him?"

"Why, he has these skills; but one might say he overprides
himself on them. He has an attitude that sticks in my teeth. We
almost had it out at that inn I told you of—particularly after what
he said to me concerning Geronde."

"He said something concerning Geronde?" said Jim. This must
have been a part of the story Brian had not been able to finish at
Malencontri. Jim had not been here three years without coming
to understand the extreme touchiness of people like Brian, where
certain words and phrases were concerned. "What did he say?"

"I don't remember his exact words," said Brian, "but the burden
of them was all too clear—as he intended it to be. The fellow as
good as accused me of troth-breaking."

"Troth-breaking?"

"Yes, yes," said Brian, keeping his own voice down, but showing a touch of irritation. "The troth I pledged to Geronde, of
course. A most foul insinuation. Surely a man can glance for a
moment at the fine figure of another woman, even though he is
betrothed? We are all Adam's sons, I think?"

Jim was about to ask what Adam had to do with it, let alone
any sons of his, when he felt his sleeve plucked; and turning, saw
Carolinus standing beside him.

"I want—" Carolinus was beginning—

But just then, the floor quivered, the walls quivered, and a
tremor like a small earthquake shook everything about them.

CHAPTER 6

"Beelzebub's daughters!" snapped Carolinus, his voice unheard among the general babble of excitement that had arisen around them, but which was already beginning to calm. "He's to stop that immediately! That's just what I was coming to tell you—no castle-shaking this week or next! You go down and tell him so, now!"

Jim had not known that Beelzebub had ever had any daughters. But, of course, he found himself thinking crazily, if Adam had had sons—which he had—it probably was perfectly reasonable that Beelzebub had had daughters. However, who was "he"?

"Who's *he*?" asked Jim.

"The giant in this castle!" said Carolinus, prudently lowering his voice now that the general level of conversation had dropped once more. Other people were assuring first-time guests that it was "only the giant in the castle." "—He's not actually a giant," Carolinus went on, "but that's not the point. You go down, Jim; and Brian, you'd best go with him—just to make sure he finds his way down and up again all right!"

"Yes, Mage," said Brian.

Carolinus turned, and went back to rejoin Chandos and the Bishop of Bath and Wells. Jim felt his sleeve plucked again. But this time it was the opposite sleeve, and it was Brian doing the plucking. Brian made a motion with his head toward the passage outside the upper room of the hall, and Jim followed him out without a word. Once outside, Brian turned and led the way toward the main staircase of the tower that anchored one end of the main hall.

"What's all this about a giant in the castle?" Jim asked; for the hall itself at the moment was deserted and there was no one to overhear him.

"Oh, there's always been a giant in the Duke's castle," said Brian. "Everyone knows that."

"And why do you call him Duke, now?" said Jim. "I remember you called him Duke the first time I heard you mention these Christmastide gatherings of his. I went around calling him a Duke myself for some time before I found out everybody else seemed to call him an Earl. Which is he?"

"Oh, he's an Earl," said Brian. He glanced over his shoulder at the empty corridor behind them for a moment, and lowered his voice slightly. "It's just he thinks he ought to be a Duke. His family, you see, goes back to ancient Roman times, here. His oldest ancestor was a Duke—or a Dux, I believe people called it then. Anyway, he longs to be called a Duke, and those of us who know him well sometimes call him that in privy talk—just between ourselves, you understand. It would never do to call him Duke in public. But it's one of the reasons, see you, behind his invitation to the Prince this Christmas. He'd like to be made an actual Duke one day; and that day may come when our young Prince will be King and make him so—if Edward ends by liking these twelve days and the Earl, himself."

They passed the floor below, and the wide entrance to the main floor of the Great Hall, where servitors were busy setting up table tops on their trestles for the banquet, and spreading the fine, fresh-washed linen tablecloths carefully over them.

"At the same time," Brian went on, "from the Prince's point of view, the more great lords he has for his friends, the stronger position he's in when it comes to a matter of succeeding his father. No man can tell from where some other claimant to the throne might appear—a distant cousin, or such like. The best way to guard against such a hap is to make sure the strength of the Kingdom is mainly on the Prince's side. So his advisors, like Sir John Chandos, will have told him. So there are wheels within wheels, you see."

"I do, indeed," said Jim.

They had now passed the floor underneath, which was where the necessary horses that the Duke and his immediate retinue rode were commonly stabled; and into which they were brought if the castle should be under hot attack and its defenders pulled back into this tower for a last defense. Daylight did not reach far in here, and the lighting provided by wall-mounted bundles of rushes had worsened as they descended. Jim was completely baffled as to why they might find any kind of giant in the stables—but his bafflement was only increased when Brian led him a short way down the stable to a farther flight of stairs that went down even deeper.

"Hup! Hey! Ho! Just a moment there! Where do you think you're going?"

Jim and Brian turned before they had put foot on the first step down this new stairway, to find themselves confronted in the dim light by a somewhat short, rotund man with a bristling gray-white mustache, a small, pointed gray-white beard on the chin of a round face, and fierce blue pop eyes under pure white eyebrows. His hair, too, was pure white. A sword belt and heavy sword hung from around the waist of his deeply red, rich wool robe. Right behind him were two tall men-at-arms, both with swords unsheathed and in their hands.

"My Lord!" said Brian, as he made out the face squinting at him in the gloom. "I think you are acquainted with Sir James, Baron of Malencontri et Riveroak, and an apprentice—"

"Apprentice?" exploded the white-haired man, drowning Brian's last words. His white eyebrows had shot up on his forehead; but Brian had already turned to Jim.

"Sir James," he went on, "you have met your host and our Earl, Sir Hugo Siwardus, my Lord Somerset."

"Apprentice?" the Earl was barking at Brian. Jim had a very sure idea why he was reacting this way. Any apprentice would be a common person; and one such among his guests, whether he was called a knight or not . . .

"An apprentice in magic, to Mage Carolinus, my Lord," said Brian.

The Earl's eyebrows dropped to half-mast at the name of Carolinus, and there was a pause.

"The Dragon Knight, of course," he said. His eyebrows relaxed to their lowest level. "My dear Sir—" He stretched his hands out to Jim, a smile on his ruddy features. "Damn happy to have you here! I've not wanted to disturb you and your Lady, after all the adventures of your trip. I hope those rascals of mine took care of you properly, the way I told them to?"

"Eminently well, my Lord," said Jim. He had been half afraid the Earl had meant to embrace him, as Brian and Giles now did; but all his host did this time was to clasp his forearm in a friendly but powerful grip and beam at him. In polite fashion Jim clutched back at the forearm behind the hand that clutched him. Then they both let go.

"But—" A frown returned to the Earl's face. "What draws you to my nether floors? Strictly forbidden to anyone to go down there! Strictly—" He puffed out his cheeks momentarily. "Even I almost never go down."

His cheeks deflated; his eyes, which had been meeting Jim's boldly, became suddenly shifty, glancing off to one side.

"—Never, actually . . ." he muttered, under his breath.

"Carolinus sent Sir James, and said I should go with him," put in Brian, "so he could remonstrate with any who might be down there."

"Hah!" said the Earl, perking up amazingly. "He did, did he! Capital notion! Yes, yes, of course. Good of old Carolinus to think of it. I wouldn't want to impose on a guest, of course; but the Dragon Knight, of course . . ."

"But," said Brian, "if your Lordship objects—"

"No," said the Earl hastily, "by no means. Follow your master in magic's orders, Sir James. Eminent magician, Carolinus. None better! Yes—do what he says. I—I must get upstairs to the rest of my guests right now; but I will look forward to seeing you later."

"Thank you, my Lord," said both Jim and Brian.

The Earl and his two men-at-arms turned and hurried off. Jim and Brian went on down the stairs.

They descended several more levels without speaking. The lighting had become almost nonexistent, and Brian had plucked a rush-light from a wall holder and carried it as they continued downward. Finally they emerged into what seemed to be an area under the very base of the castle itself, with the stone and wooden supports above them propped by great arches of more stone; and nothing but earth underneath their feet as far as could be seen.

"He must be around here, someplace," said Brian. "The stink of him is loud enough. Do you note, James, that there is fur on everything about, down here, to the height of a man?"

"I think it's hair. Maybe he rubs himself against things to scratch an itch," said Jim. He sniffed cautiously at a nearby supporting stone arch. The smell was not of the kind that would gag a person, however. It was, Jim thought, rather like a sharp, wild-animal scent. "I think it's the hair that smells."

Brian was peering around him in the torchlight. There had been no fear in his voice, but definitely a note of caution.

"Carolinus did say that the giant was not a real giant, did he not?" Brian asked, turning to Jim.

"That's what he said," said Jim.

"It is well that is so, then," muttered Brian, peering into the gloom beyond the area illuminated by the rush-light, "for the beams and stone above us here are but inches above the top of your own head, James. Well, let us look."

He led the way, apparently at random, into darkness. Jim followed.

They wandered among the stone arches for some little time, peering as far as they could in the illumination of the rush-light; but there was nothing to be seen and nothing to be heard.

"This is no good," said Brian, halting at last. "We could wander forever like this."

He raised his voice.

"Ho! Giant!" he shouted. "If so be it you are not too fearful to face us, let us see you. Come forth!"

The response was so quick that it took Jim's breath away.

Suddenly the rush-light was so pale in the new illumination that it could hardly be seen. Around them, arches, beams—even the ground under their feet—were glowing with a strange but powerful light, so that they could see for about ten yards in every direction not blocked by stone.

But it was not necessary to see ten yards to discover the individual facing them. He was less than ten feet away, and his appearance was not such as to invite them to step forward and greet him, as they might another person.

"By all the Saints!" said Brian. "A troll. But one larger than any I ever heard of! Do you speak, troll?"

"I speak, man!" came back the answer in a harsh, deep and powerful voice that made Brian's seem like that of a boy. "Tell me how you dare come here before I tear you apart and eat you!"

The giant of the castle looked as if he could do exactly what he promised. But Carolinus had been right. Technically, he was not, in fact, a giant. But he was hardly less than one.

He was at least an inch or so shorter than Jim, though taller than Brian.

On the other hand, Jim remembered, from his own twentieth century, the old saying about someone being two ax handles across the shoulder—but this was the first time he had ever seen someone who actually had that kind of shoulder-width.

This troll's shoulders, Jim thought, must be at least as wide as he was tall. This was mind-boggling. Most trolls, even the largest night-trolls, were only reputed to be about a hundred and twenty pounds in weight. This one looked as if he could match body weight with a gorilla.

In addition to that, his arms were long. His oversized hands dangled below his knees; and both arms and legs bulged with muscle. Jim had heard a great deal of trolls but had never actually met one before. He was fascinated by the head and face of the one he was looking at now. It was something like an oversized head that had been squashed down. It was broader than a human head would be, the nose large, and the nostrils flaring; the eyes were deep-set and of a dark color that Jim could not identify precisely in this light. The mouth was abnormally wide, with a powerful lower jaw beneath it. Right now the lips were drawn back, revealing sharp, pointed teeth that a saber-toothed tiger might have envied.

At first glance Jim had thought that the troll was dressed in some close-fitting suit of tanned leather. Now, he realized that what he saw was actually the troll's skin. He actually wore nothing except a sort of short, and rather dirty, kilt around his waist; upon which were black rows of single lines rather rudely marked, as if someone with very little education or practice had been keeping tally of something or other.

"Know you, troll," said Brian, "the gentleman beside me is Sir James Eckert, Baron de Malencontri et Riveroak, and a Mage. He brings you an order from his master in magic, none but Carolinus himself. Think on that. Are you so lost in this depth here that you have never heard of Carolinus?"

"Of course I've heard of Carolinus!" growled the troll. "The wolf's told me. I'll show you what I think of Carolinus. I'll eat you both and send your bones back to him!"

A low growl began in the darkness beyond their area of light. It approached, resonating deeper until it seemed to echo off or in the very stone around them.

They all turned toward its source.

"Think again, troll!" said an equally harsh voice, if somewhat higher-toned; and Aargh stepped into the light. His ears were erect, his tail was straight out behind him and his yellow eyes had a flat, murderous look as if the light behind them had gone out.

"These are friends of mine," said Aargh. "You will never set tooth in their bones."

"I take no commands from you, Aargh," said the troll. "You've been of use to me, in bringing news of the outside; and you dared come from the woods down my tunnel, up which I must go to find the food I need. But none ever came down of their own will, these eighteen hundred years, until now. None—until you. But never think you I can't eat you, too, and send your bones up with these as well—for your own sake, stand away!"

Aargh smiled. But it was not his ordinary smile. This smile was vertical, not horizontal. The lips had wrinkled back, first in the middle, and then outward, revealing the gleaming knives of his wicked teeth.

"Aargh stand away?" he said. "All trolls are fools, and clearly you, Mnrogar, as the oldest and biggest of all, are also the biggest fool. Reach for any one of us, and learn how Aargh will stand away!"

The troll growled thunderously and took a step toward Aargh. Aargh's jaws closed with a ringing snap. His lips wrinkled farther back; and he half crouched for a spring. But in that moment Jim pointed a finger at the troll, and his voice rang out among the stone and timber.

"*Still!*"

Mnrogar froze where he was, almost off balance with his stride forward barely completed. Aargh slowly relaxed and straightened up from his crouch. His jaws opened again in the more familiar, silent wolf-laugh.

"So, now what of your eating and sending of bones, Mnrogar?" he said. "The apprentice alone has made you helpless. What if you were to face his master?"

Mnrogar did not answer; but that was for the very good reason that he could not. To do so he would have needed to move his vocal cords; and all voluntary control of his body had been checked by Jim's magical command. A magician—unlike a sorcerer—might not use his powers for reasons of offense. But to render someone immobile, except when they were in a vulnerable position, was not an offensive use of magician magic. Mnrogar had become a troll-statue—still of flesh and bone, but motionless, nonetheless.

Jim walked around so that he was standing directly before the eyes of the motionless troll.

"Neither I nor anyone else here wants to quarrel with you, Mnrogar," Jim said. "But you must know that, strong as you are, you're helpless against a magician—"

"Speak for yourself, James," said the harsh voice of Aargh, and the wolf brushed past Jim's leg to lift his nose almost to the face of the motionless Mnrogar.

"Do you see that bulge under his upper arm, James? I have had to deal with, and slay, a number of trolls in my time. That is not muscle, but one of the tubes of his body through which his blood flows. A large tube, and much blood. It is close to the surface there, and I could rip it open with ease. There are other such places about his body which I know. Never think, Mnrogar, that Aargh could not kill you. You trolls all fight alike, because you are used to seizing, biting and tearing with your claws. You all move the same way; and an English wolf knows how to slash and move away from what you would do, long enough for your body to empty itself of blood. Which it would in a moment or two if one of those tubes were opened. I will die when my time comes, because I am such a wolf. You will live for thousands of years yet, if no one kills you; but I tell you now—if you live until oak, ash and thorn, together, were forgotten in this land, you would never have been able to kill Aargh."

He stepped back from the troll and out of Jim's sight.

"Mnrogar," said Jim, "I'm going to release you so you can move now. But remember that no one here has any cause against you, but if one of us did you couldn't hurt him. Your strength is nothing against my magic. Remember that. And remember this message I bring from Carolinus. You aren't to shake the castle again for two weeks, however you manage to do it!"

He waited a moment to let the message sink in.

"You're free to move," he said, then.

Mnrogar moved, but not toward any of them. With a wild howl he flung out his arms so that each one reached a seemingly impossible distance, to hook itself around one of the stone pillars on either side of him. He threw his weight against the stone he held; and everything around them shook as he continued to throw himself backward and forward.

"*Still!*" snapped Jim.

Mnrogar was suddenly frozen and the shaking stopped. Jim heard his own breathing, harsh in the sudden stillness. But that breathing was all he heard; neither Aargh nor Brian was making a sound. It took him a moment to control the sudden, reasonless anger that had boiled up inside him at the massive troll's immediate action.

"Mnrogar," he said at last, in something like a calm voice, "I could leave you just as you are now, to stand for as long as your body would hold you up. Maybe you could stand forever—I've no idea whether you'd die before your body would fall, or not. But I'm not going to leave you like that. I won't, because I'm not like you, who does things like that for nothing; only to trouble others. Now, I'll give you one more chance and let you go. But this time don't do anything that'll make me stop you again. Because if I do, this last time I'll never set you free again."

He waited a moment to let his words sink into the troll's mind. Then he spoke again.

"You can move once more," he said.

Mnrogar moved. He threw back his head and howled; a howl that rang and echoed from the stone arches all around them. His face was twisted in an expression of terrible grief. He opened his fanged mouth and howled like an animal in pain.

"For nothing?" he cried. "But it is mine! My castle, my lands! No other troll shall have them!"

He threw himself down and began beating his head against the earth floor with a force that seemed as if it should have torn that head from his body.

"Of the Lord's mercy!" said Brian's hushed voice off to Jim's left. "The creature weeps!"

CHAPTER 7

It was true. Great tears were running down the troll's ugly face; and his wide, powerful chest was racked with hoarse sobs.

"Eighteen hundred years!" he choked, looking up at Jim, like an animal caught in a cage. "Eighteen hundred years have I kept this hill, and this land, so no other troll dared set foot in it. Eighteen hundred years—"

He clutched at the kilt around his waist and pulled its bottom edge up toward Jim.

"Read! Count! Each mark—ten years, that says this place is my own!"

"I see," said Jim, for in spite of everything that had gone before, this sudden explosion of grief was so unexpected and overwhelming it tore at his emotions in spite of himself. "I believe you, Mnrogar," he said. "I see the marks. Yes, I believe you—eighteen hundred years."

"All that time!" choked Mnrogar. "And now you, all of you men and women, have brought another troll in on my land, my place—and you keep me from doing anything about it!"

The troll's suffering was so obvious and so intense that Jim found he could not stand it. Recklessly, he ransacked his mind for some magic that could ease the Natural's pain. His actual stock of spells was so small that at first he thought he had nothing. Then he realized that he did have one thing.

"Sleep!" he said, pointing at Mnrogar.

Mnrogar's grief checked in mid-sob. His eyes closed and he slumped to the ground, still. His face smoothed out, and no more tears came from under his eyelids. In sleep, his face had lost the marks of the agony it had shown before.

"What was he talking about?" demanded Brian, moving up to face Jim. "Another troll? Here? Brought into the castle by one of the guests? It cannot be!"

"I don't see how it can, either," said Jim, shaking his head. He looked at Aargh, who had also moved up close to sniff at the sleeping Mnrogar. "Aargh, can you smell a troll here in the castle?"

The ability of wolves in general to pick up scents had been known to be remarkable, back in the twentieth-century world from which Jim had come; and during his three years of knowing Aargh, he had seen clear evidence that that knowledge was in no way exaggerated. But in this case, Aargh did not even bother to lift his nose in the air and sniff.

"What else can I smell," retorted Aargh, "with a troll here, right under my nose?"

It was an obvious answer. Jim felt foolish. Happily, the wolf seemed more interested in something else.

"Do the marks on this thing he has wrapped around him actually tell of eighteen hundred years that he has kept this place?" he asked.

"As far as I can see," said Jim.

"If so," said Aargh, lifting his head to look at Jim, "he has done a great thing. I know of no other troll who has held his ground for more than forty years. You might want to think before you change him for another troll, James."

"What other troll?" said Jim, startled.

"The one upstairs—if there is one upstairs," Aargh said. "Otherwise, if he sleeps forever here, sooner or later some other troll will come down the tunnel and kill him as he lies for the sake of his land. I understand that, Jim; perhaps a human like yourself does not. They have their own ground, which they guard and keep against all comers, as my people do. But other than that, they are little like us. Each one is abandoned as soon as it's whelped by the one who whelped it. It grows up if it can and lives—and fights to win ground of its own. Then it holds that place until another comes and kills it and takes it from him. It is so with us wolves. It is so with trolls."

"Aargh!" said Jim. "Is this troll a—a friend of yours?"

"Friend?" said Aargh. "Only minutes past, you saw me ready to kill him. I understand him, only."

Jim felt embarrassed. At the same time, his mind was working. If there was a troll somehow upstairs in the castle, and Aargh's nose could be brought anywhere near it, it would be easy for the wolf to pick out the intruder. Although why a troll should be here, or why any guest should bring one in, were questions that seemed to have no sensible answers at all.

"Look, Aargh," he said, "if I can come up with a way to make you invisible—or the next best thing to being invisible—upstairs where everybody else is, so that you could use your nose up there, away from Mnrogar, you'd be able to find the other troll, wouldn't you? That is, if there is one."

"I could, but I won't," said Aargh. "You know I've no love for these things called castles and inns, and the other traps you humans huddle in. No, I will not go upstairs with you. Ask me no more such questions, James. My answer is what you have now. And also, I have no more reason to stay here. I will go."

Instantly he was gone into the darkness beyond the light.

Jim was silent—and Brian seemed to have nothing to offer. When Aargh put things like that, it would be a waste of time and tempers to try to change his mind. This medieval time in which Jim and Angie now lived was one in which almost no one ever seemed to change his or her mind.

It was not only Aargh, Jim thought. It was generally true of Brian, Carolinus—or even his own men-at-arms, castle servants and the people belonging to the Malencontri estates—who were theoretically bound to obey any order he gave them. He could control the last category of people physically, but he could not even bend the point of view of any one of them.

Curiously, it was as if they were responsible only to what they considered their job or duty—and the way they did it was the way it had always been done. He, at best, was only their temporary overseer.

It was as if he was there only to do his own job, which was to see they did theirs in traditional fashion and no other. If part of their duty required their going out and dying for him, then that was all right, too—but only if it was part of that unwritten contract that seemed to exist between them and him. They would instantly obey his wildest whim, if it did not disagree with that contract; and silently, politely, but immovably, they would resist anything that did disagree.

Both he and Angie had found this out many times, to their great despair and frustration, in trying to make Malencontri Castle a livable place from their own twentieth-century point of view.

"What will you do, James?" asked Brian.

There, thought Jim, was the contract again. Brian was his best friend in this world—after Angie, of course. He was brave beyond belief, cheerful in the face of any adversity, loyal beyond imagining; and for his duty, his given word, or his Faith, he would resist the worst possible forms of torture and death without yielding.

But he was also a simple knight banneret. Problems with Naturals like the troll, Mnrogar, lay outside the field of his ordinary responsibility. If a superior in that area was around, Sir Brian's place was merely to follow, not lead.

It was up to Jim. Then, on a sudden inspiration, Jim grinned wickedly—but internally. He wrote on the inside of his forehead a magic statement.

CAROLINUS I NEED YOU →JIM

If an apprentice owed obedience to his master, the master also owed, in return, protection and help to his apprentice. That was one of the ways in which this contract was in Jim's favor. He could use the letter of this sort of agreement to his advantage, too.

He held the magic in his mind for a moment, then let it go. He smiled at Brian, who was looking puzzled—and that was all Jim had time to do.

He had expected a certain amount of delay. But Carolinus was simply, abruptly, there. He looked at Jim, looked at the sleeping Mnrogar, closed his own eyes for a second as if re-creating what had just happened here, opened his eyes again and looked at Jim with his usual glare.

"You're not here to pamper trolls!" he said.

For once, Jim felt on firm footing with the experienced magician.

"That's not the problem," he said. "The problem's the other troll somewhere upstairs in the castle, complicated by the fact of what Mnrogar's shaking has been doing to the castle itself over the last thousand years or so—however long he's been at it."

Carolinus was very often surprising in the way he reacted—there was no rule about it, except that, sometimes, completely unexpectedly, he would react very differently from the way everyone anticipated. Apparently, this was one of those times.

"Hmm," he said, glancing at the troll and then around at the stone arches. "I can't believe . . . well, we'll have to see."

He turned on Brian.

"Brian," he said, "you can find your way back up alone, can't you?"

Brian glanced around at the darkness beyond the troll-light, which seemed to enclose them like a solid globe.

"The rush-light I brought down for James and myself along the way," he said, glancing at the formerly flaming end of the rush, now showing nothing but a sooty, cold stub where its light had been, "has burned itself out. In the darkness, Mage, I could wander, lost, for some time. Perhaps—"

He was suddenly holding a completely new, brightly burning rush-light in his hand.

"Go without delay," said Carolinus. "Go swiftly, but without attracting attention. Do not run, or move with undue haste. Go directly to Jim's quarters, where Angie may still be. In any case, have the servant let you into the outer room, and wait there until Jim joins you. Jim and I will be moving in ways magical by ourselves."

"I understand, Mage, but—" Brian was beginning earnestly.

Jim never heard what it was he might have said. The cellar winked out around him and Carolinus; and instead Jim found himself, with the elder magician at his side, standing just inside a dusty room. It was filled with old furniture, piled high against the walls, and was evidently a room above ground in the tower, for its outer wall was slightly curved; and from behind the furniture and other things piled in front of that part of it, little gleams of daylight were coming.

"Wait a minute," said Jim. "We left Mnrogar down there just as he was. I just told him to sleep. He'll sleep forever unless that order is countermanded—"

"Do you think I'm the same sort of addle-pated young fumbler you are?" snapped Carolinus. "Don't teach your grandmother to suck eggs. I told him to wake in five minutes. Not only that; but if he tries to shake the castle again, both his arms will go limp for five minutes. That should hold him for now!"

Carolinus turned his attention to the wall where the daylight was showing.

"Out of the way, all of you!" he said to the furniture piled there.

With apologetic squeaks, thumps and rattles, the furniture and other items that were there immediately began to move aside; and in a moment the stone wall itself was exposed. An arrow slit had been hidden behind them; and light was coming through it. But less than six inches from the right side of the slit there was a vertical, six-foot crack in the wall, the top and bottom of which began as nothing more than ends to a line in the rock; but in the middle it gaped widely enough to let in almost as much light as the arrow slit.

"I have never seen the like," said Carolinus thoughtfully, gazing at the slit. "Our host came to me with this problem. But Hugo is not the man to discuss solutions with, since he goes by how he feels rather than how he thinks. There are cracks like this all over the main tower—probably two dozen or more, most of them smaller than this, happily; but he has kept word of them secret until now."

After only that one brief meeting with the Earl of Somerset, Jim could well imagine the Earl exploding immediately, either in favor of or adamantly against any suggested solution, without taking time for any consideration of whether it was practical or not.

"So," Carolinus was saying, "I took into my confidence Sir John Chandos, who has a level head; and the Bishop of Bath and Wells, whose thoughts in such matters are never to be despised. Also, both men have experience and information that I lack. John has seen many castles, old and new; and the good Bishop still has architects, masons and their like laboring on his cathedral in Wells. He has now sent for some of these to come view the damage, and see what can be done. Both to repair it, quietly; and also to ensure no more of it happens. But why or how it should happen at all, was a puzzle to all three of us."

He looked directly at Jim.

"Then," said Carolinus, "it occurred to me that you—"

"Resonance!" said Jim, out loud without thinking.

"Ah-hah!" Carolinus eyed him keenly. "So I was right. There is something in that other-place knowledge of yours that applies here."

"I don't know about that," said Jim grumpily.

He was very angry with himself for speaking out before he had thought over the possible results of saying anything.

"I know as little about the actual mechanics as you or anyone else," he said, "and I'm just guessing."

"But—" Carolinus said. "Go on!"

"Well," grumbled Jim, "there's something called resonance. It's what makes a harp string, when plucked, make a sound as the string quivers to a halt. You can also set up resonance in other things, though they may not resonate as visibly. I don't remember if the practice goes back to the Roman army or not; but the rule in all armies used to be that when a mass of men were marching across a bridge, they'd change step. In other words, they'd hesitate; and instead of going forward with the left foot go forward with the right foot again—something like a sort of slow skip—which would break the steady rhythm of their feet hitting the bridge, and therefore the resonance, the vibration they were setting up in its structure by marching over it."

Jim looked at Carolinus to see if the other was understanding him.

"Ah?" said Carolinus brightly.

"Yes," Jim said, "otherwise, you see, the bridge might break under them. Even though the resonance was small, it was being reinforced and made greater each time a number of feet came down on it together as part of a pattern."

"Ah!" said Carolinus.

"Now," Jim wound up, "I don't know if there could be any connection between that and this; but I suppose it might be possible. But, over a period of hundreds of years, if Mnrogar's found two particularly shakable arches to tug back and forth, he might be repeating a resonance that'll have an effect finally that'll make the whole fabric of the tower break apart."

He stopped talking. He became conscious that Carolinus was beaming at him.

"My boy," said Carolinus, "your command of words is admirable. Half of them make no sense, but I'm willing to believe that there was probably some sense behind them in the place from which you came. If so, there might be some sense in them here, as well. Now, if you're right, what do we do about the resonance? If we stop the troll's shaking, will the tower heal itself?"

"No," said Jim. "If I'm right, the damage that's already done will just keep getting worse, even if you stop Mnrogar permanently."

"I don't know if that would be ethical," Carolinus said, plucking at his beard. "After his being there eighteen hundred years, it could be a possible forbidden interference on my part with History."

He thought for a moment, still plucking at his beard.

"You must remember, Jim," he said, "how I explained to you the position of Magick in between History and Chance. We can assist History if Chance gets the upper hand—because if Chance had things all its own way we'd end in Chaos. And we can aid Chance when History seems to be having things all in its favor and there is a danger of its pushing Chance completely out of the picture—in which case we'd have Stasis. But we're not allowed to alter the normal course of History, or change the odds in Chance. However, never mind that—you did say the present damage would go on getting worse, even if he did stop?"

"Yes," said Jim, "because the tower's already been weakened in its general structure, in addition to the cracks you see in it now; and ordinary daily wear and tear will simply increase the damage."

"Yes," said Carolinus thoughtfully. "The troll must cease shaking the castle permanently, in any case—that much is sure. But the other's also a problem; although I might—just might, understand—be able to do some mending here, ethically, with Magick. I'll have to look into it, and possibly consult with my two colleagues, the other AAA+ magicians in this world."

He stopped talking and stared off into the distance. Jim let him stare.

"Well, well, it's simply something that'll have to go through regular channels," wound up Carolinus. He turned his attention back to Jim.

"As for dealing with the rest of the situation, clearly the only way to stop Mnrogar permanently is to find the cause of it. Undoubtedly he has been doing this shaking of the foundations for years—possibly as part of his long-standing feud with the Earl, and with the Earl's forebears—but the coming of this other troll he claims is somehow in this castle with none of us knowing about it has brought the situation to the brink. I swear, by all the magic I know, that I neither feel nor sense nor can discover sign of another troll. But if Mnrogar says there is one, there probably is."

"Then how can we find it?" asked Jim.

"That, of course, was what I was getting at." Carolinus looked sternly at him. "You must get busy at once, Jim."

"Me?" said Jim. "What am I to do?"

"Find the other troll, of course. Get to it, now!" said Carolinus. "Meanwhile I'll be about my end of the matter."

With that he disappeared, leaving Jim standing. This, he suddenly realized, was the other part of the contract as it worked from the standpoint of one who is ordinarily stuck with the responsibility. You simply turn to an underling and say:

"You do it."

CHAPTER 8

"My dear son," said the Bishop of Bath and Wells to Jim, "may I offer you a little of this excellent stewed eel?"

Jim looked to his right. The Bishop was holding a deep serving dish of silver, from which he had just taken the top. Part of the top had been broken off at some time, but what was left and the dish itself were polished to a very high gloss. Jim detested eels in this form or any other. But the Bishop was showing him merely the ordinary table courtesy.

"I thank you, my Lord," said Jim and watched as the Bishop used his knife to urge a section of eel out of its sauce onto Jim's trencher, a thick slice of bread that served as his individual plate, and later would be given to the poor or thrown to the dogs; for by that time it would have been soaked by a number of rich sauces and be high in nutriment. "Just a very little, please, my Lord. It's a good food for a fasting time like this Advent, but it bothers my conscience to eat much of anything before the midnight mass tonight that ends the fast."

The Bishop solicitously took his eating knife—actually a rather sharp, small dagger—and cut off a somewhat smaller chunk of the eel than Jim had been afraid he would serve, and deposited it on Jim's trencher.

He also looked with approval at Jim. It could not be said he beamed. Richard de Bisby was not a man to beam on anyone; but Jim's words had clearly struck him as being in the right spirit.

He put the dish with the eel in it back on the table and replaced its cover.

"I must admit," he went on in a lower voice, "I asked our host to seat us side by side like this so that we might have the chance to talk privily under the general noise of the dinner. You may have wished another table companion—say, such as the Lady Agatha Falon yonder—although I vow she seems most interested in my Lord the Earl."

"The Lady Agatha Falon?" said Jim, instantly interested. He looked.

So, the woman next to the Earl was the sister of the dead man they had found in the woods. She must indeed, he thought, have been a younger half-sister; for there was clearly a gap of at least twenty years between her and the dead man they had found. She was a little above the average height, which would make her not quite as tall as Angie, who sat even farther down from Jim, talking animatedly with Sir John Chandos who was beside her, the both of them beyond the Earl and Agatha Falon.

At first glance Agatha Falon was unremarkable. She had a sort of general, somewhat bony, attractiveness; but in no way did she really resemble her dead brother. Her hair was black, her eyes were brown and a little wide-set, her nose was snub and she had a wide, rather thin mouth that looked as if it could fall into a disagreeable expression very easily—all this over a pointed chin that completed an oval, somewhat pale face.

Right now, that face was animated; and above the puffed-up upper sleeves and tight bodice of her sky-blue gown, she seemed in her animated conversation with the Earl to be almost pretty. The Earl, his eyes popping even more than usual—Jim thought that possibly both his companion and his wine had a good deal to do with that—was clearly fascinated by her, or by what she was telling him.

"Thank you for naming her to me, m'Lord," he said to the Bishop. "She is the sister of the unfortunate gentleman we were too late to rescue on our way here, as perhaps you know."

"Yes," said de Bisby, dabbing his lips with a napkin held daintily in his powerful hand, "a cowardly and unhappy end for one of good family. But I trust the good fathers at Edsley Priory gave him proper Christian burial, and his new young wife as well?"

"Indeed they did," said Jim. "But, my Lord, you were just saying you wanted to speak privily with me?"

"Yes," said the Bishop, once more lowering his voice, which had climbed almost back to its normal patient, but resonant tones. "It has to do with that matter Carolinus will have spoken to you on. The matter of this castle."

He looked knowingly at Jim. Jim looked knowingly back. They were two Powers-behind-the-scenes involved with what was almost a state secret.

"You were unhappily delayed in arriving here at dinner," said de Bisby. "But such delay is entirely understandable, since you have a young Christian soul—hopefully already baptized . . . by the by, it probably would do no harm to baptize the child again, since no one is left alive and the infant's immortal soul might still be in peril. But, in any case, I clearly understand how you might not find it easy to arrive as promptly as others, you and your Lady-wife. Still, I own I was concerned that you might not appear at all."

"Oh, there was no danger of that, my Lord," said Jim.

The delay had indeed been unavoidable. Carolinus had disappeared from the room with a crack in its outer wall, evidently forgetting completely what he had said about transporting Jim, as well as himself, by ways magical. Jim had been left to find his own way back to Angie, Brian and the banquet.

Actually, it had turned out that it was not too difficult to do this. Jim stepped out of the room, closing the door behind him. He did not know enough magic to easily move the furniture back to cover the crack in the outer wall, except by very cumbersome, short, step-by-step magical commands. He had the somewhat resentful feeling that since it was Carolinus's doing in exposing the crack, the responsibility for the crack being discovered was clearly Carolinus's—if anyone did discover it.

In the hallway outside, he confirmed the fact that the room he had just left was in the main tower, the same tower Angie's and his room was in. It was merely a matter of going down the corridor until he came to a stone wall at its end, going back again in the opposite direction until he came to the main stairway; and then trying up and down until he found the floor that their rooms were on—after which finding them was no problem at all.

Within, Brian was impatiently waiting for him, and Angie was already dressed ready to go down; also impatient, but apparently not in a mood to take Jim to task for this. Angie, of course, knew Carolinus as well as Jim did, and would have guessed whose fault it was that Jim had not shown up before now.

So, there was a brief flurry of activity, as Angie gave last-minute instructions to the wet nurse who had the baby in the next room.

"—And don't let anyone in but one of us three, until I'm back!" she said over her shoulder, coming out from behind the tapestry that covered the doorway to the other room. "I'm ready."

The last two words were addressed to Jim. They went out, heard the door barred behind them; and Jim nodded to the one of his men-at-arms he had left on duty outside.

Together the three of them proceeded down the main stairway to the floor level where the Great Hall abutted on the main tower. They entered to find the banquet already underway. The servants were hurrying around the tables with an endless number of serving dishes to be presented on bended knee, particularly to those of higher rank or more importance; and the musicians were playing merrily in their gallery halfway up one of the walls of the hall. Jim noted that among the sackbuts, lutes and tabors was an Irish harp, and felt a longing—probably a vain one—that sometime during the dinner it would play a solo.

But the musicians were all pounding, blowing and sawing away together and probably would continue doing so while the dinner lasted.

The Earl's steward captured them and led them into the hall.

Here they were separated.

Brian was taken to one of the two tables that stretched the full length of the hall, and Angie and Jim were taken on to the high table, set crosswise to the other two at the head of the hall. There, already, sat the Prince, the Earl and the other important guests.

Jim had been by no means sure that he and Angie would be seated there. It was true he was a Baron. But fourteenth-century England was a land where a Baron could be someone important, or almost a nobody.

The yearly income from a gentleman's lands could, depending on a variety of circumstances, run from less than fifty pounds a year—that was the reason Brian was so active all the time in tournaments, trying to win armor and horses he could sell to keep his own small holding going—to five hundred pounds a year, the sort of income that placed a Baron on an equal financial footing with the more aristocratic, and even some royal, inhabitants of the kingdom.

In fact, Jim himself was definitely in the lower third as far as income went. Only the fact of his being a magician, and his notoriety as the Dragon Knight who had rescued his bride-to-be (the ballad makers had loved the fact that they were not yet married—it made it more of a romance) from the Dark Powers at the Loathly Tower, were reasons to give him more attention than most Barons at his income level.

He also thought it likely that he and Angie owed their seats at the high table to the influence of the Bishop and Chandos, if not to Carolinus himself—although it was not like Carolinus to make use of whatever influence he had, in that way.

Jim woke from his thoughts to realize the Bishop was still waiting for some further response from him.

"How may I serve you, my Lord?" he asked hastily.

"With a full account of what you know in this matter," said the Bishop. He added, a little less sternly, "And your own opinion and advice where I ask it, of course."

"Of course, my Lord," said Jim.

"Well, then, Sir James," said the Bishop, descending from the more churchly level of address for the slightly more familiar use of Jim's knightly title, "I understand you went searching for the giant under this castle and actually encountered a Fiend."

"Actually, a troll," said Jim. "Very large and unusually strong for his kind; but, you know, trolls are only Naturals and not inherently wicked, so you probably wouldn't want to think of him as a Fiend."

"I am aware of the Holy Church's definitions in such matters, of course!" said de Bisby stiffly. "But it is hard for me to think of such as a troll—or perhaps one of the Djinni, which the Infidel, Saladin, sealed up in vessels and threw into the depths of the ocean, to keep them from disturbing mankind—difficult not to think there is at least a touch of the Fiend in such as they. A troll who eats human flesh—hah!"

"The sharks of the ocean also eat human flesh, my Lord," said Jim diplomatically, "but you would hardly call them Fiends."

"I am not aware of any declaration by the Church on that matter," said the Bishop. He added wistfully, "Still, perhaps in the case of trolls, it might be possible that such a creature could have been contaminated by the power of Satan, so that it might be considered partly a Fiend. If so, it would be my duty to attempt to destroy it by all means possible—from my good right arm with mace in hand, to use of the powers entrusted to me by the Church."

The Bishop's voice had mounted a little toward the end of this particular statement, and Jim thought he caught an echo from beneath the episcopal robes of the same eagerness to engage in battle that many knights like Brian exhibited. It seemed to him he remembered now that somewhere he had heard vaguely of a Sir Roger de Bisby, possibly a near relation of the Bishop's, who had demonstrated his courage and aggressiveness in the Low Countries—that area which in Jim's twentieth-century world had become known as Holland and Belgium.

"In fact," went on the Bishop again, before Jim had a chance to speak, "I myself will be glad to lead a stout force of men-at-arms down into that cellar and see the creature destroyed once and for all."

"I'm afraid the situation is such that you might have your endeavors for nothing, my Lord," said Jim, as diplomatically as he could. "I'm only an apprentice, of course, but I fear you might get down there and find nothing at all. If you come searching for the troll, he may well vanish; and you'll find nothing."

"He cannot!" said the Bishop. "I have blessed this castle and its immediate grounds. No magic—evil or good—can take place during these holy twelve days until I, myself, leave."

"Of course, my Lord," said Jim. "But, I seem to remember my master in magic, Carolinus, telling me that what Naturals have that allows them to do things we humans can't, isn't true magic. In fact it's something they don't understand themselves; and simply have no control over—such as being able to breathe water or air, wherever they happen to be. Or, as in the case of this troll, becoming invisible if a search party cornered him and he had no way to escape with his life. As I say, I'm only an apprentice. I could be wrong. My master could tell you surely."

"It is an evil strength!" growled the Bishop in a low voice. "—If true. I will indeed ask Carolinus. But there must be other ways, then, to rid ourselves of this troll."

"I don't believe it's so easy to find one," said Jim. "At the moment it seems the only answer is to find the other troll—the one that this castle's troll claims has been brought in among the guests here. Find it and get rid of it. Because by being here it challenges the sovereignty of the castle troll, who has kept all other trolls at a distance for eighteen hundred years . . . I assume my master told you about everything the troll told Sir Brian and myself?"

"He did," muttered de Bisby. "Well, then, let us lose no time finding this other troll."

"We're trying to think of how to do that right now," said Jim. "Clearly, the other troll's somehow appearing among us like an ordinary human being. Not even Carolinus has thought of a way to identify who's so masquerading among us."

"This, too, I cannot understand!" said de Bisby, in a low voice between his teeth. "The very thought that at this holy time in this blessed place, a troll could be among us in human guise! It revolts my soul!"

He glared at Jim. Jim looked apologetic and waited.

"Well, then," went on de Bisby after a moment, "can the castle troll find this other troll if he's let upstairs to search for himself among the guests? I myself would accompany him and reassure all, as he passed among them, that I would guard them from him unless one of them was indeed the troll he claimed to want. Indeed—" de Bisby's face lightened.

"Indeed, that sounds like the perfect answer!" the Bishop said. "Why didn't I think of that at first?"

"If you'll forgive me, my Lord," said Jim, "I'm not sure the troll would trust us."

"What do you mean?" The additional word "*Sirrah*!" was clearly trembling on the Bishop's lips, but he did not quite say it.

"He might be afraid," said Jim, "that he'd be slain while he was so searching, unsuspecting."

"He would doubt the word of a Lord of the Church?" de Bisby glared at Jim.

"I—I'm afraid so," said Jim. "Of course, there again you'd better ask my master in magic. Carolinus would be able to tell you more certainly."

"I shall do just that!" said the Bishop.

The angry frown had come back to his brow so plainly that Jim unconsciously braced himself as he would have, expecting a physical attack; although this was ridiculously inconceivable, particularly in view of the many diners in the hall at the present. No bishop would want to risk his dignity that way.

"Remember," said Jim, "he's just a troll and doesn't know any better."

The frown faded from the episcopal brow gradually, and the Bishop's face gradually returned to normal; and with an effort he produced a small, reassuring smile.

"In any case," he said, keeping his voice very low, "you have done well so far, my son."

"Thank you, my Lord," said Jim.

"So—" began de Bisby.

"My Lord Bishop! My Lord Bishop!" cried a sharp female voice from farther up the table to their right. Jim and the Bishop both craned out over the table to see. Agatha Falon was leaning forward and waving and looking at the Bishop.

"My Lady?" said the Bishop.

"Could we speak to you for a moment? My Lord Earl and I— could you give us a few moments of your time?"

Both the Prince—who was theoretically sitting in the center spot at the table—and the Earl were between them. The Bishop got up from his backed bench—it was no more than that, but it was padded, and a great improvement over the ordinary benches on which the other guests sat at the lower tables—got to his feet, and walked down to lean agreeably with his head between the space of Agatha Falon and the Earl. Seated on Agatha's other side, Sir John Chandos, politely ignoring her calling, continued to talk cheerfully with Angie, next to him.

The Earl said something in a rumble that was so low-voiced that Jim could not catch the words. However, the same information was shortly made obvious by the much more understandable and high-toned voice of Agatha Falon.

"We are having a debate, My Lord Earl and I," Agatha sang, "whether a true love can exist between those of somewhat different ages. Not only that, but if it may be true love at first sight."

"I would not consider myself an authority on love, my Lady," said the Bishop austerely. "However—"

"But you must have had to do with numerous couples where, say, the husband was somewhat older than the bride; and be in a position to testify—in my interest—that such distance in years need make no difference at all in feelings?"

Jim felt a plucking at the back of his cote-hardie. He had time for a mild twinge of irritation—only a mild twinge, nowadays, since he had run into this so many times before. But it had always seemed ridiculous that in this world, where somebody might split your skull with a battle-ax for looking cross-eyed at him, people had so many little small, niggling gestures. Servants scratched at your door before coming in—that is, if they didn't simply walk in without any warning at all—people of all ranks plucked lightly at part of your clothing instead of speaking up to you, or touching you in firmer fashion to attract your attention. But no. The next step up from plucking was the blow that challenged you to fight.

He turned now, expecting a servitor with another dish, from which he would be supposed to help, not only himself, but other nearby diners. But the Bishop was no longer in his seat; and the next person seated beyond him was the Prince, who did not seem to be eating at present, only drinking. That only left the middle-aged lady in the chair at his left.

But she had fallen asleep there a little while ago, and was now snoring lightly. Possibly she had been up all night at devotions, this being the last day of Advent, the day of Christmas Eve, in fact; and some of the guests were more ardently religious than others. Or, it could be she had drunk a little more wine than her body was able to handle. Jim turned.

It was not a servitor. Instead of a servant of the Earl's, Jim saw a figure in an expensive, forest-green, thick wool robe with hood, literally crouching behind his chair.

Then he recognized the robe and hood as being one of Angie's pieces of outerwear on their trip here. It could not be Angie herself, since she was sitting farther down the table, talking, with what seemed remarkable enjoyment, to John Chandos. Looking more closely into the hood, Jim saw the terrified face of the wet nurse who should have been upstairs in the tower, locked in the room with young Robert Falon until Jim and Angie, or Brian, returned.

"Forgive me, my Lord. My Lord, please forgive me!" whispered the wet nurse.

"What is it?" asked Jim, in a low voice, suddenly alert and very worried.

"My Lord, forgive me, but I thought I was doing the right thing—"

"What are you talking about? Out with it!" growled Jim.

"I know my Lady said not to open the door to any but the three of you," she said, "but this was a serving wench from Agatha Falon, who wished to give Lady Falon's young nephew a present; a ring of hers bearing the family crest. I was asked, only, to open the door enough so she could slip it in to me." The wet nurse looked almost ready to burst into tears. "I—I did."

"Yes?" said Jim. "What of it? Is that what's got you all wrought up?"

"Wrought up, my Lord?" the wet nurse stared at him.

"Upset. Disturbed!" said Jim impatiently.

"Oh no," said the wet nurse, "the serving wench did only what she said. She passed just her fingers through holding a ring for my young Lord, then pulled her hand out. I closed and barred the door again so quickly I almost caught her fingers in it."

"Well, then," said Jim. By this time he was completely puzzled. "What's all this fuss about?"

"It was only afterward, my Lord, that I thought—you being a magician, and there being many things invisible—dangerous magic things might be brought to the place of one like your Lordship; and perhaps the ring had some evil spell upon it, or somewhat, and I had taken it in. The more I thought of it, the more I was afraid. Happily, Wilfred, your man-at-arms, my Lord—"

"Yes, yes," said Jim. "I had him standing guard outside in the corridor."

"Well," went on the wet nurse, "I called him inside to stay and unbar the door on my return. I took this robe of Lady Angela's— oh, I know it was wrong, my Lord, to lay hands upon it, let alone wear it—but I wanted to come down and tell you of this, without anyone knowing who'd brought you word."

"Why, I don't see how—" Jim was beginning, when he checked himself.

Suddenly, he did see how. There were two sides to what had just been reported to him. One was the fear of most of these people about magic and dark doings beyond their control; and their belief that they would be helpless faced with such things. The other was the fact that a gift like this from Agatha Falon, who had so far shown no interest in young Robert at all, was a little peculiar, to say the least. After all, there actually was magic in this world; and a ring might have something magic about it—magic that predated the Bishop's blessing of the castle, which only blocked the making of any *new* magic.

"All right," he said. "Go back up. I'll be there in just a moment or two."

The wet nurse slipped away. Jim looked up and down the table. The Bishop was still leaning into the space between the Earl and Agatha Falon; but not leaning too far, to the extent of impairing his churchly dignity. Angie was still in animated conversation with Sir John Chandos. That last was irritating—and not a small irritation, either.

Jim liked Sir John Chandos. More than that, he admired the man. Chandos had a brilliant mind, remarkably subtle for this time in history and under these conditions. Jim also recognized the fact that to date in their acquaintance, the other had said and done nothing that might not be interpreted as normal courtly courtesies toward Angie.

But Sir John was undeniably handsome and impressive with his extra years, intelligence and position close to the Throne. Somewhere in that combination Angie had found a person she liked to be with and talk to. There was no harm to it; there was only the uncomfortable fact that what Sir John was doing was also an ordinary preliminary to that game of seduction in the guise of courtly courtesies that went on—it was not too much to call it rampantly—at gatherings like this; and something for which the Earl's Christmastide was famous in particular, along with its food, sports, tournaments and entertainments.

But all this was something Jim should worry about later, not now.

Jim took another quick glance around him. No one was looking at him.

Quietly, he rose and went off in a direction that might seem to be taking him merely to one of the castle's privies; but which would also lead him to the stairs of the great tower and a clear route up to the rooms he shared with Angie.

As he was close to leaving the hall, there was a change in its noise level. All of the instruments but the Irish harp had fallen idle; and the resonant, sad notes of its strings were beginning to lament beautifully above the sound of general conversation.

"Damn!" said Jim. "Now, of all times!"

Regretfully leaving the sound of it behind him, he hurried on out of the hall and away.

CHAPTER 9

"It seems all right to me," said Jim.

He was back up in the outer room of their two chambers, with the door once more barred, the wet nurse hovering at his elbow and young Robert peacefully asleep in the other room—after a stiff workout of waving arms and legs and making pleased sounds over his freedom to do so.

Earlier Angie had sworn the wet nurse to silence—thereby terrifying the teen-age girl, who seemed to feel she had been forced into responsibility for the equivalent of a Crown secret—and unwound Robert, as soon as they were in their room, from the long strip of swaddling that bound him tight to his backboard—a sort of short plank with the hole in it near its top, so he could be conveniently hung on a peg or nail when his nurse was busy—announcing grimly that babies needed room to *move*; and that from now on she, Angie, would decide how Robert would be kept.

She had also had Jim order some of their own men-at-arms to secretly build a sort of crib, in which the baby had freedom of movement.

"No, nothing dangerous about it at all," Jim repeated now, turning the ring over in his fingers.

The ring was a simple circle of gold, sized to a woman's finger, with a flat top face into which had been cut the crest of the Falon coat of arms. A signet ring, designed to be pressed into hot wax to seal a letter or other document, so as to attest to the rank and identity of its signer.

Indeed, it looked perfectly harmless. Jim, of course, was limited to examining it by nonmagical means, since the Bishop had now blessed the castle and no *new* magic would work until he had left. The only test he had been able to give it that approached magic had been the result of a recent talk with Carolinus, who had mentioned that an experienced magician should be able to tell by a sort of tingling in his fingers if a handled object had any magic in it.

Jim had felt no tingling in his fingers from the ring. On the other hand, it could be that he was not yet enough of an experienced magician to make that sort of test.

"But I'll keep this," he said finally. "Carolinus can look at it and tell me what he thinks. I'm pretty sure it's completely safe. The baby can't wear it, anyway; though I suppose we could fasten it to his clothing, one way or another."

"Yes, m'Lord," said the wet nurse, "I could sew a loop to it to go over a button."

"Well, then," said Jim, turning to the door and rather looking forward to getting out of the room—both rooms were stuffily overheated, with a fireplace in each merrily burning away. Brian had mildly tried suggesting to Angie that there might be something wrong in overheating the baby, or accustoming it to what was in essence a tropical temperature; but Angie had steamrollered him into silence with another grim statement that *she* would decide what was best for the child. She had sounded more like a she-wolf than anything else, ever since the moment in which she had first picked Robert up out of the snow. Neither Brian nor Jim had ventured to argue with her other than mildly.

Jim turned and reached to lift the bar holding the door shut. But as he touched it, he was stopped.

"M'Lord!" squeaked a tiny voice behind him. "Sir James! Oh, Sir James!"

Jim and the wet nurse both spun about to face the fireplace.

"Eek!" said the wet nurse, in a tone of voice admirably combining terror and extreme curiosity.

Both emotions could be justified, Jim thought. Sitting in mid-air above the flames within the fireplace itself, apparently supported on a thin column of gray smoke, was a small brown figure in rather sooty clothes, consisting of tight hose, a tight jacket, and a small flat cap, jammed down tightly on his equally small round head. His nose was stubby, his eyes were bright pinpoints and he had a somewhat timorous smile on his little mouth.

"It's just me, m'Lord. Hob, sir—your kitchen hobgoblin. I crave pardon, sir. I don't believe you've ever set eyes on me before, m'Lord. But I know you well, of course, and I'd not disturb you now, m'Lord—but it's a matter of most urgency— the dragon said."

"Hob?" said Jim. "Dragon?"

"Yes, m'Lord. A dragon called Secoh, m'Lord. He came to the castle searching for you most desperately. It was his own idea to go into the kitchen, whereat all your servants there went out; and he called up the chimney for me, so of course I came down. He sent me with a message to you—not being able, himself, to come safely to you here at this castle. Ordinarily, m'Lord, I'd never disturb your knightliness. But, I thought in this case—anyway I rode the smoke up and over the treetops to here, the way we hobgoblins do when there's need to."

He fell silent.

"I really am your kitchen Hob," he added anxiously. "It's just that we're all called Hob, all we hobgoblins."

The last words came out with a note of sadness.

"What's that got to do with it?" said Jim, a little snappishly. Too many things were being thrown at him too fast.

"Nothing! Nothing at all, great magic knight!" cried Hob in a suddenly terrified voice. "It just slipped out. Forgive me, my Lord—I'm just your hobgoblin—at your service as always. Trusty and true—though small, of course. I didn't mean to mention that about my name . . ."

"Don't you like being called Hob?" said Jim, his mind foggily trying to sort some meaning out of the little Natural's tangle of words.

"I hate it—I mean I love it. Call me just Hob, m'Lord. Forget I mentioned it. It's a fine name. I . . . I like it."

"You really mean you want a different name, is that it?"

"Yes—no, no—call me just Hob, my Lord—" Hob was becoming even more terrified.

"I'll call you Hob-One," said Jim impatiently, then regretted his tone of voice. "—de Malencontri, of course."

"HOB-ONE?" The little green-brown eyes in the brown face opened very wide. "—DE MALENCONTRI? All for me?"

"Certainly," said Jim.

A remarkable change came over the newly renamed Natural. He literally beamed.

"Oh, thank you, m'Lord! Thank you! I can't tell you—"

"Never mind that. Why do you come out into the kitchen and go on eating binges every so often?" Jim asked—more to get his thoughts back on track than anything else.

"I don't know!" said Hob-One humbly. "Something just comes over me, m'Lord. I have to come out of the chimney and throw myself around the kitchen from one thing to another, tasting everything. I don't know why I do it. I'm very sorry, m'Lord— I can't help it, though. Most of us hobgoblins go wild like that every so often. We've never known why."

"Well, maybe we can look into it; and if you don't like it, maybe I can magically help you get away from it," said Jim. "You may have to go cold turkey for a while—I mean, you may have to possibly do without your eating fits; but if you'd like to be free of them—"

"Oh, I would, m'Lord," said Hob. "I don't know. It seems to come on me when I'm feeling particularly small and lonely . . ."

Jim had a sudden insight into why Hob went on the eating binges.

"Yes," he said firmly, "from now on, all in Malencontri will be told to call you Hob-One. Possibly, just One for short. There, now you have a name. You're the number one—hobgoblin. Now, about your message—"

Beyond the door a young male voice was abruptly to be heard, raised in outrage; so that its tones reverberated through the panel of the door itself and into the room.

"What orders, sirrah?" it cried. "They do not apply to me! I am the Prince!"

"Eek!" said Hob-One, or some kind of sound very like that, and shot up the chimney out of sight.

"Now what?" muttered Jim. But the truth was, he had already recognized the voice as that of the young Crown Prince of England, whom he had last seen down at the dinner table, drinking moodily in silence. He turned to the wet nurse, who was standing, waiting beside him. "Go in the other room and wait until I call you. Try to keep Robert quiet, if you can."

She disappeared behind the curtain of the connecting door. Jim went to the outer door and unbarred it. The Prince stumbled in, crossed the room to its two padded barrel chairs and fell into one, with his elbow on the table beside it.

"Wine!" he said. "And a glass for yourself as well, Sir James. I must talk."

"No," said Jim, standing where he was and looking down at the royal young man.

For a moment, the word did not seem to penetrate the Prince's drink-fogged brain. Then it registered and he flushed, angrily.

"What I gave you was a command, Sir James!" he shouted. "Fetch me wine, I say!"

"And I said no," said Jim. In the next room, young Robert had been woken by the loudness of the Prince's voice, and was beginning to cry fitfully. But the wet nurse was quick in soothing him, evidently; for the crying degenerated swiftly to hiccups and he fell silent again.

"How dare you!" said the Prince. "I've given you a royal order. You could die for such pertness!"

He sat, staring angrily at Jim, while Jim said nothing; and slowly his face and voice both changed.

"Why do you tell me no?" he said, almost plaintively.

"You've already had a good deal of wine, your Grace," said Jim.

"How dare—" The Prince broke off and seemed almost to crumple in the chair, all his rage going out of him. He went on in an almost pitiful voice. "Sir James—my good Sir James, I need to talk to you. You're the only one I can talk to, but I need wine to do it. I'm not used to talking like this. It's against everything in me to tell private matters like this to anyone outside. But I need wine to do it. I tell you, I must talk or fall apart!"

He was suddenly very young and helpless. Jim looked at him for a long moment, and then caved in.

"I'll see if there's any around," he said, turned on his heel and walked past the curtain into the other room to where the wet nurse was rocking a sleeping Robert in her arms.

"Is there any wine here?" he asked her in a low voice.

She was singing to Robert under her breath.

"*Ba, ba, lilly wean . . .*" she sang, then raised her voice slightly to answer Jim. "In the corner there, my Lord, in the chest."

She went back to her near-voiceless singing; and Jim went to the chest, opened its lid, and found not only wine but bread and some small cakes there as well, made of pastry and rather durable. He debated taking some of the cakes as well as the wine, in hopes of getting some food into the Prince—then reflected that the Prince must have eaten something already. It would probably do no good to try to force more food on him now.

He took a bottle of wine and a leathern jug with a tie-down stopper, which held carefully boiled water to mix with the wine; also, a couple of metal cups, which he carried back into the other room and placed on the table by the Prince. Pulling up the other chair, he sat down facing the young man. He poured wine into the Prince's cup, filling it about a quarter full, and reached for the leather bottle.

"—No water!" said the Prince.

Jim ignored him and poured at least as much water as wine into the cup. Then he put a dollop of both into his cup.

The Prince did not protest, but picked up his wine and water and took a thirsty swallow. Jim put his cup to his own lips, but only wet them and set his cup down again.

"What is it that has you"—Jim checked himself in time from saying "bothered"—"concerned, your Grace?" he asked.

"Agatha Falon!" said the Prince.

Jim was puzzled. He was too ignorant of everything about Agatha Falon to understand what the Prince might mean. The young man could simply be feeling slighted, ignored or insulted somehow. He took a stab in the dark.

"Yes," he said, "I saw and heard her talking busily with my Lord Earl."

"That?" said the Prince with a wave of his hand, slumping in his chair. "What of that? She gathers trophies. It's her way. She's no beauty, but she would have the first attention of the highest she can reach. No, no, the Earl means nothing to her. It is my father!"

"The King?" said Jim. Practically every unattached—and mostly all the attached—women who came to court would be hoping to attract the royal attention. The King, still only in middle age, even though alcohol-addicted—as Edward III had not been, in the history of the twentieth-century Earth from which Jim and Angie had come—could have his pick of the available ladies. It was probable that a rich Baron like young Robert's father would have been able to spend some time at court close to the King's person; and Agatha, of course, with him. But judging by what Jim had seen of her, Jim was surprised that someone like her could become a problem; either to the King or to the first Prince of the land, because of her interest in the Prince's father.

"I wouldn't think his Majesty would be . . ." Jim was still searching for the proper word when the Prince broke in on him.

"Faught!" the Prince said.

Jim was startled. He had never heard anyone actually say "faught" before.

"That strident strumpet!" the Prince went on. "Not that he nowadays is so . . . I thought him a God once when I was younger, seeing him in his robes and crown; and on another time when he was dressed in the armor he wore for the great sea battle with the French. But he is King! And she reaches not just for the Royal favor, but to be Queen!"

Jim was more than startled—more than he would have ever imagined he could be at hearing this. Perhaps the few years he had spent here had made him more aware of the implications of what the Prince was saying.

"But she can't hope to become Queen? I mean, she's not of high enough rank," said Jim.

"Indeed!" growled the Prince. "She is hardly more than a commoner! And my mother was indeed a Queen—Isabella of France! But he, nowadays . . ."

The Prince threw himself restlessly about in his chair, reached for his cup and gulped at it again. He set it down with a bang. "How can I talk about it?"

"But how can she even hope—" Jim was beginning.

"Some will dare anything," said the Prince, "and she—give her credit, she's bold enough to dream high enough. It could happen. He is wifeless for a second time, and she never married. There are means. She could be bought a higher rank and . . . It could be done . . ."

He stopped, picked up his cup and put it down again.

"My vessel is empty, Sir James," he said.

Reluctantly, Jim poured a little more wine and somewhat more water into the Prince's cup. The other lifted it and drank it off without apparently tasting it.

"And if it comes to pass, James," said the Prince, staring at the table top, "it were not unwise for me to watch against a dagger in my back, or have someone to taste my food before I eat it myself."

"You don't mean that, your Grace!" said Jim. The Prince's last words had literally stunned him. This was England, he found himself thinking. Surely assassination at the royal level could not take place here. But then, even as he thought it, he realized it could. It could take place anywhere if the prize was large enough to make it worthwhile—and the throne of England was that.

"She will stop at nothing for the lightest thing she wants!" said the Prince. "Because she will try more, she will gain more. She will end up getting what she wants—the crown my mother wore. And I am helpless, helpless!"

He threw himself back into his chair, staring at the ceiling, and closed his eyes like someone in extreme pain.

Jim sat silently watching him until he suddenly realized that the Prince's eyes had not opened again, his tense face had relaxed and his breathing had deepened.

"Your Grace—" he said tentatively.

There was no reply from the Prince.

Jim reached out cautiously toward the Prince's arm. To even touch one of the immediate royal family without permission or command was one of the worst of crimes. But the Prince did not stir. He prodded the blue-clad arm gently.

The Prince still did not react.

Jim got to his feet, listened for a moment to Edward's breathing, which was becoming almost a snore, and went to the door that opened into the hall. He unbarred it and stepped outside to speak to the man-at-arms still on duty there.

"Do any of the castle servants, particularly those who will be serving in the Great Hall right now, know you by sight, Wilfred?" he asked.

Wilfred shook his head.

"I think not, m'Lord."

"Then I want you to go down. Enter quietly, not attracting attention if you can avoid it, circle around behind Sir John Chandos and Lady Angela at the high table, and carry a message to Sir John. Tell him quietly, so that nobody but Lady Angela will hear, that I need him urgently up here—as quickly as possible. Also, if the Lady Angela wishes to come too, say that I said that it would be better if she didn't."

"Yes, m'Lord." Wilfred unbuckled his sword belt and dropped it with his sheathed sword gently to the corridor floor; for he was allowed to wear it here by their rooms in the castle only by special permission of the Earl and because of the presence of young Robert Falon.

"You remember what I told you to say?" said Jim, although he knew the answer.

"Word for word, m'Lord," said Wilfred, grinning a fleeting gap-toothed grin. He turned and went off down the corridor, moving swiftly but silently in his heelless shoes. Jim went back into the room.

He sat down to wait; but it was not more than ten minutes before the door opened without so much as a knock or scratch and Chandos came in. Wilfred stood in the doorway until Jim nodded at him and he stepped back out, closing the door behind him.

"Your Lady would have come," said Chandos, walking over to the chair where the Prince still lay back, now obviously in drunken slumber. He looked down at the young man. "I added my words to yours to dissuade her. There are more empty places at the high table than should be at this stage in the dinner."

He turned his head and looked keenly at Jim.

"Did he say what was concerning him?" Chandos asked.

"Agatha Falon," said Jim. He was tempted to add a word about the Prince's royal father; but for a man with Chandos's perception it should not be necessary.

Chandos nodded, looking back at the Prince.

"Still, this sort of thing cannot be," Chandos said.

"I didn't know how to get him back to his own quarters without attracting notice; from servants, if nothing else," said Jim. "That was why I sent my man-at-arms for you. I hope you didn't think me presumptuous, Sir John," he said, "for involving you in this—"

"Not at all, James," said Chandos. "It'll be more understandable, and far better, if he is seen in this state with me, than with you. If you will lend me your man-at-arms from without, the two of us together can take him to my quarters, which are close here; and with luck we may not even encounter anyone else on the way. Once there, I can let him sleep. This won't happen again after I talk to him."

He looked at Jim.

"He'll be ready to listen in the morning. And it is too good a mind in that head, not to understand how something like tonight would play right into the hands of such as Agatha Falon, instead of guarding against her. Would you get your man-at-arms?"

Jim went to the door and called in Wilfred.

With Jim helping, they got the Prince on his feet, one arm draped limply over Chandos's outside shoulder and another over the outside shoulder of Wilfred, both Sir John and the man-at-arms holding a wrist; and with their other arms around the Prince's waist, holding him upright between them.

Jim opened the door and they went out into the corridor. It was empty.

Chandos turned to go, and looked at Jim.

"Heigh-ho," Chandos sighed, "and this is soon the anniversary eve of our Lord's birth. A fine Christmastide at our Lord Earl's this year—and it's just begun. Wish you good eve, James."

CHAPTER 10

"   So you see," Jim said to Angie, "none of it's really my
... business; but as usual here I am in the middle of all
this."

It was late morning of Christmas Day—almost noon. He and
Angie were sitting in the outer room of their two-room quarters.
Robert was fast asleep in the other room, and there was no one
with him. Angie had sent the wet nurse off on an errand and seen
to it that the serving woman she had brought from Malencontri
was not about either, so they could talk in privacy. Jim had been
waiting for a chance to speak to her this way since the Prince's
visit to this same room.

They had not talked until now because there had been no chance
to talk. Angie had been able to miss such duties as the midnight
religious service in the castle's chapel; but Jim had felt duty bound
to put in appearances there—luckily, since he was being treated
as a guest of high table rank, he had been able to sit down, if only
on a hard, unpadded bench seat, up front near the altar. Most of
the castle's guests had found it necessary to stand; otherwise all
of them could not have gotten into the little chapel.

So, he had been up past midnight, and had also made the
probably necessary, but uncomfortable, decision to put in an
appearance at another boar hunt scheduled for this morning of
Christmas Day—a hunt from which he had just come back.

It could be said that he had been lucky at the boar hunt, too.
They had spent several hours riding around and freezing in the

woods with the yelping hounds out in front of them and no sign of a boar; then, without warning, they had encountered one that seemed almost as big as a small bull, certainly as heavy and probably several times as dangerous.

Jim's luck had come in not being close enough so that he would seem to have held back if he did not immediately try to be one of those who reached the boar, leaped off his horse and attacked it with a boar spear. There was no lack of those among the hunters who were very eager to do just that. The boar, however, had given them no chance.

He had immediately charged them. Tearing up some of the dogs as he went through the pack like a crossbow bolt through a stand of high rushes, he bowled over two of the leading horsemen and made his escape.

The hounds would have followed, and the rest of the hunters with them; but as it happened one of those knocked over, horse and all, was the Earl himself. The Earl had no doubt been a powerful and effective huntsman and warrior in his day. But that day was somewhat past; and now he lay helpless in the snow on his back, the wind knocked out of him and his armor making it almost impossible for him to get up even if he had his breath. This brought the hunt to an early end. The reluctant dogs were called back, much against their will; for left alone they would have followed the boar indefinitely—though it was clear they had no chance at all, the full pack of them, against him.

So, that had ended the hunt. Jim was feeling the worse for wear, from lack of sleep as well as all else, and he was sitting rather exhaustedly, trying to give Angie an account of everything that had happened to him from the moment in which Carolinus had sent him with Brian down to talk to the troll in the basement of the castle.

They still had to dress for dinner, which was only an hour and a half away, but since this was a special day out of the twelve days of Christmas, everyone would be in their finest clothes; and even if Jim himself scarcely cared what he looked like, he had an appearance to keep up—while Angie very much wanted to have plenty of time in which to dress and get ready. Therefore there was a slight impatience underlying the normal concern with which she had been listening to him—and Jim could not help but be aware of this.

"I suppose," Jim went on, "I'm stuck with this business of the troll in the basement of this castle and the mysterious possible troll upstairs here among the guests somewhere, since I'm Carolinus's apprentice and I've got an obligation to him. But anything to do with Agatha Falon, or the Prince and Agatha Falon's designs on King Edward, shouldn't be any of my problem. Don't you think?"

"Does it matter what I think?" said Angie. "Isn't your real problem what everybody else will think? Carolinus, the Prince, Chandos; and the fact that we want the King to give the wardship of young Robert to someone trustworthy—you don't want to lose the friendship of the Prince, do you, if only for Robert's sake?"

"I don't think the opinion of the Prince means much to his father in the case of something like that," said Jim. A small but definite thundercloud seemed about to gather on Angie's brow. Jim added hurriedly, "but of course I won't do anything that might make arguing the wardship less likely."

"And that means you're going to have to help the Prince and Chandos and then the Earl. But, they can't expect the impossible from you; so that if you don't find this other troll, or manage to help the Prince with that Agatha Falon, then they can hardly hold it against you. I'm not surprised. That woman would try anything, let alone trying to become Queen of England—and now that we're on the subject of the ring, where is it? You didn't have it sewn on young Robert's clothes after all, did you?"

They had not been talking about the ring, Jim thought a little resentfully. Angie had simply pulled it out of thin air in mid-sentence. But he kept his feelings well hidden inside himself.

"Of course not," said Jim. He reached into the pouch that was attached to a couple of the rivets on his most dressy knight's belt, and fished out the ring. He passed it to Angie.

She examined it closely and suspiciously, even to the point of putting her nose close to it and sniffing at it.

"No," she said at last, reluctantly, "there doesn't seem to be anything wrong with it—that I can see now."

"I don't think there is," said Jim. "After all, it may be a perfectly normal gesture. She's Robert's aunt. You know how the aristocracy here feels about family. She probably simply wanted him to have the ring."

"Hah!" said Angie.

That was twice in the last couple of days, Jim thought, that Angie had come out sounding very medieval indeed.

"I told you," Jim said, "I'll have Carolinus check it out, before we bring it close to Robert."

"Absolutely!" said Angie. "Now that this Agatha knows that Robert exists, she'll see her chances of the Falon estates going completely out of her hands altogether. First, Robert's guardian will have control of them; then when Robert comes of age, he will. Maybe you better find that other troll after all."

"I'd be glad to if I knew how," said Jim. "Just how do you think I should go about it?"

"Carolinus will simply have to tell you a magical way to do it," said Angie. "I don't believe that there isn't a magical way. He's just being the way he always is about making you learn things on your own."

"We can't be sure of that," said Jim; then, hastily, because he saw that this line of talk could lead to nothing but unproductive argument between them, he added, "Also, what about this business of our kitchen hobgoblin? I haven't seen Hob-One since the Prince came in. How about this message he said he had from Secoh?"

"Forget about it for the moment," said Angie firmly. "Hob-One's not here—by the way, couldn't you think of a better name for him than that?"

But she went on without waiting for an answer.

" . . . I suppose somewhere along the line you're going to have to arrange to get far enough outside the castle to use your magic, turn into a dragon and fly to find Secoh and get the message. But you've got the rest of the twelve days for that. Well, eleven days now, if you don't count today. Jim, I think we really must get dressing."

"I'm already dressed," said Jim mildly.

Indeed he was. Besides his best belt with the painted enamel plaques in interstices of its metal links, with his best sheath and dagger hanging from it, he was wearing an almost brand-new, madder-dyed, red cote-hardie above blue hose; and his slipperlike, open-work shoes, completely heelless like everybody else's, were also dyed red.

Angie, of course, would be the showpiece of the family. She had an absolutely new formal gown, a full-skirted, tight-bodiced dress colored with the pale gold of saffron dye. The voluminous sleeves, puffed out above the elbow and tight-fitting below it down to the wrist, were of course detachable; but Angie had decided to go against the general custom of wearing a contrasting color with the saffron gown.

Instead, she wore the matching sleeves of the gown itself; but with them the enormous rubies she had been given by Rrrnlf, the Sea Devil. They had been detached from the chain that linked them, and sewed by their bezels into two rows. One row ran down the tight part of the right sleeve and the other down the left, where such sleeves normally had rows of buttons, rounded upward on their top side and often cloth dyed, or even painted with tiny scenes.

None of this was on her just at the moment. The dress, her dress shoes and everything else were waiting in the other room for her to start getting ready; and at any minute now not only the wet nurse but Angie's serving woman would be coming back to help her get into the costume. She was fairly confident her garments should match up to, or even outshine, any of those worn by other female guests present for this most important of the twelve days of mid-day dinners. Also, her position at the high table, would make her dress visible to the eyes of all.

"I think I'll roll up my travel bedroll," said Jim. He and Angie carried their own mattresses wherever they went, and avoided sleeping in the beds made available to them at most other castles and all inns, simply because these were alive with vermin under ordinary conditions. "Then I'll take it down to Brian's room, and try to catch a quick nap there before dinner. You can come by his room and pick me up when you're ready, so that we can go down to the Great Hall together."

They got up from their chairs. Angie smiled at him suddenly and hugged him.

"Don't worry," she said. "I'll be thinking of ways you could do things, too."

Warmed by this, Jim watched her go through the tapestry into the other room, rolled up his bedroll and headed for Brian's quarters. On his way down the hall, he had an idea of his own. He was seated at the high table, Brian was not. Slice it anyway you like, and in spite of the fact that Brian was a better fighter, a braver man, better in all ways that counted in this medieval world than Jim—the fact remained that largely through accident, and his own false claim to a title when he had first arrived, Jim was more in the public eye at this Christmas gathering than Brian was.

Brian would be able to move around and possibly not be missed, when Jim's moving around would be noticed and possibly even talked about. He did not see exactly how Brian's relative freedom could come in useful; but it felt as if he had the fore-runner of at least one idea if not more.

He knocked at Brian's door, not really expecting to find Brian in. However, his squire or some man-at-arms should be there, keeping the place occupied and being responsible for what was in it. Theoluf would ordinarily have been doing the same for Jim, but the baby's presence had changed all that; and Theoluf himself was just as happy to be off keeping an eye on the men-at-arms. But it was Brian himself who opened the door and summoned him in.

"Ah, James!" he said. "It's a glad sight to see you! How do I look?"

Brian turned around in front of Jim. He was clearly already dressed for the main banquet of the season himself, in a blue cote-hardie, only slightly faded, and wearing small, very clean, very recently reblacked heelless shoes that looked more like slippers to Jim's eyeing—but then all the shoes of this time did—than anything else. His knight's belt, with its sheathed dagger attached, was the one resplendent thing about him; it having been one of the prizes at a tourney where he had carried the day.

All this, of course, adorned a lean, fit, sinewy body; which, if no more than five feet nine inches tall, carried itself as if it was at least a foot taller—and did so with justification.

Brian had fought and beaten many men a great deal taller, heavier and possibly even stronger than he.

"You look excellent, Brian," said Jim, and meant it.

"Hah!" said Brian with satisfaction, turning back. "It's good of you to say so, James. I would not have it said I cannot dress to fit my station."

Abruptly he turned his back again.

"However, James," he went on anxiously, "would you look at the collar at the back of my cote-hardie? It was a touch worn. A clever woman with a needle at my castle turned it inward, somewhat—I know not exactly what she did; but the aim was to keep the worn spot from showing. Yet it seems to me that when I have it on, as now, I can reach back there, and feel a sort of roughness in the cloth, as if the worn part was still showing. Tell me, do you see it, as you stand there?"

Jim looked at the curve at the top of Brian's cote-hardie in the back. The worn spot he had spoken of was almost out of sight, but not quite. Still, anyone would have to come up and practically peer down the back of Brian's neck to see it properly.

"I don't see a thing," said Jim.

"Ah, that relieves me," said Brian, turning back. "Are you ready to go down to the hall, James? Where's Angela?"

"She's to come along here to get me when she's ready to go down," said Jim. "If you want to wait, we can all go down together."

"I'll be glad to wait, of course," said Brian. "Indeed, it may do more for my reputation with those here to see how closely I come into dinner with you and the Lady Angela and Geronde, than if Geronde and I went down by ourselves. When the steward announces you, he must needs announce me in a voice not too different, and all eyes in the hall will of course then turn upon us four."

"You underrate yourself, Brian," said Jim. "Angie and I are the ones who will be honored to enter with the well-known winner of so many tournaments. One of the premier lances of England."

"Well, well," said Brian, "I would not myself call myself one of the premier lances of England, of course; but let that be and on to other subjects—sit down and I will fetch us to drink."

"I was thinking of taking a nap—" Jim broke off, seeing the disappointment on Brian's face.

Brian very seldom invited anyone to Castle Smythe, because of its run-down condition. But he had the born soul of a host in him; and here in this one room of the Earl's, considerably smaller than either of the rooms that Jim and Angie occupied and which must necessarily hold his squire as well as himself—the squire sleeping on a pallet in front of the door—he had a chance to be a host. "On second thought, some wine is exactly what I want!"

"Well said!" said Brian, rummaging in a corner among his belongings, piled up there in helter-skelter fashion. He came up with a large leather flask of the sort that normally contained water, but was useful for carrying wine on horseback because there was no danger of it breaking, as anything but a metal container might during the vicissitudes of a journey. "I have only the two cups, and no means to wash them here at the moment. But perhaps you might be content to wipe one out, James."

Jim chose the smaller cup, poured some of the water from the leathern watering jug on the table into it and took one of the patches from the secret inside pockets of his own cote-hardie, and did as Brian suggested. The odds against his picking up any unfriendly bacteria were relatively small, in this case.

"Ah, wine," said Brian, pouring from the jug of it he had picked up, "good for the soul, good for the . . ."

He evidently ran out of inspiration. Jim reflected that for Brian, wine probably was good for his soul. In fact, good for everything, at any hour of the day or night and in considerable quantities. But it did not seem to have any great effect on him. However, this was the chance he had been waiting for.

"As a matter of fact, Brian," he said, after adding water to his own wine, "I've been wanting to talk to you. You remember the business with the troll downstairs?"

"Very well, James," said Brian, looking serious. "A stouter such being, I vow, I would never have imagined!"

"Well," said Jim, "Carolinus has given me the, er—duty of finding the other troll. The one the castle troll claims is up here. That'll be the first step in dealing with the situation with the castle troll. And besides that, other things have turned up since . . ."

He told Brian about Agatha Falon's gift of the golden ring, and the Prince's overindulgence in wine—how he had talked of fear for his life if Agatha succeeded in making herself the next Queen of England by marrying his father. When Jim had finished telling this, Brian wagged his head seriously.

"I could hardly believe that anything like that could happen—" Jim was saying.

"Strange things happen at court, James," said Brian. "Also, with wine in him, even a King might see beauty where to a soberer eye there is none; or very little at least. Who can tell? As for how the Lady Agatha might react if she once became Queen and gave our royal liege another male heir, who can say? Men and women alike can do evil things to gain the ends they want."

Jim's faint hope that the Prince had been exaggerating sank at Brian's ready acceptance of the fact the Prince might be in danger if someone like Agatha succeeded in gaining the Throne. He had half talked himself into believing Brian would immediately protest that such a thing was beyond the bounds of possibility. That it could never happen.

"But that isn't all," Jim went on. "A hobgoblin came down my chimney in the first of our two rooms—"

And he told Brian about his talk with Hob-One. Now he *did* see Brian looking incredulous.

CHAPTER 11

"This is passing strange, James," said Brian. "Certes, I have never heard of such a thing as a message from a dragon carried by a hobgoblin. Yet it seems to me that this can have little to do with the matter of the troll under this castle; nor yet of the Prince and this Agatha Falon."

"I think so, also, Brian," said Jim. "But I hate to think of our other old Companion waiting there in our kitchen to deliver some message to me. Yet I can't very well leave the castle and change to a dragon, then fly back to Malencontri and talk to Secoh myself—either there or wherever he's gone to from there."

"You think too lightly of yourself, James," said Brian.

"Not in this case," said Jim grimly. "And there's also the absence of Carolinus. I can't find him, to get help from him. I haven't seen him since he left me in the tower, and of course I can't call to him magically, the way I normally would, since the Bishop blessed the castle."

Jim realized abruptly that he was talking himself into leaving the castle, after all.

Brian looked sympathetic. Carolinus and magic were not in his area of technical authority.

"Well—no choice in the matter," said Jim. He glanced at his bare left wrist from sheer reflex. He had been here several years now, and he still could not get used to not having a wristwatch there.

However, it actually was not necessary. He had developed something of the same sense of time that most of the people around him seemed to have instinctively. He had a general feeling of the amount of time he had in which to talk to Brian before Angie showed up. Then he remembered Geronde.

"Geronde isn't coming by here to get you before going down, is she?" he asked.

"No, of course not, James," said Brian. "I was to go and find her when I thought she was ready, then we two would go down together. It was in my thoughts that you, Angela and I could go to her together."

He coughed, with a touch of embarrassment.

"I had not thought of Angela being with you," he went on, "and of course, here at the Earl's castle, she only has a single room. But you and I could wait without, and Angela could go in to her; so that neither of them would be uncomfortably waiting."

"Well, we can do that," said Jim. With the importance of this dinner, and the fact that Angie would be ready to go, Geronde would be quick to see the benefit of what Brian had mentioned— the four of them going in at the same time. She should not keep Jim and Brian waiting outside in the corridor too long before she and Angela joined them.

"While we're waiting," Jim went on, "perhaps you would be kind enough to tell me more about trolls, in general; since the one in the castle has become *my* problem, it might help if I knew more about the creatures."

"In truth," said Brian, "I know but little; only what is told in common tales."

"I understand," Jim said; "but you must remember that I did not grow up in England, and so I do not know such things."

"Yes," said Brian, "I had overlooked that." He paused a moment, then went on.

"What is said is that trolls are solitary creatures, only. They are found one by one, in secret spots of the woods, under bridges and such like. They fight each other to the death if two meet; and the loser is eaten."

"I have never seen one before," said Jim. "Are they all like the one we met under the castle?"

"As I think I said, James," Brian answered, "that one is much the largest I have ever heard of. But for that size, however, he appears much like any other such creature."

Jim paused, thinking. "So if they're strongly territorial," he went on, "that would explain the reaction of the one at the near presence of the other." Brian looked blankly at him.

"At any rate," Jim said, changing the subject, "I'll have to go talk to Secoh after all, clearly. So the problem is my having some freedom to slip out of the castle by myself when no one but a few servants will see me go. Servants, I can give some kind of a story to; but I wouldn't want to run into a fellow guest or anyone of importance on the Earl's castle staff who might wonder why I'm not at the dinner."

"Indeed," said Brian, "they will miss you at the high table."

"Not if they think they know why I'm missing," said Jim. "That's what I wanted to ask your help in, Brian."

"I will be glad to help in any way," said Brian firmly.

"Better wait until you hear what I'm going to suggest," said Jim. "See, I just need to get out in the woods far enough to be away from the Bishop's blessing on the castle—actually, just beyond the walls and on the tilting ground ought to be far enough; except that if I walked out that far and suddenly turned into a dragon or disappeared, someone on duty watching from the castle walls might see me do it, and there would be talk about why I left the banquet—particularly on Christmas Day. I'd better go into the woods. But that's not the main problem. The main problem is finding an excuse for me to leave the dinner after I've got there; and be gone long enough to fly to Malencontri and find Secoh, or perhaps manage to magic myself there, the way Carolinus does. I've got an idea how to do it, but it needs your help, Brian."

"Count on me for anything," said Brian. "What is it, James?"

"Well," said Jim, "I'd like you to do something for me—not right away, but, say, halfway through the dinner, after we've been there for the first two or three courses. You and Geronde will be sitting together, won't you?"

"We can," said Brian cautiously. "Normally, Geronde, who sees so few other ladies during the rest of the year, looks forward to sitting with some and talking; and I freely admit to liking the conversation of table-mates who are other gentlemen and tend to talk more of things in which a knight might be interested."

"Well," said Jim, "it really doesn't matter if Geronde's right beside you. Just that she's close enough to see you do this. After you've had, say, the third course, I'd like you to pretend to be sick—ill, I mean—"

"Ill?" said Brian. In the competitive social world of fourteenth-century knighthood, someone like Brian did not admit to being hurt or ill unless the cause was obvious and the hurt or illness overwhelming.

"Oh," said Jim hurriedly, "just sort of groan and fall off your bench as if you had, er"—he groped for the best possible word— "swooned."

"Oh? Ah," said Brian, thinking it over. "Fall into a swound, eh? As if I had a vision, or some such?"

"That's it!" said Jim. "You fall off your bench and into a sudden swound, or something else that will attract all eyes to you. Then I'd like Geronde to hurry to your side; and if Angie isn't already on her way down from the high table also, Geronde should get her—and that'll give me an excuse to go down to you, too. Then we can all four go out together, with possibly a couple of servants carrying, or helping you walk, or some such thing."

"Leave in the middle of the Christmas Day banquet?" said Brian, staring at him.

"I know it's a lot to ask, Brian," said Jim. Once more he glanced at his unhelpful bare wrist. Angie might show up any minute now. The way things seemed to happen to the best of his plans, this once she might very well show up early. He wanted to get Brian's agreement to this first, *then* tell Angie and make sure Brian later told Geronde. But he did not want Angie to think that the swoon that Brian had fallen into was anything but pure pretense—her reaction could upset the applecart in any number of possible unexpected ways.

"After I'm gone," he went on to Brian, "you can go back to the banquet, of course, you and Geronde; and say that what happened was just something you ate earlier, or something like that. Angie will have to go back to the high table, in any case. I know it's a lot to ask. But if you'd be willing—"

"James," said Brian firmly, "I will do it. If it will help you, you can count on me for any assistance I can give."

Not for the first time, Jim found inside him the mixed emotions of a warmth at Brian's readiness—and a feeling of guilt; guilt that this kind of loyalty was not the sort of thing that he himself had been used to receiving and giving in the twentieth century; and which he doubted he had really shown at any time back here, toward Brian.

He tried to make himself feel better with the reminder that he had not had much opportunity to show an equal sort of commitment to Brian—except perhaps for the time when he had gone to help Brian rescue his Castle Smythe from sea-pirates who had

come plundering inland and thought the half-ruined establishment
would be easily taken.

But that had been only one instance; and it was the sort of
help almost any knight would expect from a friendly neighbor
as a matter of course. Some day, he told himself, he must find
the opportunity to make up to Brian this debt of loyalty that the
other's kindness was building up in him.

"Good," said Jim. "I'm very grateful, Brian. As long as you
can do that—"

That was as far as he got. The door from the hall to Brian's
room opened without so much as a preliminary knock or scratch;
not only Angie but Geronde came in.

Now that the two were dressed, they were both anxious to go
down immediately. All four left, accordingly, Jim explaining on
the way and Brian attesting to his approval. Angie looked a little
doubtful to begin with, and Geronde seemed inclined to hunt
for flaws and possible hidden dangers in the plan; but these
eventually ran up against Brian's attitude, which could probably
best be expressed in the words, *It is my duty, and I will!*

So it was that when they entered the hall, they separated in
essential agreement. Brian and Geronde were taken to one of the
lower tables; and Jim and Angie, as on the previous day, were
whisked off to the high table.

On this particular Christmas Day, they were seated together,
much to Jim's pleasure. The fact they were side by side meant
that Angie must inevitably hear what Geronde would be telling
Jim when she brought word of Brian—which, of course, other
people at the high table were supposed to hear—and which made
it that much more reasonable that Jim should get up and hurry
down to Brian with Angie and Geronde.

As on the previous day, Agatha Falon was seated next to the
Earl, dominating their conversation and flattering that noble, if
not as young as he used to be, gentleman outrageously.

The Earl seemed to be lapping it up. He was already somewhat
under the influence of wine—possibly because of discomfort from
the ankle twisted in his fall from his horse earlier in the day. A
knob-ended walking stick leaned against the back of his chair;
so it was probably not only painful for him to get around, but
possibly painful for him simply to sit at table and preside over
the meal.

The same comfortably stout, aging lady who had sat at Jim's
left before was there again. She was eager to fill Jim and Angie in

on the high points to come of this particularly important repast.

They were to have a reenactment of the sea battle that had ended in a victory over the French navy at Sluys. Apparently the Earl, then a noticeable number of years younger and undoubtedly more active, had taken a heroic part. This reenactment would take place toward the end of the meal.

Meanwhile, as Jim and Angie had already noticed, there were jugglers out between the two long tables, juggling away; and acrobats were to follow them during the next courses. Meanwhile the musicians, perched in their gallery nest high on the right-hand wall, were sawing, pounding and plucking away, although most of the diners seemed to be paying no attention to them whatsoever.

The Irish harp was among them; but the tuneful, sad-happy notes of that instrument of which Jim was fond were lost among the noises of the other instruments. Jim sighed to himself—he had plenty of time to sigh; for Angie and the elderly lady had struck up a conversation across him and he was leaning back in his seat, so that they would have a clear view of each other as they spoke. He was, in fact, relieved not to have to make conversation.

Not only were the two women talking away happily, but they were eating and drinking at the same time. Jim was also eating—though drinking sparingly—but he was embarrassed to notice that Angie's medieval table manners were far better than his. Where and when she had found time to develop her expertise, Jim could not imagine. At home, in Malencontri, they had made use of spoons and forks rather freely, on the basis that Jim, being a magician, was likely to do anything, and Angie, as his wife, would be expected to follow suit. So, in fact, they had eaten very much as they had in the twentieth century, with some small concessions to the medieval way of dining.

But here there were no forks. Each person used the knife at her or his belt to cut up meat or other morsels—although much was ordinarily served in already bite-sized pieces—or other solid foods where you did not want the full piece on your trencher, the slice of thick bread that served as your plate. Their spoons were for use only in the case of liquid or almost liquid food—usually sauces, of which fourteenth-century cooks were particularly proud.

Jim had learned to handle his dagger at the table in fair fourteenth-century fashion; but the tricky part was that after you had carved off something eatable, or if the food was pick-up-able, you picked it up as daintily as possible with the tips of the fingers and conveyed it to your mouth that way. Getting your fingers too

deeply into the sauce was frowned on; and servants came frequently
with basins of water and towels so that you could wash off any
resultant greasiness.

So, here was Angie daintily lifting a portion of meat or tart
between the tips of her fingers, barely dipping it in a plate or
bowl of sauce, as needed, and then conveying these tidbits to her
lips smoothly and expertly.

They were indeed tidbits. Politeness also frowned upon large
mouthfuls. Both Angie and the elderly lady picked up at a time
only a sliver of whatever they were eating; but a remarkable
number of these slivers managed to make the journey, with the
result that they were both making a full meal out of what was
offered by the table's servants.

Angie had always had a good appetite. Jim had discovered
himself to be ravenous when he first sat down—these cold halls
and rooms caused the body to demand fuel. Now, however, he
had taken the edge off that; and also put the brakes on out of
prudence. Just as he did not want to have too much wine in him,
so he did not want to be loaded down with food an hour or so from
now, when he would be trying to get out of the castle and into the
woods, change into a dragon and fly back to Malencontri.

He also now took notice of another advantage in eating very
small bites, as Angie and his left-hand neighbor were doing.

This was that such small amounts in the mouth left the eater
free to keep talking. This was an academic point at the moment for
him, since he was just as happy not to have to make conversation.
In any case, he would have found it difficult to talk around either
Angie, or his other neighbor, to anyone beyond each of them.

Eating and drinking and periodically dipping his fingertips in
a ewer of scented water and then wiping them with a towel, Jim
drifted off into a reverie in which he found himself rehearsing a
number of different arguments which might convince Mnrogar to
cooperate with Jim's search for the other troll in the castle.

Angie and the elderly lady were still continuing their lively discussion—in fact, for all intents and purposes he had vanished and
there was nothing but an empty chair between the two women. His
mind moved to the problem of the troll and the Earl as hereditary
enemies. He built up a pleasant scenario, in which he brought the
two, troll and Earl, together for a conference which he himself
mediated . . . they resolved their differences, found they liked
each other and agreed to own the castle jointly henceforward.

The Earl was just telling the troll that there was a wall with a secret peephole in a corridor of the castle; and he had a way to arrange all the guests to move down it one by one. The troll could therefore watch them through the peephole, smell them as they passed, and pick out the one that was a troll masquerading as a human. Needless to say, the troll was delighted with this—

The fantasy was suddenly interrupted by something like a wild howl from farther down the hall.

Jim came back to the present with a snap and stared in the direction from which the sound had come, along with everybody else at the high table and just about everybody else in the room, many of whom were standing up in order to get a better view.

Jim and the rest at the high table had the advantage of an elevation from which to look down on the source of this strange noise; and it was what Jim had secretly feared. Brian had overacted.

Over the heads of the people clustered around Brian in a small open circle—but not approaching him too closely for their own personal and prudent reasons—Jim could see a circle of rush-strewn floor. Brian lay on his back in the center of it, legs extended and tight together. His arms were flung out on either side, so that he was in a crucifix position, lying on his back.

"It's Brian!" said Angie, looking at him with excitement and meaning.

"So it is," said Jim, his voice sounding stilted and unnatural in his own ears. "What could have happened to him? I wonder."

"Perhaps we should go down to him!" said Angie, jumping up from her seat. "I think—oh, here comes Geronde!"

Geronde it was, making good time. She reached the still-standing Angie with a fair amount of breathlessness.

"Angela, come help!" she said. "We were just talking about the Holy Sepulcher that my father was so desirous of seeing when he planned to go on Crusade; and Brian was about to say something about it, when he looked almost as if a vision had overcome him. He gave a great cry and fell!"

"I'll go right back with you!" said Angie.

"We'll both go," said Jim—loudly, for public consumption—and because Angie and Geronde had looked as if they were going to start out, forgetting all about him. "Perhaps this is something that magic will allow me to understand."

"I, too!" called a strong voice from the far end of the table. It was the voice of the Bishop. "If it was a Holy matter he chanced to have in mind when the vision took him, the Church is concerned and—"

"Hurry—" said Jim, under his breath to Angie and Geronde. They literally ran down the steps at the edge of the dais holding the high table and back along the lower table, Jim leading the way now and literally pushing his way through the crowd, the members of which gave way when they saw who he was.

Mindful of the Bishop rapidly approaching from the rear, Jim bent over the still figure of Brian, who lay motionless with his eyes tightly closed.

"A swoon, of course," he said out loud, for the benefit of the listening ears around. He surreptitiously nudged Brian's side with his toe. "I think he's coming out of it."

Brian did not stir.

"Yes," said Jim, more loudly, nudging again, "his eyes are opening now!"

Brian's eyes opened wide abruptly.

"James!" he said in a hearty voice—too hearty a voice. "What happened?"

"You fell into a swoon," said Jim. "Can you get to your feet? I will assist you."

He reached down and caught Brian's arm, just in time to stop Brian, who was about to spring to his feet with his usual vigor and liveliness.

"Slowly . . ." he hissed under his breath into Brian's ear.

Brian took the hint and allowed himself to be helped to his feet.

"He must be let blood immediately!" said a voice just behind Jim's right shoulder. He turned and saw Sir Harimore Kilinsworth, the knight who had had the verbal encounter with Brian when Jim had been with him in the upper room of the hall on their first day at the castle.

"Oh, I don't think that's necessary—" Jim began hastily.

"Sir James!" Sir Harimore twirled the almost nonexistent end of one of his mustaches. "You are a magician, as all know; but of a knight in a swound, I venture to say you may not know what is best. A good bloodletting—"

"Proud sinners, one and all!" thundered the Bishop's voice from behind Jim. "Stand back for a Lord of the Church! And you, Sir Harimore, medicine yourself and care for your own mortal soul before you venture to make suggestions for a knight who may have been vouchsafed a Holy Vision!"

He came around Jim to face Brian.

"What do you remember seeing, Sir Brian?" he demanded.

"I—I—" stammered Brian, completely thrown off his pace by a situation in which he either had to perform the impossible task of lying to a Bishop, or explain to everyone around him that he had merely been putting on an act.

"It may be he can't remember right away," put in Jim hastily. "Perhaps he needs peace and quiet—and some time in which to recollect what he saw—if indeed he can recollect it at all before it is lost."

"It must not be lost!" trumpeted the Bishop. He glared at Brian. "When were you last shriven?"

"This morning, in fact, my Lord," said Brian. "I had planned to go to confession before the last mass of Advent at midnight, but what with one thing and another—"

"This morning! Excellent!" said the Bishop. "And you have done your penance?"

"Yes, my Lord. I—"

"Good! Very good," said the Bishop. "A clean soul—we can hope."

He wheeled on Jim.

"Sir James! I believe you are best suited for this duty. See to it that Sir Brian is conveyed to his own quarters and there ensured peace and quiet in which to recollect. On this Holy Day, to have one present here gifted with a Holy Vision is too precious a thing to risk losing. Therefore I make you responsible—and I will remind you, Sir James, of the covenant under which Holy Church has permitted such as yourself with those certain arts known as Magick; and which puts you under the command of the Church at any time deemed necessary by one of authority like myself. It is my command to you that you ensure that Sir Brian has every chance to recall his vision."

"Yes, my Lord," said Jim. "If I might have the help of a couple of servants to help me support or even carry him to his room—"

"You shall have them," said the Bishop. "Stand back, all the rest of you. You there—put down that ewer and come over here; and you with the pastry, put it down immediately and come here."

Two of the servitors going about their duty around the tables, clearly interested in what was happening around Sir Brian but not daring to interrupt their ordinary tasks, happily did so now and came at a run to join Jim and Brian, Geronde and Angie.

"Should we carry you, Sir Brian?" Jim asked him. "Or with

help, would you rather walk upstairs to your quarters?"

"I can walk," said Brian hastily. He added, with an attempt at a somewhat fainter voice, "I may be a bit unsteady; but with a servant on each side of me—"

"Did I not say stand back!" said the Bishop in full pulpit voice; and the crowd of guests parted before the little party with Brian in their midst as the Red Sea had parted for the Israelites to let them escape from the pursuing charioteers of the Pharaoh of Egypt.

CHAPTER 12

Brian was understandably upset when he got back to his room and realized that while Geronde and Angie could return to the banquet, he scarcely could; considering the Bishop's injunction that he rest and recover his vision.

"I'm sorry about this," Jim told him. "I don't know how to make it up to you, Brian. But I will, I promise you. I will."

"Oh, I don't blame you, James," said Brian. "I played my part too well, that is the trouble. But I could perish up here for want of company, food and drink."

"I will stay with you," said Geronde. "Indeed, it would be expected of me."

"I can stay too, if you want," said Angie. "I'm not all that interested in the dinner, to tell you the truth."

"Oh no, Angela," said Geronde. "You go back. It'll be expected. Also you can tell all at the high table that he fell into a deep sleep, that I'm watching over him, and we have hopes that when he wakes he will remember the vision, unless he has lost it forever."

"Right," said Angie. She brightened. "Come to think of it, I can also tell them Brian said he had the feeling that the vision was some kind of lesson or message to him; and it might not return to him until some time in the future, when its lesson applies to some particular moment that's then in his life."

Both Brian and Geronde looked at her uncomfortably.

"Would you say something like that to the Bishop, Angela?" asked Geronde doubtfully.

"Certainly!" said Angie. "It could very well be true. In fact, how do we know that Brian actually didn't have a vision, even though he thought he was just acting a part? It could be that our whole scheme to have him act a part was actually intended to let him have an actual vision—which he since has forgotten and won't remember until it fits something that will happen to him in the future, where he has to make a decision."

"Right!" said Jim suddenly. "Tell me, Brian, did you feel anything different, when you threw yourself over backward and kept your eyes closed on the floor? Do you suppose that perhaps you seemed to act so well because in fact you were actually thrown from your chair and unconscious for a moment—which of course you don't remember now—and something like a vision actually happened?"

"I did seem to throw myself rather harder than was necessary," said Brian thoughtfully. He rubbed the back of his head. "And I'm not exactly sure how long I lay there, although it seemed but a short time."

"It occurs to me you actually may have had a vision, Brian; and my asking you to put on an act was a sort of miraculous accident so that you would doubt you actually had the vision and would forget it until the time came when you were to remember it."

Brian, Geronde—even Angie—stared at him.

"You think that possible, James?" said Brian, in a hushed voice.

"Brian," said Jim solemnly, avoiding Angie's eye, "anything is possible."

Brian crossed himself. So did Geronde and—in that order—Angie and Jim.

"You see," said Jim, "if that's what happened, the vision may not come back until the proper time arrives for you to remember it; so for now, you can simply go on living and acting as you usually do. Come to think of it, you could go back down after a little while up here and simply say that you have a feeling you were not to speak about it—that way the others at the table should not even question you; and you'd be back at the dinner after all."

"In especial," said Brian, "I did want to see the reenactment of the great sea battle at Sluys."

"Brian," said Angie, "Jim is just saying it might have happened that way, not that it did."

"No," said Brian. "Either I had a vision, but was meant to forget it; or else I did not, in which case I have nothing to tell anyone. I shall say so."

"Brian—" began Geronde. He held up a hand to stop her.

"I have made up my mind!" he said firmly. "I shall go back down, and tell my Lord Bishop, as well as any else, that I have nothing to tell them."

His firmness relaxed. He smiled at Geronde.

"And, Geronde," he said, "you shall go with me. You can support me when I tell of my quick recovery. You can be witness for me; that though I might have had a vision in that moment, I cannot remember it now; and feeling a sudden fresh access of happiness and energy, I chose to return to the dinner."

"Well," said Geronde slowly. "Perhaps . . ."

Brian's face suddenly sobered. He turned to Jim.

"But you, James," he said. "You were planning . . ."

"I still am," said Jim, thinking quickly. "You can tell everyone your swoon reminded me of something of vital importance, and I have to go immediately in search of Carolinus."

"What's Carolinus got to do with all this?" asked Angie.

"Well, actually it's another matter," said Jim. "But because I need to go, anyway, I can tell him about this much more important matter of Brian possibly having a vision, while I have it fresh in mind. I'm going back to our rooms now, and get dressed to go out. If you want to come along with me, I'll explain as we go."

"I'll do that," said Angie.

"Do you realize?" Angie said, as they were going back to their own quarters. "Brian's now begun to believe he really had a vision."

"Well," said Jim, "that'll make it all the easier for him to explain to the Bishop."

"That's not the point," said Angie. "He's just so impressionable. You should be ashamed of yourself!"

"It doesn't hurt anyone if he thinks the way he does," said Jim.

"Hah!" said Angie. "Nobody but him!"

Jim winced internally; they turned down the branching corridor to their own pair of rooms.

"But enough of Brian and visions," said Angie. "I've got to get back to that high table. What am I supposed to tell people about you?"

"Just what I told Brian," said Jim. "It's the truth. I'm going to look for Carolinus. He ought to be here, where he's needed.

You've noticed he's not around? He wasn't there at dinner yesterday and I haven't seen him, in fact, since just after meeting
the troll."

"I hadn't realized," said Angie. "I'm not out of our rooms
much, because of little Robert. You mean he's clear out of the
castle?"

"I'm pretty sure so," said Jim. "That's the thing. I may actually
be gone for a day or so if I have to hunt for him. Once out of
the castle myself I can use magic to try to chase him down—
after I've seen Secoh, that is, and found out what trouble *he's*
announcing."

"Well, it can't be anything so serious, can it?" she said.

"Probably not," Jim said. "But I've been uneasy about the fact
that Carolinus hasn't turned up lately." He paused.

"Would Aargh know anything about that?" she asked.

"I suppose it's possible," Jim said. "If we were back at
Malencontri, we could put out a signal. Aargh would see it;
he'd howl, and I'd go out to meet him. But there's no way to
signal him here at the Earl's. Maybe I can use magic to help
find him, if I can't find Carolinus. I really don't understand what
Carolinus is doing—is he a guest here, or isn't he?"

"This really isn't his sort of thing," said Angie.

"Mine, either," said Jim glumly. "What I'm worried about is
that he may know things he hasn't been telling me—he's done
that before. At any rate, will you cover for me with the Earl and
the other guests? Don't start out by saying that I may be gone for
a day or so, but leave it open so that you can expand on that later
on if you want."

"All right," said Angie. They halted just out of earshot of the
man-at-arms in front of their door. "I won't bother to come in
with you. If Brian and Geronde are going to come back down, I
want to be there before they are. I want to make sure Brian talks
to the Bishop first—it'll be safer."

"Yes," said Jim.

He stood and watched her for a moment as she turned and went
back down the corridor, holding the hem of her skirt carefully
above the stone floor; then he turned and went into the first of
their rooms.

There was no one there; and when he looked into the next room,
Robert was sleeping peacefully in his bed, and his wet nurse was
asleep on her pallet on the floor. Angie's serving woman was not
in evidence.

He quietly collected his heavier clothes, his armor and his sword and took them into the other room to dress before the fire there, which had been made up recently, and was blazing away merrily. He put on a number of layers of clothing, with his chain mail shirt under a jupon with his arms painted upon it; belted his sword belt and sword around his waist, put a steel cap on his head over a cushioning skullcap, and covered everything else with a long gray cloak with a hood.

He was about to go out, when he realized he had forgotten to buckle on his spurs. He would certainly want to take a horse from among those that he now had in the Earl's stables. Once in the woods, he could try magic to transport both him and the horse; but he was unsure of his ability to move around magically if under stress, the way Carolinus moved from place to place in a twinkling; besides, if trouble came at him unexpectedly, then it was better to be up on a horse than on his own two feet.

For one thing, the horse could take him away from danger a lot faster than his own two feet could.

He had just buckled on his spurs and turned toward the door, when a voice spoke unexpectedly from behind him in the empty room.

"My Lord? My Lord, don't go yet!" it said.

Jim turned sharply about; but the voice had already given the identity of its owner away. Hob-One was perched cross-legged in mid-air above the flames in the fireplace.

"I've been trying and trying to catch you, my Lord," said Hob-One reproachfully. "But you're never alone!"

"Do I have to be alone?" contended Jim. "What is it? I've got to be leaving."

"I mean, for most purposes it wouldn't be dangerous—but you never know. Also, in this case, I don't belong here, of course. When I saw you the first time, I'd had to ask the Earl's kitchen hobgoblin for permission to come and visit you in your room here."

"I see," said Jim.

"Of course," said Hob-One, elevating his snub nose proudly, "since you renamed me, I simply give him orders. After all, he's just an ordinary kitchen hobgoblin. I pointed that out to him."

"You did?" Jim said, a little startled at the results of his casual renaming of the small Natural.

"Indeed!" said Hob-One.

"And he—er—didn't object?"

" '*Varlet!*' I said to him," went on Hob-One. " '*I am Hob-One de Malencontri. I shall be visiting this castle of yours from time to time. Furthermore, I shall not bother to speak to you, unless I have need of you for some reason. If I do, I shall expect you to show the proper respect shown by one being spoken to by his betters!*' "

"I'll be—" Jim caught himself just in time. Damning yourself was not said lightly, here. He went on. "But I have to leave now—"

"Oh, but my Lord—!" said Hob-One, dropping his air of superiority instantly. "You never did hear my message from Secoh—that dragon, you know—"

"I know Secoh," said Jim. "Yes. In fact, one of the things I'm about to do is go back to Malencontri now and see him—that is, if he's still there. Is he?"

"Yes. Yes, indeed, my Lord," said Hob-One. "I heard your John Steward tell your chief server that he could have the men-at-arms put the dragon out of the castle; but he didn't think he should do that, since this dragon was a particular friend of yours. So he just stays there, eating food and drinking wine and getting angrier and angrier at me. He could snap me in half with just a few of his great teeth. He's worse than a troll. Do you know there's a troll underneath this castle?"

"I've talked to him," said Jim.

"Oh. Well, you're a great magick Lord knight, with a sword and everything," said Hob-One, "but hobgoblins—even a hobgoblin like me, Hob-One de Malencontri—we can't fight anybody. Our best idea is just to keep out of sight."

"I understand," said Jim. "However, I'm going to Secoh now; and the sooner I get started, the better. Standing here talking just delays me. If you can get there faster than I can, you might tell him I'm coming."

"Oh, I can," said Hob-One. "I can get there in just a few minutes, riding on the smoke."

"I see," said Jim. "Well, go ahead and tell him. Goodbye."

He turned toward the door.

"How are you going?" asked Hob-One behind him. "You know, my Lord, I could take you with me."

Jim stopped and turned back.

"You could?" he said.

"Oh, yes. That's one of the few things we hobgoblins can do—take people riding on the smoke with us. We generally don't do it, of course. Except, sometimes we take children. They're small like us, and usually they like us; and even if they tell the grown-ups around them afterward, nobody believes them, so it's safe enough. But because you honored me with a name, I'd like to help you, my Lord, if I can. Would you like to ride the smoke back with me?"

"I was going to take a horse," said Jim, frowning.

"You've got horses at Malencontri," offered Hob-One timidly. This was true, of course. Jim felt a little foolish.

"All right, then," he said. He looked at the merrily burning fire filling the fireplace. It looked like a rather uncomfortable thing to step over. "How do I go about it?"

"You just give me your hand, my Lord." Hob-One extended his arm, and Jim took the little brown hand in his own. A moment later he was traveling up the chimney without really knowing how he had gotten started.

He had expected the chimney to be a sooty, tight, uncomfortable matter to ascend. But this was a medieval chimney—a good deal wider and deeper than those in his twentieth-century experience—and also, some of the Natural magic of the hobgoblin may have been at work; because they whisked upward without even soiling the loose cloak he had put on. They were out of the top of the chimney before he really had time to formulate any thoughts at all.

Almost immediately, they were drifting over the tops of the leafless trees and the snow-covered ground beneath.

Jim's first impression was that they were not moving particularly fast; then he changed his mind and decided that they were indeed covering ground at something better than the speed at which he would have been able to fly, in his dragon body. But it was a very quiet, easy speed—even easier than the soaring which was the main part of any dragon's air travels; since, because of a dragon's weight, using wings to keep one aloft was an extremely tiring business. This was almost like traveling in a dream.

It was delightful. Jim remembered how, when he had first attempted flight in his dragon body, he had been completely won over by the magnificent feeling of climbing swiftly through the air, soaring or diving several hundred feet, essentially in free fall. But this was even more marvelous. Drifting—at probably better than over a hundred miles an hour, but it still felt like drifting—above the black-and-white landscape.

"No sign of the troll," said Jim out loud, without thinking, looking down at the snow blanket with nothing but an occasional animal track across it, slipping swiftly by beneath them. He tried to envision the sort of tracks that would be made by the great, naked splay feet of the troll, huge toes ending in the dents of their claws.

"That's because they're all under the snow," said Hob-One, unexpectedly, beside him.

Jim turned to look at the hobgoblin. He was riding, apparently upon a single thin waft of smoke. Jim glanced down past his legs and saw that he was doing the same thing.

"Under the snow?" he echoed. "I was talking about the troll."

"So was I," said Hob-One. He added darkly, "I don't like trolls. Or dragons. Or nightshades, or sand-mirks, or big kitchen ladies with large knives—"

"How do you mean, under the snow?" asked Jim. "Even if the snow was deep enough to hide one—"

"Oh, they don't just lie down anyplace and wait for the snow to cover them, my Lord," said Hob-One. "They pick places where the snow will blow up into a deep drift and lie down there. The cold doesn't bother them, of course—or anything else; and they can stay there as long as they like, until somebody comes by and then they jump up out of the snow and grab him—grab and eat him. Usually, of course, it's just an innocent deer or rabbit. But it could be anybody—even a hobgoblin like me!"

"Well, there shouldn't be any around here to do that to you," said Jim. "The castle troll says he's kept this territory clear of other trolls for eighteen hundred years."

"He may say that," said Hob-One. "But there's hundreds of them down there. I saw them when they were still waiting to be covered up with snow. That was when I first came looking for you, and it was still snowing."

"Hundreds of them?" said Jim. "You can't be right."

"Yes, I really am, my Lord," said Hob-One earnestly. "I know trolls when I see them, and there were at least hundreds. At least."

Jim felt a sinking sensation inside him.

"If there are that many out here why doesn't the castle troll know about it?" he said. "He was very firm about keeping his territory clear all these years."

"I don't know," said Hob. "But then, I'm just a hobgoblin."

"Why would they be there?" asked Jim.

"I don't know, my Lord," said Hob-One.

Jim caught himself on the verge of saying something sharp about the fact that Hob-One didn't seem to know much about anything.

He reined himself in. After all, he told himself, the little fellow was just what he said he was. Somebody who spent days and nights inside a kitchen chimney could not be expected to know a great deal about the rest of the world, even if he did go out occasionally. Also, checking his small burst of temper over Hob had reminded him of Angie's words after they had left Geronde and Brian. As usual, what Angie told him came back to grind away at him later on.

She was quite right, of course. He had been taking advantage of Brian's innocence and suggestibility about the vision—and that was not a good thing to do to your best friend in any century. Well, hopefully, Brian would tell people he had forgotten whatever there might have been to remember about the vision; and the whole matter would soon also be forgotten by everyone else. Still, Jim made a promise to himself that sometime in the future he would find some way of making up his misuse of Brian, somehow. Though he had no idea how.

"We're almost there!" Hob-One's voice interrupted his thoughts.

He looked ahead and saw a clearing in the trees, and there in the clearing were the walls and towers of Malencontri. He heaved a sigh of relief; and then remembered that the castle did not promise relief, but a problem waiting solution. He still had whatever trouble Secoh was waiting to drop on him.

He thrust worry from his mind for the moment. Now that he had the castle in sight, he really began to appreciate the speed with which they had been traveling. The castle seemed to be rocketing toward him.

"Down we go!" Hob-One sang almost happily; and they plunged into a chimney that Jim assumed was the one leading down to the serving room in the tower, right next to the hall of Malencontri. The serving room was where the dishes were brought and attempted to be kept warm from the kitchen; since the kitchen in most castles was outside the main castle buildings, and very often a wooden structure. Fire was the great fear of those who lived in castles and used open flame to cook by.

There was a flash of darkness around him, and he suddenly found himself coming to a halt with both heels jarring on a floor right in front of a fireplace with a comfortable fire burning in it.

But it was not the serving room nor any other room in the castle that he recognized.

It was the interior of Carolinus's little cottage at the Tinkling Water, some snow-clad miles away; and it was Carolinus himself who was facing him, fiercely, in a room lit only by the dancing shadows of the firelight, which made strange advancing and retreating areas of darkness in the further parts of the room, and a surprisingly bright glow from the upside-down fish-bowl shape of the magician's scrying glass.

"Don't ask me!" snapped Carolinus. "It's not your fault; but I can't help you."

CHAPTER 13

J im stared at the older man. Carolinus looked the same as usual, in a red robe, with the stains that always seemed to accumulate on one of his robes after a day or so; whether from food, some by-product of magic-making, or some strange other reason. But there were lines of strain around his eyes and Jim was not deceived by the fierceness. This was not Carolinus being his normal irritable self; it was Carolinus covering up something by pretending to be his normal irritable self.

"But I didn't come asking for help," said Jim. "At least not in the sense I think you meant it. I've got things to tell you and things to talk over with you; and actually I was headed to talk with Secoh first; but I'm just as glad I ran into you instead. I suppose you had me diverted to here."

"That's right!" said Carolinus.

"Well, to start off with," said Jim, "let me tell you something. There's an army of trolls surrounding the Earl's castle."

"He knows. I've told him," said a familiar voice; and Aargh came out of one of the shifting patches of shadow into the light, looking half again as big as normal, and almost demonlike himself with his yellow eyes in the candle glow and the light from the scrying glass.

"Did you see them?" demanded Jim.

"They were already under the snow," said Aargh, "but I smelled them. The whole forest there reeks of troll; and my nose is not a troll's nose, nor a deer's nose, nor a hedgehog's nose. I would smell even one of them, even under a foot of snowdrift."

"But Mnrogar didn't actually talk as if he knew about them," said Jim. "And it was only early the next day in the morning that it stopped snowing; so if they were going to be covered by snow they had to be covered by that time."

"They were," said Aargh.

"Then why didn't Mnrogar act as if he knew they were out there?" said Jim. "The only thing he seemed concerned about was this troll he thinks is upstairs in the castle among the guests."

"They were outside his territory," said Aargh. "Also, under the castle down there, unless the wind was blowing directly down his tunnel—and even then—he might not be able to smell them at that distance."

"They were there when you left us and went out?" asked Jim. "You got through and past them all right?"

Aargh laughed his silent laugh.

"They are not shoulder to shoulder under the snow," he said. "They neither love nor trust each other, those trolls. There was more than enough space between them for even a slow-moving animal to get through, with luck, let alone me. Besides, what would one of them gain by leaping out of the snow at me? Only his own death. They're there for another reason."

Jim turned on Carolinus.

"They're after the castle, the Earl and the guests inside?" he said to Carolinus.

"No," said Carolinus. His faded blue eyes burned fiercely under his white eyebrows. "They're after Mnrogar's territory. Only one of them can get it—in single combat with Mnrogar—but whether he wins or loses; whether he can hold it, after he has won, from other challengers among the other trolls, makes no difference. The very fact that they are there to try can be a thing the Dark Powers have been seeking for some time—an excuse to have you stripped of all your magical powers and leave you defenseless before them. And, as I said, in this, finally, I can't help you. I must stand aside. Because you're my apprentice I have to stand aside."

Jim blinked at him.

"I don't understand," he said after a second. "What does stripping me of my magical powers mean? And what's all this about the Dark Powers? As I understood it, once the castle was blessed—"

"The castle is safe," said Carolinus. "All in it are safe, even after the Bishop leaves. Only Mnrogar and you are at risk here."

"Well, with the people in the castle safe, that much is a relief," said Jim, letting out a breath. "You mean, the trolls won't attack the castle all together, like an army?"

"Not they!" said Aargh. "They would only fight together if all your armored men set out as a body to hunt them down, and cornered them—or else all that has always been true of a troll is true no longer and the sun and moon are gone."

"Then we don't have to worry about that either," said Jim. "Now, what's this about me being in danger and what have the Dark Powers to do with it, then?"

He was back talking to Carolinus. Carolinus frowned.

"You still don't seem to understand what I've tried to tell you so many times," said Carolinus, "about the balance between History and Chance—how that balance must always be maintained and the Dark Powers are always at work to upset it; while we, the magicians, have been on guard to keep them from doing so. That is the way of all things always—to preserve a balance.

"To begin with, Jim, the Dark Powers had no idea you could be too strong for them. They didn't expect you at all. Then you not only came from somewhere else, but with knowledge beyond their understanding. Sometime since, they've learned better; and they've been maneuvering ever since to find a way to turn your own strength against you. Now they've found it."

Jim was silent for a moment. He knew the word for what Carolinus was talking about. It was called technology—twentieth-century technology. The things he had taken for granted in the world that he and Angie had come from, the equivalent of six hundred years and more ahead of this fourteenth-century one in which he now stood. Carolinus had been right in what he had tried to tell Jim almost from the beginning—that magic was an art. Little twentieth-century ordinary things that Jim knew about mechanics, about medicine—for that matter, about people and society itself—had made the magic that he developed and learned into something that was unique, as every true magician's magic was unique to himself or herself. And that had allowed him to solve problems in ways that were not even suspected in this medieval time around him.

"I don't see—" he was beginning.

"No," said Carolinus, almost gently, "and you were probably not to be blamed for it. Do you remember when you used something you called hypnotism, as part of your magic to control the sorcerer Ecotti and the French King, long enough for you and your friends to escape and cross the Channel back here to England?"

"Yes," said Jim, puzzled by this apparent change in topic.

"And you remember, as a result I had to match myself in a magician's test with a B-class oriental magician who claimed that what you called 'hypnotism' was part of oriental magic; and that you had not been properly taught it by a magician qualified in oriental magic?"

"Of course!" said Jim. Carolinus had actually won handily in that encounter, though at the time he was despondent and the winning raised his spirits only temporarily. At the time, however, he had given Jim to understand that it was no real contest; since he had been matched against a mere B-class magician, instead of someone of his own very high rank and skill.

"—So," he was saying now, "you remember my opponent's name, of course. It was Son Won Phon; and he's been concerning himself with your status ever since—gathering a respectable number of minds among the world's magicians who tend to agree with him."

"You mean," said Jim, "he's holding a grudge?"

"Certainly not!" said Carolinus. "Magickians don't hold grudges!"

He coughed.

"That is," he went on, "qualified magickians, those above that C rank that you hold. No, the truth is he's simply somewhat conservative in his views. Take his attitude toward the transmutation of ordinary minerals into precious metals, for example—but come to think of it, never mind. You don't have the background; and we don't want to waste time talking about that just now. In fact, thinking of talking, we should do so in absolute privacy. Let me ask for a little assistance."

He held up one long finger in mid-air, and a faint musical tinkle came from the tip of it. They all stood for a moment, and then there was an answering tinkle from the shadows in one corner of the room; and what could only be described as a very beautiful winged fairy, not much larger than a hummingbird, flew out of the shadows and hovered, her wings merely wafting the air, as with one tiny hand she took hold of the tip of Carolinus's finger.

"Ah, T.B.," said Carolinus. "I hope I didn't bother you at a moment when you were busy with something important."

T.B. tinkled at him.

"Good of you to say so," rejoined Carolinus. "I have a favor to ask. It's necessary that the three of us discuss a matter under conditions where we can't possibly be overheard. Could you transport the three of us to you know where?"

The little fairy tinkled.

"Thank you," said Carolinus. "We appreciate it highly. Good of you to do this."

The fairy tinkled again.

"Not at all, not at all," said Carolinus. "I'm fully aware of the favor you're doing us. Why, if you were to do it for any magickian who asks, your island would be overpopulated all the time. I know that very well; and I appreciate your making a special case for us. Any time, then, whenever you're ready."

Instantly, they were in a small clearing surrounded by some very large, tropical-looking trees, with heavy leaves as big as elephant ears and a soft green sward under their feet. It appeared to be broad, clear daylight above the trees, but they and their leaves were thick enough so that it was pleasantly dim at ground level where Jim stood. T.B. tinkled again and disappeared.

A passing individual, rather piratically dressed in a green shirt and ragged gray trousers, with a red sash around his waist holding two pistols and a cutlass, tipped his black straw hat politely to Carolinus. Carolinus gave him a distant nod in return.

"I smell salt air," said Aargh, lifting his nose to the faint breeze that was winding its way among the thick tree trunks.

"Naturally," said Carolinus, "the sea's quite near by. But, to more important matters. Jim, pay attention to me now!"

"I have been, ever since I got to you," said Jim.

"Tut, tut," said Carolinus. "Temper! Strive to control it, Jim. Take your cue from me. Be pleasant and calm at all times."

This last statement left Jim so speechless, that he evidently gave a quite satisfying impression of having taken to heart the idea of showing the sort of calmness Carolinus wanted him to display.

"Now, where was I?" said Carolinus. "Oh, yes. As I say, Son Won Phon has gathered a number of like minds in the magicians to his point of view. Without going into the laws, by-laws and precedents on which he rests the conclusion, his point of view, simply expressed, is this: you are yourself a potentially disturbing factor to both History and Chance; and we should put it completely beyond your power to be so. If we cannot send you back where you came from, we should find some other way of rendering you completely helpless—we, the magicians, that is."

"You'd actually send us back?" said Jim, excitement suddenly leaping upward within him. If the magicians sent him back, surely they would send Angie back with him, and that would solve all their problems. He and Angie would be back in the twentieth century; and the fourteenth century on this world would be undisturbed and happy—well, happy in a relative sense—again. Undisturbed and happy, that was, if Son Won Phon was correct. Actually, Jim didn't think he was.

"What makes him so sure I'm a disturbance to History and Chance?" Jim asked.

"I was just starting to tell you, back in my cottage," said Carolinus, "when I realized it should properly be explained where no one else could hear."

"Someone like Son Won Phon, I suppose?" Jim said.

"Nonsense!" said Carolinus. "Magickians don't—but, even if they did, it'd be impossible for them to overhear our talk here as they could at my cottage."

"And where are we?" growled Aargh.

"Never you mind!" said Carolinus. "This is something wolves aren't supposed to know."

He glared at Jim suddenly.

"—Or apprentices either, for that matter!"

Actually, Jim had a fairly good notion of where they were. They were at the Island of Lost Boys in James Barrie's play *Peter Pan*. But the prospect of himself and Angie back in the twentieth century glittered so strongly in his mind that where they were did not matter.

"But why can we be sure nobody can hear?" asked Jim.

"Because what's here is fixed for all time," said Carolinus. "What you see only exists in writing and a stage play. This is neither, but the story the play tells. It's absolutely unchangeable. Past history is also unchangeable. That fact is why Son Won Phon's attitude is so—"

Carolinus paused, evidently hunting for the proper word.

"Er—so tenuous. He would have it that by being here you run a danger of changing future history. Or, just by being here, you do, you and Angie."

"He may be right," Jim said—there was no harm in loading the dice a little bit in the favor of Angie and him being deported back to their home world—"I've noticed myself there are some things about your world here that are different from what I know of the same time in the past of my own world—some historic dates, and things like that, where events here seem to have happened either earlier or later than in the histories I studied—"

"No doubt your histories were wrong," said Carolinus. "I hope you're not venturing to tell me you are always right, are you, Jim?"

"Well, no, of course," said Jim. "But—"

"But me no buts!" said Carolinus. "Son Won's arguments, in my opinion, don't hold water—or anything else, for that matter. They're porous as a sieve. But that's not the point. If even a large minority of the world's magicians agree with him, I'll be forced to dismiss you as my apprentice and strip you of whatever magic powers you have, except those that you've earned by your own right; and I believe that you spent those long ago—those, and a good deal more Magick that I arranged to have you supplied with since you became my apprentice."

"And this would make me vulnerable to the Dark Powers at least until I'd been deported?" Jim asked.

"Absolutely. You—and Angie," said Carolinus.

—Angie. That put a slightly different face on the matter. Unless they were deported while Jim still had some magic powers, Angie would be vulnerable, whatever that meant in practical terms, right along with him. By himself, Jim might have been willing to take his chances. But it was something else to gamble with that danger to Angie.

"What am I supposed to do about this, then?" he asked, suddenly very serious.

"I don't know what you can do," said Carolinus. "Things could be done if I could help you. But I can't. No magickian may help his apprentice, if that apprentice has already been spoken against by a magickian of B level or higher. I was able to take and win the test I had with Son Won Phon, simply because his statement could be read as an insult to me, rather than an accusation of you. But—"

Carolinus sighed.

"What is it?" asked Jim. For as he had sighed, Carolinus had slumped, looking suddenly like what he was underneath his magician's exterior—a frail elderly man, one possibly pushed to the limit of his strength.

"I am afraid I made matters worse by helping you," said Carolinus. "I meant it for the best; and surely you deserved and needed it. But from the point of view of the arguments Son Won Phon is mounting now, it was unwise. You remember what I did for you after you settled the business of the Hollow Men—got you a higher rating and an unusual allowance of Magick from the general fund than even any C rating is ordinarily entitled to. This rubbed other apprentices the wrong way; and inevitably their masters in magic—some of their masters, at least—were rubbed the wrong way also."

"And there's nothing I can do about this feeling among the senior magicians?" said Jim. "That's hard to believe. There ought to be something!"

"Yes," growled Aargh.

"Actually," said Carolinus, "there are three ways. Though I don't see how you could use any of them. The first would be to disprove his argument about your possibly affecting future history—and since no one knows anything about future history or how the laws of History will operate in the future, since they depend upon present events to shape them—I don't see how that could be done."

"No," said Jim thoughtfully.

"Or you could attack Son Won Phon himself, although that would be rather presumptuous, a C-level student of magic who is still technically an apprentice—and in your case actually an apprentice—accusing a B-class, or *accepted*, magician. It would raise eyebrows everywhere and probably prejudice most of the world's master magickians against you. So it would be useless.

"The third possibility would be for you to create, and add to, the store of magic in our world and time, some absolutely new Magick. Magick, as I've explained to you, moves gradually out of our professional area and into ordinary living; so we're actually losing it all the time. Only occasionally is it replenished by someone creating new Magick. So eventually Magick must disappear from our world entirely. But Jim, I really don't see you creating new Magick. No one has for eighty years, and the one who did then was a AAA magician. Also, it was very small Magick."

Silence held them for a long moment. Jim's thoughts were galloping madly. He had left the castle full of the idea that he was once again caught up in a nasty problem that was really none of his business, but which he had somehow been placed in the position of having to solve. A bad situation, but not alarming.

Now he found himself facing a problem that was very alarming, and was his and Angie's alone, entirely. One he must solve for the very personal reason of keeping Angie and himself alive and safe from possible death—or something maybe even worse, if unimaginable at the moment. Suddenly he felt as if he was at the center of a ring of spear points with no visible way out.

"I'm sorry, Jim," said Carolinus in a voice that this time was very gentle indeed. "The responsibility is mine; and I wouldn't have seen you in this position if I could possibly have anticipated it. I can, of course, go to Son Won Phon myself, and see if he will not agree simply to your immediate deportation, which I presume you'd prefer to what else might happen to you and Angie, stripped of magic here in our world. At least, if deported, the two of you would be back in a world you were used to, no matter how terrible it may be; but one where you know the rules and how to conduct yourself. Otherwise, I see absolutely no hope of your handling the situation as it is here now."

"Give him some time," growled the harsh voice of Aargh.

Jim and Carolinus both looked at the wolf. He had lain down on his side, as if what he was hearing was too boring to stand and listen to. He yawned now, and snapped at a passing fly— missing it, but not appearing to be concerned by the fact. "A hunt that leads to a successful meal is not done in a moment, Mage. Give him time and he'll have an answer, maybe one you could never dream of."

"He's got time—a little time, anyway," said Carolinus. "That much I got for him. He and Angie have until the end of the twelve days of Christmas. But if he follows my advice, he'll use it to prepare himself for what looks must happen to him and Angie. What makes you think he's got some miraculous solution in him anyway, wolf?"

Aargh yawned again.

"I can smell it in him," he said, stretching himself out lazily on his side in the grass with his hind legs extended sideways and his front legs forward, his head up above them. His attitude was one of pure disdain.

But something was tickling at Jim's mind. Aargh's support of him had been suddenly, tremendously heartening. It had brought him back from the shock of realizing what Carolinus was talking about—not so much the deportation, which Angie had wanted for some time now, and to which he was entirely reconciled himself— but the extreme danger that they might not be deported and some-thing worse might happen to them. At first, that realization had seemed to paralyze him. Now he felt a surge of body adrenaline all through him.

"As a matter of fact, I had an idea," he said. "That was one of the reasons I was looking forward to talking to you, Carolinus."

CHAPTER 14

Jim had indeed left the castle with an idea that he had wanted to discuss with Carolinus. But it was an idea that offered a solution to the problem in the castle, not one to this new, unexpected situation.

But, sparked by a tremendous warmth within him from Aargh's declaration of an absolute certainty that Jim could handle the Son Won Phon situation, a question had come to life in the back of his mind. Perhaps, if he could solve the situation with Mnrogar, the army of trolls outside, and the feud between Mnrogar and the Earl—to say nothing of the mysterious troll masquerading upstairs among the guests—it would somehow give him leverage in dealing with Son Won Phon.

Carolinus had originally sent Jim to this gathering to scout for unusual activities that might be symptoms of the workings of the Dark Powers. He, Jim, had succeeded admirably in finding strange goings-on, no doubt about it. He was not at all clear about which of them might somehow be the work of the Dark Powers—but he had to try to solve all of them, whether they were sinister plots or not. Maybe, in doing so, he could strengthen his position with the magicians. It was worth thinking about.

One reason he had hopes that his idea might work lay in the fact that before this he had successfully used his twentieth-century experience and knowledge to solve fourteenth-century problems. And it should not be necessary to convince Son Won Phon personally to retreat, if he could simply impress the world society of magicians enough so they would be willing merely to deport him and Angie—since that was what Angie had wanted anyway. Their only real danger lay not in being deported, but in Jim being stripped of his magic. He would be unable then to defend them both against the Dark Powers.

"Leaving my situation aside for the moment," he said, "the idea I was going to talk over with you, Carolinus, was a way of finding the unknown troll upstairs in the castle. Maybe, if that could be done, it would put Mnrogar in a position to scare off this challenger who may have attracted the whole army of trolls around the castle right now."

He turned to Aargh.

"What do you think, Aargh?" he asked. "If Mnrogar can defeat this challenger for his territory, will all those other trolls just go back where they came from?"

"I have never seen anything like this," said Aargh. "But if Mnrogar wins, there would be no reason for them to stay, unless they want to die at his claws, one by one."

"What do you think of Mnrogar's chances if this other troll does go ahead and challenge him?" Jim asked. "I understand his not being nearly as large and strong as Mnrogar. Or as experienced, since Mnrogar says he's eighteen hundred years or more old. So how can the challenger think he'd stand a chance of winning?"

"Mnrogar wouldn't lose because he's too weak to win, James," said Aargh. "A troll's not like you or I, who in time grow old and slow. Trolls just keep growing as they get older, getting bigger, stronger and more dangerous. In fact, one of the reasons Mnrogar's been able to hold his place so long is probably because during his first hundred and fifty years he was lucky enough not to fight another troll big enough to kill him. Also, it's luck no accident's killed him. Accidents can kill trolls just as they can kill anyone else. So he's grown so big no other troll would ordinarily even think of challenging him."

"Then why is this one trying it?" said Jim.

"He sees a chance, somehow," said Aargh. "I don't know what. But if you ask me for a guess, maybe I could tell you."

"I am asking for your guess," said Jim.

"Then it's this," said Aargh. "While a troll won't weaken with extra years, the heart and will in him may weaken. They have to be alone to live, and maybe the loneliness gets them to the point where they don't want to live—you remember, I told him that was what was wrong with him, when we all talked under the castle?"

"Hmm," said Carolinus.

"It happens to all else," said Aargh harshly to the magician. "Why not to a troll? He may see himself set apart from all other trolls. This would please him to begin with. Trolls alone do not go mad, as humans go. But he could come to feel he cares no longer what happens to him. The troll who challenges him may hope this has happened, for some reason."

Provokingly, Aargh stopped talking again.

"And if Mnrogar has? Then what?" asked Jim.

"Why, Mnrogar may not want to win—enough," said Aargh. "When the spirit goes out of human, animal, Natural or even god, they go with it. Where are now all the old gods everyone says used to be? Without spirit, all things die. A death that could not have taken them before now finds it easy. A troll who believes Mnrogar has lost spirit may challenge with hope to win. That is the only reason I can think one of them would risk challenging Mnrogar."

"When Brian and I talked to Mnrogar," Jim said to Carolinus, "underneath the castle that first day, it did seem to me he was almost unnaturally upset over the idea that another troll had somehow come into the castle. This, in spite of the fact none of us can seem to figure out—and Mnrogar gave us no reason— why it'd be possible there was another troll there. But when I lifted a *still* command from him, he threw himself on the ground and beat his head on it, like a child, as if he was helpless to find any other way to handle the situation."

"That's a long guess, Jim," said Carolinus. He in his turn looked at Aargh. "But, Aargh, you think there's a chance Mnrogar has aged within, you say?"

"There's a chance, yes," said Aargh. "No other reason I can think of. I only mention it. I'm not the great thinker that you two are."

He grinned evilly at them both.

"I'm only a straightforward, no-nonsense English wolf who deals in what I know; and I tell you this only because it might help Jim."

Aargh got to his feet.

"And now," he said, "get us back to your cottage by the Tinkling Water, Carolinus. I don't know about you two, who may wish to talk away the next three days; but I've got things to do."

"Wait!" said Jim. "I need a little more information, Carolinus."

Still upright on all four legs, Aargh pulled back the upper part of his body, elevating his head and nose rather like Queen

Victoria, in nineteenth-century England, could be imagined, as she was making her famous statement that she was "*not amused.*" It was the wolfish equivalent of a human drumming his fingernails on the table in exasperation and disgust.

"Talk, talk," he said disgustedly. "Humans like talking better than anything else I know. Well, I'll give you a little time yet."

"Thanks," said Jim. "It won't take long."

He turned back toward Carolinus.

"What I had in mind," he said, "is that I might arrange to have the Earl and the troll enter into negotiation over who owns the castle and the territory there. If they could get to see each other's point of view, they might become almost friendly. Enough, anyway, so that the Earl could arrange for the troll to come upstairs safely; and once there, while Mnrogar could stay hidden, he might be able to sniff at every guest there and smell out the troll he thinks is among us. Then, if he doesn't smell anyone at all, it'll be proof that he was wrong about there being a troll up there; and he can relax."

Both Carolinus and Aargh spoke at once.

"Utter nonsense!" began Carolinus. "The Earl would never—"

"You don't know trolls!" said Aargh; and, glancing at the wolf, Jim saw him with his jaws open in silent laughter.

"Believe what you like," he said stubbornly. "But if I could get the two to sit down together at the same table—say, somewhere outside the castle—can I count on you both to help me once I've got them there?"

"How do you want help?" demanded Aargh.

"I don't want them to fight!" said Jim. "They can say anything they like to each other, but I don't want it to break down into a fight, because after that there'd be no hope of ever getting them together—"

"After that," put in Aargh, "you'd have Mnrogar, but no Earl."

"Exactly," said Jim. "Or perhaps—an Earl and no Mnrogar."

Aargh snorted disbelievingly.

"At any rate," went on Jim stubbornly, "Aargh, the troll might listen to you. Carolinus, you might be able to use magic to keep them from actually touching or hurting each other. That's why I thought I'd get them to talk, sitting down at a table out in the woods, or something. The idea would be to have the meeting outside the castle and beyond the Bishop's blessing, so magic would work."

"Well," said Carolinus thoughtfully. "Mind me, I don't believe for a moment you can get the two to sit down and—what was that word you used?"

"Negotiate," said Jim. "Well, I actually said 'negotiating,' but the word itself is 'negotiate.' It means to discuss their differences calmly and find a way to set them aside; so that they can be friends, or at least live together in something like harmony. I'll be there in my dragon body, of course, which should help to hold them both down to a certain extent, since I doubt even Mnrogar would want to fight a dragon."

"Not he," said Aargh. "Trolls aren't idiots. They hate dragons; but one of the reasons they hate them is because they're too big for a troll to kill. In fact, I think the truth is they're afraid of dragons—not that one wouldn't fight back if a dragon forced a fight and cornered him or her."

"Negotiate . . ." said Carolinus, turning the word over on his tongue as if to see how it tasted.

"Yes," said Jim. "We use it a lot where I come from."

Mentally, he crossed his fingers behind his back against either one of them asking him how often negotiation was successful where he came from. Luckily, neither did.

"Well," said Carolinus, "if you can get the two to sit down together, and if you think this will work, I can certainly stand by and use a AAA+ magician's knowledge to magically keep them from doing any harm to each other. That's clearly within our magicians' right to use magic as defense rather then offense."

"And I suppose I'll be there too," said Aargh. "Now, can we go?"

"Yes," said Jim.

Carolinus held up his finger and immediately the little fairy was holding to it.

"T.B.!" said Carolinus. "That was prompt!"

The fairy tinkled.

"Now, T.B.," Carolinus said, "you do *not* have second sight. Only humans have second sight. No Naturals, demons, wraiths, Forces or fairies have any such thing."

There was another tinkle from the fairy.

"I'm sorry, my dear," said Carolinus, "but you must recognize your limitations, for your own good."

There was an angry tinkle from the fairy.

"I say you did not!" said Carolinus, frowning. "I strongly suspect you were able to appear so quickly because you've been listening."

There was an extended tinkle, this time very angry, from the fairy.

"Very well, I withdraw that," said Carolinus. "We're deeply indebted to you, anyway; and, knowing what a gentle heart you have, I know you won't take the few words I just said and hold them against me."

A rather more pleased tinkle. And everything changed.

Jim found himself suddenly standing in the Malencontri serving room, next to his own Great Hall. Aargh and Carolinus were no longer with him.

"But she must have been listening," said Jim to himself—but, unconsciously, out loud. "Otherwise how did she know we wanted to leave?"

The ghost of a tinkle that was almost like a chuckle sounded faintly nearly inside his ear.

"She says she did," spoke the little voice of Hob-One, behind him.

He turned and saw the hobgoblin behind him in the hearth, which merely had a low fire in it at the moment, barely more than embers; but there was a waft of smoke from these, and Hob was perched cross-legged on one of them.

"I'm glad you've come, my Lord," said Hob. "He's really been getting rather desperate!"

He was looking past Jim as he spoke those last words; and Jim, turning, saw Secoh sitting just inside the archway to the short passage leading from the serving room to the hall. Secoh did indeed look desperate. He looked worn out. His ears were drooping and his whole expression, for a dragon, was abject. The abjectness of it would not have struck Jim so sharply, if he had not been a dragon himself on occasion, and necessarily learned something about dragon expressions.

"My Lord—" said Secoh forlornly; and broke off, helplessly, simply sitting and staring at Jim.

"What is it?" asked Jim, pricked by conscience, plus a sudden new alarm. "I'm sorry I've been slow getting back to you, Secoh, but I didn't know there was any great urgency about it. I've been very busy indeed the last couple of days."

In view of Secoh's tragic expression, the excuse sounded remarkably weak.

"That's all right, my Lord," Secoh said. But the tone of his voice did not match his expression or general demeanor; which was somewhat like that of a dragon just a few moments from expiring.

"Good," said Jim encouragingly. "Go ahead, then."

"Well, my Lord," said Secoh, "I bring a message from the Cliffside dragons—that is, not exactly a message. I mean, they wanted me to talk to you and explain the situation. We've been hearing for some time about this time, I mean this time right now—that is, this is the time you georges call Christmastide. You know, five hundred years ago, we didn't pay much attention to things like that because—well, five hundred years ago it was different. For one thing, we mere-dragons were as big and healthy as the Cliffside dragons then, as of course you know. But my great-great-great-great-grandfather was supposed to have said, 'Look out for that Loathly Tower. It'll be the ruin of us yet.' "

Secoh relaxed a little and his speech became less garbled.

"It seems that what he said was remembered because, as you know—well, our present condition—it's very difficult to explain this to you, my Lord; but it's very important to us. Very important, indeed. As my great-great-grandmother said—"

Secoh was getting wild-eyed again; and rapidly becoming more incoherent. He was also, Jim saw, fighting the normal dragon urge to go back to the beginning of time, when he wanted to tell something, and build up over hundreds of years of history to the point he wanted to make about the present moment. Jim suddenly had a rather shrewd idea of why it was Secoh here before him and not one of the Cliffside dragons himself.

Secoh had the stunted size of all the present-day mere-dragons as a result of what the Loathly Tower had actually done to them; just as Secoh's great-great-great-great-grandfather had prophesied. When Jim had first met him he had been the most timid and obsequious creature Jim could have imagined, with a dragon's size and natural weapons. But that had been before he joined with Brian, Dafydd the Welsh bowman and Smrgol, the grand-uncle of the dragon whose body Jim had then occupied. Smrgol had been an elderly dragon crippled by a stroke; but Smrgol had a great deal of courage, and his help had been needed to win the decisive battle with the Dark Powers in the Loathly Tower.

Secoh had never meant to make one of their party. But Smrgol had given the mere-dragon little choice.

So, Secoh had ended up fighting like a hero and being part of the victory. Ever since then, his character had made an abrupt about-face. He was now the exact opposite of timid and obsequious. He went around challenging and bullying every other dragon he met, no matter how big that dragon happened to be.

His self-image had completely changed. He was now convinced of his own courage; and as he saw it, he couldn't lose. A bigger dragon might easily be strong enough to tear him apart; but there would be nothing but more honor in his dying after challenging someone so much more powerful than he was.

On the other hand, the large dragons were steadily ducking Secoh's challenges. From their standpoint, they had no way to win. Even if they managed to beat Secoh into submission or kill him outright, they would only have conquered a very much smaller and weaker dragon than themselves. Also, berserker that Secoh had now turned out to be, he would undoubtedly cut them up pretty badly while they were in the process of subduing or killing him.

In short, if Secoh was here with whatever he was trying to tell Jim now, the reason he was here and not one of the other dragons was simply because the rest were afraid to face Jim. A curious situation.

"—Of course, they know you've been friendly to me, my Lord," Secoh was babbling on, "so they thought it would be better if I spoke to you. As my great-granduncle said once, 'If you don't ask for a share of the kill, you probably won't get any—' "

"So, they want to make some demand of me, do they?" asked Jim, to help the mere-dragon along.

"Oh no, my Lord!" said Secoh. "Not *demand*. Never demand. Plea! I'm bringing a plea to you from the Cliffside dragons. A plea for assistance, for permission . . . for help at this time of year."

Puzzled as to why the Cliffside dragons would want any help from him, particularly at this time of year when they would be happily tucked away in their warm caves, content to drink up their stores of wine, tell each other stories, and simply wait for spring to come around, Jim drove directly to the heart of what seemed to be the question.

"What exactly is it they want?" he asked.

"My Lord," Secoh turned tragic eyes upon him. "They want—we all want—to be part of Christmastide."

Jim stared at him.

"They do?" said Jim.

"And they thought"—Secoh got it out in a sort of final gasp—"that you could arrange it."

CHAPTER 15

Little by little, Jim began extracting bits of relevant information from out of an avalanche of details about Secoh's personal ancestors, histories of dragons residing both in meres and cliffs—and a fragmented account of interaction between dragons and georges, as dragons chose to call humans.

Dragons had once hunted georges as they would any other game, but eventually found out that they were difficult prey to take. They went on to become more and more difficult, turning downright dangerous by the time of the last few hundred years, in which weapons and armor—and particularly crossbows, longbows and their arrows—had come into use. Finally, the substance of what Secoh had brought him as a plea began to emerge.

In more recent centuries dragons had gradually switched from trying to hunt humans, to avoiding them whenever possible. But only just since the battle at the Loathly Tower had they begun to take a real interest in humans. An incident in which their kind fought side by side with georges was a powerful stimulant to dragon curiosity. Since then they had begun tentatively to have an occasional peaceful interaction between a dragon and a george. These had been prompted, as a matter of fact, by Secoh; who kept coming back and telling of the adventures he had had, as a result of his friendship with Jim, Brian and the rest.

The result was that some of the legends that the humans knew had begun to be known by dragons. These legends, of course, were usually acquired from people like woodcutters, solitary plowmen, and such unlettered folk—individuals who could be encountered well away from any other georges, or in a place where a trap could not easily be sprung on the dragon foolhardy enough to stop and talk. This contact had been justified by something Smrgol had said repeatedly while he was alive—that dragons and georges should get to know each other.

As with humans, the Cliffside dragons had a strong tendency to pay more attention to what a dragon had said after he was dead, than when he had been around to say it. Alive, Smrgol could only evoke an argument by making that statement to any other dragon. Dead, the others stopped to consider it; and ended up being cautiously attracted by it.

The attraction had paid off. Dragons loved stories. Stories were appreciated only a little less than wine; and wine only second to their hoards, in the list of what dragons valued. Now they had discovered that humans also loved stories. Moreover, the stories they loved best were stories about miracles and other strange or violent happenings—all very much to dragon taste.

Moreover, the best of these could usually be traced to a quantity of Biblical writing, some of it authentic and some of it by unknown writers making use of the pretense that their works were the writings of well-known saints or holy men.

This area had not been completely unknown to the dragons. They had been aware for several hundred years of the story of St. George and the Dragon. Surprisingly, after their first fifty to eighty years of indignation over the dragon being the villain of the piece—and worse yet, the loser in the fight—the legend had become an attractive story that led to enjoyable debate over how the dragon should have fought St. George so as to beat the good saint. Nearly every dragon who had lived since that time had had his own theory of how he could have fought St. George and won.

A by-product of this had been the fact that the dragons started christening all humans as "georges."

At any rate, the dragon appetite for human legends and miraculous happenings had grown by what it fed on. They had come at last on a legend that Jim managed to recognize, from Secoh's highly distorted version. It was a story that could only have originated as part of one of the apocryphal epistles of the Christian Bible's New Testament. A work by an unknown writer, referred to in Jim's world and time by the name of "pseudo-Matthew."

This legend the Cliffside dragons had somehow mixed up with the idea of the Christmas celebration of Christ's birth; and that had brought about a reaction that touched on one of dragonhood's innermost strongest feelings.

In a nutshell, the story as Jim had read it himself, in Palgrave's *Golden Treasury*, was of a time when the Holy Family was fleeing toward Egypt, to escape Herod's slaughter of the Holy Innocents—all the children in Israel under five years of age— because Herod, then the King of Israel, had heard that one of them was the Christ Child who had come and would displace him from the throne.

With kingly logic, it had occurred to Herod that he could neatly frustrate this possibility before it could get under way, simply by killing off all children who might have been born in the right time slot to occupy his throne.

Joseph, Mary and the young Christ, on their flight from Herod into Egypt—in the story Jim had read and Secoh had heard—had been escorted by a guard of all kinds of animals; the lion and the ox and the wolf and the sheep—predator and prey together, walking side by side in perfect harmony in an honor guard for Mary, Joseph and the young Christ. Then, according to pseudo-Matthew, the Holy Family had camped overnight in some rather rugged country next to a cliff with a cave in it—or perhaps it was just some large rocks. Jim found his memory was a little fuzzy on details—

But in the morning when they got up at first light, out of the cliffs, or the caves in them, unexpectedly came dragons, creatures far too large and powerful for the animal escort to protect the Holy Family from. Joseph was frightened for them.   ·

But the young Christ, who as Jim remembered should have been about toddler age by this time, reassured his father.

"Fear not," he said to Joseph. "These good creatures have only fulfilled what was spoken by David the prophet. '*Praise the Lord from the earth, ye dragons and ye beasts. Let them approach*.' "

And he had stretched out his young arm toward the dragons, inviting them to come and be blessed.

That was the legend as Jim's memory fed it back to him. It had been only six years since he had studied Palgrave's *Golden Treasury* as part of his graduate work back in the twentieth century; but a lot had happened in that time, particularly during the last three years in this world.

Secoh had the legend fairly much as Jim remembered it. But not quite; and what he did have was wonderfully mixed up with matters as they were now, as well as with a number of contemporary people and things.

However, by this time all Jim had to do was listen. Effectively, Secoh had been uncorked like a bottle of effervescent wine; and eventually the problem became to stop him from talking, rather than fizz away indefinitely.

"—You see, what they say happened," Secoh was saying now. To him, or any other dragon, "story" and "history" were the same thing. " '*Praise the Lord from the earth, ye dragons, and ye beasts. Let them approach.*' "

"Yes," said Jim.

"Well, *you* understand!" said Secoh. "You're a dragon like the rest of us, even if you have to be a george part of the time. You know how we dragons are. The trouble with georges is they think we're just some sort of animal, along with the actual animals. But we aren't. They're only animals. We're *dragons*!"

They had finally come to the mother lode at the core of all the garbled veins of legendary ore that Secoh had been working toward.

Jim did understand.

When he had first come here and been in his dragon body, even though he was at that time effectively a dragon, he would not have understood. But he did now. He had begun to understand when the crippled Smrgol, more by force of will than anything else, had literally dragged Secoh into the battle before the Loathly Tower. Smrgol had told Brian, Jim and Dafydd all about it, booming out the information in his tremendous bass voice.

" . . . *And letting a george go in where he didn't dare go, himself! 'Boy,' I said to him, 'don't give me this nonsense about being only a mere-dragon. Mere's got nothing to do with what kind of dragon you are. What kind of world would it be if we all went around talking like that?'* "

And Smrgol had tried to mimic someone talking in a high voice but had succeeded in lifting his words only into the middle-bass level.

" '*Oh, I'm just a plowland-and-pasture dragon. You'll just have to excuse me.— I'm just a halfway-up-the-hill dragon . . . ''Boy!' I said to him, 'you're a DRAGON! Get that straight, once and for all time! And a dragon ACTS like a dragon, or he doesn't act at all!'* "

—Then there had been a time, later on, when Brian and Jim had been in France on a secret mission. Secoh had appeared unexpectedly in the middle of the night at the inn where Jim was staying; and in order to keep the inn people—to say nothing of the townspeople—from discovering he had a dragon in his quarters, Jim had magicked Secoh into a human being to make him safe. Secoh had been delighted with the idea until he was actually changed. Then he had taken one look at his own scrawny human body—naked, of course, since dragons didn't wear clothes—and burst out in horror.

"Oh, no!" he had said.

The truth of the matter was, Jim had come to realize, that dragons did not at all consider themselves a lesser species than humans—just different. Most of all, they did not even begin to consider any idea that they should simply be classed as one more animal species by the georges. The very notion was shocking to them. As far as they were concerned, the hierarchy in the world consisted of dragons, georges just below them, and below the georges all the other animals. Their upset and indignation over every george they met taking it for granted that they were no more than a large animal—possibly one that was half-demon as well, but otherwise simply animal—had rankled and burned within each dragon ever since the time of the historic duel with St. George.

So now Jim knew what was exciting the dragons at Cliffside; and why Secoh had been so concerned about reaching him with the story, plus a plea for Jim's understanding and help.

" 'Ye *dragons* AND ye beasts,' " Secoh repeated. "You see, my Lord? Your Christ Child himself said it. And, since he's come down from London with your friend Sir John—"

Jim blinked. Here were some even more far-fetched elements tangling the situation. It would never have occurred to him in a hundred years that the dragons could manage to confuse Christ with young Prince Edward at the Earl's. Clearly, Secoh and the rest were firmly of the opinion that the birth of Christ either was taking place this particular Christmas, or miraculously happened over again every Christmas; and that somehow the episode with the beasts and the dragons and the rest of the legend was to take place any moment now during the rest of the twelve days of Christmas.

"So if you don't mind," Secoh was winding up at last, "we'd like you to have me and some other dragons come to this castle you're at right now, so we can be there at the right time to worship the Christ Child and have him bless us. That's what the story goes on to say, you know. He blesses us. What does that mean, my Lord? To bless, I mean?"

"It's rather like being given an invisible gift," said Jim, extemporizing hurriedly. "You can't see it, or feel it, or smell it, but it makes you happier and it means you'll be a better dragon from then on."

Secoh's eyes grew round with excitement.

"How much bigger?" he asked.

"*Better*," said Jim, "not bigger. You'll be a finer and braver dragon afterward."

"I'm already quite brave," said Secoh.

"Well," said Jim, "you'll be surprised. There's no limit to how brave you can be. Everyone will be startled by how much braver you are. Wait and see. You may even be remembered in a story yourself, as a result."

Secoh beamed.

That was one of the good things about dragons, thought Jim. They could forget their troubles and be happy at the twitch of an eyelid.

But now, for the main problem.

"As far as getting you involved in the Christmastide celebrations," said Jim, "that's more complicated than I can explain easily. I'm not absolutely sure how to manage it. But, you see, there are twelve days in Christmas, and we've only used up one so far, so there are eleven days to go and probably what you've been talking about won't happen until the last day. So we've got eleven days to go."

"Oh," said Secoh.

"Yes," said Jim, "you go back and tell the Cliffside dragons that I'll do my best to get you all involved with Christmastide if I can. There's a small chance I can't make it, but I'm going to try very hard—and I believe all of you know that when I try very hard I usually manage to do things."

"Oh yes!" said Secoh. "We never worry, if we know you're trying to do something; because you always do it."

"Well, I suppose . . ." said Jim, feeling guilty.

He cast a glance over his shoulder to reassure himself Hob was still sitting there on his waft of smoke.

"Now," he said, "I'd better have Hob-One get me back to the Earl's castle, as soon as possible; so I can get to work on this."

"Thank you, my Lord!" said Secoh. "I don't know how to thank you. None of the Cliffside dragons will know how to thank you. We'll do our best, of course."

"That's good of you," said Jim, feeling even more guilty. "Well, goodbye then, for the moment; and I'll hope to see you in the near future."

"You will!" said Secoh fervently.

The trouble was, Jim was still thinking—as Hob-One brought him back down into his own quarters at the Earl's via the chimney route—it would not be just one or two Cliffside dragons that would want to come with Secoh to the Earl's, to be part of the legendary happening that Jim had no idea how to arrange in any case.

If one wanted to come, all the Cliffside dragons would want to come. And if there was one knight among the guests in the castle who would slaver at the mouth at the thought of fighting a dragon, there was probably all of them. In short, if Jim succeeded in giving the dragons what they wanted, it was almost a sure recipe for an attack by the knights on the unsuspecting dragons; and a resultant free-for-all that would go down in history.

It would probably push back any hope of a friendship growing up between humans and dragons for the next three hundred years.

—But at this moment, Jim found himself suddenly standing on his feet in front of the fireplace in his outer room, and Angie just coming into that room from the inner room. She jumped and gave a small scream.

"I wish you'd stop being startled when I come back magically like this," said Jim peevishly. "It's been several years now since I first started doing it—"

"That's entirely beside the point!" said Angie angrily. "I can't be expecting you every minute, you know. And if I'm not expecting you, how can I not be startled when you show up?"

The logic could not be argued with. But then, thought Jim, he never had any luck arguing with Angie anyway.

"I suppose you're right," he said.

"You bet I'm right!" said Angie. She had something of a wrought-up air about her, as if she might be ready to go off like a time bomb at any moment. But she made an effort, settled down and smiled at Jim.

"But it's good to have you back," she said, going to him.

They kissed each other.

"Ah . . ." said Angie, opening her eyes and stepping back out of his arms. She pushed him down into a chair and sat down in one opposite. "Jim, you've got to do something about this Agatha woman!"

"I? Me?" said Jim. "Why?"

"She's been here twice now," said Angie. "I don't like it!"

"Naturally, of course," said Jim. "I mean—why don't you like it?"

"She came to see little Rob-ert!" said Angie, speaking in a false, syrupy voice and clasping her hands in front of her. She half closed her eyes in an exaggerated expression of angelic meekness. "Because he was now her only living rel-ative! Now that her poor brother was dead! As if I didn't know that he was only her half-brother and they hadn't hardly said a word to each other in the last ten years!"

"How do you know that?" asked Jim curiously. "About them not talking in the last ten years?"

"Oh, everybody knows it," said Angie. "That's not the point. The point is she doesn't fool me. It's not Robert she's interested in. It's his estate. She wants the wardship; and she's been making these excuses to drop by to see him, hoping to find something around here that she can use as an excuse to argue that she should have the wardship. Luckily, she hasn't found it."

"Are you sure?" asked Jim.

Angie put off the exaggerated expression, sat up straight and looked at him sharply.

"Am I sure about what?" she asked.

"Well, both things," said Jim. "That she's only interested in the wardship and that she was looking for some excuse around here that she could use to argue that you aren't taking good care of Robert, and so she should have the wardship."

"Of course I'm sure," said Angie. "This isn't the twentieth century, Jim."

"I know that," said Jim, nettled.

"She knows nothing about the child—knew nothing about it until she heard that her brother was on his way here with a new wife and the baby. So how can she pretend to have any affection or love for Robert? Let alone the fact that she hasn't gotten an affectionate bone in her body. I tell you I know the woman. I read her at first glance. Even if I hadn't, it's an open secret. She's ambitious. She's been living all these years on an allowance from her brother. But ambition takes money—or rather, money helps a great deal in furthering an ambition like becoming Queen of England. There's lots of money in managing Robert's estate until he comes of age; and she'd have no conscience about plundering it. Because later on if she was successful, no one would dare call her to book for it; and even if she was unsuccessful, that's what most people do when they get awarded the wardship of an orphan like Robert."

"You're undoubtedly right," said Jim. "How about my second point, though? I was wondering why you were so sure that she hadn't found any kind of an excuse around here that she might be able to use to get him."

"Oh, that?" said Angie. "Of course, I was expecting her. I made sure that we were being a perfect model of good care for Robert, according to this century. I even had him reswaddled, poor little fellow. That was the only thing I was concerned about. She might easily have heard that I had unswaddled him and put him in a crib; and she might be able to make something out of that. But I can't bear to keep him swaddled up all the time, just on the chance she'll come by. But our man-at-arms on duty outside has orders to delay her with excuses if she shows up and say finally he has to step inside to get permission to bring her in. She won't like it, but she can't make any capital out of that."

"I suppose not," said Jim.

"Of course she can't," Angie went on. "It's just proof we're taking extra good care of Robert. Then I always apologize after she comes in; of course, she sees through the apologizing, but there's nothing she can do about it. Anyway, that way we get time enough to get Robert out of the crib, the crib hidden and him swaddled up again. Each time she's been here, she's seen him swaddled in traditional fashion."

"Good!" said Jim heartily. "That should take care of her."

"It has so far," said Angie. "But there's no telling what she might not come up with next. I spoke to Geronde, but she wasn't any help."

"She wasn't?"

"Well, you know Geronde," said Angie. "Or you ought to by this time. She's my best friend here; but the way she thinks sometimes makes my hair curl. Her best suggestion was that we hire some outlaw types, or men like them—men who wouldn't be missed and are willing to do anything—and have them waylay Agatha's party when she leaves the castle. She's got twenty men-at-arms with her, so it won't be a simple thing to kill everybody in her party—but Geronde pointed out that they didn't need to. The attack just had to be an excuse for making sure Agatha herself was killed. Then Geronde came up with the way to tie all the ends up neatly. We'd arrange to have a force hidden in the woods to catch the men who did it. Then kill them, so they couldn't be made to tell anyone what they were hired to do. It'd look like you just came to the rescue again, a little too late, just like you did with the brother."

"I couldn't do that!" said Jim.

"Of course not," said Angie. "But that's Geronde. So, it's up to you. Jim, surely with magic and everything at your fingertips, you can come up with some way to block Agatha off from any hope of getting the wardship of young Robert; and once she realizes she's got no hope, she won't bother with him any more and he'll be safe."

Jim smiled inwardly. As usual, he was being given an impossible task; this time by Angie, when it was usually Carolinus or outside events that pushed him into something. But this time, he had an ace up his sleeve. Angie would be surprised.

"Oh, I think we probably won't need to worry about it," he said. "The whole matter's going to pass out of our hands entirely. Angie, I've just finished arranging a way to have us be sent back by the assembled magicians of this world, to our own twentieth century. So we'll be there shortly after all. How do you like that?"

Angie stared at him, her face going white. She kept on staring, to the point where Jim began to feel slightly uncomfortable. Finally, she found her voice.

"But we couldn't possibly leave now," she said. "Probably not for another eighteen or twenty years or so!"

CHAPTER 16

The medieval world he was in—and, for all he knew, the universe surrounding it—rocked around Jim.

"Eighteen to twenty . . ." he said, dazed.

"Well, maybe only eight—or six. We have to be sure you've got Robert's wardship and time enough to bring him up to an age where he's old enough to be turned over to people belonging to this time," said Angie. "Call it the foreseeable future. Of course, we could take him back with us to the twentieth century—"

Jim was not at all sure that would be allowed. Possibly, it would be emphatically not. But Angie was going on.

"—But no. Of course we can't go back to the twentieth century now," she said. "It's unthinkable!"

"Unthinkable," echoed Jim dully.

Angie got up from her chair and swooped down on him, sitting on his lap and throwing her arms around him.

"Were you counting on going so much, Jim?" she asked, hugging him. "I didn't think it meant that much to you. I mean, I thought that you liked it here a lot and you were just thinking about going home for my sake."

"Well, I was," mumbled Jim, too numb not to tell the truth.

"That was wonderful of you," said Angie. "It's the sort of thing you always do; and I should have thought you'd be doing it now. But don't you see, we have to wait at least until we have the wardship; but even after we get it, it'll be a matter of seeing

Robert started in life. It doesn't really seem to be fair to bring him up in the twentieth century as the child of two struggling academics when here he'd be rich."

"I suppose you're right," said Jim uncomfortably.

But Angie was going on.

"—You know how many babies and young children die at this time in history," she said. "There're so many things that can keep them from ever living to grow up. And Robert's such a fragile little fellow. If you'd held him in your arms the way I have, you'd know that we couldn't just turn him loose in this cruel world. He'd be left to grow up or die, by himself. There're people like Agatha, who'd just as soon see him off the face of the earth; plus all the ordinary dangers, and all the childhood diseases—that you and I know more about than anyone does here—and the carelessness of the people around him. There's even neglect, by the servants supposed to take care of him; even maybe by his own nursemaid. Or, even if the nursemaid loves him, like the little girl we've got nursing him now—ignorance on her part could cause Robert not to live to grow up. Don't you see, Jim?"

"Yes," said Jim. "I see."

"Don't say it that way," coaxed Angie. "We'll enjoy it too, you know. It'll be a happy thing to have the little boy growing up with us this way for a few years. I mean—we can't abandon him; and if we don't abandon him, then we've got to stick with him until he has a chance to survive. Wouldn't you agree to that?"

"I guess so," said Jim.

Indeed, there was not much he could do but agree. In the first place, he knew that no matter how he might feel at the moment, he was going to end up doing what Angie wanted to do, simply because he wanted her to be happy. Secondly, while he had no great attachment to babies in general, and had had very little contact with the one in the next room, everything Angie said was true. As very young children went, Robert was rather an appealing little fellow. For one thing, it was surprising how seldom he cried, and how quickly he stopped when his immediate need was attended to.

Also, everything Angie had said was true. Robert's situation was precarious, to use the most optimistic term. In any case, Jim could hardly agree to abandon him before the King had assigned his wardship to someone trustworthy.

Jim thought of telling Angie that if they did stay here, he might be stripped of all his magic; and all of them, not merely Robert, would be in a more or less defenseless situation.

For all he knew, he might even lose his ability to turn into a dragon—although that was something he should ask Carolinus about. It might be that turning into a dragon was something that he had in his own right. He had been one before he became an apprentice to Carolinus, so it might be that ability, anyway, would stay with him. It would be an asset, if so, but the only one they would have left.

Then he thought better of mentioning it. Simply put, the fact now was that he had to come up with some way of stopping Son Won Phon, along with whoever among the magicians were agreeing with him. There had to be some answer to that, too. It was up to him to find it; and there was no point in worrying Angie when she could do nothing about it. Only he could; and since he had to do it all himself anyway, he might as well keep it to himself and not upset her with it.

"You're right, Angie," he said. "We'll have to stay, at least for the moment. I don't see just how the future's going to work out beyond that, but maybe it'll come clearer later on. There're so many problems—"

"Oh, darling," said Angie, squeezing him. "I knew you'd understand. Listen! You know I told you I'd think about your problem about the troll under the castle and the other troll he thinks is up here and the Earl and so forth?"

"What?" said Jim. "Oh, that. That's right, you did."

"Well I've thought of something!" Angie sat triumphantly upright on his knees. "Would you like to hear it?"

"Of course!" said Jim, with all the enthusiasm he could muster.

"You'll love it!" said Angie. Her eyes were actually sparkling, Jim noticed with some surprise. "You know that reenactment of the sea battle at Sluys between the Prince's father and the French navy? You didn't finish the dinner, so you didn't get to see it. But you remember they were going to have it?"

"I remember," said Jim.

"Well," said Angie, "it was the most skin-and-bones, gimcrack, exaggerated, underplayed and overplayed thing you ever saw. They put it on just in front of the high table, facing all of us who were sitting there, but with their backs to everyone else in the room. But that didn't seem to matter to the rest of the guests." She paused to draw a breath.

"They brought boxes out—or something like them—for the actor playing King Edward to stand on. That was supposed to be the important high point of his ship, which was leading all the other English ships into battle. And they had things like stepladders or portable scaffolding they brought in, that were supposed to be other high parts of the ship—one of them even had a sort of basket around him that meant he was an English archer shooting with special broad-tipped arrows at the French ships to cut their rigging; and you had to pretend that somebody up on a ladder with his feet higher than Edward's head was really at a lower point on the ship than he was. Also, you had to pretend when the ships came together that they were boarding from one ship to another, but actually there was just empty floor and they started fighting across it as if they were boarding . . . and so on. It was actually hilarious. I had to fight to keep from laughing."

Jim smiled in spite of the way he was feeling.

"I can imagine," he said. "Staging and a lot of other things would be left to the audience's imagination. In fact, audiences at this time were supposed to use lots of imagination, watching a performance."

"Well, they had it, and to spare!" Angie jumped to her feet. "You should have seen the reaction of all the guests. Even though they were seeing the play pretty much from the wrong side—it wasn't completely from the wrong side, of course, because the actors had to move around and sometimes they had to face away from the high table, particularly when they were fighting. But everyone there just ate it up. I hadn't realized how much any entertainment, any kind of a spectacle, means to these people."

"I don't think I had, either," said Jim thoughtfully. He was remembering all the additions the ballad makers had added to his own actions at the Loathly Tower, in making up their songs about it.

"But you know how children are when you tell them a story?" said Angie. "They actually *live* the story. If you tell them about something frightening, they get really frightened. If you tell them about something that tastes good, you can see them actually tasting it in their mouths. If you tell them about a castle, the castle is right there, completely real as far as they're concerned. Well, the people at that dinner were just like that."

"Were they?" Jim was getting interested in spite of himself.

"Absolutely," said Angie. "I wouldn't have believed it if I hadn't seen it. But I swear that most of the men there could hardly hold themselves from rushing up and starting to fight with the actors. And the women were just as fascinated. More

than that—you know all of us who were at the high table? The
Earl, and the Bishop, Chandos, and everybody else? They were
just as caught up in it as the people at the two long tables."

"No wonder Brian didn't want to miss it," said Jim. "You know,
I didn't realize what he might have been depriving himself of. I've
been feeling kind of guilty about that whole matter of having him
pretend to fall down; and what came about as a result—I really
hadn't planned for him to have a vision—"

"I know you hadn't," said Angie. "It was the Bishop who put
the idea in his head and everybody else's. But the Earl, the Bishop,
Chandos—everybody—were just as caught up in that make-believe
battle as a bunch of kids!"

"Well, I'll have to make sure I don't miss the next spectacle
that's shown. When are we due to have one?"

"That's it," said Angie. "There're two more, but they're supposed to be only small things, compared to the battle at Sluys.
That was special because it's Christmas Day. But, Jim, it gave me
a marvelous idea. Why don't we put on a spectacle for them?"

"A spectacle?" Appearing on top of everything else that had
come his way lately, the question left Jim's mind fumbling to
understand it. "Us? Why?"

"Don't you see?" said Angie. "Everyone in the castle will
be there, even the servants. They were actually jamming into
all the entrances to the Great Hall while the Sluys battle was
going on; and no one chased them away, not even the senior
servants, because they were busy watching the battle, too. So,
with everybody in one place, you could get your troll up from
downstairs to smell around somehow and—maybe you could
make him invisible or something—"

"Remember," said Jim, "the Bishop's blessing—"

"Oh, yes. Well, I'm sure something can be worked out," said
Angie. "The point is, this is about the only way you're going to
get everybody together and be able to bring your troll upstairs
safely without anybody seeing him coming or going. Think of it,
Jim. Isn't it a marvelous idea?"

She stared at Jim expectantly.

"I'm thinking," said Jim.

"I thought maybe we could do the Crèche scene. You know,
the Christ Child in the manger."

"Yes, I suppose," said Jim, unconvinced.

"You know," said Angie, "we could build a shelter like part
of a stable; and I'll bet we could get a real ox and an ass—and

of course Mary and Joseph; and we could get real straw for the floor, of course, and then have the shepherds coming and the three Kings with their gifts—"

"I'm not sure the wise men and the shepherds came at the same time," said Jim. "It could be done, all right. It doesn't have a lot of action, though."

"Well, we can always invent some action, can't we?" said Angie.

Jim saw clouds of disappointment beginning to gather on Angie's brow.

"I'm not rejecting the idea at all," he said hurriedly. "In fact, it's an excellent idea; it's just the details. For one thing, today is Christmas Day, and something like that is supposed to happen on Christmas Day, don't you suppose? And besides, come to think of it, since it's a religious scene, I'd probably better talk to the Bishop about it first and find out if there're any religious objections to doing it."

"Why would there be any religious objections?" asked Angie.

"I don't know," said Jim. "But remember this is the medieval Church. Nobody here's ever mentioned a Crèche scene or anything like that. If they don't normally do it, they might be hesitant about accepting it for some reason."

Angie looked disappointed.

"I don't know, I'm just considering possibilities," added Jim hurriedly. "But, yes, I don't see why it couldn't be done. I don't know quite how I'd get the troll around, invisibly, to sniff at everybody—or if he could pick out the smell of one troll accurately in a room full of people. It seems to me that might be a little hard for him. But let me think about ways to do that, too. Thank you, Angie. That's really a good idea. Just let me check into the details and see how possible it is. We just don't want to charge ahead and then find out too late there was some kind of objection we'd overlooked. For one thing, if we did something like that and upset people, that might work against my getting the wardship of Robert."

"I didn't think of that," said Angie. "That's right, Jim. You better look into it carefully. But meanwhile, I can be thinking how we might dress and such."

"Yes, by all means," said Jim.

The fact was that, outrageous as the idea sounded—just one more thing to concern himself with when he had his hands full anyway—there was something definitely attractive about it tickling at the back of his mind. But too much had happened. He literally was fuzzy-brained at the moment. Something else occurred to him.

"Say," he said to Angie, "come to think of it, this is still Christmas Day, isn't it?"

"The evening of Christmas Day," she said, with her hand upon the curtain that covered the door to the adjoining room. She was obviously just about to leave him. "Why?"

"I don't know," said Jim. "I was seeming to have trouble thinking. Then I realized that I was thinking that Christmas Day was yesterday. I guess I'm just tired. More's happened today than I could tell you in the next week."

"Oh?" said Angie, letting go of the curtain and coming back into the room. "What did happen?"

"That's what I—" Jim broke off on an enormous yawn. "I guess I'm not up to even telling you right now. I—"

Voices were coming audibly through the door to the hall. Voices clearly raised above the ordinary.

"Stand aside, damn your liver and lights!" one of them was declaiming. "What do you mean by questioning me like this, anyway?"

"It's what m'Lady said to do," protested the other voice. "Ask questions until I ran out, then slowly look in the room and ask if I should let anyone in."

"Oh? Then ask, sirrah!" said the first voice—lowered a bit now, though. "You know who I am. Ask, then!"

"Yes, Sir Brian!"

The door opened and the man-at-arms in the hall snuck a pale face in.

"M'Lady—M'Lord?" The pale face stared at Jim, who had not come in past the man-at-arms but was there nevertheless. The guard swallowed, then pulled himself together. "Sir Brian craves admittance, my Lord, my Lady—"

"Let him in," said Angie.

Brian was let in. He stood with feet spread a little apart. He was not drunk; but he obviously had been doing some drinking.

"James!" he shouted in a voice that would have carried with ease if Jim had been fifty yards away. "Good to see you. You're back, then—"

"Hush!" hissed Angie, with such effective sibilance that Brian's tone immediately dropped almost to a whisper.

"I was asked to step upstairs, James, to see what news there was of you. You must come down. We're all in the upper chamber above the Great Hall. You *must* come down. What, this is Christmas Day and you sit here apart from everyone? Angela, I know you have duties here, with the orphan, but you should come too."

"I may, later," said Angie.

"Would you forgive me if I didn't come?" said Jim wearily. "Forgive me, Brian. I'll tell you all about it when I've had a little time and I'm rested a bit. But it's been a long day for me and I've been large distances, traveling by magic and other things and I—I must sleep."

"On Christmas Day eve?" said Brian. "If there was any time at all not to waste in sleeping—"

He broke off, however, gazing at Jim.

"But you do look weary, James," he said, in a milder tone. "Have no fears. I will explain to all that you had far to go to find Carolinus, but you found him and now you are back and already sleeping. We will talk tomorrow. You have not forgotten? Tomorrow we all go hawking—in different, small parties, of course, otherwise there'd be more hawks loosed on a single prey than has ever been seen in one place in Christiandom before. And you must not fail to come too, Angela. It is something for a woman's pleasure, also, this falconry—but I had forgotten, you've no bird. Perhaps the Earl will lend you one."

"I can't promise, Brian," said Angie briskly. "I may be there. Let me speak to the Earl myself, if I need to borrow a falcon. Otherwise, I may simply ride along to be with the company."

" 'Fore God!" said Brian. "And it'll be worth the coming, on a bright and frosty morning that it seems we must have tomorrow, now that with tonight the winds have blown away clouds. Well, then, I'll leave the two of you; and return to the upper hall to make your excuses. I give you good night!"

He turned toward the door.

"Good night," said Jim and Angie almost simultaneously.

CHAPTER 17

"Where am I?" asked Jim.

But of course he was on his own Angie-made-and-disinfected pallet brought from Malencontri, in the outer room of the two chambers allotted them at the Earl's; and as far as he could remember he had slept like a log through the night, not waking once. Either he'd been too deeply asleep to be wakened; or Robert had been unusually considerate about not crying or fussing all night long.

At any rate, there was full daylight coming in through the narrow arrow slit that was their window.

Jim got his eyes fully opened (they had done a ridiculously shoddy job in opening themselves only to about half-mast) and saw his clothing piled beside the pallet. He was warm under the covers that were piled on top of him; but in spite of the fire at the end of the chamber, the air in the room, fed by the open arrow slit, was not exactly balmy.

He reached out a naked arm for pieces of clothing, one by one, and dressed himself while still in the warm nest in which he had slept. Fully dressed at last, he threw off the covers and sat up. It struck him that he was both hungry and thirsty. Mostly thirsty.

He looked automatically at the small table only a few feet from his pallet. On it stood one of the leathern bottles that they carried at their saddle bows while riding, with "*boiled water*" permanently inked upon it in block letters by Angie. Propped against it was a note in her handwriting on a fragment of the costly paper Jim had picked up in France to replace the starched sheets of white linen that they had formerly used. It had been written on with a stick of charcoal.

Jim got one of the glasses on the table—clean, again thanks to Angie or possibly to the Angie-trained, older servant woman they had brought along—filled it with water from the leather bottle, drained it, filled it, drained it again and then, after a moment's thought, drank another full glass.

Immediately, he felt immeasurably better. More awake. A stronger, brighter man.

He read Angie's note. It was written in her own modern handwriting, which would have made it unintelligible to any medieval reader, even though it was neatly written in plain English.

"*Bread and cheese on the table,*" it said. "*If you're up in time, you might want to get a horse and ride out and join the hawking. Nobody will know but what you've been going from group to group most of the morning and been with them from the start, if you want to put in an appearance. I've borrowed one of the Earl's hawks—a tercel. Love, Angie.*"

A tercel could be any male hawk, but commonly meant the male of the peregrine falcon, the female being a third again as large as the male and being therefore favored for hawking. Jim munched on the bread and cheese, even going so far as to add some wine from another leathern jug on the table to his next half glass of water.

Angie was right. It might not be a bad idea to pretend to put in an appearance at the hawking this morning.

Accordingly, half an hour later saw him on horseback, dressed in some extra clothing, light armor and a weather cloak over all, trotting through the snow that in this part of the woods was barely four inches deep, in search of the hawking party to which Angie was attached.

He found her. But not until after he had drawn a blank in the shape of three other parties, all of which pointed him off in a direction that turned out to be the wrong one. The fourth party he ran into consisted of six individuals, two women and four men, at a stand at the moment because a fine peregrine falcon belonging to one of the men had missed her kill.

She now perched grimly on a branch about twenty feet off the ground, in an unclimbable tree with no lower branches—and in no mood, obviously, to wait for a climber to reach and grab her, in any case. She sat hunched and looking wickedly down at them all, her gaze now including Jim.

"Could you possibly get her down for me with magic, Sir Dragon?" asked the knight who evidently owned the peregrine. He was a large, rather burly individual in his thirties, running a little to fat.

Caught a little off balance by the request, Jim gazed up at the peregrine. He thought he possibly could, though he found himself wondering whether it would be an ethical use of his magic according to the defense-only mandate. Luckily, while he paused to think, it came to him quite clearly that the less he showed off his ability in this respect, here with this group at Christmastide, the more he left it to them to imagine; and Angie had just been talking to him last night about the quality of their imagination.

They would give him credit for a lot more such ability if they never saw a demonstration of it, than they would if they saw such a demonstration. It seemed a characteristic of all humans that the more the demonstrations, the more their respect for him would drop as his use of magic for them became an everyday affair.

Besides, he had rather a fellow-feeling for the peregrine. Things had not gone well for it, and it was naturally in a foul mood. Let them get the bird back in any way they could.

It was their falcon, and it was a common accident in falconry to have it miss its prey; for the peregrine dropped from a great height upon the bird it intended to catch and kill in mid-air, diving at around two hundred miles an hour. A slight misjudgment of its angle of descent, or its speed in combination with the speed of the bird trying to escape, could cause it to shoot past its target, its clawed feet still tightly bunched into hard knuckles for the stunning blow. An impact that, if the falcon connected, would leave the prey floundering and falling, easy to capture as soon as the falcon had checked its dive and gone back after it.

"I'm afraid not, Sir," Jim answered. "It is Christmastide, after all; and there are certain restrictions upon the use of what small skills I have. I regret my inability to be of help."

The bird's owner looked sour, but did not argue.

"As a matter of fact," Jim went on in a lighter tone, "I'm looking for my wife, the Lady Angela. I don't even know what party she's with right now. Have any of you any idea in which direction I should look for her?"

One of the other men, who had been sitting on his horse with his back to Jim, reined the animal around so that they were face to face.

"I believe I do, Sir Dragon," he said. One hand went up to twirl the miniscule end of the right side of his mustache. "Allow me to show you the way to her."

It was Sir Harimore.

"Hah!" said Jim unthinkingly.

Sir Harimore looked at him curiously.

"I'm sure," he said, "she is with a few others, no more than a small distance from here."

He had already set his horse in motion, and Jim turned his own horse to ride along beside the knight, who had not even bothered to say goodbye to the people he was leaving.

"Good—I mean," said Jim, "it's very good of you to take the trouble to show me the way like this."

"A common courtesy, surely," said Sir Harimore. He rode his horse, rod-straight in the saddle, apparently without effort and completely relaxed, completely in possession of himself, and with no particular expression on his face. "Further, I can be of no help in recapturing a loose falcon I have never flown, let alone viewed, before today."

Jim was feeling an awkwardness in the situation. He had never seen the man previous to Sir Harimore's confrontation with Brian in the upper hall chamber at the Earl's the day before Christmas; and Sir Harimore must have heard that Jim was Sir Brian's close friend. But the other seemed to be trying to be normally friendly and pleasant. Jim made an effort to fall in with it.

"You called me Sir Dragon, just now," Jim observed. "Today's the first time anyone's ever called me that. Actually, just Sir James—James Eckert—is what I'm used to."

Sir Harimore turned his head sharply and shot a steely glance at Jim.

"Sir Harimore Kilinsworth, at your service!" he said. "Did I miscall you, sir?"

"No, no," said Jim placatingly. "Not at all, Sir Harimore. It's just that I'm not used to being called Sir Dragon."

The steeliness went out of Sir Harimore's glance.

"You are commonly referred to as Sir Dragon, as I have heard from others," he said. "I perceive it must be some kind of by-name."

"No doubt," said Jim hastily. By-name, he knew, was essentially one of the terms for a nickname. "I've no objection to being called Sir Dragon. In fact, if people want to call me that, it doesn't matter. It really doesn't make any real difference whether I'm 'Sir Dragon' or 'Sir James'—just as long as I understand I'm the one spoken of—or to."

"Hah!" said Sir Harimore. "Then, if any ask me in the future, so will I answer."

"Thank you," said Jim.

"A nothing," said Sir Harimore. He looked straight ahead, guiding his horse between a couple of close trees as they entered into a thicker part of the leafless forest. "Perhaps you are also looking for Sir Brian Neville-Smythe?"

"I rather thought Lady Angela would be in the same hawking party that he was, yes."

"As to that, I'm not sure," said Sir Harimore. "I recognized from a distance only your Lady and Sir John Chandos. But there were two other men in the party, one of whom could well have been Sir Brian. In any case, we shall know shortly when we join them."

Jim found himself wondering if it were not somehow possible for him to soothe the prickliness between Brian and this knight.

"You've known Sir Brian for some time yourself, then?" he said.

"I have," said Sir Harimore. "I have ridden against him in tourney several times; and had other acquaintance at different times."

"He's a good knight," said Jim, picking a safe, normally applied statement that could be used with practically anyone who wore a knight's spurs and belt.

"He is over-proud," said Sir Harimore. "But a gentleman, I'll give him that. And a good man of his arms."

This was not too far removed from Brian's assessment of Sir Harimore's character to Jim after Jim had witnessed their meeting in the upper hall chamber. Jim became suddenly aware that Sir Harimore was looking at him again; and the steely look was back in his eyes.

"Is it that you are about to take up Sir Brian's small debate with me, Sir James?" The steely edge was back now in Sir Harimore's voice.

"No. No, not at all. What debate are you talking about?" asked Jim innocently.

"Because," said Sir Harimore, "you may have control of some magics, Sir James, but that makes no whit of difference to me. If you would that we too should deal with this debate here and now, you need only say the word."

"Oh," said Jim hastily. "I couldn't use magic in an encounter with another knight. That simply wouldn't do. No, no—impossible. But then, as I just said, I didn't have any intention of—er—debating with you."

The steeliness faded, but Sir Harimore's gaze remained fixed on Jim. Although now it seemed almost a little puzzled.

"No magic?" said Harimore. "In that case, Sir James, I am brought to wonder why you would think to challenge one such as myself."

"Well, I wasn't challenging you," said Jim, but with a bit of edge in his own voice. Sir Harimore's insistence on the fact that Jim may have been prodding the other into a fight was beginning to get a little bit on Jim's nerves. "If it's something you want, though, I'll gladly face you, any time, anywhere. Here, or any place else—yes, and I guarantee no magic."

Seeing the other still staring at him, he snapped out again.

"I've told you several times that I wasn't intending anything like that. Now do you believe me, or don't you?"

"Truthfully, Sir James," said Sir Harimore, "I find myself a-wonder at it. You do not lack for courage—but by public repute, I already knew that. Nonetheless, to consider a debate with me—you must be aware that it would be no fair match."

"No fair match?" echoed Jim, suddenly and completely at a loss.

"Hardly," said Sir Harimore. "I should be looked on as one who debated with a twelve-year-old boy. I mean no particular offense, Sir James," said the other knight. "But surely you must be aware that you could not hope to stand before me more than a moment or two. Honor must indeed always be served; but it is plain to me that you are hardly schooled to debate with one such as I—or even your friend Sir Brian—and anyone who knows me would know that I would recognize this at first glance on seeing you."

"And just how do you recognize that?"

"Come, Sir James," said Sir Harimore. "A hundred things. The way you sit your saddle, the way you walk. A certain clumsiness about you—"

Jim's temper, already heated, came dangerously close to a boil again. He knew for a fact that his physical reflexes were markedly faster than most people's; and since his high school days the smoothness and quickness of his movements on the volleyball court had been repeatedly noticed and mentioned by sports reporters. It was true that, even with Brian's teaching, he had only begun to absorb a small part of what the average knight learned, starting in the days when he was old enough to toddle around by himself and see his elders practicing with their weapons.

"Why," said Sir Harimore, "even now you have the sword at your belt slung back further than it should be on your hip, for comfort while riding, instead of forward to where it would be quickest to grasp in case of need."

Jim's temper deflated like a pricked balloon. He could not deny that what Sir Harimore had said was the exact truth. He had gotten in the habit of riding with his sword pushed back that way, to the point where he hitched the belt around a little before he mounted, almost without thinking. He could feel it hanging there now, like a badge of shame before the experienced fighter on the horse beside him.

"Nonetheless—" he began feebly.

"Say no more, Sir James," said Sir Harimore. "I honor your readiness to debate on behalf of your friend even though you knew your attempt would be hopeless. I should have expected no less from you. For I now see legend is indeed true in this case. But— lo! I see your Lady and the others we are seeking just ahead!"

Jim looked, and it was true. Only a dozen yards ahead of them, in a small open space, four men and one woman were off their horses and examining something on the ground. Another woman sat on her horse at a little distance from the three and whatever they were looking at.

The woman on the horse was Angie.

"It is!" said Jim. "I am beholden to you, Sir Harimore!"

He put his horse to a trot, and Sir Harimore's horse, without evidently needing any signal from its rider, broke into a trot to keep level with Jim's mount. All those in the clearing looked up as the two knights rode in. Sir Harimore stopped his horse about ten feet short of the three standing together; but Jim rode directly to Angie. As he got close, he saw that her face was white.

"Jim!" she said, reaching out to grasp him as best she might with their two horses side by side and head to tail of each. She leaned forward toward him, in as close an embrace as was possible, and murmured between clenched teeth.

"Get me out of here! I can't take any more of this!" She clung to him, prolonging the awkward hug, and continued, "Such a tiny little fox! Practically torn to pieces—and they act as if they'd killed a lion!"

"Right," murmured Jim. His not to reason why. "Can you hang on another moment or two? I'll have to set something up."

"Yes. But be quick!"

Jim disengaged himself from her and turned his horse to ride over to where the others stood. Nearest him were Sir John Chandos, the Bishop and Brian, and beyond them he saw Geronde and a man he did not know. Brian was looking levelly at Sir Harimore, who was looking levelly back at him. Each of them had no expression on his face at all.

"Give us joy of the day, Sir James!" said the Bishop heartily. "My peregrine has killed a fox. True, it was not in mid-air, where she should be looking for her prey, but she attacked and killed it, nonetheless. However, I fear me she has suffered the loss of more than a few of her flight feathers. The fox turned with her talons already in him and caught them in his teeth, just before he was killed. She will not hunt again for some while. But it was a brave deed!"

"I do give you joy, your Grace," said Jim, though he was more of Angie's opinion about the fox than the Bishop's. "However, I've a matter of import on which to talk privily to your Grace and you, Sir John. But my Lady is over-tired. She should not have come out today. She must get back to the castle and rest as soon as possible—"

"It will be my honor to escort her!" rang the voice of Sir Harimore, behind Jim.

"*I*"—Brian came down very hard indeed on his utterance of the personal pronoun—"am presently escorting my Lady Angela."

"Perhaps they both could escort her," said Sir John Chandos.

Jim winced inside. Brian and Harimore might be able to keep from open conflict on the way back to the castle; but they would almost certainly find some excuse to leave it again and settle their private differences bloodily out in the woods here if they made the trip back together. At all costs, the two must be kept separated. But, at the same time, Angie really did need to be taken back to the castle. He opened his mouth without knowing what to say; but Geronde was before him.

"But what is all this?" she cried, leaving the fox and literally springing into the saddle of her own horse. "I shall accompany

Angela. The two gentlemen may come with us, but I will want Sir Brian to remain handy until I see her safely cared for in her own quarters. Come, Brian!"

Jim sighed internally with relief. Quickly, he swung his own horse about and urged it back to Angie, as Brian swung himself into his own saddle and Chandos and the Bishop followed suit.

"Faint!" he whispered as he got close enough to her.

"A-aaah . . ." sighed Angie without wasting time; and collapsed upon him.

Jim caught her in his arms—ordinarily a reasonably easy thing to do; but in this particular case he had forgotten the precariousness of being in a slippery leather saddle on top of a horse.

He found the only thing that was keeping him and Angie from plunging between the two horses to the snowy ground below was the pressure of his left knee, against the opposite side of his horse from that on which Angie's horse stood. Angie was slim for her height, but she was tall to begin with, and several years back here in the Middle Ages had turned her solidly into bone and muscle. The angle at which Jim's arms had to support her threatened to put too much force on his left knee for that alone to hold them for more than a moment, even if the horse would not protest that much pressure at one point on his ribs.

But luckily, here came Geronde to the rescue.

"You can wake up now!" hissed Jim, just as his knee began to slip.

"Where am I?" asked Angie, opening her eyes wide and pulling herself back upright in her saddle.

"You're with us, sweeting," said Geronde. "Never mind. We'll have you back in your rooms in no time at all—it's all right, James! I'm with her, now. You can go about your affairs— whatever they are. Brian!"

"I'm right behind you, my Lady," said Brian.

"Come along, then. You must ride on the other side of Angela. Sir Harimore!"

"I am with you also, my Lady," said Sir Harimore, joining them. They went off.

Jim watched them go for a moment with a sigh of relief. Angie had looked badly wrung out. There must be more strain to her taking care of Robert than he had thought, even with the help of the wet nurse and the serving woman they had brought from Malencontri. Plus the double life she essentially had to live by showing up now and then at the yuletide festivities and entertainments.

He was about to turn back to Chandos and the Bishop, when Carolinus's voice spoke inside his head.

"Follow Aargh, Jim," Carolinus said. *"He and I have already picked out the best place near the castle for the negotiation you mention. Show it to the Bishop and John Chandos. I may be able to join you; but if not, you set it up the way you want it set up, and don't let the other two talk you out of anything. Look out for the Bishop; he's used to getting things the way he wants them. Stand up to him!"*

Carolinus's voice ceased. And Jim was just reining his horse around when the Bishop's voice spoke behind him.

"A demon!" the Bishop was saying as Jim caught sight of him again, with Sir John beside him. Their attention was fixed on Aargh, who was standing facing them at a distance of about twenty feet. "Church rules enjoin me against the shedding of Christian blood. But that law cannot be considered to apply to demons; and yonder is one such, or I don't recognize such when I see it! So if you will just lend me your sword, Sir John, I as a churchman will protect us all against it!"

Just then he noticed that Jim had joined them.

"Fear not, Sir James," he added. "The strong arm of the Church protects you!"

"There's no need for protection, my Lord Bishop," said Jim hastily. "May I make you acquainted with Aargh, an English wolf, without a drop of demon or Fiendish blood in him. He's an old friend of mine, and was one of my Companions when we fought the Dark Powers at the Loathly Tower—so you could say that he was on the side of the Church, even then—"

"I—" Aargh began harshly.

"Still!" said Jim, forgetting that the command could not work against the wolf. But Aargh paused, and Jim discreetly waved a hand at him, in hopes that the wolf would interpret it as the request it was. Jim went on. "And Sir John has met him, haven't you, Sir John? You remember, when we at Malencontri were besieged by the sea serpents last summer."

"Indeed, your Grace," came the smooth tones of Chandos. "A brave and helpful, true English wolf. I commend him highly to your good wishes."

"Not demon?" said the Bishop, slumping a little in his saddle. "Ah, well." Aargh's eyes seemed to blaze up in his face.

"No, my Lord," said Jim. "Further, he is here to escort us to a place I want the two of you to see. The reason for my wishing that is what I wanted to discuss with you privily; and we can do it on our way there. Aargh is already aware of the situation I would talk about; and has been most helpful. No one knows the country hereabout as he does!"

"I see I've got myself into another of these human nonsense matters, when I should have minded my own business!" snarled Aargh. "However, enough for now. If you're coming with me, follow!"

With that, he turned and trotted off through the trees.

"We must go with him, my Lord—and Sir John," said Jim. "Bear with me, please. I promise I'll explain as we go."

"This explanation of yours, Sir James—Hocking," the Bishop added to the fourth man of their original party, a lean individual well dressed, but with a subservient attitude, "fetch the falcon back to the castle."

"Yes, my Lord."

The three of them put their horses into motion to follow Aargh.

"As I was saying, Sir James," the Bishop went on, "it had better prove worthy of the situation. I will accept your word and Sir John's; but he still looks more demon than English wolf to me, a usual wolf being little more than half his size."

"Indeed, your Grace," said Sir John, "the wolf does deserve your acceptance of him."

"As to that," said the Bishop, "we shall see. Meanwhile, I await your explanation, Sir James. But what's to do, here? The wolf is taking us back again toward my Lord Earl's castle!"

CHAPTER 18

"I don't think he's taking us all the way back to the castle, your Grace," said Jim. "As I say, he knows the country around here better than anyone else; and he's been searching out a particularly good place for me to hold a negotiation between my Lord Earl and the troll of the castle."

"Negotiation?" said the Bishop. "Traffic between a human soul and a Fiend—or, what was that name you called the creature?"

"A Natural, your Grace," said Jim. "Naturals aren't really Fiendish at all. They can't help being what they are, any more than—"

He had been about to say, "—than we can help being human" when he realized that the word "human" might trigger off an unhappy reaction in the Bishop.

"—than Aargh yonder can help being a wolf," Jim wound up. "They are not quite human—"

"They have no immortal soul!" said the Bishop. His thick brows gathered together over his eyes like thunderclouds.

"No, they don't," said Jim. He found himself in a quandary. This was a world full of talking dragons, talking wolves, magicians, sorcerers, fairies, dryads and evidently every other possible thing imagined. It would be unwise to suggest to the Bishop that there had perhaps been some divine reason for them being here.

On the other hand, he could think of no other reasonable explanation for their being here. "Possibly their existence is beyond our understanding."

"Perhaps," growled the Bishop. "No doubt the Lord will deal with them in His own time."

"Yes," said Jim. "But what I wanted to talk to you and Sir John about, your Grace, was the negotiation. You see, I haven't spoken about it either to my Lord Earl, or to the troll. But for all that there was a feud between them, the ancestors of my Lord Earl dwelt relatively in peace with the troll for more than a thousand years; and only recently has he started to shake the castle. And since that, my master Carolinus pointed out to me, is doing certain damage to the castle in divers ways, the most immediate solution seems to be to remove the reason for his doing it. Now, you know about him claiming there's another troll in disguise among the guests—"

The Bishop and Chandos both nodded.

"So you know," said Jim, "how it is this that seems to be what is driving the castle troll near to madness; since the castle is part of his territory in trolldom, and no other troll has a right here. But he cannot get at the disguised troll, because he dare not come upstairs to smell that troll out. Apparently, trolls have a smell, which other trolls and animals can scent."

"I suggested that he could come up under my protection; but you told me he would not trust the word of a Churchman like myself!" said the Bishop. "In that case, why not let his misfortune be upon his own head?"

"It is the castle that will be upon the Earl's head, if he does not find this other troll, your Grace," put in Chandos diplomatically.

"True, true," muttered the Bishop. He glared at Jim. "What then?"

"Well," said Jim, "it occurred to me that there must be some other way of arranging for the troll, in secret, to scent out the disguised troll upstairs. I'm sure the Church would agree that we, ourselves, at this particular period of Holy Feasts would be more comfortable if no troll disguised as a man or woman was amongst us."

"That is true!" exploded the Bishop, lighting up. "It is our duty first of all to root out the troll among us, just as it is to root out the Satan within ourselves—within most of us, that is. This, regardless of whether the troll below the castle is satisfied or not. Perhaps we can take our own way to discover who it is."

"My Lord," said Jim, "don't you think my Lord Earl would very much rather the rest of the guests not know there's ever been a disguised troll among us, than know that one could join his Christmastide gathering? His guests in the future would be uneasy—"

"I suppose so," said the Bishop grimly. "Well, what else have you to suggest, Sir James?"

"This negotiation of which I made mention," said Jim. He held up a hand, for the Bishop was about to start speaking again. "I assure your Grace there'll be no trafficking with anything unChristian, in the process. It'd merely be a matter of the two regular inhabitants of the castle deciding how best to get rid of an impostor neither of them wants there. All they have to agree on is how to go about it. It is merely a matter of sitting them down to talk to each other until they see that this is a point of agreement they can work on together. Once they accept that, we can proceed expeditiously and quietly."

"An excellent idea, I should think, Sir James," put in Chandos.

The Bishop glanced quickly at Chandos, glanced back at Jim and then turned his gaze on Chandos again. "You really think this would work, Sir John?" he asked. "I trust more to your age and judgment than to that of Sir James. You think Sir James has something of worth here to suggest?"

"I do, your Grace," said Chandos. "Indeed, he may offer us the best hope we have for bringing all matters to a conclusion in this hap."

"Say you so?" said the Bishop. He looked back at Jim, now. "Very well, Sir James. I am listening."

Jim fervently hoped that he not only was but would continue to do so.

"You will understand, my Lord, and Sir John—" he began, as they left the close company of the trees for a little open space before they entered some trees beyond. Above the farther trees could now be seen the upper battlements, with some pennants and banners also visible flying from the higher points. The Earl's banner floated above all, a large standard of gold and green. Jim felt a budding uneasiness in him. Aargh was indeed taking them very close to the castle, if not to it. Jim himself had conceived of some well-sheltered and hidden space fairly deep into the trees of the surrounding forest. But Aargh should know what he was doing.

Jim became suddenly aware that both the Bishop and Chandos were eyeing him, waiting to hear him finish what he had started out to say. What had he started out to say? His mind scrambled to recollect.

"As I was just about to remark," he said, "when this slight tickle in my throat checked me—you can understand how on first meeting the Earl and the troll will be full of complaints each has about the other, and not ready to agree on anything at all. They must be brought to it slowly. That is the heart of negotiation—a third party is needed to lead them both gently to a point where they can begin to find reason for agreement. I am planning to be that third member, as the individual known as the negotiator, and so lead them into agreement."

"I should be there too," said the Bishop.

"If you will forgive me, your Grace," said Jim. "The history of negotiation, as I know it, is that it works best when there are no more than three parties; the two opposed and a third both the other two have some reason to listen to, even if they won't listen to each other. If there are more than three, then it is a matter of one more point of view injected into the negotiation, which can delay results, and in some cases it's even been known to confound them."

"You suggest—" the Bishop began; but Chandos slipped in before he could finish.

"It may be Sir James is right in this," he said in his calm, well-modulated voice. "I also had been about to propose myself as a party to this negotiation; but what he has just said makes good sense to me. Since I am known by many to be involved with the policies of our ruler and his oldest son, it might be thought afterward that the Crown had some hand in the results of whatever evolves from this negotiation. I would rather not put the Crown in connection with this, slight though any danger may be. And possibly, my Lord Bishop, on mature thought you might think that it would be wise to disassociate the Church also from this magical, and somewhat unusual, method of compromise between a Christian and a Natural."

The Bishop closed his mouth. He looked thoughtful.

"No doubt something like this was in your mind, Sir James?" Chandos said, turning to Jim.

Jim grabbed gratefully at the argument Chandos had handed him.

"As a matter of fact, Sir John," he said, "it was. The more so, in fact, since my plan was to act as a soothing element and buffer between the Earl and the troll, particularly by doing my part in the negotiation while in my body as a dragon. This not only takes the discussion out of any possible association with either the Crown or the Church, but with other humans generally. It seemed necessary to me to have it that way, so that in case of any unexpected difficulty or trouble there'd be no blame on anyone but those who were involved in actual negotiation itself."

"Um," said the Bishop very thoughtfully indeed.

"But are we not almost at the place to which the wolf was leading us, Sir James?" asked Chandos. "The castle itself is beyond the next thin screen of trees. In fact, if you look closely, you can almost see it through them, though I think in summer time the leaves would hide it at this point."

"Well, yes," said Jim. "If you'll follow just as you are now, and forgive me for leaving you for a moment, I'll ride forward and ask Aargh about that myself."

Without really waiting for an answer from either one them—though in fact neither did answer—Jim touched his horse with his spurs and cantered forward until he was level with Aargh. Aargh looked up at him, yellow-eyed.

"James," said Aargh, in a low growl, "never do that again. Never try to use your magic to stop me from saying what I wish to say, or our friendship is dead from that moment."

"I'm really very sorry, Aargh," Jim said. "I didn't have time to think, and it's crucial the Bishop doesn't stick himself into this meeting between Mnrogar and the Earl. So I acted without thinking. I'm very sorry. Believe me, there won't be a next time. In the future I'll always think before I do anything like that, and let you speak."

"Well, let it be," said Aargh, still in the low growl. "There's no need to crawl on your belly to me like a puppy, James. Perhaps I would have said more than was wise, under the circumstances. Nonetheless, what I said must stand. I must never be silenced against my will by anyone—even you, or Carolinus. There can be no two ways with a wolf. Either there is complete freedom on both sides in an acquaintance, or there is no acquaintance."

"I'll remember," said Jim.

There was a moment of silence between them.

"Can I ask you where this place is you're taking us to?" Jim asked. "The Bishop and Sir John back there are beginning to wonder if we're going to end up in the castle courtyard."

"You're looking at it," said Aargh. "It's not far from the outer end of Mnrogar's tunnel to his lair. He will like that." Trotting a little ahead of Jim's horse, which Jim had reined back so that its pace was that of the wolf, Aargh led him into the semicircular open space, which had one side completely unshielded by trees and completely visible from the castle. Jim reined in his horse abruptly.

Aargh had also stopped and turned to him with his jaws open in a wolf-laugh.

"You'd better get back and stop those two behind you from coming out into the open," Aargh said. "You may not be recognized from the castle wall, but I rather think they might. There's no point in drawing attention to this space unless we have to."

"But this place won't do—" Jim was beginning, when Carolinus's voice seemed to speak from right behind his horse's tail.

"On the contrary, James," the voice said, "it is ideal. Come back now, and join us."

Jim turned his horse about, rode back among the trees just behind him and saw, standing together, not only the Bishop and Sir James, but Carolinus—as usual in a red robe such as he wore in any surroundings, season and weather, apparently always with complete comfort.

"But, Carolinus," said Jim, "this place—"

"Look again, Jim," said Carolinus. "Don't you believe it'll be a good deal easier for you to convince the Earl to meet with Mnrogar if he has his castle and men-at-arms at his back?"

"Yes," said Jim. "But look—Mnrogar may not be possible to convince simply because of that. Also, I've got a hunch that he's going to be harder to convince than the Earl even if the place was to his liking."

"Look again," said Carolinus. Jim blinked. The space was now completely surrounded by trees on all sides. No castle could be seen beyond.

This time Jim did not even have a chance to blink. Suddenly, the trees that had appeared were gone; and not only was the space open again on that side, but the castle was right where it had been, only about seventy-five yards away, with a few small figures looking curiously out over it at those of their party who were not obscured from view by brush.

"When the Earl looks," said Carolinus, "he will see his castle close at hand and everything open. So will the rest of you. When Mnrogar looks, there will be nothing but deep woods surrounding—more than that, the rest of his senses, particularly his sense of smell, will tell him that he is deep in the woods; and he will be persuaded he and the Earl are speaking privily together, with only you for—what did you call yourself?—a 'negotiator' present."

"The exact word is 'mediator,' " said Jim.

"Tut!" said Carolinus with a dismissive wave of his hand.

"But you'll be creating the illusion of the deep woods around the part of this space that's open to the castle, is that it?" demanded Jim.

"No," said Carolinus scornfully.

"Well, then, you'll move us back and forth from this spot to deep in the woods, depending upon which one of them is looking in the direction of the castle?"

"No." Carolinus's tone was severe. "I sometimes think, Jim," he said severely, "you tend to forget the difference between what a Master of Magick such as myself, and an apprentice like yourself, can do with our great Art. What I do here is something you have yet to learn."

CHAPTER 19

" If you wouldn't mind," said Jim, as he was parting from
— John Chandos in the castle. The two of them were alone
for a moment.

"Not at all, James," said Chandos. Something that could almost
have been a twinkle appeared in his rather serious gray eyes for a
moment. "I will gladly play lute to your flute in convincing the
Earl to have this little talk with the troll. I find your methods of
argument not of the usual, and therefore interesting."

"I'm indebted to you," said Jim, reminding himself once again
never to underestimate Chandos; and with a slight bow on either
side they parted.

Jim went up the stairs toward his own quarters, feeling like
someone who has fought the good fight and won. True, the
business of convincing the Earl would not be easy. The business
of convincing Mnrogar would be even more difficult—but Aargh
had promised to stand by on that. It was not that Jim felt he
needed Aargh's protection, as he had explained to the wolf; but
if Mnrogar could be said to trust anyone to any extent at all, that
one—curiously enough—seemed to be Aargh. Though Jim had
no doubt they would try to kill each other on a moment's notice
if the situation seemed to call for that.

Nonetheless—those problems aside—progress was being made.
The next important thing he must do was to corner Brian and find
out exactly what the schedule of events was for the rest of the

twelve days of Christmas. As he ran lightly up the stairs, with legs that had been trained by a lot of stair climbing in the last three years, he tried to remember what it was in the song that the lover gave his true love on the third day of Christmas—the one upcoming tomorrow.

The first day, he recalled, it had been "a partridge in a pear tree." Then the next day it had been "two turtle doves." Then the third . . . his memory stuck. It was either "three maids a-dancing," or "three Lords leaping." He was almost certain that the leaping Lords belonged in the next line—"*four* Lords leaping . . ."

He turned down the corridor circling the wall of the castle tower toward the doorway that led into his two rooms, still trying to puzzle it out. The more he thought of it, it had to be "three maids a-dancing"—unless it was neither ladies nor Lords? Perhaps Angie would know.

"All Hail, Tom!" he said lightheartedly to the man-at-arms on duty outside their door as he reached to open it.

"It is hailing outside, m'Lord?" said Tom Trundle, puzzled.

"No, no, Tom," said Jim, pausing. "I was merely jesting. A merry Christmastide to you as to everybody!"

"And to you, m'Lord," said Tom behind him as Jim went through the door and closed it behind him.

Cheerfully, inside, he turned to look at his present temporary happy home, and all cheerfulness went out of him.

What he heard, in that one moment, brought him to a sudden halt.

But only for a moment. The sound he had heard was from the next room. It was of two women's voices raised in cries of rage—and one of the voices was Angie's.

He hit the leather curtain of the doorway at full speed, bursting into the other room to see Robert crying in his cradle, the young wet nurse lying on the floor, insensible or dead, and Angie locked with another woman in combat. The other woman had a naked dagger in her hand. She was being held from using it only by the grip of Angie's hand on her wrist.

Jim wasted no time trying to identify the holder of the dagger. He went for the wrist of the hand holding it.

Angie was the taller of the two, naturally athletic even back in the twentieth century, and since hardened by their years here. But the other woman, though shorter, was heavier and evidently hard as nails. She was giving Angie an even battle. However, Jim outweighed either one of them by a minimum of forty pounds;

and he hit like a football player making contact. One of his hands closed on the wrist of the hand holding the dagger while the other seized hand and dagger alike and literally tore the dagger from the fingers' grip.

His impact sent the two women reeling apart, but neither fell. A glance at Angie saw that she was disheveled but all right. He looked at the woman from whose hand he had torn the dagger. It was Agatha Falon. Her gaze was now fixed on Jim, and Jim would never have believed that any face could look so viciously enraged.

"I'll see you both lose your heads for this!" she said in a low, uneven voice.

"No, you won't," said Jim; and was surprised to hear his own voice come out almost as laden with promised violence as hers.

"Yes!" Agatha Falon hissed the words. "The King will do as I say."

"No, he won't," said Jim. "He may still have some time left for women; but what he values above everything else is being able to do what he wants—drink and amuse himself while the great Lords and advisors around him run the kingdom. Those same Lords and advisors are going to be told of what you tried here. They already see the danger of you getting any control over the King. They'll play safe. You may be the one who loses your head, lady!"

"We'll see!" she retorted. A sudden wild, unreasonable feeling shot through Jim.

"Unless," he said, lifting a finger slowly and pointing it at her, "I decide to turn you into something small and slimy right now!"

Agatha made a small animal sound in her throat and darted out of the room. They heard the door to the hall slam behind her.

Jim and Angie looked at each other across the ten feet or so that separated them. Then Angie spoke in a voice that Jim had never heard her use before.

"It's a good thing you came when you did, Jim," she said. "If I could have got that dagger, she'd be dead now."

Jim looked at the weapon in his hand. With a sudden wave of disgust he threw it into a far corner of the room. Angie fell into his arms and he held her tightly while the great shudders going through her gradually lessened and slowed until they were only a shivering, until she was not shaking at all.

"Oh, Jim!" she said.

He continued to hold her, until she pushed herself away from him and stood back.

"Would you really?" she said, suddenly shaky with laughter, dabbing at her eyes with the back of her hand at the same time. "Would you really have turned her into something small and slimy?"

"I don't think I could, to tell you the truth," said Jim starkly. "I'm not sure the defense-only rules for magicians would let me. But I'd have tried."

"It would have suited her so well," said Angie, still shakily laughing.

Jim looked at the wet nurse. As he looked she stirred and murmured something, but her eyes stayed closed.

"What happened to her?" Jim asked.

"She'll be all right," said Angie, "but we'll have to feed Robert sugar water from a cloth teat until sometime tomorrow. Agatha got her drunk."

"Drunk?" Jim stared at Angie. "On wine?"

"No," said Angie. "On brandy, I think. You know, even in this century there're some distilled liquors, though they aren't common. My guess is it was French brandy—or rather, something more like white lightning, from the southern part of France. The King's court's one place where you can find it." Jim nodded.

"I can see why you wouldn't want her nursing until that dose wears off," said Jim. "But I'm surprised Agatha would take time out to get her drunk, even on brandy."

"Remember, Jim, people of her low rank are lucky if they ever even get to taste wine in their lifetime. And when they're given a chance to, they gulp it down the way they've always gulped down their own small beer."

Her voice hardened.

"It was just a miracle," she said. "I was headed down to the upper hall chamber but I got an uneasy feeling; and I was right. When I came back here, Tom said he'd let Agatha in because the wet nurse told him she'd been let in before. I ran in. The wet nurse was already out cold and Agatha was about to smother young Robert in . . . in . . . in . . ."—her voice shook—"his crib . . ."

Her voice deepened on the last words into that unnatural note that Jim had never heard from her until a few moments before.

"You must have got to her just at the split second—" Jim started to say.

"She was trying to arrange Robert so the smothering would look like an accident!" Angie said. "That's the only reason Robert wasn't dead before I got here. Though if I'd come in and found him dead with her there, I wouldn't have needed anybody to explain to me. So I started to throw her out and she pulled her dagger."

The shaky laugh came back.

"There was my own dagger at my belt and I didn't even think of it," she said. "I punched her. She wasn't expecting that, and it stopped her for a moment; and then I began to think clearly and grabbed the arm with the dagger. She was awfully strong, but I wasn't going to let her reach me or Robert. But I'm glad you came when you did!"

"I ought to've had a premonition myself," said Jim bleakly. "Actually, I was just coming up the stairs, trying to remember some of the song about the Twelve Days of Christmas."

Angie came to him again, hugged and kissed him.

"You came," she said. "Come, let's go in the other room. Robert's fallen asleep all on his own, now that things are quiet; and I don't want even to look at this room right now."

"What about the wet nurse?" said Jim. "Shouldn't we lay her on something, or something like that?"

"No," said Angie, "let her lie. It won't matter to her for the next ten hours or so. And when she wakes, and she feels like hell, good enough for her. She should be expecting anything up to a death sentence; but I'll simply tell her I'll leave her to answer for her sin to Heaven. That'll be worse than anything that could happen to her body. Come into the other room, Jim."

They moved, and sat down in the two barrel chairs at the little table with the wine and water bottles and the glasses on them. Angie's hands had already begun smoothing her hair and rearranging her brown dinner gown—which Jim knew was her personal favorite—as if they had minds of their own.

The gown was of fine-woven wool, dyed a brown that matched her eyes. It had the boat neckline that was the fashion of this period, the tight bodice and ample, floor-length skirt; and she had caused it to be recut in some way that gave it almost a twentieth-century look. As a married woman, she was of course wearing her hair curled and rolled into two buns, one on each side of her head. But she wore a band around her head above these, and over this, the conventional flimsy net veil hung down behind her head. To this veil she had added little glitter points of silver foil.

Jim poured himself a glass of wine and a full one for Angie, not bothering to add water to either.

"I don't need that," said Angie, looking at her glass of wine.

"Drink it anyway," said Jim. "You need to do something to put a period to all this."

Angie lifted her glass to her lips, sipped at it, then took a good-sized swallow. She set the glass down, and began to talk very quickly.

"Maybe you're right," she said. "Jim—I'd just gone downstairs to the upper hall chamber, on my way to the Great Hall itself, to put in an appearance at both places—since both of us have been more or less invisible until I went hawking this morning. I really wasn't too worn out this morning, actually. It was just that all of a sudden I couldn't join them in all their happy whooping over that little fox being killed by the hawk. The fox really never had a chance. That peregrine is big; and she can hit with her wings hard enough to knock you out of your saddle, I think."

Angie ran down suddenly and sat still. Then she took another drink of wine.

"Probably not that," said Jim, slowly and calmly. He was talking more to give her a chance to recover than to say anything important. "But you're right about wing-strikes. I don't know if you noticed at the time, but it was my wings that gave me the one advantage I had over Essessili—you remember the sea serpent I did single battle with when the sea serpents surrounded us last summer? I could hit him with my dragon-wings much harder than he could hit me with anything at all. Being built the way he was, like a sort of sea snake with little legs, he was too fat to curl up like a land snake and get any power into a head-strike."

"I told you why I came back," said Angie, speaking more calmly herself now. She drank a little bit more of her wine. "Why did you?"

"I wanted to tell you what I arranged about finding the disguised troll, here," said Jim. "I was thinking I'd find you up here, resting."

Angie laughed. Now, for the first time, it was once more her ordinary laugh.

"No matter how you figure it," she said, "what you found me doing was anything but resting!" She looked down at her glass. "Jim, I didn't believe it would happen this fast, but you're right. This wine does help."

"It hits you faster after something like what you've just been through," said Jim.

Angie sipped a bit more.

"Well," she said, "go ahead. Tell me."

"I had an idea," said Jim. "It was to get Mnrogar—the castle troll—and the Earl to sit down, with me as a sort of umpire; so the two of them could talk things out and get together on a way Mnrogar could come upstairs without being seen, and have a chance at sniffing at all of the guests over a period of time."

He refilled her glass.

"I don't need that," said Angie, looking at it.

"Don't drink it, then," said Jim imperturbably. "The question is how the other troll can masquerade as a human."

"And you don't know how he's doing it—I mean what kind of magic he's using—if it is magic?" Angie asked.

"No," said Jim. "That's the puzzle. The Bishop's blessing on the castle prohibits new magic, of course; and this could be a pre-existing spell. But Naturals can't work magic. But it's hard to think of any way the other troll could do it, that isn't magical. You know, Chandos is the one who really interests me—"

In the other room, Robert gave a tentative whimper.

"Oh, dear," said Angie, getting to her feet. "Stay where you are. I'll bring him in here."

"No," said Jim, getting up himself. "I'd better go down and see if I can arrange to talk to Mnrogar as soon as possible. Aargh will have to know when to meet me down there. I want to get Mnrogar talked around if I can before I come up for dinner. Will you cover for me at the high table? Tell them I'll be a little late."

The last words were shouted after Angie, who had already disappeared into the next room. Robert's whimper ceased, in what seemed to be a relieved silence.

"All right," Angie called back. "If you see Enna on the stairs, tell her to run back here. She should never have left this girl alone with Robert, when she knew I'd be down at dinner!"

"Right!" said Jim. Ennelia Boyer was the serving woman Angie had brought from Malencontri, a reliable servant in her thirties. Stopping only to hook his sheathed sword on to his sword belt—in clear violation of the ordinary laws of hospitality, when one was a visitor in someone else's home—Jim headed out through the door.

Enna could not have planned to be gone long. She was too responsible. On the other hand, Angie would not be able to go down to the high table at dinner until the older servant got back, with the wet nurse in the shape she was.

Perhaps he should make it a point to find Enna first, before going down to Mnrogar's den. She had probably slipped downstairs to the Great Hall as soon as Angie had left, in order to see Angie in her gown at the head table there—it had been Enna who had sewn the individual glitter points of faceted silver into the mesh of the veil.

As it happened, he met her on the stairs and she went hurrying up after his first few words of explanation. But before he could follow his original plan about Mnrogar, there was Brian on the steps below, coming up and shouting at him.

"James—there you are!" he called. "Haste! You've just got time."

Time? For what? Jim wondered.

"Giles is here, after all," Brian was continuing, his voice echoing up and down the great empty center space of the tower between floors, "although he's had the ill luck to hurt his sword arm! You must come right away. I want you to see Sir Harimore in one of the bouts with blunted sword and shield against Sir Butram of Othery. They are close to being well matched, though Sir Harimore has the edge. it will be instructive for both you and Giles to see. Come quickly, they may be fighting already!"

Brian was running up the steps, approaching around the curve of the tower down which the steps wound as he delivered his message. Jim ran down to meet him—being careful to stay next to the wall, however, since, as in most such towers, there was no kind of guard or railing on the drop-off side of the stairs.

"Giles here?" he said happily.

Sir Giles de Mer had been their companion in their first secret expedition into France, to rescue the young Prince, heir to the Throne of England. Giles was a Northumbrian knight who also had silkie blood in him. Brian and Jim had saved his life by carrying his dead human body back to the sea after he had been killed and dropping him into it. He had immediately come back to life as a seal; and although there had been some difficulty with him regaining human shape at all, he had finally managed it.

He was young, square-built, fiery-tempered and blond of hair. In a dramatic departure from the custom of knights of this period, he wore a massive handlebar mustache; that, together with an oversized beak of a nose, so dominated his facial appearance that it had been some time before Jim realized that what he had taken to simply be an unshaven, though prominent, chin was actually trying to sport the equivalent of a small vandyke beard, the sort some knights wore to counterbalance a neat little mustache.

Jim reached Brian.

"You say Giles is down there now—" Jim was beginning, on reaching Brian, when a voice interrupted from behind Brian.

"Nay, nay!" it cried; and a second later Giles himself was with them. His right arm was in a sling but otherwise he looked to Jim just as usual, still in armor, spurs and the type of garments suitable to horseback journeying. "Hah! James—it is indeed good to see you!"

In the next second Jim found his lower ribs compressed by the iron-bar embrace of Giles's unslung arm, while enduring a bristly kiss on either cheek from the Northumbrian knight—Giles clearly not having shaved for at least several days.

"It's good to see you too, Giles!" said Jim, with real feeling. If Brian was his best friend, Giles was certainly the next thing to that. "How did you hurt your arm?"

"Was but a foolish fall from my horse, in dealing with some outlaws we met on the way down. This cold winter weather, they starve in the wild woods and are savage as animals—"

"Come! Come!" said Brian, stamping his foot on the stone steps in impatience.

"We'd better go, Giles," said Jim. "We'll have a chance to talk later!"

They all hurried back down the steps, Brian leading. They went down to ground level and out through the Great Hall to the area that had been kept cleared of snow for the tournaments to be held later.

Looking toward a makeshift stand for the more important people there, Jim saw the Earl and the Bishop—and Agatha right beside the Bishop, chattering away in his ear, Jim noticed; although the Bishop seemed hardly to listen to her.

The Bishop's attention was all fixed on the three sword-bouts that were going on down on the field. He, Agatha, the Earl, the boy-Bishop—a lad whose function Jim did not fully understand even now—and Chandos all sat on the top level of the stands, muffled in clothing and furs, watching the three contests.

With Brian leading the way, Jim and Giles pushed their way through the crowd standing particularly before the second fight, with Brian calling out, "By your leave, Gentles, Ladies! By your leave! My pardon; but Sir James must see this at close hand. It is a matter of importance!"

There was a regular trail of exclamations that accompanied their passage through the crowd, "Ho!"s and "Hah!"s of resentment and outrage at being rudely pushed aside. But, seeing it was Jim following Sir Brian—who was in any case respected for his own weapon prowess—and they followed by a knight with his arm in a sling, common courtesy, to say nothing of respect for the fact that Jim had been honored with a seat at the high table, kept any one of those pushed aside from making any further objection.

Brian got them at last to the center of the front rank of standing observers. Sir Harimore, Jim saw, was already busy against a somewhat older, considerably broader and heavier knight who must be Sir Butram of Othery.

"Hah! Capital! Featly done, Sir Harimore!" cried Brian, as soon as they were in a position to watch. "Did you see that, James— Giles? How he made Sir Butram miss his stroke into empty air? Watch closely, now, for it is an interesting contest. Sir Butram is the stronger; and much quicker of hand than most would think, so that it is perilous to get close to him. Sir Harimore, though the lighter man, is countering this with skill and his own quickness of movement. Watch how he will move in and move out again, to try to tempt Sir Butram into moving to follow him. But Sir Butram is old and wise in battle, and not to be cozened so easily—there, Sir Butram takes one step; but it is one step only, and he has his feet planted solidly again almost immediately. He will not let Sir Harimore wear him out easily by tempting him into too much response. He forces Sir Harimore to come to him; and then in the end Sir Harimore must take some chances. But I will wager that in the end it is Sir Harimore who wins the bout . . ."

Brian continued with a continuous rattle of comment and criticism, reminiscent to Jim of the blow-by-blow announcing to be heard from a radio announcer at a sporting event. Jim had intended to talk quietly to Giles as they watched, and find out more about Giles's accident and his late arrival; but he found Giles was in no mood to do anything but listen to Brian and fix his own fascinated eyes on the contest before them.

The same thing was true of those standing nearby within earshot. Clearly, there was a great deal of respect for Sir Brian's expertise and critical skill.

"—Sir Butram takes two steps backward. Now the ploys are reversed. It is Sir Butram who tempts Sir Harimore to follow. Sir Harimore moves in—hah!"

Sir Harimore had indeed moved in; and, quicker than Jim would have thought possible, Sir Butram was suddenly ringing blows of his broadsword—lighter and shorter than Jim, like most untutored twentieth-century people, had imagined the weapon to be before he got back into this fourteenth-century world and saw the actual weapon—from all angles upon his opponent.

"—But Sir Harimore guards himself well—note the angling of his shield, James, that which I have tried so hard to teach you, so the blade will go off at a slant. Now Sir Harimore has backed out of arm range; and Sir Butram stands where he stood, still inviting Sir Harimore to close—"

Over the sound of the other two clusters of viewers watching the other two bouts, over the silence of those around Brian who were all straining to hear his words, there rose, suddenly and eerily under the forenoon sun, the long wavering howl of a wolf.

The three pairs of fighters with their blunted weapons paid no attention. But those watching who were not already silent, suddenly fell silent.

"An omen," muttered someone behind Jim.

"An *ill* omen," said another voice.

Indeed, thought Jim, it was a common belief. A wolf's howl by daylight—among many other such unusual events—was considered by these people to foretell some coming disaster. In fact, it was an eerie sound calculated to bring about a chill in the spine and abrupt silence.

It did not chill him, however. He was no reader of the ordinary howls of wolves; but he had heard this lupine voice many times before. More than that, he recognized it as a message directed at him.

It was the howl of Aargh, less than a quarter-mile away.

CHAPTER 20

That howl could only mean that Aargh was close, Mnrogar was in his under-castle den and Aargh was ready to be with him when he tried to talk the troll into meeting the Earl.

"Giles," Jim muttered into the shorter knight's ear, in too low a voice for those around to hear.

"Eh?" Giles tore his eyes reluctantly from the bout between Sir Harimore and Sir Butram. Brian, a little in front of them now, was effectively lecturing the whole crowd, paying no particular attention to Jim and Giles as he had in the beginning.

"I'm going to slip away," said Jim, still in the same low voice. "I must leave. I'll see you both later. If any in the crowd ask about my leaving, tell them I've gone to investigate the wolf's howl by ways magical."

Giles was anything but slow-witted. He nodded without answering aloud.

Jim turned; and gently, begging people's pardons in a low voice, pushed his way to the back of the crowd. Then he moved as rapidly as he could without seeming to run, back to the castle.

He kept to this controlled pace as long as there was anyone to see him. But once he was on the stairs leading down from the stable area on the ground floor, he went as fast as he could, stopping at the last moment to snatch a bundle of burning twigs from their position at the stairhead, to light his way down.

On second thought, on the fourth and last flight of stairs before he reached Mnrogar's home, he drew his sword and went the rest of the way with its sharp blade naked and ready. Brian, he found himself thinking, would have approved.

At the lowest level the dancing flames of his burning twigs lit up the great arches and buttresses that supported the castle. He hesitated at the foot of the stairs, then advanced half a dozen steps into the lair of the troll. There was no sound, no challenge from the place's resident.

"Mnrogar?" Jim called.

No answer.

"He's here," said the harsh voice of Aargh. "And what took you so long? I was at the mouth of his tunnel in the woods just outside the castle when I called you."

"I was outside the castle myself, watching the sword-bouts," said Jim. "I came as fast as I could. Mnrogar's here? Where is he, then?"

"Right behind you, human," said the equally unlovely voice of Mnrogar; and suddenly the troll-light was illuminating them all. Jim had spun around quickly at the first syllable at his back. Mnrogar gapped his sharp front teeth in what may have been intended to be a troll version of a grin, though there was nothing humorous about it.

"Look at him," said Mnrogar, "with his little sword all ready. Don't you know a troll's skin can turn a sword's edge, human? We're not made of thin stuff like you!"

"I don't need a sword to deal with you," said Jim. "The sword was only for rats—on the way down."

"There are no rats here," growled Mnrogar. "I ate them all for a hundred years or so, and after that they stopped coming."

He looked at Aargh.

"And wolves do not see in total darkness either," he said, "only well in very faint light. Were your teeth ready too, wolf?"

"We do not see in total darkness, troll," said Aargh. "But we have a nose which sees, unlike humans and trolls. The day you can creep up on me without my knowing it will be the day after your bones have been chewed."

And Aargh moved forward in the troll-light until he stood almost beside Jim and facing Mnrogar. Jim was reassured, but only slightly. In the troll-light, the castle troll himself bulked larger than ever. He remembered now what Mnrogar was talking about. The skin of a troll was indeed reputed to be sword-proof.

He had always thought that was nothing more than a legend; but from the way Mnrogar talked, there must be some truth behind it—but, hadn't Aargh talked about opening a blood vessel beneath Mnrogar's arm with his teeth? That dirty, yellow-brown skin could not be completely unpierceable.

"There's more than just the edge of my sword, Mnrogar, remember," he said. "There's the point. Nonetheless, as I said, I don't need a sword as long as I have magic."

He sheathed it, as evidence of what he was saying.

"As for that magic, do I have to prove it upon you once more?"

"Noooo!" The troll's answer was a howl, as fierce as it was filled with inner pain. "Say what you have to say and leave. I love you not. Neither of you!"

"Who loves you, Mnrogar?" said Aargh, and his jaws opened in silent laughter.

"None. And I need none!"

"None?" said Aargh. "In the two thousand years you have kept this territory against all other trolls, it has never once crossed your mind that you might like, for a moment, only to set eyes on another of your own kind, possibly under some condition where you could talk rather than fight? You've not thought of this? I tell you, Mnrogar, I have, and my life has been short, very short indeed compared to yours—but long enough so that there have been moments when I found myself longing to greet an old pack-mate once more. If you feared me so little, why did you talk to me when I first found my way down here? Why didn't you just try to kill and eat me?"

There was a moment of silence and motionlessness there underneath the castle, in which all things seemed to hang in the balance.

"I am a troll," said Mnrogar. "Trolls do not think like wolves— or humans! What do you want from me now, magician?"

"I thought of a way you might be able to smell out the other troll upstairs in the castle, without anyone knowing about it— except one person besides me."

"Smell him out?" burst out Mnrogar. "We will do it, then. Whatever it is, we will do it—"

He broke off suddenly.

"But I will be safe up there?" he demanded. "This is not a trap for me?"

"No-trap," said Jim. "It's only a suggestion. Let me tell you about it and then decide if you want to do it. All right?"

"Right or not, how can I tell you, until you tell me?" snarled Mnrogar.

"It's just that you and the Earl sit down with me and agree—"

"Agree!" Mnrogar's roar seemed even to shake the stone arches around them. "With him? I'll tear him limb from limb and eat the marrow of his bones first! This is my castle, not his—though he claims it! Built on my land, not his! You bring him here, you bring him to his death!"

"Then you are a fool," said Aargh.

Mnrogar's roar threatened to shake the arches again.

"Fool, wolf?"

"Fool, I said," said Aargh implacably. "James, here, knows his fellow humans better than you ever will. Also, he has a brain a great deal better than yours—almost as good as a wolf's. Hear him out before you talk about killing."

Mnrogar snarled wordlessly, but that was all. He turned to glare at Jim.

"It's within the Earl's ability," said Jim, "to convey you secretly upstairs and find you a place to hide unseen; and over a space of time you can smell all the guests. That way you can pick out the one who's a troll in disguise. You may be strong, your skin may turn the edge of a sword, but there are too many swords and too many men upstairs for you. If you go up any other way, you're the one who goes to your death—unless the Earl's your friend and makes it possible for you to do that safely. Think about it for a moment."

Mnrogar had half lifted his arms with the wicked claws on the ends glittering in the troll-light, when Jim had mentioned the possibility of his going to his own death. But now he let the arms sink down again and stared at Jim without a sound.

Jim waited. The troll was obviously thinking; and very probably that might be a slow process. In fact, it was. It was a good several minutes before Mnrogar lifted his eyes, which had wandered down to stare at the floor and arches beyond, back to Jim.

"Tell me, then," he said. "Why? Why will he do this? He will want something of me. Why else would he do it?"

"He wants only a truce between you," said Jim, mentally crossing his fingers, since he did not yet have the Earl's agreement to this, and it was entirely possible that the Earl would balk at the idea as much as Mnrogar had. "He doesn't like having a troll hidden among his guests, any more than you want one here at all. By working together, you two can find out which guest it is, and get rid of him. Alone, you can't and the Earl can't. Something odd is going on, too. Did you know there's an army of other trolls, together, without fighting and eating each other, gathered around us here?"

"NO!" exploded Mnrogar. "There is not. There could not be. If they were on my territory, I'd know it!"

"They are just outside your territory," said Aargh. "Never have I heard of trolls gathering together like that. But they are there."

"Exactly," said Jim. "And their being where they are has to have some connection with the troll, here in the castle right now. As things stand now, we've no way of understanding how this troll can make himself look so much like a human being that he's been accepted as one of the guests. But once you've told us who he is, we'll find out how he does it. That's what we magicians want out of this.

"But Aargh is right. The gathering of trolls just outside your territory must have something to do with the one upstairs. Both things are impossible, the sort of things that never happen. When they happen together, they just about have to be connected."

"Yes," growled Mnrogar, his eyes beneath their heavy brow ridge glittering but abstract. "Gathering like that—how many of them are there?"

"Perhaps a third of a third of the many years you've lived," put in Aargh.

"That many?" said Mnrogar; and for the first time Jim heard a new, strange note, in the huge troll's voice. "But why so many, without fighting? It's not our troll way—and in any case, only one can hold my territory, if I'm slain."

"They call you King of the Trolls," said Aargh.

"And I am!" Mnrogar lifted his head. "There is none like me, who has lived so long, who has fought so well, who has always won. When I have been full fed, sometimes I have hidden close to what is left of my meal to see if some smaller troll would come to try and feast on my leavings; and at times during the long years I have caught such a one and told him that I was King of the Trolls and let him go, alive, to tell all others that, so that they will know and stay clear of what is mine."

"So you've no idea why these other trolls are there?" Jim asked.

"I?" said Mnrogar. "How should I know?"

"Perhaps they have gathered to do you honor," said Aargh wickedly.

"They do me honor by running at the sight of me," growled Mnrogar. "I do not know why they're there. I do not like their being there. But more than that I do not like the hidden troll upstairs. Let me talk to this Earl of yours who claims my castle and my lands!"

"We'll have to make the arrangements first," said Jim. "The meeting's going to have to be held in a neutral spot."

"What is that?" Mnrogar's voice was loaded with suspicion.

"A place in the woods where there's no one else around, where you can be privy and secret in your talk, with only me, you, possibly Aargh and one other. But only you, I and the Earl will sit at a table; and I'll try to help the two of you talk peaceably. I'll be wearing my dragon body—of which you may have heard— just to make sure that the Earl's temper does not get out of hand— or yours, Mnrogar."

"Dragon?" snarled Mnrogar. "No troll in a thousand, thousand years has been able to stand a dragon. They are ancient enemies of ours."

"Because," said Aargh, "one on one, they can eat you, instead of you eating them."

"That is a lie—" Mnrogar broke off suddenly. Aargh's jaws were hanging open again in his silent laugh. "We have other reasons for hating them!"

"Say," said Aargh softly, "other reasons for fearing them."

"A troll fears nothing!" Mnrogar's roar rolled again.

Aargh laughed.

"I said you and your kind were fools," he said to Mnrogar. "What you said just now proves it. He who is wise is always wary. Wolves, too, fear nothing. But neither do they choose to go to a battle they can't win."

"No," said Jim thoughtfully, thinking of times in his own twentieth-century history, "only humans do that."

But neither Aargh nor Mnrogar was interested in the foolishness of humans.

"Very well, then," Mnrogar demanded. "Where do I meet this Earl? It better not be where he has twenty others all in metal at his back!"

"I just told you there would only be you, he, me, Aargh and possibly one other—the magician who is my master, and who will only observe for the community of magicians, not take part in the discussion. But you understand the reason for meeting is to find a common reason for not fighting, for working together to find this hidden troll above us? You understand that?"

"I understand," rumbled Mnrogar. "See your Earl understands. All right, those you mentioned do not worry me—though I do not like you as a dragon. It may be I should not go unless you come as what you are, a human."

Jim felt an odd little spark of anger touched off inside him. He had discovered some time back that dragons were very proud of being dragons and would not be anything else for the world— humans or any other kind of creature. Jim had also discovered that he, too, had become rather proud of being a dragon. It was as if his dragon-thinking had somehow bled over into his human-thinking. He would not be other than what he was, but he was proud of his humanity and he was proud of that part of him that was dragon, as well.

"You will take me as a dragon," he said, "or there'll be no talk and you'll never find the troll upstairs!"

"Very well," Mnrogar growled. "But it will be just the ones you mentioned. In the woods—you say?"

"Yes," said Jim.

Mnrogar turned his head to look at Aargh.

"In the woods?" he repeated to Aargh. "You have seen the place? You will be there too?"

"I will," said Aargh.

"And it is in the woods, as the magician says?"

"Yes," answered Aargh.

"My woods? The woods on my territory? Not near these other trolls you say are gathered around beyond my borders?"

"Yes, to all," growled Aargh.

"Magician," said Mnrogar, looking back at Jim. "When?"

"I can't say certainly right now," answered Jim, cautiously. "Probably in the next day—or two. I don't think longer than that. I'll let you know; or maybe Aargh will?"

He looked at Aargh.

"If I'm close," said Aargh. "Now, enough of this. If that's an end to questions, as I hope. I've more to do than stand and talk with the two of you. Is there more?"

"Not from me," said Jim.

"I will wait," said Mnrogar.

Aargh turned and was gone from the troll-light.

"Well," said Jim to Mnrogar, feeling suddenly, in spite of his knowledge of magic, singularly unprotected here alone with the troll, "I'll be leaving too, Mnrogar."

Without waiting for an answer, he turned and went back to the stairs. Behind him the troll-light went out—and he suddenly discovered that while they had been talking his torch had burnt itself out. His magic would not work once he had left the space under the castle; so in the darkness he groped upward until the blessed light of the stable, filtering wanly down the flights of stairs, reassured him that there was a world above ground.

Now to get the Earl's agreement to a meeting. That could be a trickier job. The Earl was no physical match for Mnrogar—and knew it.

CHAPTER 21

"Why?" demanded the Earl.

The Earl was as stubborn as a twenty-mule team in which all twenty mules were out of temper at once; and Chandos had been little help to Jim so far except to mildly second some of Jim's reasons why the Earl should meet privately with Mnrogar in the woods.

"Because," said Jim patiently, "as I pointed out before to your Lordship, it's better for you to have one large troll down below your castle, than a number of smaller trolls roaming your woods, eating your game—and possibly some of your cattle, if not some of your tenants or serfs. This particular troll, having all of these lands to hunt in, never needs to prey on anything but wild game; and, in spite of his size, he eats less than half a dozen to a dozen smaller trolls would eat of that."

"It's my land, damn it!" said the Earl. "It's my duty to keep it free of trolls—any trolls. Instead of talking with him, I should hunt him down with a stout band of men-at-arms and slay him."

"He claims it's his land," said Jim.

"Nonsense!" fumed the Earl. "Trolls can't own land! My family's been here since the Romans!"

"According to what he says," said Jim, "and his size tends to prove he has that kind of age, he's been here for eighteen hundred years. That would put him in possession of this area before the Romans came."

"Trolls can't own land!" said the Earl.

This was the point they had been coming back and back to. The Earl had entrenched himself on that point of argument, and refused to be budged.

The fact of the matter was, thought Jim, that while the Earl had been brave enough, once, to begin to go down under the stable floor with only two men-at-arms, to face the "giant" that was reputed to be down there—he now had had time to think it over, to remember his age, his weight, and the relative rustiness of his sword arm; and had decided that there was a great deal more to be said for facing the troll with a small army of his own men at his back. Particularly if he was doing his duty.

In short, prudence had registered its ugly presence in the Earl's otherwise fearless heart.

Jim had thought of mentioning that Carolinus with all his magic would be there invisibly to protect them, as well as to observe proceedings. But he knew very well that the moment he mentioned anyone else might be there, the Earl would seize the opportunity to name one or more people *he* wanted to be present, also—and the negotiation as a practical reality would fall apart.

Undoubtedly, Mnrogar would not stay around if anyone else than he had been told of appeared to be present. The troll might put up with the presence of Aargh. But if anyone else was visible, he would probably be out of sight before you could pronounce his name properly.

The real problem was that neither Mnrogar nor the Earl had any real intention of coming to terms with the other. But come to terms, they must. Jim went back to his own one unanswerable line of argument.

"If you got rid of Mnrogar, my Lord," he said to the Earl, "you'd not only be faced with the fact of a number of other trolls inhabiting your woods, but you never would be able to find out who the troll is that's in disguise among your guests."

"How do I know there is any?" growled the Earl. "All we've got is this Mnrogar—or whatever he calls himself—his word for it. The word of a troll—faught!"

There seemed, Jim noted, to be a lot of "faughting" going around. Or maybe he had just never noticed it before.

"It does hardly seem likely your castle troll would be that desperate about pulling these walls down around his own ears, if there was no other troll up there," put in Chandos mildly. The Earl turned to him.

"No, Sir John. But—" The Earl, who had been looking angry all through the interview, looked a bit angrier, finding himself at a loss for a good reply to this. "So that might be. But I've no certainty. I am certain there's this troll below us."

"Yes, my Lord," said Jim, "but what you can do about the troll downstairs is rather limited. If you go down the stairs with your men-at-arms after him, within his own den he has the power to vanish. Outside it, he can't vanish, but he only goes out to hunt for food; and catching him then would be nothing but chance. He can go some days between meals, since he eats such an enormous amount when he does eat. Your only certain way would be to find where his tunnel comes out in the woods; and not only will that be hard to locate, but if you did and set a guard there, he'd smell the guard before he was all the way out and dig off in another direction, starting a new escape route from his den. In short, you have much to gain by at least talking to him; and little to gain by any other means."

"But I have my duty!" snapped the Earl. He looked at Chandos. "Have I not my duty, Sir John?"

"Undoubtedly, my Lord," said Chandos soothingly. "On the other hand, duty may be approached from a number of angles. It may well be that this business of first entering into conversation with your troll beneath the castle is the best of the ways to go about executing it."

"Say you so?" answered the Earl. He had no long beard like Carolinus's to chew on to express his frustration in moments like this; but he looked to Jim very much as if he would have been chewing if he had one.

"Yes indeed, my Lord," said Jim quickly, hoping that he had seen a crack in the stone wall of the Earl's reluctance. "You are after all the only one the troll would deal with. He would certainly not talk to anyone but yourself; and preliminary conversations are probably absolutely necessary to the kind of end you have in mind—which is no more shaking of the castle, no more cracks in the castle wall."

"You know about that?" shot out the Earl, swelling with incipient rage, his eyebrows bristling.

"Yes, my Lord. Carolinus told me."

"Ahh . . . hmm," said the Earl, deflating.

"As I was about to say, my Lord Earl," went on Jim; "for that kind of end and the discovery of the unknown troll among us upstairs here, some preliminary conversation is undoubtedly necessary; and it can only be at the highest level, between the castle troll and yourself."

"Preliminary conversation?" The Earl stared, a little pop-eyed.

"Pourparlers, my Lord," explained Chandos.

"Ah, pourparlers," said the Earl. "Well. I suppose there's that . . ."

"True," said Chandos, dreamily, almost as if to himself, "there's no precedent. I doubt if any Earl anywhere in the world has ever parleyed with a troll of such a great age—one who was around when the Romans ruled this isle. In fact, I'm sure of it. History would have recorded such a resounding event. The name of the Earl would be written large not merely in monkish journals, but in the minds of all the common people as well . . ."

"Hmm . . . ?" The Earl cleared his throat questioningly, looking at Chandos, who, however, was staring off into the distance and not meeting his eye. "Remember his name? Yes, yes—I suppose they would—if there had been, that is. Yes, you're quite right."

Jim's mind was galloping. The crack he had exploited in the Earl's reluctance had been used by Chandos very cleverly to tickle the Earl's vanity. In this version of the fourteenth century, Jim had discovered, there was one major thing about the people: they were all frustrated actors. The Crown Prince, for instance, would strew favors and gifts right and left, as the spirit struck him; and that in spite of all attempts to restrain him— because it was "royal" to do so. And whatever role a person found himself or herself placed in, he or she acted their part to the hilt.

Each king grabbed every opportunity to appear more kingly than any other king. Each prince, more princely, and so on, right down the line to the Earl. And actually, the trait continued among those of smaller rank, as each person wanted to show themselves as bigger and better than anyone else of the same rank. Right now my Lord Earl of Somerset, standing in front of him, was already seeing the monks writing up his name in their chronicles. The prospect was a great temptation.

He was, after all, a knight, and had been a knight all his life. And the way a knight got to center stage was to do dangerous and daring things. Consequently, by the time they were old enough to graduate from being squires to knights, men like the Earl, Sir Brian and Sir Harimore were conditioned to take any kind of chance just to get the spotlight upon them. Literally, the cost in possible wounds or death could be easily forgotten in the excitement of the moment—and it was clear that excitement was gripping the Earl right now.

But it had acquired a strong foe in the last decade or so, during which the Earl had become aware that there were other things in life than wielding sword or couching lance. That awareness, combined with an equal awareness that life was good, and he would just as soon go on living it for a fair number of years yet, was fighting a stern battle with the temptation of a chronicle entry.

Jim decided to gamble. The Earl was on the fence and now, if ever, was the time to push him over in the right direction. He had intended to tell the Earl as little as possible about Carolinus's involvement in the meeting, or Aargh's, in picking out the ground—quite frankly, simply because he did not trust the Earl not to let what he had said leak out and become common knowledge.

If the Earl were to swear an oath that he would divulge it to nobody, of course, the information would be safe. But it would be the worst of insults to ask the Earl to take such an oath. He would take the position that his word should be good enough for anyone; and so it should be—but Jim was uneasy about it.

"My Lord," he said, "would you step over here to this arrow slit?"

They were in an upper room of the tower, and the arrow slit gave them a fine view of the front part of the castle, the cleared space beyond its curtain wall and the first of the trees of the forest.

"Why?" snapped the Earl.

"I would like to show you something, my Lord," said Jim. "This is a matter of the utmost importance and secrecy. If you would indulge me . . ."

The Earl made a noncommittal noise, but moved over to the arrow slit and peered out.

"You see, my Lord," said Jim, "beyond the curtain wall there, and beyond the cleared space where the forest trees begin, that spot where there is a small opening into the trees themselves; not quite perhaps big enough for two gentlemen to ride at each other with lances, but otherwise a fair space? It is surrounded thickly on all sides by trees and bushes, except that side which faces the castle. The reason secrecy is involved in this is that my master Carolinus has arranged to use some of his great magical ability there, outside the area of my Lord Bishop's blessing of the castle, to make the best possible place for the discussion between you and the troll, with myself sitting with you and Carolinus standing by. Note we will be within full sight of the castle curtain wall, which is less than a bow shot away; and from the top of that wall, your men-at-arms can be observing all three of us at all times, ready to come instantly, if necessary."

"Hah," said the Earl, somewhat doubtfully.

"The only difficulty," Jim went on, "is that the troll would naturally never agree to a meeting there if he realized it was such an open spot. Therefore Carolinus has offered to use magic to make it seem to the troll that trees fully enclose that area, so no eye can see; and the two of you, with me standing by in my dragon body just in case of any problem with the troll, are completely privy and unobserved."

The Earl stared at the spot, turned and stared at Jim; then after a moment his face lit up.

"Hah!" said the Earl.

Jim's spirits bounced upward. It was the tone of voice he wanted to hear, in that "Hah!" But then the Earl's face clouded over once more.

"But my duty—" he began, hesitated and cast a glance at Chandos.

"My Lord," said Chandos smoothly, with hardly a heartbeat of delay between the Earl's last words and his own, "duty is certainly something that must always considered first. On the other hand, there are situations above and beyond the ordinary—"

His eyes flitted temporarily to Jim and then back to the Earl, so smoothly that for a second it was hard for Jim to be sure that Chandos had glanced at him. But better to break in, than pass up the opportunity.

"Forgive me for interrupting," said Jim, "but perhaps there are points of this that you, my Lord, would rather talk over alone with Sir John. Perhaps I had better leave you, accordingly, and you can always send for me if you wish me again."

The Earl grunted, Chandos nodded and Jim ducked out of the room into the corridor, headed toward his own rooms and a little bit of peace—if there was any down there—with Angie.

"—When duty concerns matters of high import, not easily understood by ordinary folk—or even, mind you, the lower gentry, my Lord . . ." Chandos was saying as the door closed behind him.

Jim headed downstairs, feeling vastly relieved. He had no doubt whatsoever that Chandos would succeed in coming up with the excuse the Earl was seeking. Because that reaction of the Earl's, once Jim had pointed out that he would have his men-at-arms close at hand, ready to help if they saw anything go wrong between him and the troll, had removed all doubts. The Earl was not afraid of hard knocks. The Earl was only afraid of losing what was left of his life, or sustaining the kind of physical damage that would keep him from enjoying it to the full—to the full, possibly including Agatha Falon?

That last thought came to Jim and left him wondering. Had the Earl and Agatha merely been playing the usual party games, or had there been more at stake? Prince Edward had been sure she had been aiming at the King himself. Possibly that was one more question he should look into; but there was absolutely no time to add any extra problems right now. What he needed, Jim thought sourly going down the stairs, was a holiday from this holiday.

"Guess what, Angie," he said walking into their own quarters and seeing Angie in the front room, sitting in a chair, leaning back with her eyes closed.

"—Up? What's up?" cried Angie, her eyes flying open. "Robert—"

She started to rise from her chair.

"No, no, no—" Jim waved her back down again. Guiltily, he suddenly realized that Angie had been taking advantage of a rare chance to rest from her own obligations. She sank back in the chair, looking not at all pleased in his direction.

"What did you wake me up like that for?" she demanded.

"I'm sorry, Angie," said Jim. "I didn't realize you might be napping."

He was indeed sorry. But part of his mind told him that, just as he had been trying to do everything asked by Carolinus—and it seemed everybody else as well—a lot of Angie's fussing over Robert didn't have to be done by her alone. If Angie had been like almost any other woman of her rank and authority in this particular age, she would be leaving Robert exclusively to servants, and all but forgetting him completely in the amusements of this gathering.

Not, of course, that either Angie or he particularly enjoyed what passed for amusements in this period of history. Certainly Angie had not enjoyed the hawking. Also, certainly she had not enjoyed being woken up just now.

"What is it?" she said. "I just sat down for a minute and, bang—here you are!"

"I didn't realize you'd dozed off," said Jim. "You really ought to get out more, you know. The wet nurse and Enna can take good care of Robert; and in case anything comes up, one can stay and the other can run and find you."

"Perhaps," said Angie. But she still looked a little like a cat whose fur had been rubbed in the wrong direction. "Anyway, what is it? What did you come to tell me?"

"I live here, remember?" said Jim.

"That's right," said Angie, "you do."

She began to look less annoyed.

"But I could swear," she said, "you were trying to tell me something just when you woke me up."

"As a matter of fact," said Jim, "there's a lot of things I'd like to tell you; and I just haven't had the chance. Who's in the other room—besides Robert, I mean?"

"Enna," Angie answered. "When Robert naps, everybody naps. Well, sit down and tell me whatever it is you want to tell."

"Several things," said Jim, seating himself. He reached automatically for a wine glass and the wine and water bottles.

"You drink too much," said Angie.

"Everybody here drinks too much," said Jim—meaning everybody in the Middle Ages. He filled his glass with half wine and half water. "In this case, I need it. I've been arguing with the Earl, trying to set up a conference between him and the troll in the basement, Mnrogar. I did tell you about him."

"Yes, I'm up to date on Mnrogar," said Angie. "But why did he want to talk to the Earl?"

"He didn't," said Jim. "And the Earl didn't want to talk to him. I wanted them to talk so that maybe they'd get along together enough to let the Earl allow Mnrogar upstairs without killing or hurting him, and let him try to sniff out who the secret troll is, in disguise among us."

"I can't really believe there's a secret troll among us," said Angie.

"I know," said Jim. "It's hard for me to believe too. It was even hard for Carolinus—and it can't get much more unbelievable than that. But Mnrogar swears there is one. More than that, he's really upset over it. I explained how this was his territory and no other troll ought to come into it, didn't I?"

"Yes," said Angie.

"The hard part is," said Jim, "that they've got to meet outside the castle some place, and it's got to be a place where the Earl feels safe and Mnrogar feels safe. I think we've finally got that much worked out; and just now, with the help of Chandos, I've talked the Earl around."

He told her about it.

"Well, then," said Angie, more cheerfully awake and normal, "then you don't have anything more to worry about."

"Hah!" said Jim.

"You're saying that a lot lately," said Angie.

"Well, everybody else says it," said Jim.

"The men say it," said Angie, in a tone of voice that clearly described the miniscule amount male conversation had developed since they all lived in caves. "But you mean you've got other things to worry about, too?"

"Yes," said Jim. "Our castle hobgoblin has been visiting this room here, too. The dragons all want to come to the Earl's party. Giles is here; and Brian is still expecting me to want to break a lance with him sometime so he can show me the finer points of jousting. The fact that I might break my neck in the process is, of course, beside the point."

"Tell me about it," said Angie. "Tell me about all of it."

He did.

"Our own serving room chimney hobgoblin," said Angie thoughtfully, when Jim was finished. "I wonder why he never put in an appearance back at the castle?"

"I think he would've, once he grew used to us, and if the two of us had been in the room alone—with no one else with us," said Jim. "He's very shy and timid. But it was Secoh who made him seek me out, with the message for me; and I suppose that was all he thought of. You don't generally expect Naturals to have remarkable intellects."

"That's true," said Angie. "I like Rrrnlf, but even with a head as big as his, and you'd think a brain the size to match, he does seem in some ways pretty simple-minded. That is, I don't mean simple-minded in the ordinary sense. What I mean is, he's a little childish and innocent."

"Maybe all Naturals—" Jim was beginning, when there was a scratching on the outer door. "What is it out there?"

Taking this for permission to stick his head in, the man-at-arms on duty there in the corridor opened the door and did so.

"Sir Brian is without and would wish to come in, m'Lord," he said.

"Certainly," Jim was beginning. But Brian had already pushed past the man-at-arms and was coming in himself.

"James—Angela," he said, and dropped into the room's one remaining chair. Jim, or just about anyone else except another knight, would have been said to have collapsed into the chair. But Brian, like all his belted brethren, had been so trained by years of saddle, stool and bench sitting that it was literally impossible for him to lounge. He certainly rested in the chair; but he did it sitting as upright as if he was on parade.

"Here's a pretty pass!" Brian said.

"What now?" asked Angie.

CHAPTER 22

"I t's Giles," said Brian. He cast a thirsty eye on the wine jug, and Jim pushed both it and a cup over to him.

"Would you help yourself, Brian?" Jim said. "I don't know how much water you'd like with it."

"Oh, water won't be necessary," said Brian, filling his glass to the brim with wine and swallowing it down. He smiled happily at them both. "Ahh! I was much in need of some wine. Yes."

"So Jim was saying when he drank some a little while ago," mentioned Angie. "But what's this about Giles? Jim mentioned he was here, but that was all. Has something happened to him?"

"Nothing *to* him," Brian said, "though he hurt an arm in falling off his horse during a small altercation with some outlaws on the way here. No, he's the best of lads, you know, but he will keep talking."

"Talking?" Jim asked. "What about? There's no harm in just talking."

He said the last words with a touch of relief. He was aware of Giles's hair-trigger temper and his penchant for challenging anyone at all upon the slightest cause—the more important or more dangerous the opponent, the better.

"No, no," said Brian, as if reading Jim's mind. "He's on good terms with everyone. They all like him—however—he's the best of lads, as I say; but he will talk!"

"If what he says offends nobody," said Jim, "his talking can hardly do any harm."

"Hah!" said Brian.

Angie got up and went into the other room. Brian stared after her, puzzledly.

"Did I—" he was beginning; but just then the curtain was whisked aside and Angie came back and sat down, smiling kindly at Brian.

"Go on," she said.

"Well—as I was saying," said Brian, "or rather, James was saying that he could offend no one by talking. But offense is not the matter. The matter is that they're entirely too happy to hear what he has to tell them. He's been talking to them about us, about our adventures in France, with that magician and so forth. And they keep urging him to tell more."

"I still don't see how this can cause any kind of problem," said Jim. "But I got the idea that he was causing some kind of problem from the way you first talked when you came in."

"He is causing a problem, James," said Brian. "Though it's not all his fault. To be truthful, James, you—and even you, my Lady Angela—oh, I know you have good reason for it; but the rest of the guests have hardly seen you, except for a short while seated at the high table, where there is no chance to speak and become acquainted with you. But you do realize that they all came here, looking forward to meeting the Dragon Knight; and his Lady, who was carried off by dragons? The ladies particularly want to talk to you about what it was like being carried off by dragons, Angela. The gentlemen, of course, want to hear from you, James, about our battle at the Loathly Tower and the various things that chanced to hap in France and on our way there and back again. They had hoped to hear this from you before now. But—"

"Well, that's true," said Jim. "I'm sorry. It's just that there've been so many other things. Still—"

"Still me no stills!" said Brian sternly. "It has caused something of a problem. Forgive me for saying this to you, but it does seem to more than a few of them as if you might be deliberately holding yourself apart from them—almost as if you did not regard them as equals, only such as the Prince, the Earl, the Bishop and Sir John."

Brian's voice dropped to a nearly apologetic note on his last few words, for this was a stiff thing to be saying to old friends who were also members of the gentry.

Jim and Angie looked at each other.

"I can't blame them, really," said Jim slowly. "The ones you just named are about the only ones I've been free to talk to since we got here; and of course Angie's been busy."

"Oh, I can get loose more than I have been," said Angie. "You're quite right, Brian—they're quite right. I can get loose more. We will, won't we, Jim?"

"Absolutely!" said Jim heartily to Brian.

"Excellent!" said Brian. "I knew your answer would be that. Well then, James, you can begin today, by staying around after dinner—Angela needn't stay, of course, beyond a reasonable time. Most of the—er, polite ladies leave fairly shortly after the eating is done. But the gentlemen always sit around for some time—on occasion into the evening. Stay with us today, and all of them will feel they've had a chance to get to know the Dragon Knight. There are none who wish you ill, James, you know that. There are just some who have become a little unsure of their welcome where you are concerned. Which reminds me; you should probably be getting ready for dinner right now."

"Dinner?" said Jim, like someone just woken up. He rubbed a hand over his eyes. "Forgive me, Brian, but what day is this?"

Brian looked at him with a certain amount of puzzlement.

"Why, good Saint Stephen's Day, of course," said Brian. "No more than the first day after Christmas Day, itself."

"Only the day after Christmas?"

"Indeed," said Brian. Then his face lit up. "Oh, I see what you mean, James. There are no special masses for this day, and the Earl has nothing planned for sport following dinner. We may sit at table as long as we like. But—hadn't the two of you best be dressing? I will take my leave, of course. You will come by my room on your way downstairs?"

"Why don't we meet you at Geronde's room, instead," said Angie, "say, in half an hour?"

"By all means," said Brian, and took his leave.

All of them together, a little less than an hour later, entered the dining room. For once, they were early; and on stepping into the Great Hall, it was clear that neither the Earl nor the Bishop were at the high table themselves yet, which meant that the dinner had not officially started, although the seats in the room were three-quarters filled, and most of the people there were doing a certain amount of eating and drinking.

Foreseeing this, Brian had suggested on the way down that they put the time to good use, with Geronde introducing Angie to some of the ladies she knew, and Brian presenting Jim to some of the other gentlemen. In consequence, they did not go directly to the high table, but split off, Geronde and Angie together, Brian and Jim together; and headed toward different parts of the two long tables. Jim found himself being led first by Brian to—of all people—Sir Harimore.

"A pleasure to see you again, Sir James," said Sir Harimore, standing up from the table to face them. "—Sir Brian."

"Sir Harimore," said Brian. "Sir James was with me when we reviewed your splendid exercise with Sir Butram of Othery. I had another good friend with me, also—a Northumbrian knight named Sir Giles—who does not seem to be in the room with us right now. But both Sir James and Sir Giles much applauded your sword-work. I also. Sir James and I wanted to wish you joy of your winning the bout."

"The merest chance," said Sir Harimore. "A lucky stroke, in a moment when Sir Butram's shield was a trifle down. I was concerned for the good knight, when he fell, for all that we were playing with blunted weapons. But he seemed dazed, no more, when he woke, after a few moments; and I hear he had nothing but a headache in consequence. I would not have done him any real harm for a wealth of moneys."

"Nor I," said Brian. "He is a good knight, and has proved it many a time."

"Well, in any case, I thank you and Sir James for your kind wishes," said Sir Harimore, looking keenly at Jim.

"They were certainly earned," said Jim. "I was considerably impressed by your skill."

"Oh, a mere trick or two," said Sir Harimore. He half turned back toward the table. "May I make you gentlemen acquainted with my Lady of Othery, who sits next to me, here? Sir Butram has been let blood and is keeping his bed."

Jim and Brian acknowledged the introductions. The Lady of Othery was considerably younger than the man Jim had seen matching swords with Sir Harimore. She had blonde hair, lively blue eyes and a merry face.

"—Also, on the other side of the table, across from us, are Sir Henry Polinar, Sir Gillian of the Burne, Sir Alfred Neys . . ."

Jim acknowledged the introductions as the gentlemen named also rose and bowed. He summoned up pleasant words to speak to the new acquaintances; and after a little more conversation Brian led him to another part of the table, where more introductions were made to more knights and ladies, none of which Jim knew, but all of whom, it seemed, knew Brian. Risking a glance across at the other table, Jim saw that Geronde and Angie were now part of a cluster of about half a dozen ladies, all of them on their feet and evidently having a happy conversation, since laughter was ringing out from time to time above their group.

All in all Jim met fifteen or twenty of the other guests, the names of which remained all jumbled together in his mind. He was sure that they would not come readily to his tongue when he ran into these people again. But they all seemed to enjoy being introduced to him; and the guilty conscience he had felt earlier when Brian had spoken about those who wanted to see him began to fade somewhat. In any case, matters were put to an end when the Earl came in with Agatha Falon and the Bishop.

This gave Jim an excuse to break loose from the current business of meeting people and take his seat with Angie at the high table.

It was a relief to be away from the business of meeting seemingly innumerable people who obviously wanted to know him and talk with him in his—possibly very legendary—guise, as the Dragon Knight.

"Well, sir," said a voice at his side opposite to where Angie was sitting. He turned; it was the middle-aged lady who had been his dinner partner through all the previous meals together here.

She had clearly seen him being sociable down on the floor of the hall and was not going to let the opportunity go to waste. "It's good to have you with us again, Sir James," she said. "I have been longing for a chance to learn from you about your adventures as a dragon. Tell me, when was the first time you discovered you were a dragon?"

Jim searched hastily for words that would translate the actual happenings into something more understandable and innocuous.

"It just happened one day," he said, "when I discovered my wife was missing."

She smiled encouragingly. "And then, Sir James?"

"Well, this was at my barony of Riveroak," Jim went on, "a long, long way away from England. I guessed that an evil sorcerer had been at work—and of course he had. I went in search of him, and forced him to send me to wherever Angie had been taken.

When I got here I found that she'd been captured by a dragon and I was a dragon, myself."

"Indeed! Fascinating!" said the lady. "And then what?"

Jim resigned himself to a full-fledged telling of the story of the Loathly Tower.

He did not get a chance to talk to Angie for some time. When he did, he found her deep in conversation with the Bishop, who was on her left—Jim was never sure how the seating arrangements were decided, but this was a change. The good Lord of the Church was now between Angie and the Earl. And at this moment he was doing most of the talking and Angie was listening with every sign of deep attention.

While Jim might have ventured to interrupt Angie, he could hardly in politeness interrupt the Bishop. He pretended to be absorbed in his food; and, happily, the lady who had been questioning him had now herself gotten interested in eating—clearly she was no finicky trencher-woman. In fact, once engrossed in her food, she also became interested in her wine, and between the two of them she went from eating to dozing and had no more questions for Jim that day.

The result was that Jim, kept from Angie by the Bishop's loquacity, after being somewhat socially overwhelmed found himself with nothing to do but eat and drink—both dangerous activities for anyone who did not want to stuff himself or get drunk.

It was not until three hours later, after Angie and most of the other ladies had left—a good number of them going off with Angie in a group, as if they intended to attend some small conclave of their own—that the dinner took on an entirely different character indeed. In fact, it became something that so far in the fourteenth century Jim had been lucky enough not to encounter.

He was used to sitting around talking after the medieval noon meal, which was usually taken in early afternoon among the gentry, and could run on into early evening, or at least until lighting in the way of candles or torches was necessary. But in all his earlier experiences, these sessions had either been with small groups, where decorum was enforced by someone like the iron-handed Herrac de Mer, the father of Giles; or they had been dinners with close friends, who naturally kept their manners more or less with them, and the talk remained at least sensible until the gathering broke up.

But these dinners during the Christmastide gathering at the Earl's, as he had heard before, were of another kind.

Jim was not entirely innocent. He knew that such situations were likely to develop in extended parties where there was drinking going on and those involved were nearly all male—and not necessarily all on the best of terms with each other. In fact, he had encountered somewhat similar situations in his own twentieth century in certain rather rough-hewn bars, or at teen-age parties where there was a large availability of alcohol and the participants had energy to burn. Such gatherings were almost bound to be drunken, noisy and, on occasion, combative. He had been prepared for some of the after-dinner sessions at this annual gathering at the Earl's to be along these lines.

But he had vastly underestimated these people.

Without thinking too much about it, he had somehow expected that the iron pattern of manners among the gentry would keep them under control at all times, even when away from home and enjoying themselves. It turned out he was wrong about that—though this was not visible until the eating part of the dinner had not so much ended as eventually trickled away; with morsels of food still being offered at tables, but completely replete diners looking at them with popping eyes and a complete inability to swallow another mouthful.

However, if the guests could not swallow any more food, they certainly could continue to swallow wine; and the water jugs that stood on each table, handy to dilute the wine in their cups, were ignored more and more often.

Also, Jim had expected the few women who stayed to act as something of a reminder of the necessity for manners on the part of the gentlemen. He had forgotten that the ladies of this time were quite as outspoken and free of action as the men.

What actually developed was a drunken, bawdy uproar.

The one redeeming feature of the uproar was the fact that it was surprisingly melodious. When the party reached the stage where people felt like singing, these people sang remarkably well. Jim had never gotten over being surprised at this. The characteristic held good right down to the merest plowman.

He had told himself many times that it should not be surprising, but he was always surprised. Singing was one of the few things that didn't cost money, and consequently everybody got lots of practice singing—to the point where almost any casual gathering could harmonize like a veteran barbershop quartet.

The only problem with the singing here was that several different songs were going on in different areas, with different groups of singers, at the same time, inevitably clashing with each other.

Relief came from an unexpected source.

"—Silence!" The Earl was roaring, pounding on the table in front of him. "Silence, damn it! I said—SILENCE!"

He kept shouting and the noise gradually diminished as the message went down the hall. The laughter and talking stilled, the singing groups dwindled off into discordances, and eventually there was not a whisper in the room.

"That's better!" shouted the Earl. He had clearly not been mixing too much water with his own wine. "Let's have some order here. One song at a time and all can sing together with the singer after the first verse. I'll name the singers. Sir Harimore!"

As the voices in the hall had quieted, so too, the people who had been making the noise had been regaining their seats at the table. Now they were all seated. Sir Harimore stood up and began to sing, completely unself-consciously, in a bright, true tenor.

> *Deo gracias anglia,*
> *Redde pro victoria.*

> *Oure kyng went forth to Normandy—*

—Jim recognized the song at its first words. It was the Agincourt Carol that he knew from his medieval studies. His magical (or otherwise) translator was giving it to his ears in modern English, rather than in whatever dialect of fourteenth century English Sir Harimore was singing it in. Mentally, Jim translated it into what he remembered of the Chaucerian London English of his studies—helped out with twentieth-century English when his memory failed him.

> Oure kyng went forth to Normandy
> Wyth grace and myght of chivalry;
> Ther God for him wroghte merveilously,
> And so Englond may calle and crie:
>   *"Deo gracias!"*

—Everybody else evidently knew the song too. It was about King Henry V's victory over the French at the battle of Agincourt in 1415—Jim checked himself suddenly.

He was, he had long ago decided, in the fourteenth century of English history on this particular alternate world. Theoretically the battle of Agincourt hadn't been fought at the time they were now singing about it.

But, on the other hand, he had already uncovered a number of instances in which the history of this world did not agree exactly with the history of his own twentieth-century world. At any rate, those in the room not only all seemed to know it, but to be having an excellent time singing it.

All their voices were joined together now on the succeeding verse, telling how King Henry had besieged Harfleur town. They blended marvelously, the few women's voices among them soaring above and giving a carol of victory a nearly angelic sound. Jim could not resist singing along with the rest of them, although he kept the volume of his voice low, so that its lack of quality should not disturb the ears of the rest of them around him. They wound their way through it to the final verse in which everybody joined with extra hardy goodwill.

> Now gracious God let save oure kyng,
> His peple, and alle his wel-wyllyng,
> Give him good lyf and good endyng,
> That we with mirth may safely synge:
>   "*Deo gracias!*"

A silence fell on the hall; and Jim sat back in his backed and padded chair with pleasure. All of them ringing truly together on a song that he recognized from his own studies, but of which he had never known the melody—it had touched his emotions.

But the Earl was already calling on someone else for another song. A rather heavy, middle-aged knight stood up and sang, with a resounding baritone, a song that was familiar even from Jim's twentieth century, where it had become a folk song in modern English.

> I have a yong suster
>   Far biyonde the sea;
> Many strange things
>   That she ther sente to me.

Jim's head was already ringing with the modern version of the succeeding lines.

> She sent me a cherry without a stone
> > she sent me a chicken without a bone . . .

The whole room was singing again. Obviously they knew this too, as they probably knew most of the songs that would be sung here. Jim sang along, sometimes in modern English, sometimes along with the Chaucerian English that he heard all around him.

But now the song was coming to its end. The Earl was standing up and looking around the room again for his next victim. His eyes ranged up and down the long tables, came back to the high table and stopped on Jim.

"Sir Dragon!" he shouted.

Jim's stomach suddenly felt hollow. He got to his feet. He had no idea what kind of song he could sing to these people that would be both understandable, and not offensive to something in their life, manners or religion. Obviously, a Christmas carol was in order; but there was hardly one he could think of that seemed to fit. He had an uneasy feeling that he, known as a magician, should be very careful how he was speaking of not only Christmas but the major religious figures involved with it. Then inspiration struck.

He opened his mouth, with a desperate wish that they would excuse the fact that his voice had never been anything but a sort of kitchen baritone, and began to sing.

> Good King Wenceslas looked out
> On the feast of Stephen
> Where the snow lay round about
> Deep and crisp and even.
>
> Brightly shone the moon that night
> Though the frost was cruel
> When the poor man came in sight
> Gathering winter fuel.
>
> "Hither page, and stand by me
> If thou knowest telling.
> Yonder peasant, who is he?
> Where and what his dwelling?"
>
> "Sire he lives a goodly league hence,
> Underneath the mountain.

Right against the forest fence
By Saint Agnes's fountain."

"Bring me flesh and bring me wine
Bring me pine logs hither,
Thou and I shall see him dine,
When we bear them thither."

Page and monarch forth they went,
Forth they went together.
Through the cruel winds' wild lament
And the winter weather.

"Sire, the night grows colder now,
And the wind blows stronger,
Fails my heart I know not how
I can go no further."

"Mark my footsteps my good page.
Tread thou in them boldly.
Thou shall find the winter wind
Freeze thy blood less coldly."

In his Master's steps he trod
Where the snow lay dinted.
Heat was in the very sod
That the saint had printed.

"Wherefore, Christian men make sure,
Wealth or rank possessing,
Ye, who now shall bless the poor
Shall yourselves find blessing!"

Jim came to the end of his song. Nobody had joined in at
all, all the way through; and it seemed to him that a particularly deadly silence held the whole hall. The faces of all those
there were staring at him; and he could not be sure whether it was in anger, shock or amazement. Self-consciously, he
sat down.

The silence persisted uncomfortably. Then suddenly it was
broken by a single powerful voice that could have drowned out
the Earl's any day, from behind Jim.

"*Deo gratias*, indeed!" thundered the full voice of the Bishop, who evidently had just rejoined them. Jim turned instinctively and was instantly engulfed in the powerful arms of the Bishop himself, and kissed resoundingly on both cheeks. Then the Bishop all but flung him aside, turning to the room.

"Thank God indeed, ye men and women of substance and rank!" cried the Bishop. "That a knight who is also a magician puts you all to shame, by singing so beautifully of God's charity on this, one of the most holiest days of the year! What, have you no response to it? No acknowledgment of your own failure in charities?"

The dam of silence broke in the room. With an intuitive flash, Jim realized that they had been silent out there, not so much because the song displeased them, or they did not understand it, but because they were unsure of how they should react to a magician who sang what was very obviously a carol.

There was hammering upon tables. Voices shouted. "Again, Sir Dragon! Sing it once more!"

Hardly believing the happy way things had turned out, Jim opened his mouth and sang. This time, to his surprise—though it should not have been—other voices joined in, until the whole room was singing with him; seemingly, everyone there had remembered his every word. It was something almost incomprehensible from a twentieth-century viewpoint; but these people had the necessarily retentive memory of those who for the most part could not do more than sign their name and must often carry verbal messages correctly word for word; plus the ear for music that he had already been made fully aware of.

Jim sat down again glowing with happiness and success.

CHAPTER 23

Jim came back to consciousness with the vague feeling that he had for some reason been trampled by a herd of elephants. He swam upward from the murky darkness of his slumber—not because he wanted to but because he couldn't help it—gradually remembering the last things that had happened to him.

He remembered singing "Good King Wenceslas," the Bishop praising it to the other assembled guests, and his singing it again to general applause and agreement. But that had been only the beginning of the evening, not the end. Now that they had him, the guests were not about to let him go. They wanted him to sing some more. They wanted him to sing another song they'd never heard before. Another, different song.

Jim had insisted that some other people had to take their turn for a while, but eventually they came back to him with insistence. But during that time he had had a chance to do some hard thinking. He stood up and sang to them the ballad of the Martins and McCoys, with appropriate changes to make the Martins and McCoys into two families of fourteenth-century knights. Instead of:

> Oh, the Martins and the Coy's
> They were reckless mountain boys
> They could shoot each other quicker
> Than a squirrel's eye could flicker . . .

they got:

> Oh, the Martins and McBytes
> They were gallant fighting knights
> They could slay each other quicker
> Than an arrow shaft could flicker . . .

The words altered from the original lyrics of the ballad varied from awkward to nonsensical; and sometimes to mere noise, when Jim had to make them fit the same rhythm and line length as the original ballad. But if anything, this song went off with more success than "Good King Wenceslas" had.

After that his memory of the evening became more and more patchy. He was aware of being there for quite some time, and singing a number of songs more or less altered to fit the time and place in which he was now living. They were all very much liked by his audience. He gave them "The Face On The Barroom Floor," as a romantic ballad that started out with a knight on a sorcerer's floor—manacled there and about to be tortured to death—who somehow broke his bonds and managed to rescue the princess in the tower after all. Nonetheless he ended up losing the princess—which gave it a sad ending, over which he had worried somewhat before singing it.

He should not have. He discovered that these people liked tragedy almost as much as they liked blood. And their appetite for blood was remarkable.

He sang them "Casey At The Bat" to a tune pulled at random from his memory, transforming it into the story of a knight who is a champion on one side in a melee, and who is the last one left alive, but died immediately of his mortal wound when there was no one else to fight.

After that, he had a vague notion, he had sung some more—and that was where memory ceased. Somehow he had gotten to where he was now. As he rose from the murky darkness of his slumber he came into an awareness of a splitting headache and a feeling that he had become something that had crawled out of the woodwork to die; and slowly he began to realize that he was in the outer of the two rooms that he shared with Angie, the servants and Robert.

He was lying on his own mattress on the floor and there was a piece of paper beside him with something written on it in what looked, to his bleary gaze, like Angie's handwriting; but he was not up to reading it right at the present moment. He crawled to his feet, staggered to the table, found the water jug and drank it almost dry; then collapsed into one of the chairs.

He wished most desperately that he could go back to sleep; but he could not. He felt too uncomfortable for sleep now.

It was bitterly ironic, he found himself thinking on a note of self-pity. He normally did not get hangovers. But on the other hand, normally he did not let himself slip into the depths of drunkenness he must have hit somewhere along the line last night—and, from the feel of it, simply kept going on down.

He remembered how once before he had had a hangover after an incautious evening and gone outside to find Sir Brian and John Chandos examining Gorp, his so-called war horse.

Both Brian and Chandos had been drinking; and with the cheerful malice of their kind, they had insisted he immediately swallow a large, full cup of wine with them. He had just managed to get it down; but he remembered now that, once down, it had helped. He looked at the wine jug presently on the table before him, and shuddered.

No, life was not worth it. He would become a hermit and live on water and dry bread. He needed help.

He looked toward the leathern curtain that covered the entrance to the other, adjoining room.

"Angie!" he croaked.

There was no answer from the other room and Angie did not appear. He called again, but still there was no answer. Painfully, he bent down and reached for the piece of paper that had been lying by his mattress, pulled it up, rubbed his eyes and with effort read it.

Jim—

If you're going to stay up like this on other nights, would you see if Brian will put you up for the night.

None of us got a wink of sleep last night after you came back—except Robert. We'd just manage to drop off, and you'd start snoring again and wake us up. I've never heard you snore like that before in my life. Robert, the little darling, somehow slept right through with no trouble at all. But the rest of us are all worn out and Geronde has been good enough to let us catch up on our sleep in her room; since she's going to be out of it all day long.

*If you want anything, don't forget you can send the sentry
at the door for just about anything you need. I'll be back up
to the room to dress for dinner about an hour before noon.
I'll see you then if you're free.*

I'm sorry about this, Jim, but you do snore. *If you had to
lie and listen to yourself all night, you wouldn't be able to
put up with it either.*

> *Love,*
> *Angie*

Jim let the paper drop from his fingers. There was a scratching
at the door. He closed his eyes against the noise.

"What is it?" he called, sending a stab of pain through his
temples.

The door opened a crack and the man-at-arms on duty outside
stuck his face in.

"Sir Giles is here, m'Lord," he said. "He's been here several
times, but he didn't want to disturb you. Can he come in now?"

"Who? Giles?—Yes. Yes," said Jim, every word an effort and
accompanied by an extra stab of headache. "Let him in."

The door opened and Giles came in, carrying a large pewter
flagon, with a green cloth tied over its top. He walked softly with
this to the table and set it down carefully there.

"Sit," said Jim, remembering his manners.

Giles sat. He himself, except for the arm that was still in the
sling, was looking very well—but concerned.

"We were all up rather late last eve," he said, in a carefully low
tone of voice, looking interestedly at one of the blank walls of the
room and avoiding Jim's eye.

Jim was caught in a dilemma. Would it hurt more to nod his
head or just say yes?

"Yes," he said. He had been wrong, of course. To talk had
evidently been the worst choice.

"All are speaking today about how finely you sang last night,"
Giles said, looking earnestly back at Jim, "and what an honor
it was to speak with you. Many were concerned that you had
over-tired yourself, when you—er—could not finish a song and
needed some assistance in leaving the hall. The Lady Angela
has been explaining to us this morning that the evening we
had came on top of a very hard morning of necessary magic
duties, that normally you would have rested from for at least
twenty-four hours. All understand that you must rest today; and

all are concerned that you soon recover your strength."

"Oh," said Jim bravely, ignoring his headache. A knight, of course, could not admit to any weakness; and theoretically would never become drunk enough to be helped out of a room. Only theoretically, of course, for it happened almost daily. A sort of *The Emperor's New Clothes* situation. "That's very good of them. I should be all right in another twenty-four hours."

"I'm overjoyed to hear it!" said Sir Giles, as earnestly as if he really believed that Jim had been nothing more than overtired the night before. He looked away at the wall again, however, before returning his gaze to Jim. "By the way, I thought I might bring you a draught that in our family has been known as a remarkable cure for fatigue such as yours."

He gestured at the flagon with the green cloth tied over it.

"You merely drink this down without stopping—you must not stop, it would be mortal otherwise—it will greatly help an over-tiredness such as yours."

He untied the thong holding down the green cloth over the top of the flagon, and pushed it with the cloth still on it toward Jim.

Jim eyed it with suspicion. It was undoubtedly one of the noxious brews that went by the name of medicine in this particular age. On the other hand, it might just possibly turn out to be one of those types of folk medicines that actually helped. Almost anything would be welcome. Also, he suddenly remembered, he was on the horns of a dilemma.

As a knight, he could not admit to having been drunk; therefore he could not possibly admit to having a hangover. Officially, he could only be "over-tired," as Giles was delicately insisting. Therefore, as a knight he could not in politeness refuse the restorative medicine that his close friend Giles had just brought him.

Jim stared at the flagon for another minute. There was really no choice at all. He held his nose with one hand, whipped off the green cover with his other, grasped the flagon and poured what was in it down his throat, swallowing desperately until it was all gone.

"There," said Giles after a long moment during which Jim had sat absolutely without movement. "Do you not feel better now, James?"

"Hhrrrllp!" wheezed Jim, managing to get some air into his lungs. "Wasser!"

Giles reached for the water bottle on the table, took the cork out of it and peered into its interior.

"Here is some small amount—" he was beginning, doubtfully, when Jim threw proper manners to the wind, snatched the vessel out of his hands and drained everything that was in it. He shoved the empty jug back into Giles's hands and pointed at the door with his free hand.

"More!" he gasped.

Giles stared at him for a moment, then got up, carrying the water bottle, and went to open the door.

"Get this filled immediately, sirrah!" he said to the man-at-arms on duty.

"But, Sir Giles," protested the guard, "I'm not permitted to leave—"

"Next room—" husked Jim as loud as he could, from the room behind Giles, pointing desperately to the leathern curtain.

"Look in the next room, numbskull!" said Sir Giles to the sentry.

"Yes, Sir Giles."

The sentry took the jug, ran with it past Jim, through the leathern curtain—and there was a moment of silence, followed by the provokingly slow sound of water being carefully poured from one water jug into another. It ended, eventually, on a gurgle that implied the first jug was empty; and the sentry came triumphantly back with the refilled water jug Giles had handed him. He set it on the table before Jim. Jim glared at him. He went out and closed the door behind him.

Jim snatched up the jug, filled the closest empty cup, drank it empty, filled it again, drank that off and finally found the extraordinary fire that had been ravaging all the areas of his interior beginning to gutter and go out. He put the glass down and looked at Giles, who had come back to sit down again in his chair and peer concernedly at him.

"Thank you," said Jim, with raw vocal cords.

"A nothing," said Giles, waving one hand airily and sitting back in his chair with relief.

Jim was getting himself back under control. In the process he was discovering that most of the ill effects of his hangover were gone, including the headache. The cause of this, he told himself, was probably simple shock, rather than any anesthetic qualities of the liquid dynamite he had swallowed. Because what Giles had given him had been the rawest of possible raw distilled liquors he had ever run into in his life.

In fact, nothing in his experience approached it. It must have had a proof of about a hundred and eighty. His mouth, tongue and throat still had that "white" feeling he remembered getting on occasions when he had seared those parts with some near-boiling soup or coffee. It was the last sort of cure that Jim had expected someone like Giles to produce.

"Where did you get this?" he croaked, wondering as he asked if this was the liquid of which the wet nurse had drunk so deeply. It couldn't have been. That must have been diluted to a certain extent. "Is it some of what they're calling French brandy?"

"Indeed!" beamed Giles. "The Earl had some and was so good as to give me some when I told him it was for the Dragon Knight."

"Ahh," said Jim, pleased at having his guess justified. Then an ugly thought struck him. He pushed it away from him—surely not even Agatha Falon would be reckless enough to try to poison a magician; who might not only be aware that what was being offered him was poison before he ever tasted it, but could retaliate with all sorts of magical violences. This must be the real, uncut stuff; and its source be the Earl, himself, rather than something Agatha Falon had brought down from London and the court—unless she had brought it down and had been using it to get the Earl under her control.

Giles was speaking again, but Jim did not catch what he was saying, because just at that moment a long quavering howl was heard. It was off in the forest, and its sound reduced by distance and the shutters, which were still shut on the room that Jim and Giles were in; but it was unmistakable. Aargh was calling for Jim again.

Jim's mind scrambled for some excuse that would let him part from Sir Giles without any waste of time. It was still scrambling when Carolinus walked in the door. The guard had not attempted to stop him, which was remarkably sensible, Jim thought.

"Never mind, never mind all this!" said Carolinus testily. He waved a hand in the general direction of Giles, looking irritated. "Your friend can't hear us now. But we need you right away. The meeting between the Earl and the troll will have to be this afternoon. In fact, it has to be now."

Jim darted a glance at Giles, who was sitting, apparently frozen, with his mouth open and a friendly, inquiring look on his face. Before Jim could speak the elder magician went on, in a more cheerful tone.

"My, that hypnotism of yours can be quite handy!"

"Why right now?" Jim said, deciding that he could only handle events in serial fashion.

"You just heard Aargh," Carolinus answered. "He was telling us that Mnrogar is on his way up to the meeting-place. The Earl's awaiting us at the castle gate, and we want to get him there before Mnrogar appears. You have to be there too."

"But why all of a sudden this way?" demanded Jim. "Did something happen?"

"Only that the Earl decided that he wanted it right away," said Carolinus. "He suddenly realized he didn't want any of the guests watching except the Bishop, who's been told to watch from the battlements secretly. This is the time when all the other guests will be down in the hall at dinner, expecting the Earl to come in at any moment. The Earl doesn't want the guests to see the troll, which is reasonable. In fact, you should have thought of it beforehand."

"I should?" said Jim.

"Of course!" said Carolinus. "That's an apprentice's responsibility—deal with the details! At any rate, you're to come right now."

"But what shall I do about Giles?" said Jim. "I can't just leave him here like this."

"Of course you can," fumed Carolinus. "He won't remember anything except what you last said to him. The talk can't take too long, and we should be back in plenty of time for the Earl and you to get to the dinner and nobody know the difference."

"It's not right just to leave Giles this way," said Jim stubbornly.

"All right, then!" said Carolinus angrily. "I'll wake him up and you tell him to go away. Then we'll go." The magician turned to Giles and spoke, too softly for Jim to hear.

Movement came back into Giles. He blinked at Jim.

"It's the strangest thing, James," he said. "I could have sworn I was about to say something to you; but it has escaped my memory completely."

"I'm not surprised, Giles," said Jim hastily. "What happened to you is just something that happens when a magical message is delivered to somebody else in the room. I've just gotten one. I must go immediately."

"Go?" Giles stared at him. Then his face saddened. "I was hoping we might have a chance to talk, James."

"I'll look you up the moment I'm free; and we'll have all the time we need to talk, Giles. I—I give you my word," said Jim.

"Well, well." Giles got slowly to his feet, trying to smile. "Duty is duty, of course. But I'll see you soon, James?"

"Yes," said Jim, also getting up. "You have my word on it."

"Oh, I trust your word, of course," said Giles.

"I didn't mean that, either," said Jim. "Forgive me, I'm a little hasty because of the urgency of the message I just got."

"Oh. I see," said Giles quickly. "Forgive me—I won't hold you a moment longer. I'll look forward to seeing you soon, James."

He was already in movement as he spoke. He opened the door and went out and the door closed behind him.

Jim looked balefully at Carolinus. Carolinus looked mildly and inquiringly back at Jim. Jim changed his mind about saying to the elderly magician what had been on the tip of his tongue a moment before.

"Well, then, we can go now," he said.

They did.

CHAPTER 24

It was not long before Jim found himself standing in snow in the woods, because Carolinus had magically transported him to the meeting spot, once they gotten outside the castle. He was standing next to a table that consisted of a flat wooden top laid on two trestles—exactly like those in the dining room, except that it lacked the linen tablecloth that was to be found right down into the households of well-to-do tenant farmers. The table, with its picnic connotations, seemed sadly out of place here, three-quarters surrounded by wild woods.

The removable top was of seasoned wood and at least three inches thick, four wide planks joined together—probably by pegs in the edge of one plank, fitted into holes into the edge of the plank next to it—and of a uniform gray color that testified to the fact they had been in use for a large number of dinners. There were also the trees he remembered surrounding three sides of the clearing, with the fourth side open, giving a good view of the castle, half a bow shot away, and the bright steel caps of archers and men-at-arms clustered on the curtain wall in plain view there. Aargh was nowhere to be seen. Neither was Carolinus, or Mnrogar, or the Earl.

Jim became suddenly aware that he was freezing. A few years in this period of history had accustomed him to loading himself with clothes in the winter and still having to endure a fair amount of chill. But in this particular instance, he did not have even the usual extra layers of clothing. Caught up in Carolinus's haste and yet, he now suspected, still dull with the aftereffects of his night of revelry, he had not bothered to think about the fact that he would need to be dressed to withstand the weather. Even though it was a bright, sunny day with only a few clouds above the snow which had fallen overnight, the wind was keen and the temperature was a good number of degrees below freezing.

Grumbling to himself, Jim went to work on magic that would get him the clothing he needed. He had never exactly worked out a procedure for doing so, though he had worked up one particular magic command to remove his clothing before he turned into a dragon; and another to replace the clothing magically just before he turned back into a human. He tried variations of this command without luck. Finally he had to settle for simply naming the articles of clothing he wanted and ordering them to appear in front of him.

This they immediately did, in a neat pile in the snow. Still grumbling, he brushed them off and put them on; but necessarily over the clothes he was already wearing. The result was probably going to make him look a little bit odd to the Earl; but he consoled himself with the fact that the Earl would probably have his attention fully occupied by Mnrogar.

Still, none of them were in sight yet. Jim wondered if Aargh was close by among the trees. After a moment's hesitation he tried calling.

"Aargh!"

There was no reply. Either Aargh was not there; or he considered it beneath his dignity to reply to a shout for him, as if he was a common dog. —It suddenly occurred to Jim, that after all his hurry to get warm clothing on himself, it was now going to have to come off him. He was supposed to be in his dragon body for this particular meeting.

Reluctantly he spelled out the magic command in his head to make him a dragon and to carefully store what he was wearing in some odd continuum, from which he would regain it after everything here was over.

He stopped himself just in time from giving the final *execute* command, as he realized that he would be making the transformation in full view of the men-at-arms and anyone else who was up on the wall. He turned around and tramped off to one side of the clearing, until the trees screened him from the view of those in the castle, then gave the *execute* command.

As a dragon he waddled back—waddled, unfortunately, was the only honest word for the way a dragon progressed when traveling on his hind legs—back to the table. It was set up so that it would be crosswise to the view of those watching from the castle wall. There were three stools around it, one on either long side and one at the end. Mnrogar must be seated with his back to the illusory, magic-produced trees that would seem to screen his view of the castle in any case. That would also give those on the high castle wall a good view of the Earl over Mnrogar's head from behind.

The stool at the far end of the table was obviously for Jim, himself.

He stumped around to it now, looked it over and decided to ignore it. He had seen Secoh do the same in the Great Hall at Malencontri, when joining Jim, Angie and other people for a session of talk and drinking and eating. Secoh would choose simply to squat on the floor. He was big enough, even with his stunted mere-dragon body, so that his head came above the board of the high table almost as high as those of the humans who were seated around it.

Jim unobtrusively pushed the stool to one side and squatted in the snow at the head of the table. He was pleased, as usual, to rediscover the fact that as a dragon he was pretty much immune to cold and other physical discomfort. Thickness of hide probably had something to do with it. He was beginning to search his mind for arguments as to why the troll and the Earl should work togeth-er, when Mnrogar appeared out of the trees directly before him, at the far end of the clearing. The troll was still, at this spot, out of the sight of those on the castle wall; but he stopped immediately after emerging from the trees and stared at Jim.

Jim had forgotten how suspicious the other would be, out of his den and under the circumstances.

"Mnrogar!" he called. "It's just me, the Dragon Knight, in my dragon body. On an official meeting like this, I have to be in this body. I'm just sitting, waiting. Also, I never did have anything against trolls. Come and sit down."

Mnrogar hesitated, then slowly came forward, scowling at Jim all the way and looking as if he could either spring at Jim's throat, or turn and bolt for the woods again, at any moment.

Jim said no more and did not move a muscle. He simply sat where he was. After a certain amount of coming forward, hesitating and then coming forward again, Mnrogar reached the one of the two stools that had been deliberately set a little farther down the table from Jim than the one at which the Earl should sit. He sat down there with his back to the castle, leaving the last unoccupied seat for the Earl.

"Where is he?" growled Mnrogar.

"The Earl?" said Jim, as innocently and mildly as he could manage with his dragon voice. "He should be along at any moment—in fact, I see him coming out of the trees to your left, now."

Jim did indeed see the Earl coming. Carolinus was with him; and not only Carolinus—there was another person walking on the other side of the Earl.

Happily, dragon's bodies did not jump when dragons were startled. They weren't designed to do so; and in this particular case there was a good deal of benefit to the fact. The person on the other side of the Earl was Angie.

Both she and Carolinus seemed to have something like halos around them. Jim blinked, but the halos stayed, undeniably in place. Mnrogar turned his head and looked, but seemed to see nothing extraordinary about the three figures that were advancing. His gaze was clearly solely upon the Earl, who was glaring back at him ferociously.

"It's all right now, James," called Carolinus, as soon as they were close. "Angie and I are both invisible to Mnrogar, and for that matter to the Earl and those on the castle wall." He and Angie were not, Jim now realized, leaving any tracks in the snow they traversed.

Carolinus stopped somewhat short of the table. The Earl and Angie came on, the Earl still glaring at Mnrogar. He took his seat at the side of the table and Angie came up alongside Jim and put her hand on his dragon shoulder.

"Angie—" he began.

"Nobody can hear me except you and Carolinus," she interrupted quietly in Jim's ear. "Don't turn your head to look at me when you speak. I saw you and Carolinus as you left the castle, and caught up after he had sent you here. I made him tell me what this was all about, and then told him that I didn't intend to be left out of all this. Go ahead and talk to me if you want. The others won't see your mouth move as long as you're speaking to me."

"You shouldn't have, Angie," said Jim.

"Why not?" demanded Angie. "Neither the Earl nor the troll can see or hear me, so how could I be in any danger? But I might be able to help you with a suggestion or two, Jim. You know I can help that way."

It was true, of course.

"Well, all right," said Jim. "But try not to be helpful unless you're absolutely sure it won't throw me off balance."

"Don't worry," said Angie soothingly. "My, I'd forgotten what a fine-looking dragon you are, when you're being one. The troll must be shivering in his kilt, or whatever he calls it. Why doesn't he freeze to death out here?"

"Probably for the same reason I don't freeze to death as a dragon without any clothes," said Jim. "I can take cold, rain, wind, sleet, probably even hail—it's the heat that gets me when I'm being a dragon. Now, let's not talk. I've got to get on with this meeting before these two start to savage each other."

He returned his attention to Mnrogar and the Earl. Mnrogar was still sitting without moving a muscle and, at least in human terms, no expression on his face. There was a certain amount of built-in threat in the actual bones and flesh of his face; and the pointed teeth that could just be glimpsed between a slight parting of his thin lips. But beyond this he was not giving a sign of any emotion at all. The Earl was another matter.

He did not look at all intimidated by the shockingly inhuman strength revealed in the troll's massive upper body; in the potential of the barely glimpsed teeth and the wickedly curved claws that grew from the ends of his massive fingers as they rested on the table, where human fingernails would ordinarily be. The Earl's white eyebrows were bristling, his slightly protruding eyes were glaring, as he came up to the table and took his seat.

There was obviously nearly a snarl of contempt and fury on his lips, and his chin was jutting pugnaciously. Aside from this, he only looked a little fatter than usual; but Jim suspected with some certainty this was because he was loaded with clothes underneath his armor, to the point where the thongs that tied breastplates to backplates and fastened the other parts of the joined metal about him seemed ready to snap.

He was wearing a bastard sword—otherwise known as a hand-and-a-half sword—half as long again as an ordinary broadsword, in a scabbard on his right side, the side away from Jim as he sat down. Jim had not thought that the Earl was left-handed. In fact, he had been under the impression that the nobleman was right-handed. But there the scabbard and the hilt of the sword within it were, now in plain sight not only of Mnrogar, but of those watching from the castle wall over and around Mnrogar's bulky upper body.

In fact, just at the moment Jim was thinking all this, the Earl stood up again from his stool and drew the sword with his left hand. With the hilt in both hands he jammed its tip down into the table top so that it stood upright, quivering slightly on its blade before him.

"Observe, troll!" he shouted at Mnrogar. "A cross stands between me and you!"

Mnrogar neither blinked an eye nor moved a muscle. He might as well have been deaf. Jim began to feel definitely uneasy.

"Carolinus?" said Jim, carefully not turning his head. "A cross won't do him any good against a Natural, will it?"

"No, no," said the voice of Carolinus behind him, "of course not. Somewhat useful in the case of shades, ghosts, vampires and some classes of demons—but against Naturals? He might as well have stuck a willow wand into a crack in the table, upright between them."

"You don't want to tell him that though, Jim," said the voice of Angie.

"I know that," grumbled Jim. "Don't worry, Angie; and please only talk to me if you think it's really necessary."

There was silence from his right side, although Angie's hand still rested on his shoulder. Jim felt a small spasm of guilt. She had only been trying to help; but he needed to concentrate on the two before him, and that was going to be hard enough, even if Angie spoke to him only at times when she could help.

Meanwhile, Mnrogar had neither moved, nor changed his expression. A human being might have fidgeted, or reacted. Either trolls didn't, or Mnrogar had himself completely under control. Jim decided to take advantage of the moment of silence that followed the Earl's sitting down again on his stool and once more taking up his glaring past the blade of his sword at the troll.

"My Lord Earl," he said, "may I make known to you Mnrogar, the troll who has occupied the underneath of your castle, before even that castle was built; and has kept other trolls away from your territories and those of your ancestors all that time."

The Earl snorted.

"And, Mnrogar," said Jim, "may I make known to you my Lord the Earl of Somerset, the gallant and renowned knight, Sir Hugo Siwardus?"

Mnrogar growled deep in his chest, but otherwise showed no reaction. Jim went on.

"We are met here today," he said, "to determine how best to work together to deal with another troll, who has got into the castle by somehow managing to adopt human appearance. This is something that not even my Master in magic, S. Carolinus, can conceive being done. Perhaps you, Mnrogar, know how a troll would be able to make himself look like a human being?"

"No," said Mnrogar. He was undoubtedly trying to speak as expressionally as he was looking, but such was his voice and his general physical make-up, that the word came out as much like a threat as the Earl's display of his sword.

"Why not?" demanded the Earl. "If one troll can do it, all trolls ought to be able to do it! If all trolls know how to be able to do it, this one—what's your name? Mnrogar? You should know it, too. Or are you lying to us?"

"No," said Mnrogar, again. And once more the word, in what Jim was becoming more and more positive was an attempt by Mnrogar not to be provoked unnecessarily and not to give provocation if he could avoid it, came out with a much more threatening ring to human ears than was comfortable to hear.

"Hah!" said the Earl.

"What is 'hah'?" said Mnrogar harshly.

"It means 'hah'!" snapped the Earl. "It means—I do not believe you, Sir troll!"

"I cannot make myself look like one of you," growled Mnrogar. "If I cannot do it, no troll can do it!"

"Then what makes you say there's a troll among my guests?" the Earl flung at him.

"Because I smell one up there!" retorted Mnrogar.

"And I'm to take your word for that? A troll's word, hah!"

"A human's word," snarled Mnrogar, "hah!"

The Earl's cheeks began to turn purple.

"What do you mean," he demanded dangerously, "hah?"

"I mean what you mean when you say 'hah'," said Mnrogar.

They were now both beginning to lean forward over the table toward each other. *Blessed are the peacemakers*, thought Jim, and hurried to try to calm the waters.

"I think what the Earl was getting at, Mnrogar," he said as gently as was possible with his dragon voice, "is that if you say a troll can't be up there in human guise, then how can it be that you smell one? Because unless the one you smell there is in human guise, everyone in the castle must have recognized him as a troll, on sight."

"How do I know?" said Mnrogar. "Maybe one of your magicians helped him do it."

"The poor fellow doesn't realize what he's saying," said Carolinus's voice in Jim's other ear. "Don't let yourself be offended, Jim."

"I'm not offended," said Jim.

He had forgotten, however, to direct his thoughts and his voice to Carolinus alone; and clearly both the Earl and Mnrogar had heard him. They were both staring at him now, the Earl obviously startled and baffled; Mnrogar very possibly so.

"As I was saying," added Jim hurriedly, "I'm not offended by anything about this; and I strongly suggest that neither you, my Lord Earl, nor you, Mnrogar, be offended either. We'll never get anywhere unless we discuss this calmly and reasonably, all of us searching for an explanation and a means of resolving the situation."

It was, Jim thought, a pretty good point he had made. But the Earl did not seem to have accepted it in the proper spirit; and Mnrogar, to Jim's concern, replied with another deep, wordless growl that this time seemed to leave no doubt about how he was feeling.

He had plainly come here, ready to accept any agreement that would help to get rid of the visiting troll in the castle. But clearly, also, he could be pushed only so far; and the Earl had been doing way too good a job of pushing.

"Forgive me, my Lord Earl," Jim said hastily, "but we did come here to discuss ways and means of getting rid of the intruder troll among the guests. Perhaps we should be talking about those ways and means now."

"Very well," growled the Earl. "What is the plan, then?"

There was, of course, no plan. The plan was what they had come here to decide on. This was, Jim decided, the equivalent of Carolinus saying that apprentices should take care of the details. However, there was only one way Jim could imagine anything could be achieved in this situation, so he plunged ahead.

"The only possible way, it seems—" said Jim, looking at the troll, "—with Mnrogar's agreement, of course—is that he be put in some position where he's able to smell all of the guests, and so pick out the one that smells like a troll."

"Excellent plan," said the Earl. "We'll do that. Then, once we have the creature, it will merely be a matter of making him admit that he's a troll—"

He broke off suddenly, a dismayed look on his face.

"—But what if he turns out to seem to be one of the more important guests? Someone of high rank and repute?" He stared at Jim. "I would not like to—er, put strongly to the question—some gentleman of worth and reputation. It might be—most difficult. Embarrassing. Particularly if he wasn't a troll, after all."

"Let me come face to face with him," snarled Mnrogar. "He will be a troll; and, being a troll, will know what I am come to do with him; therefore he will instantly turn back into a troll, and fight me with teeth and claws, instead of with one of the toy swords or other weapons you humans carry around. If he is a troll, he will fight like a troll."

"Well, then," said Jim quickly. "Since we're agreed on that, the question becomes one of ways and means—details, that is. Naturally, Mnrogar will want to be sure of being safe once he is up among humans; and I have a suggestion. There is a wolf I know that he trusts to a certain extent who I was going to suggest might go with him—"

He turned to Mnrogar.

"I haven't mentioned this to Aargh, and of course he'd have to agree, but if he was with you, with his nose and ears to warn you of any attempt against you while you're upstairs, would you feel safe about coming upstairs to sniff out the other troll?"

Mnrogar growled uncertainly, hesitated, finally spoke.

"I'll come if Aargh will," he said.

"Who is this Aargh?" demanded the Earl suspiciously.

"A trusty wolf and a good friend," said Jim. "Sir John Chandos will vouch for him, if you care to ask Sir John."

The Earl growled uncertainly in his turn.

"Well, then," said Jim cheerfully. "Now that all that's settled, my Lord Earl, do you have a place where Mnrogar can be out of sight, but still able to sniff at every one of the guests over a period of time, without any one ever knowing he is doing so or that he is upstairs at all? Ordinarily, with the help of my Master, Carolinus, we could disguise him, using magic for this trip up among the guests; but there's the good Bishop's blessing on your castle. I don't think he'd be agreeable to any lifting of that blessing to let Mnrogar upstairs."

"Er—no," said the Earl, "I don't believe I'd want to ask him that. No. Our Father in God and our Lord in the Church, you know?"

"Yes," said Jim. "Well, if you have the place to hide Mnrogar, perhaps I can figure out some way of getting him and Aargh upstairs and back down again unseen. So, my Lord, do you have some observation place for him then where he would be out of sight?"

"I don't know," grumbled the Earl, frowning fiercely at the table. "There are certain spots in the castle—places with spy-holes—"

He looked up at Jim.

"Purely in need if an enemy fights their way into part of the castle and we need to spy out the portion he holds, you understand. Also, for the same reason, there are some passages between walls, up and down through the castle . . . very private, of course. Ordinarily, never divulged to anyone outside the family. Never used by anyone outside the family . . . I don't know . . ."

"I'm afraid something like that may be needed, my Lord," said Jim. "The point is, however, could you come up with the means to let Mnrogar sniff at all the guests to find the one who is there in disguise?"

"Yes, damn it, I suppose so!" said the Earl. He glared across the table at Mnrogar. "A damn troll in my damn castle to catch another damn troll—I never thought I'd see the day!"

"I don't like you either, human!" said Mnrogar, on a rising growl.

"Hah!" said the Earl. "What you like means nothing. What I like means everything. Know your place, troll; and be silent until I speak to you. You are here on my land without my permission. Be glad you are still alive!"

"It is my land!" roared Mnrogar, shooting to his feet. The Earl likewise shot to his feet.

"Trolls can't hold land!" he shouted back. "Speak to me no more of it being your land, troll, or you'll die for it!"

"Die? I!" thundered Mnrogar. But the Earl was already reaching for the handle of his sword that was stuck in the table—and unseen by the troll, men-at-arms started to pour out the sally port of the castle and approach them at a run. Jim suddenly realized that from the beginning, the Earl's sword stuck into the table had been a signal to his waiting men; and pulling it out was meant to call them to his aid. He cursed himself for an idiot for not realizing that sooner. But already things were happening faster than he could stop them.

Mnrogar batted the Earl's hand away from the hilt of the sword as if it had been the hand of a child reaching for something forbidden on a table. Instead, his own huge, horny hand engulfed the top end of the sword, hiding hilt and crosspiece alike; and with one furious motion he drove it not merely into the table but through it, clear down to the point where the bottom of the hilt clanged against the top of the table and the point was buried—not only in the snow but in the frozen earth beneath that.

The Earl snatched out his poignard and reached for the end of the buried sword, as Mnrogar let go. But all the Earl's tugging could not move it. It was firmly fixed, too firmly for any ordinary human hand to remove it. He let go, lifted his head, looked toward the castle and shouted.

"Hola! To me! Haste, haste!"

The men-at-arms, swords in hand and running toward them, were already about halfway between the castle and the clearing. Mnrogar, however, did not even bother to look in the direction in which the Earl had shouted. He turned swiftly from the table; and, crouching, so that the hands at the ends of his long arms literally touched the ground, he ran, bounding like a deer, with incredible swiftness off into the trees and disappeared.

Jim found he had got to his own feet in the excitement. He sat down again with a thump.

"Well, my boy," said the voice of Carolinus dryly in his ear, "you failed!"

"Damned coward!" said the Earl, looking off at the woods into which Mnrogar had vanished, as something like forty men-at-arms came swarming to their liege lord's aid. "All bloody damn cowards, these trolls!"

"Never mind," said Angie, in Jim's opposite ear. "We can think of some other way."

Jim hoped so. But right now, he not only did not feel like trying to think of another way of solving the situation; he sincerely did not think he could.

CHAPTER 25

Jim, Angie and the Earl went to dinner. There was no choice in the matter, at least for Jim and Angie, since as Brian had pointed out, they had been absent too often and too long. Of course, they were a little late coming in; but the Earl was a law unto himself as far as that went, and Jim and Angie would have looked far more laggardly if they came in without him.

Jim was out on his feet. True, he had had a full night of slumber, but it had been drunken slumber, and it seemed to him he had been traveling at ninety miles an hour from the moment he woke up; only to end by smashing up against—as Carolinus had not hesitated to point out—a complete failure to reconcile the Earl and Mnrogar. Nonetheless, he did the best he could to seem as if he was enjoying the meal.

It helped that Angie was free to talk to him this time. It was the middle-aged lady who usually sat on his left, who was missing. Her seat had been filled by a thin cleric in a black robe, about fifty years of age, who peered keenly at everyone around him, and then ignored them completely. The result was that Jim was almost as free to talk to Angie as if they were back up in their rooms, the only drawback being that Jim was really not up to talking about anything much at the time.

"I don't think I can keep my eyes open for five minutes longer," he murmured to Angie, after they had been sitting at the table for nearly three hours.

"Try to hang on until the last of the food is over, anyway," murmured Angie. "It won't be long now. They're bringing the Troycreme right at the moment."

"Oooh, good!" squeaked a juvenile voice from the far end of the table, its high tones carrying it through the adult conversation intervening. Jim leaned forward to see the boy-Bishop—that youngster from the Bishop's cathedral who had been brought along in the real Bishop's retinue. It was part of the season that a boy should be dressed up like a miniature Bishop, fed at the high table with the rest of them and servitors bowing to him, treating him in every way like Richard de Bisby himself. Right now Jim saw him happily digging with his spoon into the bowl just set before him. There was nothing wrong with him, Jim thought darkly; he was probably a good kid, but his high-pitched tones seemed to override all other conversation.

Thankfully, tomorrow would be the end of his role-playing. Today was the day of Saint John the Evangelist. Tomorrow was the day of the Holy Innocents—with the children's mass—and after that the little imitation Bishop would go back to being an ordinary boy again. Meanwhile, his voice seemed to pierce Jim's head from ear to ear, for his headache had returned.

Jim sat back, grumpily. One more dish. In fact, at that moment a servitor put a bowl before him. He looked at its contents with distaste. It was pretty enough; a swirl of gold, red and white colors of some kind of thin pudding or thick soup. He picked up his spoon to go through the motions of eating it, and took a small amount on the spoon.

Provokingly, it tasted delicious; and very sweet. The sugar, for some reason, seemed to tickle an appetite that Jim thought he had lost a couple of hours before. The red color was probably from quinces; and the other two were honey and plain heavy white cream, whipped until it had thickened. The trick evidently was to mix the taste of all three together in one spoon-load. He found himself cleaning up the bowl; and the sugar in it seemed to bring him to, momentarily.

However, it did not improve his mood.

"Look at them all down there at the long tables," he growled to Angie, "slavering to have me sit around and drink and sing with them, all night long!"

"Nothing of the kind," whispered Angie soothingly. "I don't even see one of them looking right at you, as a matter of fact.

By the way, were you thinking of going to bed right away when you got up to the rooms?"

"Yes, I was."

"Then why don't you take your mattress down to Brian's room?" she asked. "He won't leave the hall for some time; and he may be more able to bear your snoring than we are."

"I'm not going to snore tonight," said Jim.

"Let's play it safe," said Angie. "Besides, if you move down there, you won't be disturbed by us or Robert. Don't go yet—"

Her last words were prompted by Jim starting to get to his feet.

"Not yet?" growled Jim.

"Drink a little hippocras first," said Angie.

Jim shuddered. He had been avoiding any real drinking from his very well-watered cup of red wine all through the meal. But he made the effort, swallowing some of the hippocras from his maser, a square-looking, pedestal cup that had been placed in front of him.

"Now smile," murmured Angie. "That's right. Now stand up. Kiss me—no, no, Jim! On the cheek, Jim—the *cheek*! Manners! We're in public. Now you can go."

Jim went.

Jim came swimming up slowly from deep, deep sleep with a feeling of marvelous comfort and lack of urgency, but with a slight tickle of something different. This gradually solidified into the memory that he had slept the night in Brian's room, rather than one of the two he occupied with Angie, Robert and the servants.

He was in no hurry to open his eyes. Undoubtedly he had slept well beyond the normal dawn period for wakening. Brian would long since have gotten up and gone out—undoubtedly rising and dressing quietly so as not to disturb him. Good old Brian. As for anything else he ought to do today, it didn't really matter. Maybe he'd just spend the whole day lying where he was and dozing . . .

But evidently his body had other ideas. It seemed it was determined to come all the way to consciousness, whether the rest of him felt like it or not. Reluctantly he opened his eyes; but an explosion of light from a sunbeam directly through an arrow slit across the room made him squeeze them shut again.

Slowly and cautiously he opened them once more. As his vision slowly adjusted, he made out the figure of someone sitting at the table in the room just a few feet from him—and a few seconds later he realized the person in question was Brian, completely dressed, and sitting there with a cup that probably held watered wine—not even his old friend was likely to start drinking straight wine early in the morning, except on special occasions—and looking thoughtfully at him. The rest of the room was a maze of light and dark, his eyes still too dazzled by the sunlight to see what was there, besides Brian.

Of course, there would be nothing else to see but the bed and another chair or two—

"Ah, James," said Brian gently. "Awake, are you?"

Jim was strongly tempted to say "no" but common sense told him he could hardly deny the fact, as long as his eyes were open and his own gaze was on Brian.

"Yes," he said, and was pleased to hear his own voice come out in its own normal tones, instead of the sort of peevish croak he had woken up with yesterday morning.

The light from the arrow slit was still in his eyes. He rolled off the mattress, hitched it up so that the back half of it was upright against the wall of the room, and sat back on it, pulling the attached covers over him again. The room had been cooler than he had stopped to realize it would be. Sitting up, he gazed at Brian.

This was better. A few sunspots still danced before his eyes, seeming more dazzling than they really were because, the only illumination of the room being that one shaft of sunlight through the arrow slit, most of the room was dark by contrast. But the deep shadows hardly mattered in a room as small as this.

Brian, he noticed, was not dressed as if he was just about to go outside for some outdoor activity like hunting or hawking, but merely sitting comfortably in his shirt. It was true the shirt, of bright green knitted wool, was thick enough to have been classified as a sweater in the twentieth century; but for this period it represented just about as light a piece of clothing as a man could wear and still be dressed politely, if he considered himself a gentleman.

"Would you like a cup of that hot drink—what is it?" Brian asked. "Carolinus drinks it, you know. Tea."

"Tea?" echoed Jim.

Then he realized that on the table stood a very large leathern jug with the legend *BOILED WATER* largely printed on it in Angie's handwriting; and his ears told him that singing gently on the fire in the fireplace was their travel kettle.

Coffee was apparently was not to be found in the England of this time under any conditions. But Carolinus had his tea; and somehow Angie had talked him into keeping her supplied with a limited quantity of tea leaves. He had firmly resisted Jim's entreaties for instruction to magically acquire either coffee or tea, and would not explain why. Jim guessed that perhaps for some reason, other magicians frowned on Carolinus drinking of it. But it was only a guess.

At any rate, one of Jim's lingering hungers from the twentieth century was for something hot to drink when he first woke up. Coffee by preference, tea if that wasn't available. Cocoa would do in a pinch—but that again was unheard of, in this particular time and place.

"Why yes, thank you, Brian," he said.

"Well, in that case," said Brian, "perhaps you'd be good enough to make it for yourself. Angie did show me what to do; but I'm not sure about how I . . ."

His voice trailed off.

"Be glad to," said Jim. He got himself to his feet—a little creakily, but not in bad shape otherwise. He stumped over to the kettle, brought it to the table, discovered a cup with a homemade tea bag of tea already in it (the one thing that was available to them in this era was people who could sew) and it had been relatively easy for Angie to have some of their tea leaves made up into small, light, porous bags. These were handy, particularly on a trip like the one here. At home at Malencontri, they made their tea several cups at a time in another small kettle.

At any rate he got his cup of tea, returned to the comfort of his mattress and covers, and sat drinking it, feeling generally that all was right with the world.

As he woke up even more, it began to dawn on him that this morning had been made unusually comfortable for him. Not only had Angie supplied the safely boiled water for mixing with wine, the tea and the cup, she had even tried to show Brian how to make tea; and Brian himself had been ready to give up any other morning activities. Instead, he had sat around here, waiting for Jim to wake, as solicitous as if he was taking care of a wounded comrade.

Ordinarily, Jim would have felt embarrassed on realizing this. But right at the moment, he was entirely too comfortable drinking the tea, warm under his blankets in the pleasantly dim room with its one dazzling shaft of incoming daylight no longer in his eyes.

There was a sort of half-buried feeling in him that, after all, perhaps he more or less deserved this kind of comfort after the way things had been going for him.

"How are you feeling, James?" asked Brian.

"Fine!" said Jim; then was suddenly aware of a deep urge in him to talk about his worries. It occurred to him that if there was one thing he had been needing, it had been a sympathetic ear to talk to—an ear that was not Angie's.

Some of what was bothering him, he had been determined not to tell Angie. Also, he was used to living with his own thoughts and his own concerns, here in the Middle Ages. But even if Brian did not understand—and it was a hundred to one he would not—it would be a great relief just to tell him about it.

"I mean 'no,' " he said.

Brian's face took on an expression of extreme concern.

"Oh? You are not ill or hurt, James? Surely Angela would have told me. What troubles you?"

"A few hundred—that is, a number of things," said Jim, correcting himself with the realization that Brian would take the idea of his facing several hundred troubles quite literally. "I never knew so many things could go wrong at the same time."

"Indeed!" said Brian with gratifying concern. "Who is the lady?"

"Lady? Lady?" Jim found himself sounding like a parrot in his own ears. He stared at Brian. "What's a lady got to do with all this?"

"Oh!" said Brian. "Ah . . . forgive me, James. I just thought—this being the Earl's party, and you being gone so much of the time and not even Angela knowing always why or where—well, clearly I was mistaken. I . . ."

He was obviously highly embarrassed.

"Good Lord, no!" said Jim. He found himself laughing. "Aside from everything else, I wouldn't have had time to get tangled up with any other—but in any case, it'll never happen as long as I have Angela. Cheer up, Brian. I'm the one who ought to apologize. I've given you the wrong impression. No, these are perfectly polite troubles; but bad enough in spite of that!"

"Oh?" said Brian, recovering. "Well, however I must still crave pardon for suggesting—"

"No, you needn't," said Jim. "My mistake, as I say. Forget that for now. The other troubles are bad enough."

"Well, of course. That troll, I would venture for one thing," said Brian.

"Yes," said Jim, his earlier comfortable feeling clouding over. "I don't understand this. Carolinus acts as if it's one of the most important matters in the world that the Earl and the troll come to some kind of agreement, so the castle stops being shaken and damaged—"

"Damaged?" said Brian.

"Oh—sorry, Brian," said Jim, suddenly remembering. "That's something I shouldn't talk about. At any rate, as I was saying, Carolinus seems to think it's that important; but he simply leaves it all to me with a wave of his hand. And it's not that simple a matter. After all, the troll and the Earl's family have been at swords-points for eighteen hundred years, or so."

"You are Carolinus's apprentice, James," said Brian reasonably. "He's teaching you by letting you find your own way to do it. Doubtless, the Mage could, with a twitch of his finger, manage the affair. But he wants you to learn by doing. It is always so with Masters and apprentices."

"Well, he didn't twitch his finger at the Loathly Tower," said Jim. "He was there with his staff to hold back the Dark Powers, themselves. But we were the ones who had to do the fighting. You and I, Dafydd, Smrgol and Secoh—you haven't heard from Dafydd, recently, come to think of it?"

Dafydd ap Hywel was their archer friend, who had since married Danielle, daughter of Giles o'the Wold; and who already had either a son and a daughter or two sons. Jim could never remember exactly which.

"Not since we both saw him last," said Brian. "Last summer, if you recall."

"We'll miss him and Danielle—Angie and I," said Jim sadly. "But even more we'll miss you and Geronde, Aargh, and all our friends."

"Miss?" said Brian suddenly. "How? Miss? Were you and Angela going some place?"

"Not willingly," said Jim grimly. "And probably, possibly, not at all. We just might have to go back where we came from; or I might be stripped of my magician's ability. In which case the Dark Powers might be successful in destroying Angie and me. But it's a long, involved story. I shouldn't bother you with it."

"Certainly you must!" said Brian. "What? I am your comrade-in-arms! Your Companion in more than one essay—and I should not know when to come to your aid, if you need me? By all means you must tell me. It is your duty, James!"

Jim had forgotten how seriously Brian and many of the people of this period took such things as friendships and enmities. To Brian, not letting him know when he was in trouble and Brian could help was the next thing to deliberately slighting him. He, himself, was as duty-bound to tell Brian when he needed Brian's aid; as he also would be to go to Brian's, if Brian needed him.

"Forgive me," he said. "I didn't think. It's just that so much of this is secret. The matter about the magic and leaving is something I can't really in honor tell you, even now. Also, I shouldn't be so hard on Carolinus. I've got an idea he's been working as hard for me as possible. But as I say, we might be forced to leave; or I might lose my ability to work magic."

"Could that happen?" Brian stared at him.

Jim nodded.

"Evidently," he said, "neither one is something you could help me with, or that I can do much about myself, according to Carolinus. Also, as it happens, since we found young Robert Falon, Angie very much doesn't want to leave. She wants to stay here and bring up the boy to the point where he can fend for himself, to some extent anyway. Of course, that's assuming the King gives me Robert's wardship. You see, Agatha Falon also wants it; and she's considerably closer to the King personally than I am. I understand she'd inherit, if anything happened to Robert."

"The Lady Agatha Falon?" said Brian. "The one who has been paying all attention to the Earl?"

"Yes," said Jim. "As I think I told you before, it's really the King, back in London, she's supposed to have her eye on. Prince Edward is worried she might succeed, with the King ennobling her to the point where he could take her as a wife—in which case Edward would be doubly threatened, both with the possibility of a second heir, and by having Agatha as a powerful enemy, in her own right. Apparently they don't like each other; and both of them know it. Anyway, Agatha tried to kill Robert, and came very close to killing Angie . . ."

He went on to tell Brian all about it.

"But surely," said Brian, when he had finished, "Sir John Chandos told the Earl about this for you—or Carolinus did? If so, what did the Earl say?"

"I'm afraid Angie and I didn't tell anyone," said Jim. "We really haven't had the chance so far, anyway, because of the situation with the Earl and the troll. The time hasn't been right to bring up anything like that when either of us talked to the Earl—a matter of bothering the Earl with one thing at a time."

"That troll is still troubling the Earl?" said Brian. "I had guessed you or Carolinus had put a stop to that. Then, the matter is what? Or perhaps you should not tell me that, either?"

"I think I can," said Jim. "After all, you were the one who went with me in the first place to talk to Mnrogar below the castle."

He told Brian everything concerning the Earl and the troll and the castle, with the exception of exactly what damage the troll was doing to the castle.

When he was done, Brian shook his head.

"Indeed, James," he said. "It passes understanding. Three such coils—this magic problem you cannot tell me of, and the enmity of someone such as this Lady Falon seems to be, as well as the problem with the troll and the Earl."

"Oh," said Jim, "did I tell you about the army of trolls just outside the territory of this troll, waiting for something?"

"You did," said Sir Brian. "I had forgotten that. But surely they pose no problem to us, since they are only concerned with one of their number replacing the castle troll?"

"That's the obvious reason for their being there," said Jim. "But the thing that concerns Carolinus and me is the fact that trolls ordinarily never gather like that without fighting to the death among themselves. This is something that's against troll nature—and that in itself is frightening. If they'll act differently than they ever did before in that way, might they not act different in other ways too?"

"By the Holy Innocents, whose day this is!" said Brian. "But I had not thought of that!"

"Well, maybe the reason's something we'll find out about later on. It might mean they could give trouble in other ways," said Jim.

"But such a storm of evil haps!" said Brian. "I have never heard the like. It angers me that in none of this can I be of any use to you!"

He brought his fist down on the table, and then absent-mindedly caught his wine cup in mid-air before it completed its bounce to the floor. Jim felt a warmth at Brian's obvious emotion.

"I don't expect you to do anything, Brian," he said. "That's one reason I didn't tell you about these things before. Probably, I shouldn't have disturbed you, even now."

"No, no," said Brian. "I wish to hear of such things from you, James, always. I had a feeling that something was toward. Ah, and I had looked forward to your being at this party as such a happy time! I would have the chance to show you many things about the holding of the lance in tourney, and the use of other knightly weapons—you and Giles both, but particularly you, James; and we haven't had a moment for it. Nor does it seem we shall have."

The warmth in Jim was replaced by a guilty feeling.

"I know, Brian," he said—the guilt he suddenly felt was not so much from not having time for what Brian had just mentioned, but for being able to dodge those particular activities. He had no eagerness to couch a lance in the lists; or to practice, even with blunted weapons, with other knights. For that matter, Brian himself had showed no gentleness at all to him in the training sessions he had given Jim up till now. Brian's way was to hit just as hard in practice as he would have in actual combat; it being up to Jim to get his own blunted weapon or shield up in time to block the blow.

The sense of guilt faded; but, still, Brian's unhappiness had triggered off in Jim a melancholy where the comfortableness and warmth had been earlier.

"Don't worry about any of it, Brian," he said. "I'll come up with something—or Carolinus will come up with something; or things will work out one way or another. The one thing that really bothers me is the result if I should lose my magic or if Angie and I have to leave."

He sighed.

"But you know, Brian," he said, "maybe our leaving'd be for the best after all. You know, even after these several years, and with the help of you and Geronde, Giles, Dafydd, Aargh—and even Secoh and others—I really haven't reached a point where I fit in here. I'm really nothing much of a magician, as Carolinus often points out; and you, yourself, know I'm nowhere near being competent with any kind of knightly arms—and probably never will be. Also . . ."

He caught himself just in time. He had been about to confess to Brian that he had lied to the other knight when they had first met about the fact that he, Jim, had been Baron of a place called

Riveroak; and let Brian believe that he was already a knight. Brian, he knew, would try to field any informational blow that he aimed at him; but there were certain automatic social reflexes in him. If Jim was not a knight, if he was not a Baron—was he a gentleman at all? And if he was not a gentleman, then he, Brian Neville-Smythe, had been in the position of introducing an impostor as his closest friend to other genuine knights.

The revelation would be hard enough on his friend, even if he kept Jim's secret—which his honor probably would not let him do. It was unthinkable that he should ruin Brian's own opinion of himself as one of those entitled to bear sword and wear the golden spurs of knighthood.

Not that they were always golden, of course. Quite the reverse. Many knights could not afford golden spurs, and in any case they were hardly practical for everyday use, gold being the soft metal it was.

But Brian was already remonstrating with him.

" . . . James, you take these small lacks in yourself too seriously," he said. "You will learn the use of arms—I will teach you and you will learn, I promise you—and any other unimportant matters will eventually be taken care of."

"But," said Jim, so deep in melancholy by now that he was almost enjoying it, and using the one phrase that he knew Brian could not talk away, "after all, you know, yourself, Brian, I am no Englishman."

"True!" said Brian bravely. "But you are a valiant knight. You have fought and been victorious always in good causes. All gentlemen and ladies are proud to know you. I am proud to know you!"

"Pride!" said a harsh, contemptuous voice from a dark corner of the room. "One of the human toys, and nothing more. Among the things that count, pride is nothing."

Jim looked. His eyes were fully adjusted now to the dimness of the room, aside from its single shaft of bright sunlight, and he saw what he should have seen before. In one of the deeper shadows of the farthest corner, lying lazily on his side, was Aargh. The wolf got to his feet and paced forward, until his large, fierce head almost intruded between the faces of the seated Jim and Brian.

CHAPTER 26

"Aargh!" said Jim.

He was only too aware of Aargh's reluctance to go inside any building if he could avoid it. It evidently went against all reasonable wolf caution to enter anything that might resemble a trap. A den, or small space in which he could curl up and there was no room for anyone, any enemy, to come at him except from the front, was fine. A place like that was a cozy, personal fortress. But the habitations of humans, particularly castles, were merely large places where a wolf might be attacked from all sides at once; and where a flood of strong smells could make him miss a warning his nose would otherwise have given him, of someone or something dangerous nearby.

"How long have you been here, Aargh?" Jim asked.

"I came with Brian," said Aargh. "We met in Mnrogar's den and came up the stairs, through the stable and up the tower stairs. The servants were all busy working, or eating and drinking, themselves; while the guests were doing the same in the hall. We saw no one. No one saw me. If they had, we had been ready to make pretense I was only a large dog. No one asked."

"Well, I'm glad to see you, Aargh," said Jim. "The sun from that arrow slit was in my eyes or I'd have noticed you sooner. You, probably even more than Brian, will understand how poorly I've fitted with all of you."

Aargh snorted.

For a second he seemed about to turn his tail on Jim and walk away, a wolf's strongest expression of contempt; but he did not.

"If you want my friendship for you to end," the wolf said, "you're saying the right words, James. What is this whining, like a three-day cub? Before you were here you were some place else, you've said. Am I wrong?"

"No," said Jim, "you're not wrong. I just—"

"And when you were there you were a man, were you not?"

"Of course," said Jim.

"Not a dragon?"

"No," said Jim. "What are you driving at—"

"I am a wolf," Aargh interrupted him. "I have been a wolf all my life. I will be a wolf until the day I'm killed. After that the ravens may pick my bones. It will not matter. You were a man wherever you were before, you say. You are a man here. Continue a man, and what else matters? The time will be when what comes against you is something you can't kill. Then you will die. All things die. But nothing can take from you the fact that from birth to death you were a man. Nothing else matters."

Brian made a sound in his throat as if he would begin to speak. Aargh looked at him, and he sank back in his chair, his chin in his hand.

"If you were about to tell me that James's situation is one of these human things a wolf cannot understand," Aargh said to the knight, "I'll answer you. That also means nothing, compared to the fact that I am I and James is James, and you are you. We are what we are. We do what we can. When we can no longer, we are done and we go down, having had our years and filled them; and what can we ask more than that?"

He looked back at Jim, who at the moment was feeling very conscious of how he had let himself fish for sympathy from these two friends.

"You're right, Aargh," was all he could manage to make himself say.

"Of course, I'm right," said Aargh.

He looked at Brian.

"Will you still dispute me, Brian?"

"Hah—well," said Brian, "a gentleman is something more than just a man. Honor, duty . . . but there is much in what you say, Aargh."

Indeed, Jim was thinking, there was. Surprisingly, there was a good deal of comfort in it. His spirits had begun to rebound toward their more cheerful, normally enthusiastic level; and something had just occurred to him.

"By the way, Aargh," he said, "do you know much about hobgoblins?"

"Very little," said Aargh. "I have seen them from time to time, riding their smoke some place through the woods; but they are house-bound beings and I ordinarily would have nothing to do with them. I know they are timid, however, like field mice."

"Too bad," said Jim, half to himself. "I was just wondering what makes them tick. The one from the Malencontri serving room chimney showed up here the other day to tell me about the Cliffside dragons."

"The dragons?" said Brian. "What have the Cliffside dragons to do with this moment?"

"Oh, Secoh brought me word," said Jim. "I didn't tell you about this?"

"I do not remember you telling me, James," said Brian. "Surely this is not another difficulty that you have been faced with?"

"As a matter of fact, it is," said Jim. He had already told Brian so much that he might as well tell him anything else he was free to talk about. "The dragons want to come here, to the Earl's party."

"Dragons? Here?" Brian stared at him. "Surely they must know better. There is not a gentleman in the castle that would not wish to attempt the slaying of them, if they came. But why should they want to come?"

Jim found it harder than he had thought to explain.

"Well," he said, "because of what Smrgol talked about before the Loathly Tower fight—people and dragons getting to know each other better. It's because of that; and Secoh having so much to do with us, and telling stories about what we'd done together. Some of the younger dragons, particularly, have taken to talking to single humans when they meet them safely away from other humans—charcoal burners off in the woods and people alone like that. And they've picked up a story about the dragons meeting Christ, Saint Joseph and Saint Mary, when they were fleeing from King Herod's plan to kill off all the young children, so as to make sure that Christ didn't arise to challenge his kingship."

"Indeed!" said Brian. "An evil plan!"

"Yes," Jim went on. "So, for some reason, the dragons have Prince Edward all mixed up with Christ, and they know the Prince is here at the Earl's party. In the story they heard, Christ blesses the dragons; and they think this is going to happen, or should happen this Christmas at the Earl's. So they feel they ought to be here so they can be blessed. Something like that."

"A strange tale," said Brian. He crossed himself.

"Oh, I think they're just mixed up," said Jim. "The thing is, though, they're looking to me to arrange it for them to come here safely to be blessed."

"You must certainly tell them not to come!" said Brian.

Aargh's jaws gaped, showing the double, arched row of teeth. Brian, however, had known the wolf long enough to recognize the wolf's private, silent expression of humor. He turned on Aargh.

"And what do you find so laughable about that?" he snapped.

"Only the idea of telling dragons not to do something; and expecting them not to do it!" said Aargh.

"I'm afraid he's right, Brian," said Jim. "For a number of reasons, it wouldn't do any good to tell them that; and anyway, there're sensible reasons not to. What I've got to do is come up with some good reason why it's better that they don't come. But so far I haven't been able to. If I could only get them here under some conditions where everybody thinks they're just part of the scenery for some reason—or, even better, if I could have them come at a time when everybody else is so busy that they won't be seen, or any attention paid to them—"

He stopped abruptly.

"You know," he said, "maybe there's an idea there. Brian, I've forgotten. This is, let me see, the day of the Holy Innocents? So the next day is the day of Saint Thomas . . ."

He ran down, his memory for the names of various saint's days failing him. The calendar of the Middle Ages was more often kept by such days than by numbers.

But that was not usually a social problem for Jim. Magicians had a reputation for being absent-minded.

"Then after the day of the blessed Saint Thomas," Brian helped him out now, "is the Octave of Christmas, and then, the next day, Saint Sylvester's—and after that the Circumcision of Our Lord on January first; and, heigh-ho, then another year ahead of us—"

He corrected himself abruptly.

"Though, to be sure, in law and numbering the new year actually starts on Ladyday, which is the twenty-fifth day of March. Forgive me, James. I did not mean to preach to you on the days of the year."

"You weren't preaching. I needed to know. Thanks, Brian,"

said Jim. "But which of these days is the one that the tournament's to be held on?"

"Well, as a matter of fact," said Brian, with what looked like a touch of embarrassment, "it has happened in the past that there are usually some small hurts resulting from a tournament. So that all those invited here should be able to enjoy themselves to the utmost for most of the twelve days of Christmas, some years since it was judged best to hold it on the last, or twelfth day of Christmas, the Epiphany of Our Lord, which is January sixth."

"Well, that's fine," said Jim, his spirits really beginning to rise. "That gives me plenty of time to sort out this problem of the Earl and the troll first, and anything else that needs attention. I could have the dragons come in on that last day, when everybody's at the tournament—everybody will be at the tournament when it's happening, won't they, Brian?"

"No one would miss it," said Brian. "Gentleman, lady, noble, meanest servant, tenant or serf."

"That's excellent, then," said Jim. "As I say, I can have the dragons come while the tournament's going on; and get the Prince away for a short while to go through the procedure of letting them all feel properly blessed. Then they can take off; and no one will know they've been here. That's magnificent!"

He poured some wine into the nearest cup and drank it in self-congratulation.

"But you're sure everybody will be at the tournament?" he asked Brian.

"Did I not just say so?" said Brian.

"That really couldn't be better," said Jim, talking as much to himself as Brian and Aargh. Suddenly another inspiration woke inside him. There could be the possibility of killing two birds with one stone.

"That gives me another idea. Brian," he said, "did I tell you that Angie said that all our guests very much enjoyed the reenactment of the battle of Sluys at the dinner on Christmas Day?"

"Did we not!" said Brian. "I could hardly hold back myself from rushing forward to join in the battle. Though of course I knew it was but a play and an acting; and also, of course, I was carrying no sword wherewith to fight, or any other parts of battle dress. But it was more real, James, than you can imagine!"

"So Angie said," Jim answered, thinking a little uncomfortably about how he had smiled at hearing about the primitive acting and staging Angie had described. "But it gave Angie an idea.

She thought perhaps she and I, with your help, Brian, and of course yours, Aargh—and Carolinus and some others—might put on some such play for the amusement of the guests on one of the days of this gathering. The last day, maybe, after the dinner that will undoubtedly follow the tournament, would be an ideal time to do it. What she wanted to do was the Crèche scene."

"Crèche scene?" Brian frowned.

"You know," said Jim, suddenly realizing that Brian was unfamiliar with the idea, "the moment just after the birth of Christ, in the stable, with the donkeys and the oxen, Saint Mary and Saint Joseph, and the shepherds coming to worship the newborn King."

"Oh, indeed?" said Brian, in a tone of wonderment and admiration. "I had not realized—but, it is a marvelous notion, James. You should do so, by all means. I will be only too glad to help. So will you, won't you, Aargh?"

"Why?" asked Aargh.

Brian hastily turned his attention from the wolf and went on talking to Jim.

"But it would be an excellent thing for the last day," he said. "Particularly, since normally the twelfth day dinner is the end of all, and never before have they had something more to look forward to. You would put it on in the hall during the dinner, as the battle of Sluys was represented?"

"As a matter of fact," said Jim, "I was thinking that, if it was outside we'd be away from the castle, which is under the Bishop's blessing, and the scene could be improved upon because both Carolinus and I could possibly make it even better with a little magic—"

He broke off abruptly.

Both Brian and Aargh fixed their eyes on him.

"I just thought of something else that might be done—even better. At the tournament, itself," he went on, after a second, "I could perhaps solve the question of who the disguised troll is, with something else that also would be an entertainment. Brian, what would you think if, near the end of the tournament, a large knight riding a black stallion and armored entirely in black should appear, refusing to give his name—even better, refusing to say a word—but somehow he proclaims his challenge of any knight present who dares to cross lances with him?"

Brian's eyes lit up.

"It would be a great thing indeed, James!" he said. But then his face fell. "But whoever would play the part of the black knight would quickly be known by the rest of the guests, by their noticing who has been missing from among them up until now—for the black knight will have had to leave early, secretly, to armor and horse himself before he rides in."

"But what if the knight could be someone who is not one of the guests?" asked Jim. "Then they'd have no choice but to believe that he was what he seemed to be. He would be the largest knight in armor they had ever seen, on the most large and fierce war horse they had ever seen."

Brian's breath caught in his throat. The glow in his eyes reached new levels of illumination. But then it faded again.

"But if not one of the guests, who could this dark knight be?" he asked. "There are no gentlemen nearby who could play such a part, who would not have been invited to the castle for this Christmastide already."

A look of uneasiness came into his face.

"I hope"—he hesitated—"you are not thinking, that you or Carolinus, James, would raise some unholy spirit to ride against Christian gentlemen—and this was the reason you wanted to make this happen at the tournament grounds, because they are outside the blessing of the Bishop on the castle?"

"No," said Jim, still bubbling inside with enthusiasm, "no evil or dark spirit at all. Merely a Natural."

Brian's face became literally glum.

"I'm afraid it will not do, James," he said. "No gentleman should be cozened to a passage of arms with anyone less than another gentleman—let alone a mere Natural."

"But I've got an idea," said Jim. "Suppose the black knight does not pretend to be a gentleman."

"In that case, no one would deign to fight him," said Brian, promptly.

"Wait. Wait a minute," said Jim. "Listen to me, Brian. The creature would look like a large black knight in armor but he would not say a word, even to give his rank. Then someone among us guests might wonder aloud if he was not something from the nether regions. Then someone else—it could be me—could say something about, if the black knight was really an unholy creature, then it would be a gentleman's Christian duty to show that no such being should be allowed to pretend that he could stand against a true Christian gentleman; and I myself would be glad to ride against him."

"By Saint Brian, who is my namesake!" said Brian, lighting up. "You make a very cogent point, James. It is indeed the duty of a Christian gentleman to destroy such creatures of darkness. You need not offer yourself. I will do so."

"Well, actually," said Jim, "I was hoping that if I offered to ride against the challenger, in spite of his not being anything but possibly a dark spirit, other knights there would be eager to do so also; and since I'm known to be no great expert at arms, the others would take precedence over me, and I could politely let them all try first, if they wished—"

"I doubt not there would be those who would *wish*," said Brian.

"You see," went on Jim, "I'd hope to have this black knight win against all comers, so that he'd end up by winning the prize of the day—the crown, or whatever such reward is offered by the lady whom the Earl will name to hand it to the winner. That would give the black knight the chance to come up to the stand where all the guests will be seated—for I imagine the seats will be built by that time. He can pass by them slowly on his horse and come close to them all."

He stopped, triumphantly. Brian and Aargh looked at him.

"Don't you see?" said Jim. "That's why I'm thinking of making Mnrogar the black knight. It'll give him that chance to pass close to every one of the guests and smell out the other troll among them. Then, challenge him, or otherwise expose him. That'd solve his problem and the Earl's, too."

He waited.

Brian and Aargh did not move a muscle. They both stayed as they were, still looking at him. After what seemed to be a very long moment, Brian leaned toward him and put the back of his hand lightly against Jim's forehead, looking upward at the ceiling as he did so. After a moment he took his hand away.

"Strange," he said, in a thoughtful voice. "To the touch you are no warmer than usual. Have you been feeling a fever lately, James?"

"I'm perfectly all right!" said Jim. "What's the matter with you? It seems to me it's a good idea."

"A troll to joust with knights?" said Brian slowly, staring at him. "It would be easier to teach a mountain to wait on table."

"Well, as I say, I know there'll be problems," said Jim. "But surely in the time between now and the last day of Christmas we can handle them—"

A thought erupted in Jim's mind, and he broke off suddenly. "Let me think a minute," he said to the other two.

Brian sat back in his chair agreeably. Aargh lay down on his side on the floor with every indication of going immediately to sleep; although, from past experience, Jim guessed that the wolf was still awake and continuing to watch him alertly.

What had occurred to Jim was the memory of Carolinus specifically saying that he could no longer be of help with any problem Jim might have, because of the current uproar in Magickdom about Jim having the privilege of extra magical energy. The big question was whether this meant that Carolinus could not even help him by giving advice. If it did mean that Carolinus could not advise him, then that explained why the elder magician had been completely out of touch with him lately—theoretically, it might endanger Jim's already fragile position.

Advice might be all that Jim could get right now; but he would need that. He had no idea of how to go about magically producing armor for Mnrogar, or producing a war horse for him. He had vague ideas of transforming an ordinary horse or something else into the necessary steed. These were things surely Carolinus could do—and if Carolinus would point him in the right direction, Jim ought to be able to work out how to do them himself.

But if he couldn't talk to Carolinus, there was a problem. He had gotten the impression from Carolinus before that there was no way he could talk privately to Carolinus without other magicians of at least the higher levels knowing that the two of them had been in contact. That would be the only reason that really explained Carolinus's staying away from him the way he had. But just now a remarkable thought had occurred to Jim. He could talk to Carolinus in the magician-proof secrecy of the Island of Lost Boys in the story of *Peter Pan,* as they had once before. All he had to do was call Tinker Bell—

He stopped himself abruptly. He had just remembered that he was still inside the castle, where his magic could not work. He stood up and began to dress.

"Come," he said. "I need to be elsewhere to try some magic." Brian's face momentarily showed the uneasiness about magic that was the reflex of the period; but he instantly rose to follow Jim. So did Aargh, though without readable expression.

Within minutes they were down underneath the castle, back in Mnrogar's den. Jim suspected that even this place smelled better to Aargh than the human habitation they had just left. But he set himself to his task, driving irrelevancies from him.

Mentally, he attempted to write, in capital letters on the inner side of his forehead, the magical spell:

ME TO TALK TO→TINKER BELL

Nothing happened. He tried it again. Still nothing. He tried concentrating very hard on the remembered sound of Tinker Bell's tiny silver-bell toned voice speaking in his ear . . . but it did not come.

He relaxed for a moment.

A new idea came to his rescue.

It did not have to be the island in the story of *Peter Pan*. Why couldn't it be any place in any story? Also—Carolinus was always hinting that he was trying to do his magic the wrong way. Magic, Carolinus kept saying, was an art; and Jim must remember that. And it was a fact that Jim was strongly influenced in the making of his spells by thinking of them as like something produced by a desktop computer on its screen as a result of his finger movement on the keyboard.

Carolinus had been trying to tell him something, but the difference between fourteenth- and twentieth-century thinking got in the way of Jim understanding. Perhaps magic actually was a matter of artistic concept, rather than an actual spell or message or command? Jim had already been able to transfer himself magically to Malencontri from somewhere else, or to where Carolinus was, successfully; and always he had done it by writing a spell; but also—he realized now—by visualizing the place to which he was going or the person he was seeking.

He tried again.

ME TO HOME OF→SHERLOCK HOLMES

In his mind he concentrated on imaging the room that had been described so well and so often in the stories about Sherlock Holmes—

And he was there.

It was the room as he had always pictured it. There were the nineteenth-century overstuffed armchairs. There was the mantelpiece with the curved stemmed pipe and ample bowl, thickly carboned inside; and the wall above it with the bullet holes spelling out S M.

Sherlock Holmes himself was nowhere in sight. A shorter, heavier man than Jim had ever imagined Holmes to be was standing with his back to Jim, facing a writing table.

The words "Dr. Watson, I presume?" sprang almost irresistibly to Jim's lips; but he forced them back. Just in time, too, as it turned out. For as he opened his mouth to speak, the figure before him walked backward from the desk toward the door in one wall of the room. The door opened before he touched it, he backed out, the door closed and Jim was left alone.

A slight glitch in his magic, Jim told himself. He was about to go back to where Brian and Aargh waited for him and start over again, when it occurred to him that there was another, possibly easier, way.

If spells were a matter of concept . . . he experimentally tried visualizing an analog watch, with the numbers of the hours arranged in a circle and the hour and minute hands sweeping by them—also a sweep second hand that he could clearly see was moving. He formed his mental vision with the second hand visibly sweeping backward. Then he stopped its turning, and started it circling forward again.

The door opened. The short, rather stout man came back into the room, stopped and stared at him.

"I say," he said in the exact voice of Nigel Bruce that Jim remembered from a number of Sherlock Holmes movies, "how did you get in here without Mrs. Hudson announcing you?"

"My name is James Eckert," said Jim. "It's vital that I talk to Mr. Holmes at once. Is he in?"

"A moment," said Dr. Watson. He stepped out of the room again, closing the door behind him. Through its panels Jim heard his voice calling, "Holmes? Holmes, there's someone . . ." The rest of what Watson had to say was in a lowered voice that did not come audibly through the door.

Jim waited. After a moment the door opened and Watson stuck his head in again.

"Mr. Holmes will be with you shortly," he said, took his head out and closed the door again, firmly.

Jim hastily did his best to visualize Carolinus, along with a desperate need to speak to him—he tried to confine himself only to the visualization and the emotion of needing to talk, without putting it into words. Surely Carolinus would sense his need, being the Master Magician he was; and not only understand that Jim wanted to talk to him, but where he was to be found.

He was not wrong.

There was something like a small thunderclap in the room. Suddenly, there was Carolinus, looking very much like a thundercloud himself, as he glared at Jim.

"How did you manage this?" he demanded. "I've been doing my best to keep my distance from you, because I knew you'd try to drag me in by the ear somehow. You might ruin what little good I might have been able to do you in this magical matter that concerns you and Angie! But how did you manage this?"

"Then I have got us in a place where we can talk without other magicians knowing?" Jim asked eagerly.

"Of course!" said Carolinus. "But how did you do it? Answer me at once, because your future and Angie's may hinge upon it."

CHAPTER 27

Jim told him.

"I see," said Carolinus, brightening. "I imagine you've discovered for yourself by now why you didn't get an answer from Tinker Bell when you tried?"

"Because I only tried to call her?" Jim said. "Because I didn't try to visualize her, the way I visualized this place and you, and visualized time stopping to run backward and starting to run forward normally?"

Carolinus's face fell.

"Well," he said. "I suppose I should congratulate you anyway."

"Why, anyway?" Jim stared at him.

"Anyway, because you at least passed the requirement for being an actual Class C magician—still apprentice level, mind you!" said Carolinus. "An apprentice graduates from Class D to Class C when that apprentice stops using words to make spells and takes a step forward toward directly making Magick. So you're now a qualified C-class apprentice; instead of having a special appointment to that Class."

"Good!" said Jim.

"Worth something," growled Carolinus. "For a moment I'd hoped you'd achieved more than that."

"What more?" asked Jim.

"That," said Carolinus, "you'll still have to find out for yourself. But what you've done at least takes care of one of the complaints I've been faced with: that you'd been unfairly favored by being over-classed as a C. I still wonder how you managed to pick this as a place where we could speak privily. The stories concerned with it haven't been written yet."

"They have back where I came from," said Jim. "Just like the story of Peter Pan."

"Ah? Oh!" said Carolinus. "Hmm. It's a good thing we are where we can't be overheard right now. There are others in Magickdom who'd say merely the fact you know such future stories was another unfair advantage you had over other apprentices. But the answer to that, of course, would be that you did not deliberately come here, knowing you'd have the advantage. You came here voluntarily, but with no thought of Magick in mind. However, the larger question of your being favored with extra Magick in your account, even beyond the C level, is still the greater charge and problem."

There was a moment's silence.

"Well, thank you anyway for the congratulations," said Jim.

"You're welcome," said Carolinus glumly. "What did you want to talk about?"

"Well, I got this idea for letting Mnrogar get close enough to the guests so he could smell out the troll among them; but when I told it to Brian and Aargh, it appeared that there would be some technical problems involved—"

The door behind Carolinus opened abruptly and a tall, lean man with a thin face and keen eyes came briskly into the room. He was wearing a somewhat worn, flowered dressing gown.

"What is the nature of your problem—" he was beginning to say to Jim, when his gaze fell on Carolinus.

"Ah, Carolinus," he said. "It's pleasant to see you again."

"I could say the same thing to you, my dear Holmes," responded Carolinus, with more cordiality in his voice than Jim had ever heard him use in addressing any other human, animal, Natural, supernatural, Force or Functionary. "May I introduce Mr. James Eckert? Mr. Eckert has been studying with me."

"Ah, yes," said Holmes, his sharp eyes seeming to pierce right through Jim. "You will be an American, clearly, Mr. Eckert. From the Midwest?"

"Why . . . yes," said Jim. "How did you guess?"

"I never guess," said Holmes. "I deduce. From what I heard of your accent as I came in, you are American, but from a region there, the speech of which I have never heard before. There is the barest touch of French influence, but none of the Scottish inflection that could imply that you might come from farther northward in the American continent. On the other hand, you have none of the characteristics of any of the various southern or western regional American accents with which I have made myself familiar. Therefore there is no place left for you to have come from, but from somewhere in the middle of the continent between north and south in America."

"Remarkable!" said Jim. "Your deduction, I mean, Mr. Holmes."

"Not at all," said Holmes. "My real interest lies in what you have to tell me. If it is also what you are about to tell Mage Carolinus, perhaps you'd favor us both at the same time with the problem."

"Well—" Jim caught himself saying again; and made a mental vow to banish the word from both lips and mind for the rest of the time he was in Holmes's company. He had no idea how well the detective would understand the background; but the only reasonable course was to go ahead and tell them both what he had been just about to say to Carolinus.

He did.

It turned out to require more explanation than he had expected. Carolinus listened in silence, without moving. But Sherlock Holmes wandered over to his pipe on the mantelpiece, stuffed tobacco into its bowl from a persian slipper, lit the pipe and wandered back, beginning to fill the room with clouds of smoke.

When Jim finally ran down and stood waiting for a reaction from either or both of them, Carolinus remained silent, frowning. But Holmes, taking the pipe from his mouth, spoke up decisively.

"Both the problem you describe, and those involved in it, are outside what I normally encounter. Today, of course, Carolinus and Mr. Eckert, you realize we live in a modern world. Many of the things and individuals you mention, Mr. Eckert, have long since vanished from society. Also, in any case, Moriarty is once more in London—I have just gotten a telegram informing me of this—and I must give my attention to dealing with him first; so I don't have freedom to involve myself in your concerns at the moment."

He turned, stepped back, knocked out the dottle of his pipe into the ashes of the fireplace and placed the pipe itself back on the mantelpiece.

"However," he said, "there are inevitable patterns in all such matters. I would suggest, Mr. Eckert, that you make an effort to locate the secret witness, who has been keeping silent until now."

"Secret witness to what?" asked Jim.

"That remains to be seen," said Holmes, starting toward the door. "However, a secret witness exists, and you will save time in the long run by finding whoever it is and making public the knowledge kept hidden until now."

With these last words, he went out the door, closing it behind him. Jim and Carolinus were left looking at each other.

"What did he mean?" Jim asked Carolinus.

"I know no more than you," said Carolinus. "But his advice is always correct. However, on a more important point, what do you want from me?"

"I was hoping you could help me with some advice," said Jim. He added hurriedly, "I don't mean you should help me magically, but show me what I need to do magically to produce armor for Mnrogar, and find a horse for him to ride in the lists."

"Jim, Jim . . ." said Carolinus. "When will you understand? You come from a far and strange place, where things are done that would seem magical to anyone of us here. But still, you're infected by the popular superstition about Magick—even such as I control. You believe it capable of almost anything."

"Isn't it?" asked Jim. He had almost added *here*.

"Far from it!" Carolinus glared at him. "Actually, as I've tried to explain before, Magick can actually do very little. Certainly we magickians can make things appear and disappear. We can ourselves appear and disappear. We can even disappear in one place and appear in another; thus saving us the ordinary discomfort and time of traveling. Magick can heal wounds. But you've already learned it cannot help with disease; otherwise I'd have used it to cure myself, the time that bunch of ragged outlaws held siege around my cottage. But I could not; and so you, Angie and your men-at-arms had to come to my rescue. The wonder isn't how much Magick can do. It's how little it can do, that's of any real use in ordinary human affairs. Most important matters have to be dealt with by human—or animal—means alone, as they always have been. Witness your individual battle with the sea serpent Essessili. At its utmost, Magick can merely be a sort of aid to ordinary human subtlety; or by influencing a situation by illusion."

"But it's an illusion I'm after," said Jim, snatching at the opportunity. "I want Mnrogar to give the illusion of a black knight in armor on horseback, so he'll ride down any human knight who dares to face him, win the crown for the day, and get to ride slowly past every guest watching; and that means every guest of the Earl's, because of the importance of the occasion. It'll give Mnrogar a chance finally to smell out the disguised troll among them. I'm only asking you to help me with some instruction on how to work magic that'll create the illusion of the black knight and the horse. I'm hoping Brian'll agree to train the two of them. But it'd be a great help if magic could also make it easier for Mnrogar to learn how to carry and use the lance."

"And you were counting on me to produce that Magick for you?"

"Unless you can't, of course," said Jim.

"Can't? Can't?" said Carolinus.

He checked himself abruptly, glaring now at Jim.

"That is to say," he snapped, "something may be possible in Magick and still be impractical in reality. To begin with, you forget I'm still trying not to have anything to do with you, so that no one can accuse me of helping you."

"But if I can arrange for Mnrogar to find the other troll," said Jim, "then that will probably unravel whatever scheme the Dark Powers had for disturbing this particular holiday season at the Earl's. Aren't I right?"

"Well . . ." Carolinus became suddenly thoughtful. "You *have* suddenly made it to C level . . ."

His voice faded away. He stood, staring off into the distance.

"Could I get Aargh and Brian here to help us talk about this?" Jim asked him.

Carolinus came back to himself with a jerk.

"What? Oh, certainly, if you want to. No. Wait a moment . . . let me do it . . ."

He looked hard at the other side of the room. The fireplace mantelpiece and the wall with the bullet holes in it vanished. In its place was a section of Mnrogar's den under the Earl's castle, with Brian and Aargh still in it. Brian blinked and stared at them. Aargh was instantly on his feet. But neither one of them seemed to pay any attention to the different appearance of that part of the room at 221B Baker Street where Jim and Carolinus stood.

"Brian, Aargh," said Jim, "forgive me. I had to find a place where we could all talk with special privacy; and with Carolinus joining us. We're all now in a place like that one Carolinus took Aargh and myself to before, the one where there was the little tinkling invisible person he talked to and who took us there and back—only this is a different place. I'm talking to Carolinus about the difficulty of having Mnrogar appear as the black knight."

"James," said Brian, "how can this be? You and the Mage are here, with us. We are not some place else with you."

"*Jim,*" said Carolinus's voice in Jim's head, "*they can't see any of Sherlock Holmes's room. They aren't hearing me say this either. Just ignore the whole thing and we'll go ahead and talk.*"

"Carolinus thinks we should ignore things like that and simply go ahead and talk," parroted Jim, trying to keep straight in his own mind everything that was going on. "I've just been telling him about the plan to have Mnrogar enter the lists at the tournament as the black knight; and he's concerned about some of the practical difficulties."

"Concerned indeed!" said Carolinus out loud—and Jim saw the eyes of both Brian and Aargh fasten upon him.

But Carolinus was continuing.

"For one thing," Carolinus was saying, "where are you going to find a horse to bear his weight and behave in proper fashion in the lists? Don't bother to try to answer, you can't. You're counting on me to do it for you. But if you couldn't get me, you were willing to go ahead and try it yourself; and, Jim, that would have made the most unbelievable coil not only of real things, but of the whole fabric of Magickdom—and this at a time when you're in enough trouble there already! In anything approaching actuality, the idea is as far-fetched a plan as could be imagined. How can a troll be expected to ride and act like a knight?"

"As well ask a brute beast to put on an armor and do the same," put in Brian.

"A brute beast," growled Aargh, "would have better sense."

Jim's head whirled again. It seemed as if he was being attacked from all sides, by those he had most counted on to support him. He reached out to snatch at and deal with one point at a time.

"But I'm not expecting a great deal," he said. He turned to Brian.

"Look, Brian, all that would be necessary, if we could get Mnrogar into the armor and on the horse, would be to teach him and the horse itself to go through certain motions—just a few motions that'll make them look as if they know what they were doing. They won't even have to know why they're doing it. I was thinking of magic, of course. With a little help that way, possibly it could all become a simple matter of training—"

"James," said Brian sadly, shaking his head. "You know that you, yourself, are really not ready to ride in the lists with any seriousness against any knight of experience at all. This, after several years in which I've tried hard to teach you many things— many things out of the many, many more things that one who fights either on foot or a-horse must know. Certainly magic must be able to do wondrous things. But how can it help me to teach more than I ever taught you, to a troll; and in a matter of a few days only! Even if he was willing and able to learn?"

"Which he won't be," said Aargh.

"Now there," said Jim, recovering some of his self-confidence, "is where I think all of you are wrong. I think Mnrogar wants that other troll so badly that he'd be willing to do anything. Not only that; but I also think he'd rather enjoy being an unknown knight in armor and trying to put a lance point through a human being. It's his nature. All he has to be taught is that instead of leaping on somebody from a place of hiding and using his teeth and nails, he's going to ride toward someone with a long, pointed lance and knock whoever it is off their horse. It's just another way to attack, that's all."

"That's *all*?" echoed Brian. He shook his head from side to side, slowly.

"And as for the armor and the horse," said Jim, turning on Carolinus, "you really could help me with that, if you wanted to, couldn't you, Carolinus? What I mean is, magic could make something appear like something else?"

"Of course it can!" bristled Carolinus. "But that's not the point. The point here is that the level of Magick required for that could only be done by a magickian of my skill. Magickdom will realize this instantly."

"Would they?" said Jim. "After all, you said yourself I suddenly jumped to a true C level by my way of arranging my transfer to Sherlock Holmes's rooms. In fact, you acted almost as if you thought I'd jumped higher."

"I implied no such thing!" said Carolinus. "In any case, I can't lie to my fellow Master Magickians."

"You wouldn't have to," said Jim. "I don't suppose any of them are likely to try to pin you down on how we got these results." Carolinus's mustache bristled briefly.

"Hah! No," he said. "But they can suspect."

"But will they be sure?" said Jim. "You yourself say that since I came from somewhere else I sometimes get results that someone who belongs here shouldn't. It could be my responsibility, rather than yours. Particularly, if the whole thing works. Couldn't it?"

Carolinus stared at him, opened his mouth and hesitated.

"It's barely possible," he said finally. "But only if the whole insane scheme works. It'd be the next thing to showing you could make new Magick anytime you wished. You did do it that one time at the Loathly Tower by defeating the Dark Powers with only human strengths. I only refereed in that instance, giving you a clear area to fight in. Of course, all Magickdom thought it was a single, fortunate accident . . ."

He abruptly fell silent for a second, staring past Jim's head at nothing.

"Still," he continued, on a note of new interest, "if you could do something like that, none would question you. Once could be an accident; twice would indicate a gift. You'd have to be put in a class by yourself. And what with all of us losing Magick all the time as bits of it become something anyone can do—like sewing skins and cloths together to make clothes, as I once told you— that which used to be high and most secret Magick grows less by the day. We badly need more. Magickdom would welcome you with open arms if you had the gift of making some."

He grew thoughtful. Suddenly, he threw up his long, thin arms with his hands held wide.

"Well, why not?" he said. "The world is turned upside down. Masters serve their apprentices, instead of the other way around. Trolls become knights because a troll needs to be in disguise. Perhaps this is World's End and Chaos has finally routed the orderly process of History completely. Yes, I can do it. I might as well do it—if you can manage your part of it. But I don't see how you can."

"Mage!" said Brian. "You would countenance this?"

"Why not?" said Carolinus. "The Wild Hunt has passed over your heads in this castle each night of the Twelve Days of Christmas, as it does each such season of the year. Yet no man or woman has so far been caught up and carried away by it. This plan of Jim's is no wilder. If it succeeds, and the troll under the castle destroys or drives off the troll among the guests that would challenge him, then mayhap the army of trolls gathered around us will run off in all directions from one another once more and the Dark Powers will not have succeeded in disturbing

this Holy Season after all. That at least may speak in Jim's favor
and justify my argument he deserves special consideration. There
is just a chance it might save him; and also settle the troll and
Earl situation here, once and for all. One chance among many,
like one star among all those in the heavens. But why not?"

"There, Brian," said Jim quickly. "If Carolinus will help, will
you help too? Can't we work out something simple for the troll
and whatever we find him in the shape of a war horse?"

"If you could find him a war horse," said Brian. "In any case,
what is he to ride? He must weigh twenty stone or more—"

Jim made a quick calculation in his head. Twenty stone would
be right around three hundred pounds. His own guess was that
Mnrogar, probably with oversize bones inside that big body of
his, might weigh even more than that.

"He would break any horse's back, even if we could find one
who would carry him," said Brian.

The truth was, Jim had been holding back an inspiration he had
had as far as solving that much of the problem went. He had just
been waiting for the best moment to bring it up.

"With Carolinus helping," he said, avoiding the magician's
eyes, "perhaps with magic we could transform that large boar
that upset both the Earl and his horse the first morning when
the guests at the castle here were out hunting. I was told he
was as weighty as a bull. If magic could make him look like a
horse, he ought to be able to carry Mnrogar's weight; and, not
only that, but his natural instincts as well would be to charge
anyone or anything in his way; which would make it a natural
thing for him to adapt to charging down one side of the barrier
in the list."

"Yes, I was out that morning with the rest of them and saw
him," growled Brian. "A fine beast; but how are we even to find
him again, let alone train him?"

"I know the boar you mean," put in Aargh. "There's only one
that size around here. I can find him, if that's all you need."

"Fine. Then—" Jim risked a glance at Carolinus, and was
startled at what he saw. Carolinus's expression had changed completely. A cheerful wickedness had made its way onto his otherwise stern features. Jim had been about to ask him whether
Aargh's being able to find the boar meant that Carolinus would
be willing to help train the boar; but it did not seem necessary.
The elder magician was looking past them all at something off
in the distance.

"Reminds me of when I was a young magician," he was saying, more to himself than to them. A faint smile that could only be described as machiavellian touched the corners of his lips. "Yes, yes, indeed . . . Jim? You were about to say something to me?"

"Just whether you'd be willing to help make the boar act like a horse as well as look like one. We'll have to trap him first, I suppose, or trick him into some position where he can't get away from us—"

"No, no," said Carolinus, still smiling a little evilly to himself, "that won't be necessary. If Aargh knows where he is, I can simply bring him to wherever the rest of you are going to work with Mnrogar."

"But, there's this business of making him look like a horse and act like a horse—" Jim was beginning again.

"Oh," said Carolinus. "But that's no problem. I'll just have a little talk with that boar. After that, I think he'll do more or less what you want him to do; that is, as far as a boar can act like a horse. There are physical limitations, you know."

Aargh snorted. Just what the snort was supposed to indicate, Jim was not sure. But he was sure it would not be the wisest idea to ask what the wolf had meant.

"Then there's the matter of the troll, Mnrogar," said Carolinus, almost dreamily. "I can have a small talk with him, too. It won't make him into a knight, you understand, but like the boar, he'll be more amenable to suggestion. Aargh, you say you know where this boar is now?"

"I know where to look for him," said Aargh.

"Excellent!" said Carolinus. "We'll both go look now, then."

Carolinus and Aargh disappeared. Brian looked rather blank. At the same time, Jim became aware that the portion of 221B Baker Street that had seemed to contain Carolinus and him had vanished. He was completely in Mnrogar's den with Brian. Carolinus, having now made up his mind, was evidently spending magical energy with a vengeance.

CHAPTER 28

As Jim sat at the high table, with the cressets flaring to light the Great Hall—and the air already stuffy and overheated, in spite of every arrow slit and window having their shutters thrown wide open—a slim female figure in a worn old brown cloak, with its hood completely over the head and held tight closed to hide the face within, glided into the empty seat beside him.

"It's me," said Angie, letting the hood fall open enough to show her face. "You're sober! Good. I got worried; and I didn't want to send either Enna or the wet nurse down to see if their Lord was passed out drunk, so I took this robe of Enna's and came down myself."

She untied the cord around the waist of the cloak and threw the garment off her, showing herself in a green gown more suitable to her status as one of the honored guests here in the hall, merely sitting and talking to her husband.

"I was worried," she said.

"And well you might be," said Jim.

And well she might be. The dinners had run later steadily as the Twelve Days of Christmas passed, the wine become less watered, the behavior more licentious. It was somewhere between nine and ten o'clock at night—the equivalent of three or four in the morning by twentieth-century standards. Those still left in the hall—as it happened, a majority of the guests, simply because the Earl himself was also still here—were down to a hard core of those who enjoyed unlimited partying. They had, effectively, been at dinner since between one and two o'clock in the afternoon. The decorum had long since passed from the normal to the uproarious, and by now had added a certain amount of downright dangerousness.

"You *are* sober, aren't you?" asked Angie. "You're not just sitting there stupefied, but acting bright-eyed and normal, are you?"

"No," said Jim. "This time I outfoxed them. I've been managing to drink mainly water, with just enough wine to color it. Now we've reached the point where as long as I go through the motions of drinking, that's all anybody expects—oops, here comes one now."

A plainly very drunk middle-aged knight dressed all in brown, his cote-hardie straining over his portly figure, was lurching up to the opposite side of the high table. He reached it, a large square mazer in his hand with red wine slopping in it.

"A cup with you, Sir Dragon!" he said thickly, waving the mazer and slopping his wine about. "Dragons forever!"

Jim lifted his own mazer to his lips and drank and then lifted it again.

"Sir Randall forever!" he said.

"Y'honor me," said the knight, and lurched away again.

"Wouldn't it have been better to toast his family name? Or is Sir Randall the first name of someone else?"

"No, it's his," said Jim. "I can't remember most of their last names. If I can't remember either one, I offer a toast to some part of the coat of arms that they're all wearing somewhere about them. In an emergency, I mumble. Don't look at me that way, Angie; I'm just trying to last until the Earl leaves or passes out; and I think he's close to passing out now."

"I hope you're right," said Angie. "I really don't think it's safe for you to be here with all of them in this condition."

"Probably not," said Jim.

He looked out over the hall. Perhaps a third of those there were either unconscious from the amount they had drunk or so close to being unconscious that they could hardly stir from their seats. But there was a sufficient core of people like Sir Randall who were still on their feet and moving about, or able to go through the motions of being their usual selves; and within these was the truly dangerous core.

These were the male guests who had been careful not to get drunk beyond a safe point; and now sat around, stiff-backed, upright and smiling with glittering invitation on all and sundry who might approach them.

The smile, particularly on the faces of such as Brian and Sir Harimore, was something like the smile on the face of the tiger, on whom the Lady from Niger mistakenly went on for a ride.

"*I am too much of a gentleman to start a fight*," that smile said, "*but if you would care to offend me, I would be happy to satisfy any desire you might have for a small encounter.*"

"You know, Angie," Jim said thoughtfully, "remember how our spring breaks used to be at the college back at Riveroak? We had ten days; and the first day or so, it seemed that we had time unlimited; and those same first few days had so many things going on in them that it seemed we could live half a lifetime before we had to go back into academic life again? And then, all of a sudden, we'd wake up to the fact that there were only two or three days left of the break, and it was all going to be over in no time at all? You remember?"

"I remember," said Angie. "I also remember that, looking back on it, the latter days of the break were just as filled with things to do as the first ones, only by that time we weren't paying any attention to time at all, and acting as if we were going to have a lifetime that way. Then we came down with a bump on the last day. You know—"

She broke off to glance around the hall. Everybody there was immersed in their own conversation scene or argument.

"—You know," she said again, "come to think of it, this is the best chance I've really had to talk privately with you for days. Our rooms aren't the best place, with Enna or the wet nurse in the next room with little Robert; and every place else we're with people. I don't believe anyone in this time even knows what privacy means."

"It's uncommon enough," said Jim, looking around the hall and silently agreeing with her view on medieval privacy.

"Well, it's a chance for me to say something to you," said Angie. "Do you know Agatha Falon's been bribing everybody's servants right and left to keep an eye on our room—'because of course she'd like to visit little Robert when it was possible, but she didn't want to disturb us more than was necessary. I was such a good keeper of the little boy'?"

"At least she admits it," said Jim, trying to think of a way to lift the anxiety that was clearly on Angie's mind.

"You aren't very perceptive, Jim," said Angie dryly. "That's an ultimate fourteenth-century put-down. What she's doing is talking about me as if I was on the servant level, with Enna and the wet nurse. The message is that I'm actually no Lady. That's about as insulting as you can get in this society; particularly talking about another woman who outranks you."

"Oh, well," said Jim uncomfortably. "I don't imagine she can do anything, so she's taking it out in insults. She's been here at table with the Earl since the dinner started."

"She's here now?" said Angie, trying to peer past Jim, two empty seats and the bulky body of the Earl, without appearing to do so.

"That's right," said Jim.

"I came in from the side entrance," said Angie, giving up the effort. "I didn't think to see her still at table. Is she drunk?"

"Not that you could tell," answered Jim. "From what I can see, she can really hold her wine—better than the Earl, for all his body weight."

"The Earl's in for a surprise from her, one of these days," said Angie darkly. "Anyway, the point is, Jim, there's only a few days left for us all to be together here; and I'm sure she'll try something against us or little Robert. I want another man-at-arms actually inside our first room, except when you or Brian, or someone like that's there. And he's not to talk to the wet nurse or Enna, or they to him. We can have that, can't we?"

"Another man, armed?" Jim asked.

Angie nodded.

"Theoretically, I suppose it's going beyond the permission the Earl gave us out of courtesy to have an armed man at the door," he said. "But I don't think, this late in the twelve-day period, it'll matter. What have we got? There's just tomorrow and the next day, isn't there?"

"Don't tell me you've forgotten?" asked Angie.

"I haven't forgotten," said Jim. "I remember what day it is, in spite of what I said earlier. But I've been pretty busy, you know, with Mnrogar and that boar. Brian has been doing his best, but it's going to be a miracle if both the boar and Mnrogar act like they ought to at the tournament. Also, we've got another problem. Mnrogar doesn't dare say anything and probably wouldn't say it right anyway if he did. What he needs is a page or herald to go ahead of him and announce that he's there to challenge everybody."

Jim cleared his throat.

"—I don't suppose, if you put on hose and a doublet—"

"Don't be insane, Jim!" said Angie. "I'm a married Lady. Maybe at the court in London, under special conditions with the King approving it, something like that might be done. But here, everybody in the county would start pretending they couldn't see us, after something like that. Would Brian put on a clown suit and start doing somersaults on the floor to make people laugh?"

"No," said Jim, stunned by an image of Brian in a clown suit doing any such thing, "but he's a knight."

"And I'm a knight's Lady. A Baroness," said Angie. "Nice Ladies have a lot less freedom to do things than nice knights; and anything that isn't done *really* isn't done! You should know that by now, Jim."

"Probably no one would ever find out it was you, dressed up like a page," said Jim.

"And possibly just one person would," said Angie grimly. "Then all the world would hear. No."

"Well, possibly you're right," said Jim.

"Of course I am," said Angie. "And, speaking of people dressing up and doing things: have you forgotten you're going to be Joseph in my Crèche scene the last evening here? I've been trying to set up some kind of rehearsal, but I can never catch you."

"Angie," said Jim, "I simply can't do it. I've got the Mnrogar tournament thing earlier that day. The problem of handling the dragons is still up in the air. I've got to think of some way to get them here briefly, even if they don't see anybody but the Prince for a moment or two before having to leave again. Then there's still that whole mob of trolls circling out beyond the edge of Mnrogar's territory and the rest of us here; and nobody knows what they're likely to do. I've got to be free to move around that day. I can't be tied down to being with you when that scene goes on."

"If you don't," said Angie, "there won't be any scene. I've got to have a Joseph."

"I told you," said Jim, "I can magically get someone here from Malencontri. We can put a costume on him and I can magic him to go through the motions and say whatever words you want to say."

"Have you ever had anything to do with amateur theatricals?" Angie asked.

"You know I haven't," said Jim.

"Well, you know I have," said Angie. "And the chances that things will go wrong are just about ninety-nine to one. Whoever's Joseph may have to ad-lib, to handle whatever suddenly happens to change the performance when it actually goes on. Your magic man from Malencontri won't be able to do anything but parrot the speech he's been given ahead of time. You're the only one who can do the ad-libbing."

"Well, I'll say what I did earlier," said Jim. "I'll do my best to be there when the time comes; but you'd better have somebody else ready to step out and stand there anyway. Maybe I can come up with some magic that will let you do your lines and his, too, if something goes wrong."

"Jim, does my voice sound like a baritone to you?"

"I can make your voice for Joseph sound like a baritone," said Jim. "But—let me forget about it for now, anyway. There's too much else to deal with."

"That's all right. You'll come up with solutions for these other things," said Angie. "I trust you. And when you start to get in control of them, then we'll talk again about your being Joseph. Forget it for now. What exactly is your biggest problem with Mnrogar and the boar?"

"Simply the fact that Mnrogar's a troll and the boar's a boar," said Jim.

"You mean they want to fight each other?" Angie asked.

"Not that. In the sense that the two of them never want to do the same thing at the same time," said Jim, "I suppose you could say they're fighting each other; but they're not doing it deliberately. Carolinus took care of that by whatever magic he used when he had his little talks with them—whatever he did or said then. They came in like lambs. The boar turned into a good-looking horse; Mnrogar turned into a huge but believable black knight in armor, riding the boar. But it's from that point on things've become difficult. The boar may look like a horse; but he's a horse that wants to act like a boar; and Mnrogar may look like a knight in armor, but he wants to act like a troll. Carolinus was right. There're certain basic problems—"

"Oh, wait a minute!" said Angie. "I forgot Hob-One is upstairs wanting to talk to you, and he did say he was in a hurry. Secoh is evidently waiting for him to come back with some message from you. Hob's in the chimney of the fireplace of the first of our two rooms, out of sight of course, of Enna and the wet nurse."

"They won't hurt him," said Jim.

"Tell him that," said Angie. "He only trusts me because I'm connected to you. Anyway, the point is he wanted to talk to you right away; and that was what decided me finally to come down here and check on you—though I'd been thinking about it earlier."

"It's ridiculous!" said Jim. "That hobgoblin carries caution too far. Anyway, he'll just have to wait. I made up my mind not to leave here until the Earl did; and he can't last much longer, but—"

He broke off suddenly.

"Oh, no!" he said.

"Oh, no what?" said Angie, turning to look out through the hall in the direction that Jim's eyes had suddenly been directed. "What is it? I don't see anything going on that hasn't been going on anyway. Brian's just sitting down there now, talking quietly to another man who seems as sober as he is."

"That's what worries me," said Jim. "That other man is Sir Harimore—you remember him?"

"Oh," said Angie, "you mean the other knight who offered to escort me back from that hawking on one of the first few mornings and actually did ride along with Brian to escort Geronde and me back to the castle? What's wrong with their talking?"

"As long as they do nothing but talk, nothing," said Jim. "But they don't like each other; and I think they both got a little tired waiting for somebody else to come pick an argument with them; so Sir Harimore seems to have gone over to Brian, and that could very well end in the two of them slipping out together for a quiet little sword fight—by mutual consent."

"But why would they want to do that?" said Angie. "I thought they were looking forward to meeting each other in the tournament the last day of the party."

"Well they were and probably are," said Jim, "but there's more going on there than appears on the surface. You know how Brian depends on winning tournaments to get prizes he can sell or pawn for the extra money he needs to keep Castle Smythe going? Well, Sir Harimore is well enough off so he doesn't have to worry about income, but he knows Brian lives on the edge of poverty all the time. As it stands, they've each won two of the four tournaments in which they've ridden against each other; and one of them is almost a sure bet to win the prize this time."

"It'd better be Brian," said Angie. "He's going to need a lot of money before long, Geronde tells me—she won't say what for."

"He always needs a lot of money," said Jim. "Anyway, Sir Harimore knows that; Harimore himself is one of these people who's always determined to be better than anyone else—do you remember when there was the invasion of the sea serpents and Sir John Chandos was with us in the castle and all of a sudden what seemed to be a fight broke out in the courtyard?"

"Yes," said Angie.

"Well, you remember it turned out that they had just been play-fighting?" Jim went on, "With Brian heading up a bunch that was trying to beat their way in through the door of the Great Hall; and Sir John was head of another group that was trying to keep them out?"

"I remember," said Angie. "Yes. What's that got to do with it?"

"Well you remember I stopped it simply by appearing; and both Brian and John Chandos apologized to me—since I was their host. But in the process of apologizing, Chandos highly complimented Brian, including him in a reference to the best swords in the kingdom."

"That's right," said Angie. "I remember now. He did. Brian was thrilled. I was thrilled for him, too—and of course Geronde—"

"Well that's it," said Jim. "The word spread, of course, and reached Sir Harimore; and he can't stand the idea that people might think that meant Brian was a better fighter than he was. So he's ready to do almost anything he can to chop Brian down. That's why I'm afraid what looks like them talking quietly together is working up to an agreement to slip out and settle things with swords right now. They've got just enough wine in them to not have ordinary prudence."

"Surely," said Angie, "they wouldn't kill each other? Not while they're guests here in the castle, would they? I know an awful lot goes on here; but the guests won't actually try to kill each other, will they?"

"No," said Jim, "of course not. That'd be a violation of the Earl's hospitality, to say the least; and simply not done in any case, but what I'm afraid of is Harimore has been planning this, maybe only pretending to drink all evening, so he could catch Brian half-drunk and wound him—not badly enough to keep him out of the tournament, but enough to handicap Brian as far as being at his top effectiveness, when they ride against each other in just two days from now."

"Well . . ." said Angie. "Maybe you ought to tell the Earl, or—"
Jim shook his head.

"No. That'd never work," he said. "It'd only embarrass the Earl, make a deadly enemy of Sir Harimore and possibly ruin my friendship with Brian. But you're right. I've got to stop them somehow—"

He suddenly lit up inside.

"Angie!" he said. "In your purse at your waist there, do you have paper and those scissors that you had our blacksmith at Malencontri make for you?"

Angie, like some of the other women, carried a purse at the decorated belt around her waist; and among the things in that purse, there was always a folded length of French-made paper and some of the charcoal sticks they used for writing messages to each other. The scissors, among other things, were for cutting off a piece of the paper on which to write.

"Bring it along," said Jim, getting to his feet, "and come with me. I think I know a way I might be able to stop them. It's critical from my point of view. Without Brian, I'll never get Mnrogar to ride that boar the way the Black Knight should ride his horse and handle his spear. So this has got to be stopped."

They both rose and walked off to the side, down off the dais that held the high table, and started around the corner of the long table at which Brian and Sir Harimore now sat, only a few steps from a door that led to a hallway that ran the length of the hall and would reach a door that opened on the courtyard.

"How much of this do you want?" said Angie, as they went along. Jim looked.

She already had the scissors out of her purse and was pulling out the end of the rolled-up paper, about six inches in width and maybe three feet in length. She had about six inches of it out of her purse. Jim considered it for a second.

"About a foot of it, I guess," he said. "Yes, twelve inches."

"What are you going to do with it?" asked Angie. "Look, can we stop for a moment? It's not easy to cut it off while we're walking along like this."

"You're right," said Jim. "Come to think of it, I need to sit down at a table for a moment, anyway. There's a lot of empty seats right there. We can talk without being overheard; and none of these people are paying attention to anyone but themselves right now, anyway."

They stopped and sat down. Angie cut off the length of paper. Jim took it from her and began to fold it in accordion pleats of about two inches in width.

"You didn't answer me," said Angie. "What are you going to do with it; and why are you folding it up that way?"

"You remember folding a piece of paper this way and then cutting out a paper doll through all the thicknesses—then you unfold it and you have a chain of paper dolls holding hands?"

"Of course," said Angie.

"Well, I can't work any magic in this castle with the Bishop's blessing on it," said Jim. "But maybe I can sort of invoke the idea of magic to help me stop Brian and Harimore from doing anything foolish."

He stood up, tucked the folded paper and the scissors into the purse at his own belt, and started toward where Brian and Harimore were sitting—but they weren't.

"They're gone!" he said.

"They're just heading for a door, now," said Angie. "See there?"

"I see," said Jim, beginning to stride in that direction. "We can catch up with them outside. That'll be better anyway. Hurry—but don't look as if you're doing that."

"That's all right for you!" panted Angie. "Your legs are longer than mine!"

"Hurry!" said Jim. Ahead, Brian and Sir Harimore passed through the door into the relative dimness of the passage beyond, where it was also lit by cressets, but spaced at larger intervals. He and Angie came through the door right behind the two knights.

They were only half a dozen steps down the corridor ahead; and they did not turn at the sound of feet behind them. Jim went more swiftly, leaving Angie a little bit behind as he tried to catch up with them just as they passed under the light from one of the flaring cressets.

"Gentlemen!" he said. "A moment!"

By the time he had said the last syllable Angie had caught up with him and he was right behind the two of them. They stopped. He stopped; and they turned, each pivoting on his heel in the same direction, as if they had been trained members of a drill team from a latter age.

Jim looked into two pairs of eyes, neither pair of which was plainly overjoyed on seeing him and Angie.

"Forgive me for interrupting your conversation, Sirs," said Jim—neither Brian nor Sir Harimore had been talking at all, but this was beside the point—"but I was on my way to see if I could unravel the reason for the omen I have just received. I will probably not know for another day at least, but I thought I might pass a small warning to the two of you; though I doubt either one of you are likely to be endangered by whatever I may find. It is highly unlikely that either one of you would find someone picking a quarrel with you before the tournament; and if they did, I have no fear as to your safety in any such encounter. However, forewarned is never a bad thing to be."

"Omen, James?" queried Brian. The glitter Jim had noticed in his eyes as he sat in the hall earlier was still there, as it was in Sir Harimore's eyes as well, but there was the tinge of a note of immediate caution in Brian's voice.

"What omen?" demanded Sir Harimore.

"The omen," said Jim, slowly and impressively, "of the Dancing Dolls!"

The two knights stared at him. Brian it was, of course, who asked the inevitable question.

"I've never heard of an omen of Dancing Dolls," said Brian. "What is it, James? And what does it mean?"

"Let me show you," said Jim, still in the slow, portentous voice in which he had spoken a moment before. "Both of you know that under the good Bishop's blessing, there can be no magic made in this castle until the Twelve Days of Christmas are over and the Bishop has left. But such things as omens are not necessarily magic."

He lifted the paper.

"Observe!" he said. "I cut into this paper at random, letting the scissors go whither they will."

It had been a long time, thought Jim, since he had been young enough to be fascinated by this sort of scissors-trick; but he still knew generally how it needed to be done.

He put the open scissors against the upper edge of the folded paper and cut into it, making an arm, a shoulder, a round head, a shoulder, another arm leading down to the folded edges; then off them and back again to cut the underside of the arm, on down the body, out to the folded edge once more for the leg and feet, and finally back again for the underside of the remaining foot and leg—hacking out something that looked rather like a snowman with legs.

Still holding the paper tight, he put the scissors back in the purse at his belt; and, ignoring the cut pieces of paper that had fallen to the floor, with both hands he extended the paper to its full length, revealing a chain of doll-like figures joined at hands and toes.

"The Dancing Dolls!" he said ominously.

The glitter in both pairs of eyes before him had definitely changed. It was still there, but it was a wary glitter. He hesitated portentously a moment before going on. "What this will actually mean, I won't know, as I say, for some little time; but in general it's a warning of ill fortune for someone. Naturally, I wanted to warn you, Brian; and I feel fortunate to find you with Sir Harimore. This gives me the chance to pass the warning to him, too; and that pleases me because of the great respect I've developed for him, particularly after watching his swordplay with Sir Butram."

"What sort of ill luck, Sir James?" demanded Harimore.

It struck Jim that the knight was either more driven by his desire to excel over everyone else or less credulous than most of the medieval people Jim had dealt with so far. Probably, he thought, it was simply the desire to excel, and what was driving the knight right now was simply a sort of baffled fury at something that could interfere with his hope of crossing swords with Brian.

Jim deliberately paused a moment, looking at him.

"That," he said then, as impressively as he could, "I can't tell you, Sir Harimore. I only know that the ill luck forewarned by the Dancing Dolls usually strikes one who least expects it; and from a quarter where it is least expected. So there's no defense against it, except to be cautious of all ventures, particularly where there might be a chance of ill luck befalling you."

He paused again for a moment, then carefully folded the Dancing Dolls back together, put them back with the scissors in his purse and turned to Angie.

"Well, m'Lady," he said, "we must be getting upstairs. A good eve to you, Brian and Sir Harimore. Be of good cheer, Sirs. The chances are the omen deals with someone entirely else. I've simply mentioned it to you because it's my belief it never hurts to offer a warning in these cases. A good eve and a good night to you."

"Good night, James," said Brian. "But stay, perhaps I will go up with you, since our ways lie together—"

He broke off, turning to Sir Harimore.

"Am I right, Sir Harimore?" he said. "You are of my mind? We can have our little discussion at some other time?"

"Indeed," said Sir Harimore, "that is undoubtedly wise. I will look to see you again soon."

"Do not doubt it," said Brian.

"Then, good evening to you all," said Sir Harimore, "m'Lord, my Lady, Sir Brian."

He gave them all a brief bow and turned, going back down the corridor and in through the door into the hall.

"Come on, Brian," said Angie, linking her arm through Brian's as well as Jim's. "That's enough for all of us, for one day."

CHAPTER 29

"Last night..." said Jim, as he and Angie sat at the table in the front one of their two rooms, drinking from their life-giving cups of hot, strong tea. The early morning sun was filtering in around the still closed shutters over the window, giving them a muted but still bright morning illumination. "...did I tell Hob-One to tell Secoh that the dragons should come along to Malencontri, after all?"

"You did," said Angie.

"I was afraid I told him that. Now, why—" said Jim, shaking his head like a non-ticking clock. "Why would I say that?"

"I don't know," said Angie. "You didn't tell me. I supposed you had some reason up your sleeve."

"Hah!" said Jim bitterly.

"Please," said Angie, "can we dispense with the medieval-isms—at least when we're talking between ourselves, and this early in the day."

"I'm sorry," said Jim, rubbing his eyes and forehead with the heels of his hands. "It's just that I hear it so much all the time it comes to my lips without thinking. I didn't have anything up my sleeve."

He took his hands down from his eyes and saw Angie looking at him across the table sympathetically.

"Why did you say it, then?" she said.

"I don't know," said Jim. "Maybe I thought I'd be coming up

with some kind of an idea in time. Maybe I just wanted to get rid of one problem. I did ask them to come and see the Crèche scene, on the evening of the last day, didn't I?"

"That's right," Angie said. "That's the message you told Hob to carry back to Secoh."

"Well, it's too late now, then," said Jim. "I doubt if they'd stay away after that, even if I went to see them in person and told them not to come. I tell you, Angie, it's having to do eighteen things at once that's driving me crazy. And it wasn't the wine, in case that thought had crossed your mind. I really didn't drink hardly any at all. But sitting there for all that time wore me out. All I wanted was to get things over with and forget them for a while. Like jumping out of a plane without knowing whether the parachute will open or not, but not caring any more."

"You're sure," said Angie, "there isn't something bothering you, you haven't told me about? Something you should have been telling me about?"

"Certainly not," said Jim.

Angie looked at him from under her eyelashes with a steady gaze.

"Well," said Jim, "there's one thing, perhaps. It's just a possibility, of course; and I didn't think it worth giving you anything to worry about as long as you had Robert to take care of, and all that. And anyway—"

"What is it?" asked Angie gently.

"Well," said Jim, "you remember there was that magician Son Won Phon who had questioned my use of hypnotism, claiming it was an oriental magic and I hadn't been properly taught by a magician who was an oriental instructor?"

"I remember it perfectly," said Angie.

"Well, anyhow," said Jim, "it seems he and some other magicians were a little upset over my being promoted to C rank when I really wasn't qualified for it—oh, by the way, you'll be happy to know I've just qualified for C rank. Just the last time I saw Carolinus, he told me I had."

"When was that?" asked Angie.

"Oh, a day or so ago, maybe a bit longer than that. Several days back, perhaps. It didn't seem particularly important, since I was being treated like a C anyway, and I've had so much to do. I should have told you, but it slipped my mind. Forgive me."

"That's marvelous, Jim!" said Angie. "But that isn't what you were about to tell me. Is it?"

"Not exactly," said Jim. "Or rather, it's part of it. To make a long story short, Son Won Phon and some other magicians evidently got upset because of that unusual promotion of me to a C-rank magician, when I technically still wasn't any more than a D—which is no problem now that I've qualified—but also because I was given that unlimited drawing power on magical energy. Their apprentices felt that they ought to have had a chance at something like that; and, well you know how it is . . ."

Jim let his voice trail off and smiled at her.

"Go on," said Angie.

"Oh," said Jim, "yes. Well, the rest of the story is that there's been something of a fuss about it; and there's a possibility, just a scant possibility, you understand, that a majority of the magicians might be brought to vote that they didn't want a couple of twentieth-century people like us interfering with the way history is developing here; and they might decide to deport us back to the twentieth century. When Carolinus first told me, it was before we'd decided to keep Robert; and of course I'd been thinking you'd be happy to be able to go back to the twentieth century. But, since you've found Robert . . ."

He ran out of words again.

Angie sat silent for a minute, looking more or less past him.

"Yes," she said. "Of course, Robert changed everything. I couldn't leave him to that Agatha Falon. I know what she'd do. She'd push him down a well, or smother him while he's sleeping; the way she started to do here before I walked in on her."

She got up suddenly, came over and sat down in Jim's lap, put her arms around his neck and kissed him.

"Poor Jim," she said, pressing her cheek against his. "No wonder you've been worried to death. You should have told me a long time ago you had this worrying away at you."

"There were some other things," said Jim guiltily. "I mean, it wasn't only that. I mean that wasn't, well—"

"Don't worry any more," said Angie. "Carolinus can take care of that problem, I'm sure of it; they won't send us back. You can relax and be sure of it, too."

"Yes," said Jim. "The thing is, though—"

He hesitated. Angie pulled back her head and looked at him suspiciously.

"Is there something more about this you still haven't told me?"

"Like what?" said Jim uneasily.

"Certainly, if they let us stay here, none of these other things will be all that important in the long run, will they?"

"Yes, and no," said Jim uncomfortably. "You see, there's a drawback to their leaving us here. If they did, they might take away any magic powers I have. I'd be left without any at all, permanently."

"Well, what of it?" said Angie. "We've done without it before. Most of the last three months, for example, you've been out of magic—or thought you were, before Carolinus told you you could get more from your unlimited drawing account. We'll hardly miss it. Maybe you can even stay home a little more, now."

"It's not that simple," said Jim. "You see, evidently the Dark Powers could want to get back at me. Because of the way I've spoiled things for them in the past, you understand."

Angie stared at him.

"You don't mean all the other magicians would just leave you defenseless to face the Dark Powers? And, even if they would, come to think of it, I thought Carolinus gave us the idea that the Dark Powers weren't like a human individual. I mean, I didn't think they'd want something like revenge, the way humans would. Like Sir Hugh de Bois, for example, would, because we took Malencontri from him?"

"Maybe not," said Jim. "But I don't know if, even without magic, I still wouldn't be something the Dark Powers would consider in their way. I mean, you and I are making a difference, in small ways anyway. Like the fact everyone here at the Earl's now knows all the words to 'Good King Wenceslas' and sings it, years before the carol was written. And besides, we've made differences even in Malencontri itself—in the castle, I mean."

He paused, waving his free hand in the air a little. "Plus, we may have made a difference in some of the vital elements of history, as when we all rescued the Prince from Malvinne. The Dark Powers wouldn't have to attack us for revenge. It'd be enough if they felt I was still a piece of grit in their machinery. They'd simply want me out of there. The way they do things, that would mean destroying me—possibly both of us—even Malencontri itself, and even close friends of ours, like Brian, Giles and Dafydd."

"And Robert!" said Angie, suddenly stiffening. She jumped up from his lap and stared down at him. "Jim, you've got to do something!"

"There you are," said Jim wearily. Angie swooped down, hugged and kissed him again.

"I didn't mean that the way it sounded," she said. "I mean *we'll* have to do something. I'll help as much as I can. What can I help you with?"

"Actually," said Jim, "nothing I can think of. The only possible things would be to let me off from being Saint Joseph, and you being the herald for Mnrogar. But you're right about my being needed for the Joseph role, and the fact that you couldn't be the herald—and they're small things compared with the bigger problems. I think probably the best you can do for me is just talk to Carolinus, as you said you'd do just now. If anyone can make him exert himself to the utmost, it'll be you."

"I'll talk to him, all right!"

Jim felt a little uneasy. Angie was like a loaded gun in one respect. You didn't want to point her at anyone you didn't want shot. On the other hand, she couldn't do any harm; and it just might be that with a little boost, Carolinus could be pushed to get them out of the current situation with the other magicians. Meanwhile . . .

He finished his tea.

"Well, I'd better get going," he said. "Brian will already be out with Mnrogar at that secret practice ground that Carolinus fixed somehow so nobody will ever blunder in on us to see what we're doing. And, for that matter, Carolinus himself might show up. If he does, I'll tell him it's important you see him right away. If it's anything less than important, he's likely to put it off or forget it. Sometimes I think he's getting more absent-minded all the time. Where's my sword belt and sword? Oh, there they are."

He belted them on.

"Well, I'll see you later in the day," he said, heading for the door.

"You might want to put on some more clothes," said Angie. "It's still winter outside."

"That's right," said Jim, brightly and falsely, making a U-turn. "I was just about to do that."

It was only a ride of five minutes or so from the castle to the area in the woods where Brian had been working so hard to get Mnrogar and the transmuted boar to behave like a proper Black Knight and horse at the tournament; but Jim made the trip on Gorp, his war horse, and with armor, shield and weapons.

There might be no need for all this martial preparedness; but no knight ventured far into woods, as they were at this time, without at least his sword; and in unfamiliar woods, he went prepared for anything—and preferably not alone. The fact that on the morning when Angie had gone out for the hawking Jim had encountered nothing but small parties of several people together, was not merely because these people were so fond of each other's company. It was a habit. If you had people with you, you had automatic allies in case something came up.

So Jim had gotten over feeling foolish about getting all dressed up to go a short distance like this. But even if he had not, he had reminded himself that he was not exactly sure where the practice area actually was.

Close to the castle as it seemed to be, it might actually be a good distance away. Because at no time in any of the days since they had first tried to get Mnrogar to behave properly in a suit of magic armor, and the boar to behave properly like a war horse, had they been intruded upon by any other guests, or ordinary denizens of the castle.

It was a question whether Carolinus had set up magic to transport them from a certain point close to the castle to some distant spot; or set up magic wards of some kind around the practice area that shunted off anyone who might be passing by close enough to see what they were doing.

On this morning, as usual, Brian was there before Jim and already at work with the magically transformed troll and boar. Both his squire, John Chester, and Theoluf, Jim's squire, were also there, to assist as needed.

Jim tethered Gorp with Brian's and two other horses, at some little distance from the very real-appearing lists, which had been created by a few sticks stuck in the snow, supplemented by Carolinus's magic. They looked for all the world like an actual jousting area with a barricade down the center, which was there so that two opposing knights could ride at each other on different sides of it, and so avoid the danger of their horses blundering together.

The whole space, except for the surrounding trees, was a perfect match for how the lists outside the castle would look tomorrow— Jim winced at the thought that the actual tournament was now only some twenty-four hours away—and that resemblance was both good and necessary, because the boar and Mnrogar both had to be trained under conditions as close as possible to those under which they were going to have to perform.

Most of this barricade, of course, was mainly illusion. But the central twenty feet or so of it had been made hard and actual by

Carolinus's magic. It was the only way to protect against the boar's natural tendency to try charging right through it at the opposing horse, and Mnrogar's natural tendency to get to close grips with his human opponent.

The thought of Mnrogar diving from the boar's back over the barricade at the last moment to grapple with a knight approaching him with spear and shield from the opposite direction had been a nightmare to both Brian and Jim. In fact, it was not exactly certain that they had trained both boar and troll into proper list behavior, even now. The trouble was, as Carolinus had pointed out earlier, that certain things in the animal and the Natural were instinctive; and so were not easily controlled, either by training or magic.

However, Jim headed toward Brian, who turned to meet him with a weary smile.

"Well, you know," said Jim, as he came up to his friend, "you have to admit they really look the part."

In fact, they did. Mnrogar was close to being believable as the Black Knight, in complete plate armor with a jousting helm—rather like an upside-down bucket, the bottom of which had been round rather than flat. A bucket with a slit cut into it for its wearer to not only see out of, but try to breathe through.

It was no wonder that knights who had to wear such full head-coverings in action avoided full beards in favor of being clean shaven, or perhaps wearing a small, neatly trimmed mustache and goatee, a manly display of hair that would not interfere with their breathing in the already confined space of the helm. The near unbelievability of Mnrogar, Jim decided, lay mainly in the inhuman width of his shoulders. His magically produced armor made them bulk even larger. But then it also made all of him look larger, so perhaps he would seem possible to the viewers at the tournament, after all.

At the moment, he was sitting completely still in perfect horseman fashion on a black horse the size of one of the massive Percherons Jim had seen once in the twentieth century pulling a brewery wagon in a parade. The towering, slim length of his jousting spear stood upright from its socket by his armored right toe.

The transformed boar between his legs was no less impressive. He also stood perfectly still, overwhelming in his size and utter blackness; and Jim felt a moment's yearning for such a horse himself—only a real one that size and a trained war horse to boot. Neither made a sound.

"Do they seem to be getting the idea at all?" Jim asked Brian.

"They have gotten better over time," said Brian. "Sometimes I think they may act without fault on the morrow. But no sooner do I think that, than Mnrogar will try to use his spear like a club, or the boar-horse will try to go through the barricade instead of running beside it. James, I don't think they can ever be completely trusted. We must take our chances when the hour comes, and only hope they behave as they should."

"Maybe Carolinus'll show up; and we can get him to give them some final finishing magic of some kind to make sure they don't misbehave," said Jim.

"By the Holy Trinity!" said Brian. "I hope so!"

"How have they been acting so far today?" asked Jim.

Brian scowled at the motionless armored figure and his black charger and turned away from them. Jim turned also to continue talking with him.

"So far today, I have not run them," said Brian. "We can do so now if you like."

"Let's," said Jim.

They turned back.

The knight and horse were still silent. But while Brian and Jim had turned their backs, the horse had lain down—not on its side in normal horse fashion but by doubling its legs underneath it. The knight was still in his saddle, but had his legs splayed out to keep from standing. Brian stamped over to the head of the horse.

"Get up!" he roared.

Clumsily, the horse climbed to its feet again and the knight put his feet back in the stirrups. Brian took the reins and led the horse forward a few paces, turning it slightly so that it was facing down along the right side of the barrier, which resembled nothing so much as a plank wall about four feet in height. Jim peered along it, to see if he could tell where the illusion part joined with the solid section in its middle; but he could find no seam or line to indicate a joining. Probably, he told himself, that was not surprising, seeing the whole thing was the result of magic— just one part was more solid than the other.

Brian was handing the reins back to the knight, who took them and held them in proper position in his right hand between his second and third fingers.

"Dress your shield!" snapped Brian.

Mnrogar already had his left arm through the straps with which it held the shield, and now he brought it forward into protective position, so that Jim managed a glance at the back of it, as well as at the blank blackness of the front. He had been curious as to whether it was all one solid piece, as he suspected the barrier was. But the shield seemed instead to be a duplicate of the real thing, obviously made of several layers of laminated wood with leather over it, the whole held solidly together in out-curving triangular kite-shape, with glue and rivets.

It could be the plate armor Mnrogar was wearing was also a faithful copy of the real thing. It would probably evaporate into nothingness after a certain length of time—probably after the tournament had been over for a day or so—as did all magic-made things, sooner or later. But for now it looked about as actual as everything else in sight.

"John!" Brian was calling to his squire. "Ready to sound the trumpet!"

Jim looked over, and saw to his surprise that John Chester was holding a long silver horn, of the kind that royal heralds used, but which were otherwise seldom seen.

"Where did that come from?" he asked Brian.

"What? Oh, the Mage," said Brian, "of course. John, one note!"

John Chester put the trumpet to his lips and sounded a remarkable silvery tone on the bright morning air. Nothing, however, happened, and Jim looked at Brian questioningly.

"When they're actually at the tournament," said Brian, "there will of course be a delay before another knight rides to the far side of the list to oppose them. It was Carolinus's thought that we should stay to an exact time in everything that the troll and the boar do, so that they will not be confused by differences between the practice and the real."

Jim nodded. They waited a few more moments, and then the figure of another knight in armor, with helm over his head and riding a bay-colored war horse, appeared on the other side of the barrier at its far end.

"Sound the ready note, John," said Brian.

Once more the horn pealed. The knight at the far end of the barrier—or the image of a knight—took his spear from its upright position in its socket and leveled it across his horse's neck with its blunted point aimed ahead and over the barrier.

Mnrogar did the same. His horse, however, now began to paw the ground and make small diving motions with its head right and left down at the earth.

"Is he still doing that?" demanded Jim.

"Of course!" said Brian disgustedly. "Once a boar, always a boar. All the magic in the world can't keep him from wanting to tear up the ground with his tusks to frighten his foe. I tell you, I've given up on that, James. I think it does no harm. It is somewhat strange behavior for a horse; but then Mnrogar with the width of his shoulders and all else is strange enough anyway, so that no one will think anything is amiss. The greater problem is the delay that occurs while the boar does this. But there's no help for it. However, you must remember to have the troll's herald insist that he be the one to sound the three separate notes to start the spear-running . . . there, the boar is done at last."

The horse had stopped his unhorselike antics.

"Sound for the running, John!" called Brian. "Now!"

A third note of the horn rang out, the figure of the knight at the far end of the list urged his horse forward, and Mnrogar and his black steed also went into movement, rapidly accelerating to a gallop. Mnrogar was now holding his spear level in proper position, across his saddle and pointed over the barrier where its point would make his first contact with the oncoming knight, as soon as he should come within reach.

Jim watched with fascination. He had seen this for some days now; but the whole thing was almost a little too real to be watched comfortably. The two armored figures sped at each other. They came together, the spear points contacted both suits of armor an instant before the horses passed each other; and the shape of the other knight went flying from his saddle, while his spear broke against the breastplate of Mnrogar's armor.

Mnrogar rode on, apparently not even jarred in his seat by the impact of the other lance.

It took twenty yards more for Mnrogar to rein his charger to a halt. Even then he had to jerk the head around, as the boar element of it strained to savage the illusion of the farther barrier with its presently nonexistent tusks. But Mnrogar's strength was more than equal to the task. He pulled the horse around, away from the barrier in a complete turn, and trotted back up to the end where Brian and Jim stood.

"There's nothing wrong with that!" said Jim happily.

"Yes," said Brian gloomily. "But will it always go off so smoothly at each spear-running? In short, James, have they learned their duty once and for all, or are they still capable of getting it wrong somehow, without warning?"

"I don't know," said Jim. "I don't suppose we'll ever know. We'll just have to risk it. Turn them a few more times and see if they're still doing it right."

They did. Mnrogar and the transformed boar performed beautifully.

"I don't really see anything wrong with it," said Jim. "Why don't we just consider them ready—unless you can think of some specific other thing that needs to be worked on?"

"Well," said Brian, more cheerfully than Jim had heard him speak so far, "you may be right, James. Perhaps it would be just borrowing trouble to look for anything else. I agree with you. So far today they've done everything excellently. There are little things, of course—"

He broke off, looking past Jim, who had his back to Mnrogar and the boar-horse at the moment, the two having just returned from their latest run and come back to take up position in the same spot where Jim had seen them when he had first ridden in this morning.

"There's that, of course."

He nodded at whatever was behind Jim and Jim turned. What he saw was that the boar-horse had lain down again, but completely on his side this time. Mnrogar appeared to have gotten off on time. He was standing, wide-legged, a little back from the animal—an even more impressive figure if that could be imagined, now that he was on his feet instead of in the saddle.

The boar had evidently decided to roll. He proceeded to do so now, grinding the saddle on his back into the snow and frozen earth beneath.

"Stop that!" shouted Jim, stepping toward the imitation horse. Brian caught his arm and held him back.

"It's all right," he said. "He does that every time he loses interest in running the list and decides to take a rest. But for some reason, magic, no doubt, it does no hurt to the saddle and gear."

Jim relaxed. Of course, the saddle was as much a piece of unreality as all the other out-of-the-ordinary things around them. Mnrogar was taking off his helmet; and in a moment his menacing troll face glared at them from above the steel-clad shoulders.

"John! Theoluf!" snapped Brian. "Assist Mnrogar from his armor."

The two squires came forward and began to obey.

"But there is one matter, James," said Brian. "One point you must make most clear to any herald you find to do the troll's speaking for him. It must be made very clear that Mnrogar will not accept whatever prize is offered to the winning knight of the day. He must say he scorns any such token, wanting only to show those here that none have any hope of unhorsing him."

Jim stared.

"But Brian, that would ruin the whole point of doing this!" Jim said.

It was as if the world had just come tumbling down around his ears all at once. The Black Knight had to win the tournament prize. How else could Mnrogar have the chance to ride slowly past all the guests in the stand and smell out the disguised troll among the guests?

Surely, Jim thought, he had gotten this clear to Brian earlier? Or had he?

CHAPTER 30

Clearly, decided Jim, he had not.

Brian was staring at him with a stern, cold look on that usually cheerful, friendly face, a look that Jim had never seen on him before.

"Surely, James," Brian said, "you did not think I would lend myself to the making of an occasion on which a troll, unfairly kept in magic armor and mounted on a magic steed, and trained beyond anything of which he would be normally capable, would win the day against belted knights who have won their sword and spurs, each by proof of courage and virtue in true combat against their equals? It is one thing to make a play or a show for some good end, or for the amusement of all; but to appear to shame all chivalry and true, brave gentlemen by making them to seem less than a denned, foul creature, which all men rightly normally destroy on sight—and which, by Saint Anthony, without magic armor and magic horse, would run like a hare from an armored knight with lance in hand and a-horse!"

"Of course! Yes, I know what you mean," said Jim hurriedly. His mind was scrambling desperately for the proper answer. "You're quite right, Brian. I'll admit my own fault, and shame for that matter, for not having thought the matter through to what should have been so obvious to me. Of course, you're right. Mnrogar must not win the day. At the same time, Brian, he has to have a chance to ride up along the stands to smell out the disguised troll there. Let me think."

He thought desperately. Brian waited, his face still stern and judgmental.

"I have it!" said Jim, on a sudden flash of inspiration. "Of course! There wouldn't be any shame to any of the knights being overcome, once it was realized that the only reason they failed to win was because there was unfair magic on the side of their opponent. Would there?"

For the first time, Brian's face relaxed a little.

"If all present know," he said. "But, James, what is the purpose of keeping his real person and nature hidden in the armor and with the blank shield, if it is to be revealed afterward that it was all only magic?"

"He only has to stay hidden up to a point," said Jim eagerly, "because if he didn't, the troll in the stands could suspect what's up, and decide to escape. Whoever the disguised troll is, he'll want to get away the minute he, in his turn, smells Mnrogar inside the black armor. It's true, trolls don't seem to have the nose for things that Aargh has; but if the breeze is from the list to the watchers, the troll in the stands could scent Mnrogar as soon as he appears—"

"There is no guaranteeing the direction of the wind tomorrow morning," said Brian grimly. "I fear me what you hope for, James, is impossible—"

"No!" said Jim. "No, it's not. I just thought. Just before Mnrogar comes out of the tent or appears on the scene—however we bring him in—I can magically deprive everyone in the stands of any sense of smell they have."

Brian looked startled, then baffled.

"Everyone, James?" he asked. "Why everyone? Why not just the troll who is in disguise?"

"I would if I knew who the troll in disguise was," said Jim. "But since I don't, I'll simply take away the sense of smell of everybody in the stands for as long as Mnrogar is jousting with the other knights; in fact, until he comes close to the stands. The troll we want to uncover may notice that his sense of smell is gone, since it's keener than a human's; but I don't think he'll take alarm from that alone. Everyone else—the real humans— probably simply won't notice they aren't picking up odors. Would you, Brian, if you suddenly stopped smelling anything?"

"Sooner or later I would," said Brian slowly, "but, it may be you're right; in special, with the excitement of the tourney before them."

"And even if they do," said Jim, carried away on his own inspiration, "there's nothing in that that would make them suddenly get up and leave the stands, now is there?"

"Leave, while spear-runnings are going on?" said Brian. "Just because they smell nothing? Such a thing as a sense of smell suddenly lost may be cured, or not—as God wills—after the tournament. No one would certainly leave, even if they were aware."

"That's what I was thinking!" said Jim.

"But you have not answered my first concern," said Brian, becoming stern again. "If Mnrogar should carry all before him, then he will surely come forward to claim the prize, since that is what you intend; and the unfairness of knights being conquered by unfair means of magic stands. So what use this keeping all there from smelling anything?"

"Oh, as far as the unfairness of it goes," said Jim, "remember what I just asked you. If it was known the Black Knight was a troll in magic armor, and with a magic steed, who because of these unfair advantages had been able to unhorse true knights—then any shame to anyone who'd been unhorsed by him would cease to be. How could there be any reflection on the knight who lost, when, against magic, he was helpless to win? You agree to that, don't you?"

"True," said Brian, frowning. "But how to have matters happen so all discover that Mnrogar is, indeed, but a false knight?"

"It should be easy, Brian," said Jim. "Look—Mnrogar wins over everyone who rides against him and comes forward as if to claim the prize. But before he can, I'll have him take off his helm—and everybody's going to see he's only a troll. So the only way he could have won had to be with magic—which makes him unfit to win any prize. Otherwise, how could gentlemen of prowess be unhorsed by a creature that knows nothing of riding or lance-work? All there will understand at once."

Jim held his breath, staring at his friend, mentally crossing his fingers that Brian would not suddenly find some further objection to this solution to the problem.

For a moment Brian's frown deepened. He stared over at Mnrogar, then down at the snowy earth at his feet, trampled and marked by human footprints and horses' hooves. But then he looked up at Jim, with a smile forming on his face.

"You will surely be able to do this, James?" he said. "Not merely take away the fact that those present might smell anything, but that Mnrogar should lift off his helm for all to see?"

"That's what magic's for!" said Jim, beginning to breathe again. "But I swear to you, if anything goes wrong, you've got my word for it, that I'll acknowledge to everyone there, to the Earl and every guest—I'll explain the magicking of the boar and Mnrogar; and about the other troll in disguise among them. All, except that I won't mention that you were the one who trained Mnrogar and the boar."

"Ah?" said Brian. "Yes. Yes, that would be good of you, James."

"There won't be any need to mention that part of it, even if I have to explain—and I'm sure I won't have to," said Jim. For the first time in days he had an irrational feeling that everything tomorrow would go the way it should. A faint memory troubled him for a moment with the thought that every time he could remember feeling like this before, something had gone wrong. However, enough of a sense of relief was bubbling inside him now that he positively beamed at Brian.

"Also, Brian," he said, "the excitement over Mnrogar's finding the troll hidden among them should take their minds off anything else."

"To be sure," said Brian. "There is that, too. To say nothing of the fact the troll and boar both ran through their paces this morning without a fault. If you're satisfied now about the way Mnrogar is to act, then I believe I, too, can trust them. We can look forward to tomorrow with confidence."

He was his old, cheerful self. It was, thought Jim, an excellent moment to end their conversation. He struck his forehead with the heel of his hand.

"Good Lord, Brian!" he said suddenly, "I just remembered. I'm supposed to meet Angie back at our rooms. She may be waiting there for me now. Can I leave everything here in your hands, then? You'll forgive me if I leave suddenly, now?"

"Certes!" said Brian cheerfully. "Tarry not. On your way!"

Jim went.

As it turned out Angie was indeed waiting for him, in the front one of their two rooms, when he came into it.

"Hah!" said Angie. "There you are. A good thing, too. You'd better start getting dressed for dinner right away. We've come in late too many times. This is our next to the last dinner; and for once we're going to be among the early-birds."

Jim thought of pointing out to her that she had just used the medievalism she had made a point of asking him not to use; but he decided against it. Discretion—always the better part of valor, he reminded himself. But this dinner business was something else.

"Angie," he said, shedding his sword belt and sword, and beginning to get rid of the extra clothing he had put on against the temperature outdoors, "I've got three days' work to do yet between now and tomorrow morning. There're all sorts of problems—"

"Enough, so you don't need any more," said Angie. "The rest of the guests are beginning to talk again about how little you're around; and make guesses as to what you're doing when they don't see you."

Ahah! thought Jim; and undoubtedly some of those guesses would be like Brian's mistaken one—that he had become involved with another lady among the Earl's female guests. Angie should know better, but in any case the rumor could not be pleasant for her.

"A lot of them disappear from time to time," said Jim. "They either disappear, or they talk about it."

"You aren't them," said Angie; and Jim decided to steer clear of the subject. She went on. "You'll notice I'm already dressed."

Jim hadn't.

"Your saffron gown? The one you wore Christmas Day to dinner? I thought you'd save that for the last big meal, tomorrow."

"Most of them will be up all night tonight, or nearly all night," said Angie, "and probably in no shape to pay too much attention to how people are dressed at the last dinner. In fact, some of them are leaving right after it, because they have to be back home by some date or other. Anyway, this is all beside the point. The point is that they're beginning to notice and talk about you being missing so much. Agatha Falon may have had a hand in it—or in starting it, at least. At any rate, there're questions; and all I can say is, Mnrogar's uncovering of the castle troll had better explain everything to everybody; or there's going to be a lot of gossip circulating about us in the county during the coming year. Your clothes are laid out on your mattress there on the floor."

"I see them," said Jim, and started to put them on.

"What, exactly do you have to do between now and tomorrow?" Angie said, sitting down carefully in one of the chairs, with due regard for her dress, to watch Jim as he dressed. "And what happened this morning? You were going to go see how Brian was coming with Mnrogar and the boar-horse, weren't you?"

"I did," said Jim. "They went through their paces perfectly. But Brian almost upset the apple cart by reminding me it had to be made clear that any knights that joust with Mnrogar hadn't risked their reputations; and that if Mnrogar won, it was by magic and other unfair ways. I got it settled with him, though. The herald is going to announce the Black Knight isn't the least interested in any prize. He just wants to show that he can overthrow anyone who comes against him in the lists."

"Yes, that herald," said Angie. "Have you found someone to be a herald for you?"

"Not so far," said Jim. "I'm going to go back to Malencontri and see if I can't find somebody who can at least sit up there on the horse while I put words into his mouth, magically or otherwise. I did think of May Heather. I could magically make her over so that she'd make a good-looking little imp—you know, to match the devilish appearance of Mnrogar and his horse—but I don't really trust her to follow orders."

"No," said Angie. "For an eleven-year-old she's got got too much independence for this particular period in history."

They were both silent, thinking about it. May Heather was the youngest of the table service staff. She was not quite the youngest of all the servants who were concerned with the castle's food—there was a boy on the cooking staff who was actually two days younger than she was, but a little bit bigger—which wasn't saying much, since May Heather was not large.

The kitchen staff, of course, was usually in their wooden building in the courtyard, outside the castle proper. The actual presentation of the food at table was done from the serving room, next to the Great Hall, by the serving staff alone—after the food had been cooked in the kitchen and separately transported to the serving room.

The two staffs were independent, but there was a continuous movement back and forth among them, as dishes were carried from the kitchen to the serving room and what was left of what had been on them back to the kitchen again; and a rivalry had developed between May Heather and this particular boy, whose name Jim could not remember right now. It had escalated; and finally developed into a battle royal between the two of them in the courtyard, encircled by most of the other servants; who, medieval fashion, urged the combatants on, rather than doing anything to separate them.

Both May Heather and the kitchen boy had fought themselves to exhaustion, with May being adjudged the winner. Since then they had been very good friends; but with relative rank now established, May Heather being the superior and the kitchen boy her admitted inferior.

"No, not May," said Angie; and they both sighed.

May Heather would be an invaluable person to have around the castle, if she ever reached the point where she could be trusted to follow important orders—and managed to grow up in this dangerous world she had been born into—a sort of female Sir Brian in residence.

"Chances are, though," said Angie, echoing the thoughts of both of them, "she'll marry somebody and go off. In fact, we can almost count on it."

"She might marry someone else who's a retainer in the castle, or on the castle lands," said Jim.

"There's that," said Angie. "Why don't you sit down to put on your hose?"

"Because I want to keep my sense of balance in training," said Jim. "How many men do you know my age who can still stand on one foot and put something like this on one leg while he's doing it?"

"How many men do you think I've watched dressing since we came here to this fourteenth century?" said Angie. "Oh, Jim, that reminds me. I'll need one of the men-at-arms as a stand-in, to just be there and represent Joseph. I want to hold a rehearsal tonight, secretly. Enna can help, but I'll need the ox and the ass, and would you magic-up the walls and back of the stable for the scene? I assume you've already picked a secret place out in the woods where we can put on the play. Don't forget, the area of the manger has to be heated—you can do that with magic, too, can't you?"

Jim lost his one-legged balance completely. Luckily, there was a chair close enough so that he managed to fall into that. He stared at her.

"When do you expect me to get all this done, with everything else I've got to do?" he said. "Heat the manger? Why?"

"Because little Robert will be in it, of course," said Angie. "That's going to be the greatest, concluding effect of the play.

After it's all over, we'll invite the Earl and some of the chief guests up to actually step into the stall. They'll see all the way into the manger, then, and there'll be a living baby inside it. But it's got to be safe and warm for Robert there, as much as if he was in the other room here. Don't tell me there's any problem with that?"

"Any problem with that?" said Jim. "I don't know if I can even make the stable scenery by magic. Can't somebody else get the ox and the ass? Did you ask Theoluf?"

"Of course I did," said Angie, "but he said that somebody like you would have to get permission from the Earl, and one of his staff would have to go get them. I thought you could just magically bring some here from our own castle."

"I—Angie," said Jim desperately, "I may have all the magic energy I could ever need at my fingertips right now; but that doesn't mean I know how to use it. I've never used magic to build anything. I've never used it to warm anything—to make a sort of indoor temperature when it's outdoors. And I've only used it to move myself from place to place. How do I use it to go get an ox and an ass for me from forty miles away, or whatever it is, when I don't know which ox or which ass, or where they are about our castle or lands right now?"

Angie, who had gotten up from her chair a little earlier, sat down in it again and looked at him.

"Jim—" she said.

"Well, now, wait a minute," said Jim; for, clearly, she was seriously upset. "I haven't explained that to you before, and so maybe it's partly my fault; but you could have asked me a little earlier."

"Evidently, I should," murmured Angie.

"Well, it isn't the end of the world," said Jim. "First, let me talk to Theoluf myself."

He visualized Theoluf standing in the room in front of him, having come from wherever Theoluf happened to be at the moment. This new visualization method of his of making magic was a lot faster and easier, he told himself with some satisfaction— and right upon the heels of that idea came the sudden realization that he, Jim, was now inside the castle, where his magic was prohibited. He sighed, and went to the door to have the guard there send for the squire.

But in fact, Theoluf was already outside the door, having apparently just arrived by his own doing. Jim wondered fleetingly if some sort of instinct was at work inside that useful head.

"Theoluf," said Jim, and cleared his throat, "ah—come inside."

"Yes, m'Lord."

"Now, tell me," said Jim, when they were inside the room with Angie, "what you know about getting an ox and an ass for Lady Angela's play. There ought to be some way we can get those two animals locally."

"Oh, there's no trouble getting them here, m'Lord," said Theoluf. "I talked to the Earl's High Steward; and he said there was both an ass and an ox that could be brought here within the hour, if he had authority from the Earl to bring them."

"Well," said Jim, deflated, "that takes care of that."

"Oh, no, m'Lord!" said Theoluf. "A couple of silver shillings should do it, though you might have to give him three."

"Oh? Oh!" said Jim, waking up to the fact that Theoluf was simply talking about the commonest way of getting things done unofficially in this particular century. "You're sure the steward would bring them for three shillings?"

"Oh yes, m'Lord," said Theoluf.

"Do you know where he is now?" said Jim, fishing in his purse for coins, and bringing out a handful from which he separated three silver shillings. "Offer him two first, of course. You know where to find him?"

"Oh yes, m'Lord," said Theoluf, "he's just downstairs. And of course I will only offer him a shilling first, and then work up. Undoubtedly he will have the beasts brought to the stable, and I will take them from there. Where did you wish me to take them, m'Lord?"

Jim looked at Angie.

"Did you have any place particularly in mind, Angie?" he asked. "It'll have to be a place near the castle, of course, so the guests can get to it easily. Also it needs to be a place that both you and I've seen if I'm going to—er—handle it."

"How about that indentation in the woods where the Earl and Mnrogar had their talk?" said Angie. "You'd have to fix it somehow so that people in the castle couldn't see us rehearsing or anything like that. But it's easy to get to. If it wasn't for the fact that I don't want them to get any idea of what I'm going to show them ahead of time, I'd have liked to have it where they've got the tournament set up. The people watching could sit in the stands and watch, then. The trouble is, there's that barricade down the middle there; and I don't suppose you could take that away—

you know, the way you're going to do the other things?"

"I could not," said Jim. "It'll be a problem anyway, making sure nobody tries to wander into that area where Mnrogar and the Earl did their arguing. Carolinus has some trick of his own for keeping people away from things; but I don't know it. Carolinus?"

He looked appealingly and hopefully at the empty air of the room; but Carolinus did not appear.

"He's been deliberately avoiding me," said Jim to Angie. "No, it'll have to be the Earl and Mnrogar's meeting place; and I'll see what I can do about setting up some kind of wards that perhaps just make people uncomfortable if they come close to it. Also I'll have to magic-up a screen of trees to hide you; but I can do that because I remember how it looked from Mnrogar's viewpoint. Carolinus did show me that. See, Angie, anything I can visualize in my mind's eye, now, I can make by magic. But if I can't visualize, I'm helpless."

"Ah," said Angie.

Jim stopped talking for a moment and half closed his eyes, building a picture in his mind of how that space at the edge of the woods, with the table at which he, Mnrogar and the Earl had sat, had been. For a moment, there was only his effort to imagine it; and then suddenly he saw the clearing, as if it was being seen by an inner eye, sharp and clear.

"I think I've got that firmly in mind," he said. "Of course I can't work the magic from here, but if I step outside and do it right, you and anybody with you, or Theoluf by himself, can go out to that indentation in the woods; and seem to vanish from the sight of anyone looking out from the castle. All they'll see will be as if the woods had closed in that space."

"As I remember that clearing," said Angie, "there'll be enough space to hold all our guests of rank, and still have a good forty feet or so between them and the other end of the clearing—where we'll set up the manger scene."

Jim and Angie spent a few more moments discussing the manger scenery. Jim wanted to have his mental image clear for the moment when he could step outside the castle and implement his magic production. It was a matter of putting together part of an actual barn belonging to an uncle of his, as modified by information gained from Theoluf; and replacing the cows in two of its stalls, one with an ox and the other with an ass. In between was a larger open stall, with a manger built against the wall to hold food for whatever beast was in it. It was a bit of a struggle to make all the changes. But he ended up with a clear, sharp mental picture in the end, right down to some straw on the plank floor.

"Don't forget the heat," said Angie.

"Heat . . ." said Jim.

Well, that was not difficult. The original barn he remembered had been almost hot from the body heat of the large animals enclosed in it. Of course, it had also smelled of cow; but after a little effort, he was able to delete the smell, and just keep the warmth. Abruptly the visualization firmed up, the way the clearing in the woods had before; and once more he had the feeling that the necessary magic to produce it had been set in his mind, ready for release. He glowed inside.

"There, I've got it, trees, manger and all. It's a good thing you're having a rehearsal tonight, though," he said to Angie. "You'll have a chance to look at it and see if you want any last-minute changes. I won't be with you. I've got to go to Malencontri after dinner, as I say; and then possibly to the dragons at Cliffside, to see if I can talk them into coming to the right spot and doing what I want them to do, so that they won't trigger off an attack on them by the knights here—Angie!"

"What? What is it?" said Angie. "You made me jump!"

"I just had a magnificent idea!" said Jim.

He checked himself, realizing that Theoluf was still standing there, patiently waiting.

"Off you go," he said to the other man, "and if you mention any of this to anyone in the castle—"

He stopped himself just in time from uttering the words "I'll flay you alive!" Such an exaggerated threat would have been proper—even expected—if Theoluf had still been a man-at-arms; but now that he was Jim's squire, he was assumed to have acquired gentlemanly tact and responsibility.

"Fear not, m'Lord," said Theoluf. "None shall know."

He went out.

"What was it you were so excited about just now?" asked Angie.

"I just had a magnificent idea!" said Jim. "This will take care of what the dragons want, keep them safe, and do everything else to take care of them in one fell swoop. Angie, you remember the story also had dragons coming out and Saint Joseph being fearful until the young Christ spoke up and reassured him—"

"Of course," said Angie.

"Well," said Jim, "we can actually have a few dragons take

part in your Crèche scene. Actually, I think Christ must have been about two years old at the time of the Slaughter of the Innocents—but nobody's going to bother about that. The voice of the Holy Child can just speak from within the manger. He'll be out of sight of the audience. That was why I was so surprised that you wanted Robert there, instead of just a doll, or something like that. I was just going to make a voice come from inside the manger . . ."

His voice ran down, whatever else he was going to say lost in the spreading glow of triumph that had come to him with the inspiration of using the dragons in the play.

For the second time today, he felt in control of matters, instead of at their mercy.

"Now I know what I'll say to them at Cliffside this afternoon," he told Angie. "It couldn't be better if I'd planned their coming from the start. Everything's falling together the way it should."

"Of course," said Angie. "I said you'd always be able to handle any trouble when it came to a pinch."

He opened his mouth automatically to argue this—to name instances when he hadn't—when he suddenly understood what she was doing. He saw her smiling fondly at him. He smiled back. He loved her.

CHAPTER 31

Jim appeared on the dais holding the high table at Malencontri right in front of Gwynneth Plyseth, the mistress of the serving room staff, who was carefully examining the wooden surface of the high table for splinters that might snag one of her best tablecloths, once Jim and Angie were returned and a tablecloth was in use daily.

She screamed at the sight of him; but it was a purely automatic scream, since she had recognized him almost the second he had appeared; the staff of Malencontri had almost gotten used to their magician Lord appearing out of nowhere at unexpected times.

There had been some grumbling about this at first; and a deep suspicion that perhaps Jim was attempting to catch them doing something they shouldn't, or failing to do something they should. But time had convinced them of Jim's innocence in this regard; and they had all come to take a proprietary pride in Jim's appearances. Very few castles could boast a Lord and master who might suddenly appear before you at any hour of the day or night.

In short, while it was a feather in their cap to have a magician as their overlord, it was even more so to have an *active* magician. Anyone lucky enough to have Jim appear within a few feet of him unexpectedly had a story to tell for the rest of his life.

Jim became aware that Gwynneth was bobbing a curtsy at him. It was a rather abbreviated curtsy, neither her years nor her figure being adapted to anything more extensive.

"Would my Lord care for a bite and sup?" she was asking.

"No, no," said Jim.

He had become expert, these last eleven days, in the art of appearing to eat one of the lavish holiday dinners, without actually overstuffing himself. Nonetheless, at the moment he felt as if he was not likely to want any more food and drink for another twenty-four hours at least.

He looked at Gwynneth. She was a sensible, experienced woman, who was knowledgeable about every person in the castle and on the Malencontri lands. He could probably do worse than to at least listen to her opinion.

"Gwynneth," he said, "I need someone from the castle or the lands who could act as a herald for me at the tournament that's to be held tomorrow at the castle of the Earl. Who do you think would be best for that purpose?"

"Herald, m'Lord?" echoed Gwynneth, frowning. "I know little of tourneys and heralds and such, m'Lord. They blow horns, I think. The one man who might be best at blowing a horn at Malencontri would be Tom Huntsman."

Jim winced a little, though internally. There was a community feeling among the servants, he knew, and a definite conviction on their part, that among Jim's faults was the fact that he did not seem to care for hunting the way someone of his wealth and rank should. In fact, he had already gathered that they felt sorry for Tom Huntsman, who was himself feeling slighted and unhappy because the lack of use of the castle's pack of hunting dogs. He had a deep suspicion that it indicated to the world, if not to Jim himself, a feeling that he and they were inadequate in some way.

Jim took a padded and backed bench at the table and sat down with his chin on his fist.

He considered Tom Huntsman. The man was very reliable; but hardly the image of the slim, tabard-clad figure Jim had been imagining. Tom Huntsman was a short, spare but erect, man in his forties; in superb physical shape from running with his hounds during a chase. He was clean shaven, his hair was gray and he usually smelled rather strongly of the kennels.

The one thing in his favor was that he had a remarkably resonant, carrying voice. Also, thought Jim, come to consider it, there was the fact that he could blow a hunting horn, which was ordinarily simply a cow's horn, fitted with a nipple. If he could do that, he probably could blow a herald's trumpet as well. Of course, Carolinus had already created a trumpet by magic; perhaps Jim could cause it to make its noise magically as well.

But actually, Tom Huntsman was a far from impossible suggestion. It was a shame, Jim thought, that he had to be responsible
for a situation that put the man in an uncomfortable light. The
truth of the matter was that neither Jim nor Angie liked hunting
at all. They had been brought up in the twentieth century, grown
up with loved pets and cartoon movies of cuddly animals, and
surrounded by a general attitude that one should be kind to
all creatures, feed the birds in the wintertime and help any
animal that had been hurt. Medieval hunting, with its break-
neck pounding after the chase, the savage yelping of the dogs,
their even more savage tearing at the chase once it had been
surrounded and pulled down and before they were beaten off
by the huntsmen—all this went directly against something deep
in both of them.

On the other hand, Jim knew very well that from the fourteenth-
century viewpoint, such feelings were nonsense. The meat from
beasts hunted and killed was a needed addition of protein to
winter-bound diets—if not that of the lord and lady in the castle, then at least to the servants in that same castle and even
those outside it. Wild game, from rabbits to boar or even bear—
although bears had just about become nonexistent in the south
of England by this time—was not only worthwhile but a necessary thing.

Still, he and Angie could not help feeling that the chasing
and killing was too much like a Roman holiday with games
in the arena—at this point in his thoughts Jim felt his elbow
nudged.

He lifted it and his head, to discover that a cloth was being
spread on the table and pitchers of wine and water, with a large
glass cup, had been set in front of him, together with some small
baked pies.

"Just in case your Lordship should wish something after all,"
murmured Gwynneth in his ear.

Jim managed to contain the sigh that started inside him. It was
no use. He had to sit here with food in front of him, if only because
that his servants would be uncomfortable if he didn't. However,
the interruption had joggled his thoughts off hunting back to his
problems; and it occurred to him that while Tom Huntsman might
not be the ideal herald himself—as someone who was deeply
involved with hunts, which meant deeply involved with the noble
class—he might have more knowledge of heralds than anyone else
in the castle at the moment.

Besides, at the moment he was the only lead that Jim had.

"Send him to me," said Jim to Gwynneth.

"Yes, m'Lord."

Jim waited. He never usually had to wait long for anyone who served in the castle, because normally they came at once, and came at a run. Absent-mindedly, he found himself dumping a little bit of wine into his cup. He stopped and filled it up with water. It was almost tasteless in the proportions in which he mixed it, but that was all to the good. He sipped at it, thoughtfully. His mind had automatically gone off to things he would need to tell the dragons at Cliffside.

One of the things to get very clear was where the dragons would stay, until it was time for them to come forward into the play— or some of them, Jim corrected his thought. There were over a hundred Cliffside dragons. That was a lot of dragon. Probably, the answer was just to have four or five of them come forward as representatives of the whole group.

Also, it would be a good idea to have them all warned to stay back among the trees, and not make any particular show of themselves. That would help keep the fighting men among the guests from getting either nervous or combative. In fact, it would be best if he announced to the assembled guests that dragons would be there; but he was putting a magic wall between them and the dragons, so that they could not get to the dragons, or the dragons get to them—on second thought, it had better be expressed only as "the dragons could not get to them"—

"M'Lord?"

He woke up from his contemplation of his cup and his thoughts to see Tom Huntsman standing in front of the table, with his cap in his hands.

"Ah, Tom!" said Jim as genially as he could make himself sound. "I'm afraid I haven't paid as much attention to the kennels as I should, what with being away from the castle, and having so many other things to do while I'm here. I trust the hounds are all right?"

"They do well, m'Lord," said Tom.

"How many of them are there now?" asked Jim.

"Twenty-nine, m'Lord," said Tom. "Harebell and Gripper died this last winter. But just a week gone, Styax, one of the younger bitches, gave us a good litter of nine pups, five of which I wager will make the pack, if they last through this winter."

"Good!" said Jim. "Very good. And they're all in good health, and that sort of thing?"

"They need exercise, m'Lord," said Tom.

There was not the least note of reproach in Tom's voice. Jim was quite aware that Tom exercised the hounds daily, taking them out for long runs, and in fact running with them through the woods. But he did not hunt with them. He called them in if they started on the trail of any scent at all. Actually hunting with the dogs was an occupation for people of higher rank than just the castle huntsman; even though he knew much more about it than any of those around him at any given time. So there was no sound of complaint to be heard in his words, now, but a sort of aura of censure radiated from him.

"Well, well," said Jim, "I must find time to go out with them soon. Yes, soon. However, Tom, that isn't the reason I wanted to see you. Lady Angela is arranging for a play to be given during our visit at the Earl's castle."

"Indeed, m'Lord," said Tom.

"Yes," said Jim. "And a need for someone to play the part of a herald has arisen. I thought you might know of someone who could act the part. He would have to know how to sit a horse, and to blow a herald's trumpet."

"There is no one in or about Malencontri who can blow a trumpet, m'Lord," said Tom decisively.

"Oh?" said Jim. "I thought it was very much like blowing a hunting horn."

"Not so, m'Lord," said Tom. "The nipple of the horn makes a note. The note is made on the trumpet when it is blown by the way the herald's lips are set on the open mouthpiece of the trumpet."

"Oh," said Jim again.

It occurred to him abruptly that he might be using that conversational sound a little too much. But in any case, if the huntsman was correct, Jim was going to have to make sure the trumpet was blown magically. But he still needed someone to sit in the saddle and hold it. He had already been planning to do the herald's speaking for him, in any case. He merely needed a body properly clothed on a horse—and even the clothing, the herald's tabard, could be provided magically.

"Well, never mind that, then," he said. "But who do you know we have in the castle, or on Malencontri's lands, who is fairly young—between fifteen and twenty, say—who can ride and sit straight in a saddle? Someone who could look like a herald, if he was properly dressed and placed as to appear one?"

"Well, there's Ned Dunster, m'Lord," said Tom. "He's a bright one, and bidable. He remembers his orders well. It's in my mind that he's seventeen years, now, but it may be he is a year or so younger. Shall I send him to you, m'Lord?"

"If you would, Tom," said Jim. "And—oh, yes, I was glad to hear about that new litter. If I can ever get around to using the pack, we should have some interesting hunts."

He felt like the sleaziest of dishonest politicians in saying what he did; but people of Tom's class were used to people of Jim's class promising things and then forgetting about them completely—and he did have to have someone to stand there and fill the part of herald when he introduced Mnrogar to the crowd watching the tournament. He felt even more guilty, as he saw Tom's face light up with at least a ray of hope.

"I'll send him to you right away, m'Lord," said Tom, and ran off.

He was back within minutes with Ned Dunster, a bright-eyed individual only a few inches taller than Tom Huntsman himself, and clearly on the knife-edge between the last of youth and the first of full manhood.

He was sturdily built, with straight, light hair that was brown and eyes of the same color, a square chin and an open face that was one of the naturally happiest faces Jim had ever seen.

There was a merriment like an aura around him. Not the slightly mischievous merriment that Jim was more used to encountering in a great many of these medieval people at moments, but a sort of continuous wonder and happiness—even surprise—at everything about him. It was as if, even after nearly two decades of life, he was still finding the world crammed with wonderful and interesting discoveries to be made. He came to a halt with Tom Huntsman in front of the high table.

"M'Lord," said Tom, "this is the kennel lad I told you about, Ned Dunster."

"M'Lord," said Ned, pulling off his very scruffy headgear, which might have looked something like a beret at one time but now was unrecognizable, except as a rag that would cling to the head, instead of falling off with the first nod or bow—the second of which Ned had just clumsily attempted.

"Ned," Jim said, "Tom Huntsman tells me that you can ride a horse."

"Yes, m'Lord," said Ned. "I started riding the miller's horses when I worked for him as a tiny lad, before I ever came to the castle."

"Good," said Jim. "I'll also want you to go through the motions of blowing a herald's horn."

"A herald's horn?" said Ned, staring at him. "Crave your pardon, m'Lord, but what's a herald's horn?"

"Like a hunting horn, you numbskull," growled Tom, "only made of iron or brass, but much bigger and not blown the same way."

"Yes, that's right, Ned," said Jim. "Because it's blown a different way, I won't need you to blow it. You just put it to your mouth and I'll make the horn blow itself. What I want you to do is ride out on a horse in front of a knight in black armor, put the horn to your lips, let it blow itself, and then sit still there while some matters are announced; then, when I tell you, turn around and ride back past the knight, and behind a tent from which you both came. Do you think you can do that all right?"

"I'll surely try, m'Lord," said Ned, half stammering—but, as Jim noticed, apparently more from excitement than from doubt of his ability to do the task successfully.

Jim's ear, sharpened since the matter of his singing to the other guests at the Earl's party, was barely aware of the actual speech of Ned, which the usual magic or whatever of this world normally turned into modern English for him. It seemed he was catching a faint hint of what might have been even a twentieth-century Somersetshire accent behind the actual sounds Ned was making, as if he was speaking in a broader dialect than that of Tom Huntsman. A slight emphasis on the *s*, sounding it almost like a *z*, seemed just at the edge of the young man's voice.

"Well, good," said Jim. "I'll count on you then. Now, in a short while I'll be leaving here; but I'll be back later this day to get you and take you magically to the castle of the Earl of Somerset. That's where we're going to put on a play in which you'll be a part actor."

"Me, m'Lord?" said Ned.

"Yes, you," growled Tom.

"So, stay around the kennels, where I can have you sent for quickly, when I next come," said Jim.

"He'll be there," said Tom. "There's a lot to do around the kennels, more than enough to keep him busy the rest of the day."

"Very good," said Jim. "I'll see you later then, Ned. Thank you for finding him for me, Tom."

"An honor, m'Lord," said Tom.

The two of them went off. Jim got up from the table and went into the serving room. He expected to find Gwynneth Plyseth there as usual; but it was between meals and she was gone. Pleased to be alone, Jim went over to the fireplace, in which a fire was always burning winter and summer; with its arrangement of suspended chains, swing-out handles and other devices, to hold laden platters of food close to the warmth, while they were waiting their turn to be served. There was nothing in the way of food waiting there now. Jim pushed aside a few of the swinging handles and yelled up the chimney.

"Hob-One!" he called. There was no answer. After a moment he called again.

"Hob-One!" he called again, more sharply. "Hob, I know you're there. This is your lord, James. Come down immediately."

Hob's face peeked into the room upside down from inside the top edge of the fireplace.

"You're really alone, m'Lord?" he asked.

"Do you see anyone with me?" said Jim, a little more snappishly than he had intended to. "Hob-One, when I call you, you come. You know with me you're safe, whether there's somebody with me or not."

Hob popped out of the fireplace and hovered in sitting position on a waft of smoke that had suddenly decided to go just outside the fireplace chimney.

"I'm very sorry, m'Lord," he said. "Pray forgive me. It's just a lifetime of having to be cautious . . . but I'll always come right away from now on, m'Lord. You can count on me."

"That's good," said Jim. "Because that's just what I intend to do. Now, I'm going to bring Secoh here to join us, and then we're going to go off and visit a number of other, larger dragons."

"Other dragons!" cried Hob, and leaped to Jim's shoulder, wrapping his arms around Jim's neck, and holding so tightly that Jim found some difficulty in speaking.

"Relax, now, Hob-One," he said. "Remember who you are, and where you are. You're Hob-One of Malencontri, and you're in Malencontri itself."

Hob's hold loosened.

"That's right," he said, with a fine combination of fearfulness and awe.

Jim visualized Secoh appearing on the floor before him. For a moment, as with his visualizations earlier, there was a feeling of effort—and then all of a sudden Secoh was there, looking startled. The startled look faded as he recognized Jim.

"M'Lord," he said, sitting down and trying hard to do his dragon equivalent of a courtly, human bow. "How did I get here?"

"I brought you—with magic," said Jim.

"Magic?" said Secoh.

"Magic!" said Hob-One, clutching Jim's neck tightly again. He had ducked around so that Jim's head was between him and Secoh. "Is Secoh there?" he whispered in Jim's ear.

"You know he is," said Jim. "Now you come around to my other shoulder and we'll talk with him."

"Oh, m'Lord," said Hob-One, trembling. "I couldn't," he whispered in Jim's ear. "I always stayed well out of his reach, before. He's so close, now. I don't dare—"

"Yes, you do," said Jim firmly. "Remember I'm with you. You're even holding on to me. There's nothing to be afraid of."

There was a pause, and then he felt Hob inching around the back of his neck until he gradually moved to where at least most of him had to be visible to Secoh.

"Hello, Hob," said Secoh.

"H—Hob-One de Malencontri," said Hob-One, but his voice trembled as he spoke.

"Greetings, Hob-One de Malencontri," said Secoh.

"G-greetings, Secoh," said Hob-One, still tremulously.

"Hob-One," said Jim, "is going with us, you and I, Secoh— to talk to the Cliffside dragons about how they're to come to the Earl's castle tomorrow and how they're to act at the Earl's tomorrow afternoon. It's very important they get things straight and do exactly what they're supposed to do. After I finish telling them, I want you to stay with them until they're ready to come. Then fly over with them, and make sure they follow my instructions exactly. You can handle that?"

"Of course, m'Lord," said Secoh grimly. "They'll obey, or else!"

"Now, there's something more," said Jim. "Hob-One here, is much braver than most hobgoblins, but he's a little bit worried at meeting all the Cliffside dragons at once. He doesn't know them the way he knows you—"

"That's right!" said Hob.

"—And I thought maybe you could assure him there's no need for him to be afraid; using yourself as an example of someone who has no fear of anything."

"That's true," said Secoh. "I fear nothing—and, hobgoblin, I

too used to be fearful. But I learned that there is never a need
to be."

"No need for you, maybe," said Hob-One. "You're a dragon."

"I'm a small dragon," said Secoh. "A mere-dragon. One of a
line of our race that's been badly stunted by the evil effects of
the Loathly Tower, in the meres where we've always made our
home."

"The Loathly Tower?" echoed Hob-One. "The *Loathly* Tower?
Is that near here?"

"Some little distance," said Secoh offhandedly.

"Oh, my!" said Hob.

"Why do you whimper?" demanded Secoh. "Near or far, it
makes no difference. Large dragon or small, it makes no difference. I was with m'Lord James and other Companions, including
Smrgol, a wise old dragon, who taught me that fear is something
to be disregarded. With him I fought a dragon much larger than
myself, and won."

"Oh!" said Hob. "Are there dragons much larger than you?"

"Many," said Secoh. "And very much larger. They don't bother
me. If one of them offends me, I go for his throat!"

"You do?" Hob stared. "But if they're bigger than you, don't
you realize what one of them might do to you?"

"No," said Secoh, "never think about that. There's only one
rule in fighting. Don't wait—go for their throats!"

"That's all right for you, of course," said Hob. "You've got all
those big teeth."

"You've got teeth," said Secoh.

"Well, yes," said Hob. "But they're very little teeth."

"What does the size of teeth have to do with it?" said Secoh
fiercely. "It's going right at them that counts!"

Hob clutched Jim's neck tightly.

"Oh, m'Lord," he said in Jim's ear, "I could never do that! We
hobs aren't dragons."

"That's the sort of thing I used to say," said Secoh. " '*Oh, I'm
only a mere-dragon*,' I used to tell everyone. Hah! When we go
to the Cliffside dragons, just watch me—how I talk to them, how
I deal with them! You'll see!"

"M'Lord," said Hob in Jim's ear again, "do I have to go?"

"I'm afraid so," said Jim. He had been working up the
visualization of the main cave where the Cliffside dragons all
got together on important occasions, and now he had it firmly
in mind. "Here we go now, all three of us."

CHAPTER 32

Jim visualized his goal; and they were instantly in a place that at first seemed very dark, but got brighter as their eyes adjusted.

It was an enormous cave with a high arching roof and a bowllike floor with a single vertical rock wall between them, so that the whole cavern was like a natural amphitheater, deep in the rock that was the Cliffside dragons' home.

The wall and ceiling were of some dark granite. But they were patterned with a perfect lacework of streams of what appeared to be molten silver, each stream no thicker than a pencil, but all together covering the walls thickly. Each of the slim lines of silver radiated light—something more than a glow, and something less than the more customary illumination such as a candle or even a low-wattage light bulb might give.

The result was—and it became apparent as their eyes finally reached full adjustment—that the full cavern, including its dark, overarching natural roof, was generally lit by these streams. It was not as bright as a day—or rather, it was about as bright as a day overcast with thunderclouds. At the moment there were only a few dragons present, a couple of them talking and the rest simply passing from one of the many entrances into the cavern over and out by another of the entrances.

Jim summoned by magic one of the padded and backed benches from his own Great Hall, and sat down. Hob-One was still on his shoulder. Secoh sat down on his haunches—not a normal position for a dragon to adopt, but he had stuck to it steadily since he had been visiting Jim at Malencontri and had to do with Jim and other humans.

"What happens now?" whispered Hob-One in Jim's ear, but also looking over at Secoh as he spoke.

"We wait," said Jim.

They waited.

Little by little dragons began to drift into the cavern. These came in through all the different entrances, and tended to gather together near the entrances to talk in low voices, so that only a deep rumbling but no intelligible words reached Jim, Hob and Secoh, waiting down at the low point of the bowl-shaped floor.

However, as more and more came in, those near the wall moved farther down into the cavern; and there was a general shift in the direction of Jim, Hob and Secoh, happening as if it was nothing more than the result of casual movements among the dragons wandering from group to group of their fellows.

Still, in about fifteen minutes, the cavern had reached the point of being about three-quarters filled. By this time Jim estimated that most if not all of the dragons of Cliffside were present; but they still tended to cluster up close to the surrounding wall.

But then a new movement began. A sort of leapfrogging from position to position in groups; and the tide of great bodies flowed forward down the slope of the floor until the whole mass was solidly in place before Jim, Secoh and Hob-One. All this was accompanied by more of the low muttering among the dragons. But when at last they were packed solidly around the visitors, the muttering died away; and there was a dead silence in the cavern.

"*Jim!*" cried a large dragon in the front row, his incredible bass voice making the single word bounce off the walls of the cavern. There was a note of surprise in it, as if Jim had just that second materialized in front of his eyes.

"Gorbash!" replied Jim. Gorbash was the only dragon there who called Jim by that version of his name, rather than "James." It was a special mark of intimacy between them.

Indeed, they had been intimate, since it was Gorbash's body Jim had occupied; controlling it, in spite of Gorbash's own wishes, from the moment Jim had arrived in this fourteenth-century world right up through the ending of the fight at the Loathly Tower.

Gorbash was a dragon who had been generally considered not too bright by the other members of the Cliffside community, and unimportant. But he had gained remarkable stature in their eyes by his association with Jim; and he had exploited this to its limit, to the point where the other dragons at least listened to him before arguing with him nowadays—and listening was something any dragon found hard to do. Argument was built into them, so to speak.

Whether the Cliffside dragons, as a community, liked Jim himself, Jim did not know. They were perfectly capable of liking another individual, as Secoh and Smrgol, the now-dead great-uncle of Gorbash, had demonstrated. They just never gave any indication of it. Also, they were very touchy, and inclined to be wary of Jim. It was hard to believe that creatures so large and fierce should need to be wary of anything. But the fact was that only lately—in the last few hundred years—they had become aware that there was an even fiercer and more dangerous species, in this world, than they were.

This was the species to which Jim belonged, which the dragons called "georges" after the Saint George who had gone down in history by slaying a dragon single-handed. Even now, it was only the younger dragons that would risk stopping to talk to a george if they found one out in the fields, or away from other georges, or the buildings in which georges usually lived.

The thought of that, now, reminded Jim that if anyone here did really like him, it would be the younger dragons.

For that he had Secoh to thank. It had been Secoh, with his storytelling of the battle at the Loathly Tower, including his own part in it—and other adventures in which he had been with Jim, Brian and other nondragons—that had won the imagination and admiration of the young dragons. There were no young dragons down near the front of the crowd that faced him now. Young-sters—dragons under a mere hundred years of age—were crowded to the back of any gathering like this, since they were still juvenile and unimportant.

Gorbash, on the other hand, was a sort of fair-weather friend, Jim was aware. Gorbash's connection with Jim had given him status; but he would back Jim only so far—and then, only as long as it seemed useful to him.

"Well," boomed a short, broad dragon, also in the front rank, about three bodies over to the left of Gorbash, "when do we get to go to the Earl's castle?"

It was very like dragons to be slow about getting around to speaking and then immediately jump right into the heart of whatever was to be discussed.

"That's why I'm here—" Jim searched his mind frantically for the name of the dragon who had spoken. A white scar along the upper part of his muzzle happily brought back the elusive memory. "—Lamarg. I made this trip specially to tell you all about it. It'll be tomorrow—"

All at once the whole dragon community was talking among themselves at once.

"What did he say?" "He said tomorrow." "It should have been before this!" "No, at the end is the best. He was saving it for us." "Shut up, Maglar, you never know what you're talking about!" "Tomorrow—that's just after *tonight*!—"

Eventually the interchanges died down and there was quiet in the hall again.

"We don't have to pay for any of this, do we?" demanded Lamarg.

There was a growl from the assembled dragons, seconding this pertinent question.

"Not a thing," said Jim. "All you have to do is follow what I tell you to do, exactly. I want you to go there and come back safely; but to do that you're going to have to do precisely as I tell you. And Secoh's going to go along with you to remind you if you happen to forget any of the things that you have to do."

More general conversation at this. Some cries of "He's only a mere-dragon!" from anonymous members safely hidden in the crowd. Secoh bristled, dragon fashion, half raising his wings.

"Why does it have to be him, James?" protested Lamarg. "It could be one of us. He's not even a Cliffside dragon."

"Because I know more of things like this than any of you, Lamarg. Who else here has a tenth of my experience with georges?" snapped Secoh.

Lamarg growled wordlessly, but did not continue the argument.

"Also," put in Jim to calm tempers, "because Secoh's been with me and fought alongside me so many times he's the most likely one to know which way I'd want you to do things, if an emergency comes up. Now that makes sense, doesn't it?"

The Cliffside dragons talked it over for two or three minutes. Finally they came to the conclusion that it did make sense.

Jim waited patiently. The process of doing anything with the Cliffsiders as a whole was always a lengthy one, but there was nothing to be done about that. Meanwhile, however, it gave him a chance to speak a private word to Secoh.

He leaned over and spoke in the mere-dragon's ear.

"Secoh," he said in a low voice, "I'm going to tell them you'll give them the word when it's time to go to their place by the Earl's castle. It'll be near a clearing you'll see from the air. There'll be a lot of people standing at one end of the clearing, then there'll be Lady Angela, myself and possibly some other people, plus an ox and an ass, putting on a play near the other end—"

"A play?" asked Secoh in a deep, but relatively quiet, conspiratorial whisper.

"That's when a story is acted out," said Jim. Then, as Secoh still looked doubtful, frowning at the word "act," Jim added, "Acting is when people do what was told about in a story. As if we went through the motions of the fight at the Loathly Tower all over again for people to see."

Secoh's head came up and his eyes lit up.

"Could we, m'Lord?" he whispered.

"Maybe," said Jim incautiously—and then hurried to add, "but it'll have to be sometime pretty far in the future before we think about it seriously."

A little of the light died in Secoh's eyes, but some was left.

"Yes, m'Lord," he said. "Where by this clearing do you want the Cliffsiders?"

"That's the point," said Jim. "I'd like them to come down in the woods—see if you can't find a smaller clearing some place, not too far away, and then come in on foot until they're right next to the clearing, behind those of us who are putting on the play. They should be far enough back in the trees, though, so that the people watching from the other end of the clearing can't see them. They can take advantage of the things that will be built for the play to more or less hide behind; but they have to keep their voices down."

"Why, m'Lord?" said Secoh.

"So none of those watching the play hear them. In fact, they should whisper," said Jim, "from the time they get there until the time they're called out. You'll hear my voice speaking in your head, telling you to come forward with five—only five of them—when the time's right. But until then they'd better whisper; because the whole point of the play is that there are supposed to be dragons in the story, but the people watching won't expect real dragons to be there until they come forward. It'll be just as it is in the story when Saint Joseph sees the dragons coming and is afraid; and the young Christ tells him there's nothing to fear."

"I see, m'Lord!" said Secoh. "I understand, now!"

"And you'll remember all this, won't you?" said Jim.

"M'Lord! A dragon never forgets!"

It was true enough—in fact, only too true. They not only remembered, they kept on talking about what they remembered over and over again for hundreds of years. The discussion among the Cliffsiders had quieted down again by this time, and they were waiting to hear more from Jim.

"Secoh will tell you where and when to go, and how to behave yourself when you're there," he said. "But there's one important thing. No, two things. The first is that you stay hidden among the trees around a clearing until Secoh gives the word for a small number of you to move out, as representatives of all of you. Remember now, none of the rest of you are going to be forgotten. The representatives Secoh chooses will be allowed closest to the young Prince; but his blessing will be for all of you."

The Cliffside dragons had to talk this over too, but since there was apparently no choice in the matter, they finally quieted once more—all but Lamarg, who was still looking stubborn.

"What was this second thing you were going to tell us, James?" he demanded.

"Oh, that," said Jim. "I was just going to mention to you that when you're there in the woods, you just might by chance smell some trolls, or see a few around—"

An immediate growl erupted from the whole audience, mounting to almost a full-sized roar before it settled down again into near silence.

"We hate trolls!" said Lamarg; and there was a roar of agreement.

"I know you do," said Jim soothingly. "But I don't think any of them are going to get close enough for the rest of you to pay attention to them; and if you did start doing something about them, you might give your presence away to the people who are watching the play. That would spoil everything and, of course, you'd never get blessed."

"It would spoil the blessing?" asked a dragon voice from the crowd.

"It would," said Jim.

"Then they just better not come too close," said Gorbash. "If they spoil everything—"

This, coming from the dragon who—in spite of the fact that he was always careful to hide the fact—was probably the most peaceable of all the dragons there, gave a pretty good index of the dragon reaction if the trolls encircling Mnrogar's territory showed up. Jim winced internally. A free-for-all of the dragons against the trolls would be almost as bad as a mêlée between the dragons and the Earl's guests.

Jim wished he had given this aspect a little more thought earlier. But there had been no time. It all went back, Jim knew, to something the dragons had always considered an insult: the fact that the early Vikings and other Scandinavian seafarers had used to take down the dragon-heads of their ships when they came into shore, because they thought the sight of the dragon heads would infuriate the trolls of the land.

"I repeat," Jim said, "the trolls are nothing to worry about. I just mentioned them because I was concerned some of you might say something out loud if you saw them, or do something that would let the people watching the play know that you're there ahead of the time you're due to come out and be blessed."

The dragons muttered, but agreed—all except Lamarg, who still seemed in a bad mood. He was staring at Hob-One now.

"And what's that little thing got to do with our going to the castle? This is our business, isn't it? How's he come into it?" demanded Lamarg abruptly.

"This," said Jim, "is Hob-One de Malencontri. The hobgoblin of Castle Malencontri, who is my special messenger; and if need be he can carry a message between me and Secoh for all of you, when we're all gathered together tomorrow at the scene of the play."

"What's a hobgoblin?" growled Lamarg.

Secoh moved forward a couple of steps toward the other dragon.

"He lives in a fireplace in Malencontri, Lamarg!" he said. "That's all you need to know."

"What's a fireplace?" snorted Lamarg.

"A place where a fire is lit and is kept burning," said Secoh, his wings half lifting. "Hob-One lives with and just above the flames of a lit fire. How would you like to do that, Lamarg?"

"I'd be a fool to get close to fire," said Lamarg. "And I'm not a fool, Secoh. You're going to push one of us too far, mere-dragon—see if you don't!"

"I'm not pushing," said Secoh. "I'm just pointing out something. You wouldn't like to get close to fire, but it doesn't bother Hob-One de Malencontri. What does that tell you about what he's like? Do you think he's so little and unimportant, if he can be happy in a place that you wouldn't get close to? I repeat, he lives with flames, Lamarg!"

"A fire-imp!" said Lamarg, abruptly backing up half a step—which was as far as the dragon bodies behind him allowed him to retreat.

On his shoulder, Jim felt movement. He looked. Hob had stood up, clinging to Jim's helm, and was literally inflating his tiny chest and squaring his shoulders.

"You'd like it if he was just a fire-imp, wouldn't you, Lamarg!" said Secoh, taking another step forward himself. "You'd be lucky if he was only a fire-imp. But he isn't. He's much more than that. He's a hobgoblin!"

"Hah!" said Hob-One, on Jim's shoulder.

"What did it squeak?" asked several dragon voices at roughly the same time.

"It said, 'Hah!,' Lamarg!" said Secoh. "Now you've made him angry."

"I'm not afraid of him!" said Lamarg, trying to retreat farther and finding it impossible.

"No. It's all right," said Hob, in the lowest tones he could manage. "I'm not angry."

"That's good," put in Jim hurriedly. "We mustn't have any ill feelings on a great occasion like this. I'm sure Lamarg and you will get along nicely, Hob-One. Now I think it's time Hob-One and I went. Secoh, I'll be in touch with you about final details by the way I mentioned between now and when you leave tomorrow. You'll be here, won't you?"

"Certainly, m'Lord," said Secoh. "I'll be ready and the Cliffside dragons will also be ready."

The hall erupted in a clamor of Cliffside voices, starting to announce just how ready they would be.

Jim took advantage of the hubbub to visualize the serving room at Malencontri again and—in no time at all, he and Hob-One were back in the serving room.

This time Gwynneth Plyseth was there. She gave a polite, small scream and curtsied to Jim.

"What would m'Lord like?" she asked.

"I would like Ned Dunster, if you can find him for me," said Jim.

"Immediately, m'Lord," she said. "He didn't think it was proper, a kennel lad like him, waiting inside the hall, though Tom

Huntsman had let him off from working any more at the kennels, since m'Lord might need him at any minute. I'll fetch him in a moment."

She ran out of the room.

"Hob-One," said Jim, "come down off my shoulder and perch some place in front of me, would you?"

The light weight of the hobgoblin vanished from Jim's shoulder and there was Hob-One, riding a waft of smoke from the fireplace, at eye level about a foot in front of him.

"I was hoping for a chance to speak to you alone in any case," said Jim. "I want you to come back to the Earl's castle with me, and stay there. I need you there in the chimney of the fireplace in the outer room the Lady Angela and I have there, to give the alarm, if anyone who shouldn't be there comes in. When you're above the fire in a fireplace, can you hear everything that's going on in the room, or even come down and take a quick look and go back up again before anybody could get a good look at you?"

"Easily," said Hob-One, with what was almost a tone of authority. "I mean—easy, m'Lord. I can be up the chimney out of sight and still know everything that goes on in the room."

"That's good," said Jim. "Because I'll want you to keep a watch there as long as we're using that room; and send me a warning—all you'll have to do is think of me and talk to me in your head; and I'll hear you and answer you. Do you think you can do that?"

"Without a doubt," said Hob-One. "What sort of people who shouldn't be there do you fear—I mean, do you expect, m'Lord?"

"Anyone who's not usually there," said Jim. "The usual people are the Lady Angela, myself, a serving woman named Enna, a wet nurse and young Robert Falon, who is a baby. People who are unusual visitors would be any man-at-arms not normally stationed inside the room, or any visitor, even if Enna or the wet nurse lets them in—or, for that matter, any servant who wants to come in, and is let in by Enna or the wet nurse. There is a Lady Agatha Falon among the guests there, who's an aunt of young Robert, and whom we suspect of having ill intentions toward him. She probably would not come herself, but she might send somebody else to do him harm. So you simply let me know the minute any person comes in who isn't usually there. You can do that?"

"Certainly, m'Lord!" said Hob-One. He was still sitting on the waft of smoke, but Jim now noticed he had his shoulders squared, again, and his chest inflated, as they had been in the dragons' cavern, after Secoh had hinted to Lamarg that Hob-One might be related to a fire-imp—one of the servants of the King and Queen of the Dead—and normally never seen by above-ground living creatures.

Rumor had it that the fire-imps were either beings made of fire, or were continually on fire, themselves; so that they would reduce to ashes any ordinary individual who was touched by them. But suddenly Hob-One's chest deflated. "I mean—I'll do my best, m'Lord," he wound up.

"I know you will Hob, Hob-One," Jim said, "and in any case—"

But he was interrupted by Gwynneth bringing into the room Ned Dunster. Having delivered the young man and done her duty, she curtsied and went out, leaving them alone.

"Well, Ned," said Jim, "we're going to take a short trip, now."

"Yes, m'Lord," said Ned. But his gaze had left Jim and focused upon Hob, perched on the waft of smoke. The young man's eyes widened.

"You!" he said to Hob-One. "You took me for a ride on the smoke once years and years ago when I came to the castle with the miller to deliver flour!"

"I never did," said Hob-One.

CHAPTER 33

"But you did!" insisted Ned. "It was nighttime, just about this time of year, and there was snow on the ground; and I'd been let in to sleep to keep warm, and I woke up and I wandered in here, and there you were and you took me. We went out over the snow and among the trees and I was warm all the way and it was the most great thing that ever happened to me. You can't have forgotten!"

"I never did," said Hob. "I never did!"

"Come on now, Hob-One," said Jim soothingly. He turned to Ned. "Ned, have you ever told anyone about being taken for a ride by Hob-One here?"

"Never, m'Lord," said Ned, staring from Hob to Jim and back again. "The big people would never have believed me. Anyway, I didn't want to tell anyone. It was so wondrous great I wanted to keep it all to myself."

"And you have, all these years, haven't you?" said Jim.

Ned nodded slowly.

"You see there, Hob-One?" Jim said. "Ned's never told anybody; and he never will. It's quite all right to admit if you did take him out when he was small."

Hob relaxed slowly.

"Well, yes," he said, after a minute. "I remember him because he was so happy riding the smoke with me. He was the most happy with it, I think, of any child I ever took."

"I was?" asked Ned, his face lighting up.

"Yes, you were," said Hob-One. "I really remember that. They always enjoy it, of course. But you just seemed to take everything—the night, the woods, the snow, the stars—it was just as if you took them all into your arms and held on to them."

"That's the way I felt," said Ned, in a low voice. "I'd like to feel like that again."

"Well, we're going to be traveling a little too early in the afternoon for you to see stars, Ned," said Jim, "but I think it's about time we started for the Earl's castle. Are you ready, Hob-One?"

"M'Lord," said Hob-One timidly, "I'm not sure if the smoke will carry two extra people besides me—and one of them a grown Lord."

"That's all right," said Jim, "you ride the smoke. I'll take Ned with me by magic; and we'll keep pace with you, so we all travel together."

Jim half closed his eyes and visualized himself and Ned suspended in air just above the chimney that led directly up from the fireplace beside them. This visualization was an amazing improvement over his old method of spelling out his magic. He certainly should have thought of it sooner. It was an improvement like that of writing on a computer rather than a typewriter. But, as fast as the magic was, Hob-One had been faster. He was already waiting for them a few feet above the chimney tip on his waft of smoke.

"Fine, Hob-One," Jim told him. "You lead off and we'll keep up with you."

Hob immediately began to travel, again at what seemed like a fairly lazy drifting speed, over the outlying parts of the castle, the open ground beyond, and finally the first trees of the forest. But that speed was again deceptive, and Jim knew that they were going much faster than it appeared.

It was strange, because he could look down and the trees below did not seem to be blurring past him. It was as if he was involved with a double time-track. One track gave him the certainty that he was moving at almost twentieth-century aircraft speed; while at the same moment the other track insisted that he was drifting above the forest at no more than four or five miles an hour at the most.

But he, Ned and Hob-One all stayed together. Jim had visualized all three of them traveling along side by side; and so they did.

"Well, Ned," Jim asked the stable lad, "how do you like it, this time?"

"I like it fine," said Ned, glowing. "It's not—quite as pretty like, though, m'Lord—I mean, there was a full moon the time before, and all those stars."

He ended on an uncomfortable note, looking at Jim with a certain amount of embarrassment.

"That's all right, Ned," said Jim. "I understand."

He did. This was not night, as Ned had said, but late afternoon of a cloudy day. The sky above them was clouded over, but not heavily, so that there was plenty of light to see what was below them, but no feeling of gloom such as might come before a storm or with late twilight. The snowy and treed landscape over which they passed was eerily silent. There was no breeze to rustle the branches together and no animals visible on the snowy, forest floor below them—nor any sign of tracks.

It occurred to Jim to wonder, with so many trolls gathered together around Mnrogar's territory, whether they might not be sweeping the countryside clean of game to feed them all. But there was no sign of troll tracks, either; and it had not snowed for a couple of days now. Between and below the bare branches, the ground he looked at could have been painted, for all the life or evidence it showed.

Thinking of trolls, however, brought another idea to mind. He looked to his right, over at Hob, riding his waft of smoke; for they were moving abreast, Hob to his right and Ned to his left.

"Hob-One," he said, "do you know if the trolls are still in position around the edge of Mnrogar's land?"

"Who's Mnrogar, m'Lord?" asked Hob-One.

"He's the castle troll. The troll in the Earl's castle," Jim said.

"Oh, that troll!" said Hob. "I never knew his name!"

For a moment Hob seemed shaken, and then he squared his shoulders and lifted his head again.

"Are the trolls still there, around that troll's territory?" he asked.

"Yes. A whole army of them," said Jim.

Hob wilted visibly; and as visibly pulled himself back together again, upright chest lifted and shoulders back.

"That's right," he said. "They don't dare go in, do they, m'Lord, until one of them is brave enough to fight the castle troll? But why are there so many of them there?"

"I don't know why," said Jim. "And I'd like to know. But it suddenly struck me, as long as we're going to be passing over where they used to be, I'd like to check and see if they're still there; or if they've moved away, or moved in closer, or anything like that. I was just going to ask you—can you smell a troll?"

"Oh yes, m'Lord," said Hob-One.

"You can? Fine!" said Jim. "Would you be able to smell him even if he was pretending to sleep under a snowbank, waiting for some prey to come along?"

"I—I think so, m'Lord," said Hob-One doubtfully. "It would depend on how deep the bank was; and how close I was to the top of the snow."

"I remember," Jim said, "when you brought me from the Earl's castle to Malencontri on the smoke last time you started mentioning seeing them waiting for the snow to fall on them. Do you know where that was?"

Hob-One puckered up his little brow.

"I think so, m'Lord," he said. "Maybe if there's a lot of them together, then it'd be easier for me to sniff them out."

"Do you remember where you smelled them before?" Jim asked.

"Oh, yes, I remember," said Hob. "I may not have told you before, m'Lord, but hobgoblins never forget anything."

Neither hobgoblins nor dragons, thought Jim. Also, judging from his experience, neither did wives, wolves, sea devils nor fourteenth-century humans—only poor old C-class magicians from the twentieth century named Jim. But, there was no point in grumbling to himself over that now.

"Well, that's good," said Jim. "Because when we pass over them again now, on the way to the castle, I'd like you to tell me if they're still there."

"Oh, I'll be happy to, m'Lord," said Hob-One. "It won't be long now. We're pretty close to it. In fact, we're almost on top of it."

It was less than five minutes after that before Hob-One spoke to him again.

"We're getting to where I smelled them before, m'Lord," he said. "It's not exactly the same place we crossed over, last time; but if they're all around—"

"That's right, they are," said Jim. "Just see if you can get a whiff of them."

He sniffed the air himself. For a moment he was tempted to turn into his dragon body, since the dragon nose might be as good or even better than Hob-One's. But if Hob-One could do the job, it was just as well that neither Ned nor Hob-One should suddenly find themselves traveling with a dragon. In spite of the fact that their common sense would tell them that the dragon had to be Jim—and of course he would speak and reassure them of that, right away—they couldn't help reacting emotionally. If there was a choice between disturbing people and not disturbing people, then all things being equal it was much better not to disturb them.

"Do you smell anything at all yet?" he asked Hob-One.

"Not yet, m'Lord," said Hob-One, staring hard at the ground below. "I almost think—no, I don't. I almost think there's some smell of them, but maybe it's just from their being here some time past."

"Forgive me, m'Lord, Hob-One," said Ned diffidently, "but maybe we're too far up from the ground. If Hob-One would go down closer . . ."

Jim looked keenly at Hob-One. Hob-One was not exactly happy over the prospect of going closer to the ground, he saw. Jim remembered the hobgoblin's graphic description of how a hidden troll would let himself be covered by a snowdrift, and lie there until he smelled a prey come by, then explode out of the drift before whatever it was had a chance to escape.

"I don't know," said Jim. "Hob-One, do you think you might want to go down a little closer to the ground and see what you can smell then?"

"Well, no—I mean yes, m'Lord. Yes, of course," he said. "Of course I can go down closer and sniff harder. There's a drift right up ahead there—"

Before Jim could say anything more, Hob's waft of smoke had dived at an angle toward the snowdrift at the base of a large oak some fifty feet ahead. It was a drift that had piled up, Jim guessed, at least four feet or possibly more at the base of the heavy old oak. Either that, or there was a rise of ground right around the tree, which had caused the snow to make a hump up there. At any rate, Hob and his smoke slid down toward it as Jim and Ned came to a halt, some fifty feet above.

"M'Lord!" called up Hob-One triumphantly. "You were right. There is—"

The snowdrift exploded; and not one, but two—unthinkable to encounter two together at once!—night-trolls, the larger, silver-furred breed, erupted on either side of the hobgoblin; and before

Hob-One could escape one of them had grabbed him up in one wide, long-taloned hand.

"What is it?" asked the troll who was not holding Hob of the one who was.

"I don't know," said the other, looking down at Hob-One. Neither of the trolls had evidently thought to look up; they seemed unaware of Jim and Ned overhead. "Some little thing. Hardly a mouthful."

Hob-One had not called for help. He was valiantly biting at the web of flesh between the taloned thumb and forefinger of the troll that held him, gnawing away with his little teeth at skin that was supposed to be able to turn the edge of a sword.

"M'Lord—" began Ned, in an alarmed voice; and the two trolls looked up. But Jim had already exploded, himself, in one of his rare fits of rage. In almost the same moment he was down on the ground with the two trolls and stabbing a pointing finger at both of them.

"*Freeze!*" he commanded. The two trolls were instantly motionless; their mouths, which had been opened to speak or snarl, making no sound whatsoever. They both glistened, now, as if they had been covered with a layer of molten glass.

Jim glared at them. It took a moment for his mind to come down from its rage and realize that, in his excitement, he had used the wrong word. The word he had meant to use was the familiar magic command of *still*. But twenty years of growing up with television not lacking in cop-and-crooks dramas had made him produce its twentieth-century equivalent; and the magic command had operated literally.

The trolls were indeed frozen.

Immediately his eyes jumped to Hob-One, expecting to find him coated in ice and motionless also. But Hob was not. The magic command clearly had struck, like lightning, only at the point at which it had been aimed. However, he was now struggling to pull himself out of an icy grasp, but without being able to.

Jim pointed at the troll-hand holding Hob-One.

"*Unfreeze! Relax!*"

The ice around the troll's hand shattered into a small shower of shards and the hand half opened. Hob pulled, but could not quite get free.

Jim reached out, spread the rough hand farther, and lifted Hob out, laying him against his chest in an automatic protective movement. Hob clutched at Jim's jupon, and Jim could feel the small body trembling against the palm of his supporting hand. He looked down and saw Hob staring off to one side.

"M'Lord! Ware!" cried Hob. Jim looked around him, and saw trolls coming at him from every side.

"Up, m'Lord!" Hob was calling to him. "Up!"

Jim felt a pressure between his legs, and looking down saw that there was a waft of smoke there, trying to lift him. But he did not feel like going up.

"You go up, Hob," he said; and he tried to put Hob down on the smoke, but Hob clung to him.

"I won't leave you, m'Lord!" The hobgoblin's voice was shrill. "Mount! You must up, and fly!"

"The hell I must!" He visualized himself and Hob enclosed in a glowing aura, of which the inner part that touched them was cool, but the outer part was at the temperature of boiling water. Just in time; the first few trolls reached him and stretched out their arms to take hold of him, plunging their hands into the glow and recoiling with howls of pain and anger.

"That's better," said Jim, turning to face them, still holding Hob to him. The unusual anger in him was flaring to a new high. "You'd like to take hold of a magician? Go ahead, help yourself!"

By this time he was surrounded by trolls, but none of them were within arm's length of the aura. The ones farther back had been roaring and growling, but as the silence of the ones standing immediately around Jim began to impress its way backward through the crowd, they too fell silent until there was no sound at all from any of them.

"That's better!" said Jim. He half turned to the two trolls who had captured Hob-One.

"Unfreeze," he told them. The ice around them shattered; they moved, stretching their arms and legs almost as if they could not believe that they would move again.

Jim turned back to the crowd.

"Never," he told them, "never attack a magician or a hobgoblin. Do you hear me?"

There was still a dead silence from the trolls around. Their eyes glittered; and as far as any expression could be read from their savage faces, they were baffled, but in no way intimidated.

"You," said Jim, picking out the largest troll in the front rank of the crowd that had come to surround him. "What are you all doing here? What are you here for? Answer me!"

The troll looked right and left, down at the ground, up again at Jim—and said nothing.

"I will speak!" shouted some voices from the back of the crowd. There was a swirl of movement through it and bursting suddenly through into the front rank, thrusting those immediately in front of it to right and left, came two identical trolls. They stopped just outside the nimbus, not only looking exactly like each other but standing exactly alike, with fist on hips.

"What are you doing here, magician? This is my territory!"

Jim stared. It was not what they had said that had startled him, but the fact that both had said it in exactly the same words at the same time, both of them using the word "my."

"Make me go, then," Jim answered.

The two stared at him savagely. Jim stared back, equally savage, but torn between two attractive possibilities—one of them being to make himself as big and tall as Rrrnlf the sea devil (though he would still only have the same strength he had as a human being; the trolls wouldn't know that)—or to freeze them all and simply leave them there as living troll-statues.

No, maybe that second choice was a little too brutal. But in any case, he was in no mood to mince words with them. He waited for them to speak again.

Both the two trolls, moving eerily in the same moment and without saying a word, reached out cautiously toward the aura, felt the heat before they touched it, and pulled their hands back. They continued to stare at Jim.

"All right now," said Jim. "You two tell me. What are you doing here?"

"I wait for Mnrogar," they said.

"So, you're waiting for Mnrogar," said Jim. "Why are all the other trolls around, then? Are they waiting for Mnrogar too? And just one of you speak. I don't need both of you talking at once. Either one, but just one speak."

"I must speak with both mouths!" said the two trolls in perfect chorus. "I am one person. That's why I will fight Mnrogar and eat him. His territory is mine!"

Jim found himself staring a little at them.

"What do you mean, you're one person?" he snapped. "I can see there're two of you."

"No, I am one. My mother tore me into two when I was born; but I have always been one. I am one. I live as one. I eat as one—and I fight as one. Mnrogar will die. No troll can win against me.

I can take what territory I want at any time; and now the time has come for me to take his from he who calls himself the King of the Trolls."

"What good's that do?" asked Jim.

"Then there'll be no question about who's King of the Trolls. Because when I can take his territory, as I can any other, then all territories are mine. It is a new time for trolldom; at last under a new King. We will take all—all; and we will crack the bones not only of Mnrogar but of all such as you and any others who pretend to show strength in this island. All will be mine. Mine, forever!"

Jim discovered his anger was evaporating in the face of this new curiosity. Big as Mnrogar was, the two before him—who were indeed, individually bigger than any of the other trolls surrounding them—stood a good chance of together pulling him down. Particularly, since he seemed to be weary of living, after nearly two thousand years, and—if Aargh was right—with being alone.

This, it came to him in an unexpected flash of understanding, could be the source of the Dark Powers' thinking that they could disturb the Earl's party and, in essence, act against History during a Christian feast from which they were themselves shut out. They could not do anything here directly; but free-acting agents like the trolls could do it for them, since Naturals had the ability to affect History, at least to a certain extent.

This strange pair, that spoke simultaneously and used the first person when they spoke, must actually have been joined at birth— "Siamese" twins. That is, if they'd been telling the truth about being born as a single individual and their mother biting them apart.

Whether they actually believed they were one person in two bodies, or this was a clever plan of theirs to give them an advantage, did not really matter. The only thing that mattered was that other trolls were accepting it. If they actually were united in mind as well as personalities, of course, it would explain a lot of things. Working as a pair, instead of as individuals, they would indeed be able to overcome any other troll; and possibly to pull down larger game and generally get more food—even as they were growing up—than ordinary trolls. That would help to explain why they were larger now than the others of their kind, standing around them right now.

"You said you were born as one, and your mother tore you apart!" said Jim. "How can I believe that?"

Without a word, the two turned as one; presenting, one his right side, the other his left side, to Jim; and Jim saw the long ugly puckered scars from just below the ribs to the hip on each one.

Again, without a word, they turned back to face him.

"But if you've been separated," said Jim, "you can't consider yourself one person any more."

"I am one!" the two voices rang together.

Jim found himself inclined to believe that at least they believed it—and, judging from the trolls that surrounded them, these believed it also. If so, then the victory of the twins over Mnrogar might really create a danger, if the twins had enough wisdom to use the other trolls as a united force against even humans. Even if they did not, if the other trolls would take commands from these two, then game could be surrounded and driven, an area could be absolutely cleaned of all the animal life within it. And the same tactics, used against outlying farms or even small villages, could enable the trolls to live off livestock, or even groups of humans.

This would disrupt the kingdom of Britain in the fourteenth century of this world, so that human History would be distorted in a way that had never been foreseen.

The two now said something more; but Jim paid no attention. His mind was too busy examining this entirely new aspect of things. No wonder the Phoenix had not flown as it should. No wonder anything.

But this was not the sort of situation that could be, or ought to be, dealt with offhand. He needed to get away and have some time to think about it—above all to speak to Carolinus, if he could ever get in contact with Carolinus again—about what measures to take.

The worst of it was, he found himself thinking, that as a magician, he and all other magicians might be forbidden from interfering with the trolls under these circumstances. By the laws under which they as magicians operated, whether they could do so, or not, was another question he needed Carolinus's help in answering. There was no point in standing talking to these two, and the other trolls, further.

"I tell you," said Jim in the most ominous tone of voice he could manage, staring at the pair before him, "and I speak as a magician speaks. Take heed to what I say. If you go against Mnrogar, you are doomed!"

Deliberately, he looked down at Hob-One, whom he still covered with his hand.

"Come, Hob-One," he said. "We'll leave these trolls to learn wisdom. Let's continue our journey to its destination."

With that, he visualized himself and Hob being back up in the air with Ned—and immediately they were. A sudden roar of outrage and frustration came from the trolls on the ground below them; and looking down Jim saw their faces up-turned. Jim let go of Hob, who slipped from his jupon and was instantly astride a waft of smoke, between him and Ned. Ned was still in the air where he had been left; but had somehow managed to turn over on his stomach, as if he had been trying to swim down to the ground.

"Did you see him? Did you see our Lord?" burbled Hob-One to Ned. "He stopped them. He frightened them. They couldn't do anything!"

"Forgive me, m'Lord," said Ned, still struggling to pull himself back into an upright position. "Forgive me, m'Lord," he said, "I could not come down to you. True, I only have my knife, but I would not have you think that I—"

"Not at all, Ned," said Jim. "I wanted you to stay up here. I'd have called you down if I needed you; and you'd have been able to come. Forget the trolls now, both of you, we need to get on to the Earl's castle. Tomorrow's not that far away, and there's a lot to do."

CHAPTER 34

The morning sun shone brightly down from a perfectly cloud-less blue sky on the tournament area before the castle, brilliant with the colors of the banners and pennants around the lists and in front of the wooden stands, like football bleachers crowded with warmly dressed spectators; the barrier itself running the length of the field crosswise before them so that the two opposed knights would each ride down his own side of it. Large, round tents had been erected at each end of the list for the knights who were next to ride against each other.

It would have been nice to say that the sun *beamed* down, but that would not have been exact. There was nothing beamish about it; nor about the sparkling, but hard, winter blue of the sky. Nor was there any particular kindness to be found in the trampled, snowy surface of the grounds, the raw wood of the barrier and the unrelieved white of the tents.

Nor, for that matter, in the crowd itself. The gentlemen and ladies there were certainly cheerful and merry—some of them were already in process of becoming merrier, even now, as they sat taking further anti-freeze protection from flasks of wine. But in spite of their good humor, they were here to see blood and violence—even possible death. As recently as the year 1318, Sir John Mortimer had been killed in just such a tournament as this, and buried with his ancestors in Wigmore Abbey.

There had been, in fact, a long list of tournament deaths even before that; going back to the notable one of Geoffrey of Brittany, son of Henry II of England, who had been killed in a tournament in 1168.

In any case, the stands were crowded. The only open seat visible was one on the left of the Earl himself, where the Bishop of Bath and Wells usually sat. But the Church officially disapproved of these rough sports; and so it would have been impolitic for the Bishop to lend his countenance to this one. Still, most of those seated there already were fully expecting him to slip in a little later, probably wearing the habit of a common monk with its hood over his head and drawn forward to hide his face.

If he had been there officially, it would have been his pastoral duty to condemn the tournament. There had been numerous prohibitions and bans; as early as the year 1130 there had been an interdict forbidding ecclesiastical burial to anyone fatally wounded in the sport. This usually happened to be quietly overlooked; but still, a tournament itself was not the sort of thing that the Bishop could officially avoid condemning, no matter how his martial heart might beat with his longing to be out there in the lists, himself; his faith and position forbade him from anything but disapproval of the sport.

No one else there was oppressed with such a sense of duty, however, unless it was Jim himself. He was sitting, eating what was, in effect, the breakfast he had missed several hours earlier, when he had gone out into the frosty air before dawn. His mission then (with no chance of refusing it) had been—with Brian, Ned Dunster, the two squires and a few trusty men-at-arms—to take Mnrogar, his armor and his boar-horse to a spot in the woods where they would be safely hidden from view; but close enough so that they could be brought out when the proper moment for the Black Knight's arrival had been reached, which would possibly be several hours from now.

Jim had taken the extra precaution of magically making both horse and troll, by means of a primitive magical technique he had invented some time ago, invisible to any eyes but those of their own little party. Not that there was much likelihood of spectators trying to sneak in for a look at the tournament from that side of the field. The way through the woods was too likely to have men-at-arms of the Earl's, on guard for any of a variety of possible troubles; and it would go hard with any tenant or other common person if he or she was caught trying to sneak close in other than the area allowed to such.

But that was beside the point at the moment. Right now, Jim and Brian were eating in relative privacy in one of the small tents clustered behind each of the two larger tents and mostly hidden from people in the stands by its bulk. The small tents were for various things, such as to store extra spears, armor, or even horses; but, also, one of them was always allotted for the use of a knight who would be next to ride against an opponent from this end of the list.

So far the first spear-running of the day had not taken place; but Sir Brian was due to ride in the second contest, and was listed for several more later in the day. The first joust was to be between Sir Oswald Aston and Sir Michael Land, two other guests.

Brian was at the moment refilling his wine cup, his usual early-morning cheerful self. Jim looked at him with hatred, his own eyes still puffy and his body feeling as if it was made of lead, whenever he had to get up and move it any place.

"Aren't you going to water that wine a little?" he said to Brian. "Particularly with your turn in the list coming up right away?"

"By Saint Ives, no!" answered Brian happily. "At times like this, the wine might as well be water itself, except for the taste—which I much prefer to that of something from a well."

Jim had to admit that Brian had a small point there. He and Angie invariably boiled any well water that they had to drink, if they had the chance to do so. But boiled or not, the water from most wells around in castles like this was a far cry from the clear and limpid stream from a spring in a mountainside.

"When were Angie and Geronde going to be in the stands?" he asked. "Do you know, Brian?"

"Oh, they'd be there by now, I'll venture," said Brian. "I can send one of the men-at-arms to find out, if you wish. But neither of them would care to miss any of this lance-play."

Geronde would undoubtedly not want to, thought Jim. But he knew very well that while Angie would be present, she would not be enjoying it. She was only too aware of the human damage involved in these encounters. However, that was not something to mention out loud even to Brian.

"She hates to leave young Robert," Jim said.

"With both her maidservants, the wet nurse and a man-at-arms without as well as another within the rooms," said Brian, "what trouble could there be? I would not say this to you but that you are an old and trusted friend who will understand I say it out of friendliness and concern only; but do you not think that perhaps Angela is worrying too much about this youngster? After all, the King may take him off your hands within a month or so; and for that matter he may go to Agatha Falon as next of kin."

"That's exactly what Angie's worried about," said Jim. He lowered his voice, for the tent was not exactly soundproof—although no one but their own people should be outside. Still it was not the sort of thing to be mentioned out loud, ordinarily. "Angela's positive Agatha Falon would as soon not see Robert grow up at all, so that she could inherit the Falon lands."

"So you've told me before," said Brian. "It would be a foul deed to do anything to the lad, of course, but—well, well, it will be as God wills—"

He broke off abruptly, putting down his glass and getting up with a look of alarm on his face.

"What with this early rising, I forgot entirely!" he said to Jim. "I am not shriven. Was not one of these tents supposed to hold a priest?"

"So somebody told me," said Jim. "Here, let me. I'll step out and have one of the men-at-arms get him right away."

"No, no," said Brian, turning toward the tent-flap opening. "There may be other knights waiting their turn with him, and I will have to take my place in line or possibly discuss the necessity of my being before them with some of those already waiting; and I have my hands filled merely to ride against those I'm to contest here today. Wait here for me, James."

He went out.

Secretly, Jim was just as glad to be alone for a few moments. He had been half asleep all through the period of dressing, going out, and moving Mnrogar and the horse. In fact, he had only begun to wake up by the time they had got the two to their new position, and Mnrogar curled up in a very small tent, which gave the troll the illusion of being safely denned.

The boar-horse had simply been tethered loosely to a tree and turned back into a plain boar while it was waiting; so it was free to root and snuffle down under the snow and see if there was anything interesting underneath . . .

Jim tried to think of what he ought to be doing next. He was sure that there was something that he should be busy about right now; but he could not seem to think of it. It was as if the general coldness about him had slowed down his mental machinery, to a point where it barely turned over, like the engine of an old car on an equally cold morning back in Michigan, five hundred years and more in the future.

Not that he was uncomfortably cold. He was layered in clothing, to say nothing of the light armor he was wearing and the sword at his belt; wrapped to a point where the cold really was not getting at him. In fact, now that he had sat a while, out of the open air, and gotten some food inside him, he realized he actually felt comfortably warm, sitting here.

He dozed off.

—And woke to find Brian shaking him by the shoulder.

"—Up!" Brian was saying. "I must armor me now, James; and here is John Chester to help me make ready. You had best be getting to your seat in the stands, with Geronde and Angela!"

"What? Oh—yes," muttered Jim. He got creakily to his feet and stumbled out of the tent into sunlight that was so bright it set him to blinking. He headed around the end of the barrier toward the stands.

His route took him close to the trees at that end, necessarily, therefore; and a voice spoke to him from out of sight in the forest.

"James!"

It was Aargh.

Jim stopped, rubbed his chin, as if he had just remembered something, then turned and walked into the woods. About twenty feet in, he found Aargh waiting for him.

"I've been downwind from the stands, as close as I could get without leaving the trees," said Aargh. "Your troll among the guests is there with the rest of them today. I could scent him clearly."

Jim looked at the direction of the stands and back at Aargh.

"You're sure, I suppose," he said, "you weren't smelling Mnrogar, himself? He's just back a little in the trees from the small tent I just came out of."

"Can you tell your right hand from your left?" said Aargh.

"Of course," said Jim, "that isn't—"

"How?" demanded Aargh.

"Well, of course—" It was such a simple question that an easy answer did not come immediately to mind. "Well, for one thing, they're different."

"So's the troll in the stands, from Mnrogar," said Aargh. "No two trolls smell alike; any more than any of you two-legged people smell alike. What do you expect?"

"I guess I asked a foolish question," said Jim.

"You did," said Aargh.

"Were you able to tell where in the stands the other troll is?"

"Not at this distance," said Aargh. "At a guess—only a guess—somewhere in the middle."

"Umm," said Jim. The information was more alarming than useful. But Aargh was as usual being helpful, without being asked to be and in spite of his frequent claim that he had no obligation to anyone but himself.

"I'll leave it to you to find him," said Aargh. "Meanwhile, you might want to know that the army of trolls has moved in on Mnrogar's territory. They now ring this place no further from where we stand than I could trot in the time it will take you to walk the rest of the way to the stands yourself."

"That close?" The news was a shock to Jim. He had somehow assumed that things could not get any worse at this point and should get better. "Do you think they might try to show up at the tourney here?"

"They are trolls. Who can tell?" said Aargh. Then the harshness of his voice softened slightly. "I don't think they will, James. They're always hungry; and from the way they look at things, there's a lot of meat there in those stands right now. But also, there's a lot of you people with swords and spears and horses. If I know trolls, they'll think twice."

"But it does mean that they're going to force Mnrogar to come out and fight for what he owns, doesn't it?"

"Yes," said Aargh.

"There're two twin brother trolls that are more or less leading them, did you know that?" Jim said.

"I knew it," said Aargh.

"You never mentioned it to me," said Jim.

"Why should I?" said Aargh.

"The two brothers were born tied together, and their troll-mother separated them," said Jim. "They believe they have the right to both fight against Mnrogar at the same time—why are you laughing?"

Aargh shut his jaws with a snap.

"It will be something to watch!" said Aargh. "I think both Mnrogar and they are going to be surprised."

"Could Mnrogar win against two of them?" asked Jim.

"Perhaps. Who knows?" asked Aargh. "We'll have to wait and see."

"You know, Aargh," said Jim, goaded finally to the edge of his temper, "I appreciate your telling me about the troll in the stands and these other trolls moving in; but you aren't being exactly helpful in other ways."

"You people go around giving each other advice," said Aargh. "Wolves don't."

There was a moment of silence between them.

"I'll say this much, then," said Aargh. "You'd better tell Carolinus about this—soon."

"I wish I could," said Jim. "He's been keeping himself hidden from me. How can I find him?"

"Your problem," said Aargh, and half turned away. "I'll be around."

He vanished among the trees and their sharp shadows cast on the snow.

Jim turned around, himself, and plodded back in the opposite direction, out of the forest and onward to the stands. Sir Michael and Sir Oswald were already in armor and on horseback, at their respective ends of the lists. Sir Oswald was still selecting his jousting spear.

In the stands, as Jim came up to them, he could see the unused seating space was still open next to the Earl. Jim looked beyond that nobleman into the farther part of the stands, went down several levels of the bleachers and found Angie, sitting next to Geronde, but with some considerable space between them and also some open space on the other side of Geronde. He walked down in front of where they sat, and then climbed the bleachers, strewing apologies right and left for pushing through the other guests already seated on the lower levels.

He got to his goal at last, and dropped onto the available opening on the bleacher bench that they had kept for him. It was only when he was seated that he realized Angie had moved over next to Geronde, so that the two were together and Geronde was holding still another space, undoubtedly for Brian, if he should join them.

On the other side of Jim, for his neighbor he had a lean, long-nosed, guest in his sixties, who was evidently one of a party of five.

"Give you good day, Sir Dragon," said this gentleman, in Jim's ear, as the roar died down.

"And a good day to you, Sir. Er . . ." said Jim, turning to him.

However, the older man seemed to take Jim's forgetting his name with good grace, and turned back to talk with others of his own party. Jim also turned back—to Angie.

"I didn't expect to see you out here this early," he said.

"I wasn't coming this early," said Angie, "but I thought it'd be better. I've arranged to get a message about halfway through the morning; so I can leave early and won't be back. It's not the warmest day of the winter. Are you cold, Jim?"

"Some," admitted Jim. "Not bad."

"Here, James," said Geronde. Her hand came across in front of Angie, passing him what looked like a cloth bundle. He took it, without thinking, and then noticed that from the top of the bundle protruded the neck of a stoneware bottle with a cork in it.

"Thanks, Geronde," he said, handing it back. "But I want to keep my head clear; and I've had enough cold wine and cold water mixed together this morning."

Geronde pushed the bundle back at him.

"Try some," she said, "you'll like it."

Under the manners of the period, it would have been impolite to go on refusing. He took the cork out and tilted the neck of the bottle to his lips, swallowing a small mouthful. To his astonished surprise, it was not merely warm but almost hot. It was hippocras, one of the few medieval wine mixtures Jim liked.

It was, in fact, red wine, simply flavored with spices. But the wine and spices would have been brought to a boil and then simmered several minutes, essentially boiling off most of the alcohol content, so what was left was simply a pleasant hot drink. He drank some more, gratefully.

"I said you'd like it, James," said Geronde, as Jim corked the stoneware bottle and handed it in its insulation back to her. Geronde checked that the cork was tight and then shook the bundle, evidently to feel how much liquid was left.

"Beatrice"—she said, Beatrice being one of the two serving women she had brought from Malvern Castle—"will be coming in about half an hour with a fresh bottle, so—"

Her words were cut off by a blast of the trumpet of the Earl's herald, now standing directly before that part of the stand where the Earl was seated, but addressing everybody in the stands at once.

"With your gracious permission, my Lord, and his Grace, Edward, Prince of England who sits with you, the next joust will be between Sir Brian Neville-Smythe and Sir Amblys de Brug!"

The Earl waved a hand in gracious assent; and the herald turned back to face the lists, putting his long horn to his lips. He blew a single blast, and two figures in armor rode out of the large round tents, one at each end of the lists.

A roar of approval went up from the stands. Brian was a favorite. Good things were always to be expected of him; and Sir Amblys was a jouster not to be despised.

Both armored figures accepted their spears from attendants and rode to the ends of their respective sides of the barricade, where they halted.

The joust was about to begin.

CHAPTER 35

The trumpet pealed again. The two knights on their horses hurtled toward each other and came together with an explosive sound, both spears splintering.

Brian sat as if welded into the saddle. Sir Amblys swayed backward slightly from the shock, but also held his saddle. Both knights turned and started to ride back to the beginning of the list they were in for fresh spears and a second running.

But, halfway there, Sir Amblys suddenly wavered as he sat and began to slump forward over the horn of his saddle. Servitors ran out to catch him before he should fall. He was caught in time, and led back on his horse to the end of the list. He and the horse disappeared into the large round tent.

Another cheer went up from the stands.

"Geronde!" said Angie dangerously. "If you keep hitting me like that I'm going to punch back. And I know how to hit!"

"Crave your pardon, Angela," said Geronde. "I was carried away. Often, it is a gentleman sitting beside me; and I can hit him as I like. Pray forgive me." Angie's eyes met Jim's for a second in a flash of *understanding*. Of course, Jim thought, it was the *impoliteness* of her hitting Angie that Geronde was apologizing for—her unladylike behavior. Not any discomfort Angie might have felt; discomfort was supposed to be ignored.

"That's all right," said Angie. "I can understand you getting excited. Will Brian be coming out to sit with us for a while?"

"I do not know," said Geronde. "Sometimes he does. In this case he may wish to ride outside the lists down to the other end to see how Sir Amblys fares. Brian is a knight of courtesy. Yes—look, there he goes now."

Jim and Angie looked and saw Brian, still in his armor, but riding a palfrey rather than his war horse, taking a circuit away from the lists, by the woods and down to the other large tent, where he dismounted and went inside.

He was not inside long, however, before he came out again and spoke to Sir Amblys's herald—or rather the herald that belonged to the tent at that end of the lists, which had become Sir Amblys's tent and herald for the duration of his joust.

The herald put his horn to his lips and sounded two notes, the second higher-pitched than the first. The stands cheered again.

"Hah!" said Geronde. "Sir Amblys is not badly hurt. But his horse and armor will be Brian's, of course. Brian should come to us now, unless he has other business to hold him there."

But Brian did not come. The joust went on. Jim tried to think of ways to get in touch with Carolinus that would not alert everyone else in Magickdom; and, not having any luck, dozed off until Angie nudged him awake for Brian's second spear-running with another knight, whose name Jim did not catch.

This time, the other knight flew cleanly out of his saddle and landed with what seemed to Jim a killing impact on the frozen ground. He staggered to his feet, though, almost immediately, to show that he was not hurt; and even remounted his horse, which Brian held for him without getting out of his own saddle. They both rode back to their respective tents.

The crowd applauded loudly. Jim, jolted to something like full awakeness for the first time today, found himself marveling, with a sense of true appreciation, at Brian's skill. It was one thing to know that your best friend was one of the best jousters in England. It was something else again to see him in action. In fact, as Brian walked his horse leisurely back toward its tent, Jim thought he read in him a sort of settled confidence, of the kind which lives in someone for whom the issue was never in doubt.

Was he imagining this, he wondered, or was it simply because he knew Brian so well that he could read the way he sat his horse, and other body language, unconsciously; even as Sir Harimore had said he could read the way Jim wore his sword and sat his horse as signals that Jim was by no means a practiced fighter at

Sir Harimore's level. Still wondering if long acquaintance might not even develop something close to telepathy—certainly, he and Angie could exchange information with a look, for example—Jim dozed off again.

He surfaced to semiconsciousness several times after that, roused by an unusual roar from the crowd, but evidently it was not Brian riding again, or Angie would have woken him. If Angie had received the message she had set to be delivered earlier and left, then Geronde undoubtedly would have woken him. But neither had. He was vaguely aware that most of the morning had gone by—then he was shaken rudely awake and looked up to see Brian's face under an ordinary steel cap, rather than his jousting helm, glaring down at him. Angie's seat beside him was now vacant.

"James!" hissed Brian in his face, "time to go!"

His mind startled to a feverish alertness, but his body still half asleep, he stumbled down the stands after Brian, mumbling apologies that were only rough approximations of those he had strewn right and left as he had climbed up. Happily, Brian's leading the way to a certain extent cleared a path for him, so most of the apologies were unneeded.

Once on the ground he fell in beside Brian and they walked back along the stands to the end of it and off a little farther, before circling out and around toward the tents at the nearer end of the lists. Brian led him past the large tent, around to one of the smaller ones behind it and inside.

Within were not only Brian's squire, John Chester, but Theoluf, his own, plus four of Brian's men-at-arms. Brian pushed Jim past them into a chair at a table on which stood a leather jug of wine and another that presumably held water, but looked remarkably untouched.

Jim collapsed in the chair. Brian uncorked the wine jug and filled one of the large metal cups on the table with wine. He pushed it into Jim's hand.

"Drink!" he said.

"Oh, for God's sakes, no!" said Jim. "No more wine, Brian. I want to wake up!"

"And I want you to wake up. Swallow it all down—that'll wake you!" said Brian. "You must wake, James! We need your wits, brother!"

It was easier to give in than argue or refuse. Jim swallowed the wine. It was only a degree, if that, warmer than the icy air inside the tent—which, come to think of it, must still be not much below freezing or else the wine itself would be frozen—but he managed to empty the cup.

"Now," said Brian, with satisfaction. "Sit there for a small while, James, and let the good wine have its effect on you. Meanwhile I'll have a few words with these lads of ours."

He turned away to the squires and the men-at-arms.

"Now, John; now, Theoluf," he said. "You and these others have been keeping a guard of at least two on the troll and the boar, have you not? Has anything untoward happened? Anything you should tell us? Because, if so, now is the time to speak."

"There is nothing that needs telling, m'Lord," said John.

"That is so, Sir Brian," added Theoluf.

"Good!" said Brian. "And the troll is still in his tent—sleeping, perhaps?"

"He was awake when last I looked, m'Lord," said John. "The boar was still a boar and lying on the ground, perhaps sleeping, perhaps not."

"Good," said Brian. "Now, you lads-at-arms, back with you all to the two beasts and stay until Sir James and I come. I know you've been under orders to keep all away in any case, but now be doubly sure that none come close—including other trolls, if you see any. If one of you catches a glimpse of any other troll, sound an alarm; and at least one other of you go to the one who sounded the alarm, out swords, and charge the troll. I warrant he'll not stand against two of you with blades." For a moment there was a glint in Brian's eye, that was matched in the eyes of those he addressed.

"So," he went on, "otherwise keep troll and boar doubly hidden until Sir James and I come. All, except one—it'd best be you, Theoluf—come with John and me to the main tent; because I am now due to ride the last joust of the morning against Sir Harimore. John will dress me. You, Theoluf, should stand by outside the big tent to watch the jousting, then come back and tell Sir James how matters have gone. You understand, Theoluf? Even if I am hurt and they keep me in the big tent, you must go directly, first, to Sir James. You understand?"

"I understand, Sir Brian," said Theoluf. "I will so do."

"Good!" said Brian, clapping the former man-at-arms on a shoulder. "I know I can trust in an experienced head like yours to follow orders." He turned to his own squire.

"When I am prepared, you go with these lads, John; and all things back with the two beasts will be at your command until we come. You also understand?"

"I understand, m'Lord," said John.

"Then we go," said Brian. He glanced over his shoulder at Jim. "Sit you quiet, James. I warrant to put Sir Harimore out of his saddle and be back shortly."

The squires and men-at-arms stood aside to let him out first and then followed him out. Jim sat alone in the tent. He sat, glad enough to be left alone, and—unbelievable as it seemed—beginning to feel a certain soothing influence of the wine he had poured down.

The feeling, he told himself, could be only a self-delusion, but it was welcome in any case. Theoretically he should not react to wine swallowed only minutes before. On the other hand, his mind was definitely calmer; and yes, there was no doubt about it, his head felt clearer and his thoughts seemed sharper. This was just the opposite effect of what a sedative like alcohol should do. But cold alcohol on a warm stomach in an icy tent under these conditions could be excused for behaving in an unlikely manner. Either that, or the alcohol had simply begun to calm him; and the adrenaline of excitement had made him alert.

His mind filled in the gaps. Brian must have angled, possibly by arrangement with and with the consent of Sir Harimore, to be the last bout of the day. It would be a reasonable request, since both were likely to be real contenders for the day's prize. Both were crowd favorites, and in a way their spear-runnings would be a climax to those of the morning. But in addition to these things, it also made an ideal situation in which the Black Knight could ride in and issue his challenge, threatening to upset the apparently settled outcome of the day.

In the stands Jim had been puzzling as to how to get in touch with Carolinus. Now that his mind was clearer, he saw the utter futility of this. If Carolinus had not let himself be contacted earlier, he certainly would not let himself be contacted now. Jim would have to deal with matters by himself.

Outside he heard the distant roar of the crowd in the stands, which must be signaling that Sir Brian and Sir Harimore, fully horsed and armored, had now ridden out of their respective tents. He waited for the time to elapse during which they would have selected spears and readied themselves to gallop down the list. After a short wait it came. He heard the crash of spears against

armor once more and the excited neighing of one of the horses;
then things were silent again.

For the first time, Jim found himself worrying about Brian.
Every instinct in him told him to get up and walk out of the tent
and go and see what was happening. But Brian had deliberately
sent out Theoluf to bring back news, which meant he had wanted
Jim to stay hidden here; and even though Jim's mind was sharper
now, he could imagine that Brian might have been seeing the
situation more clearly than he could, even now.

He sat and waited. After what seemed entirely too long a wait,
Theoluf stepped in through the flap of the tent, held it closed
behind him and spoke.

"No decision, m'Lord," he said. "Both Sir Brian and Sir
Harimore broke their spears on the other's shield; and neither
were moved from their saddles. They will choose new spears
and run a second course."

"At least Brian is all right," said Jim, half to himself.

"M'Lord," said Theoluf, "perhaps might not have worried. I
have known two knights wise and able in the ways of jousting,
without needing to make special agreement, to run a first course
in which spears would be broken, but no great test made of
either one; so that they might ride a second course for the further
enjoyment of the crowd. It has happened."

Jim looked up and saw Theoluf's eyes shrewdly on him.

"I only said I have known it to happen," said Theoluf, "in
times past when I was man-at-arms under another Lord."

Every so often, thought Jim, these fourteenth-century people—
Brian leading the list—made him feel as if he'd been born yesterday. Naturally, for more reasons than one on Brian's part, it
would be sensible to run at least a couple of courses to heighten
the tension of the crowd. Aside from anything else, it would gear
the crowd up for the arrival of the Black Knight.

"Thank you, Theoluf," he said.

Theoluf went out and the flap closed behind him.

Jim listened therefore, once more to the roar of the crowd, the
note of the trumpet that sent the knights riding at each other.
There was the sound of their meeting, and then another finger-
chewing wait before Theoluf stuck his head once more into the
tent.

"Both spears broken again, m'Lord, without decision," he said.
"A third course will be run."

He paused.

"M'Lord might be interested to know that I have never known or heard of more than three courses being run between two knights without a conclusion one way or another."

He went out.

So, thought Jim, this was to be the real thing. He got to his feet and paced back and forth in the tent. This time the wait before the noise of the crowd told him that Brian and Harimore had ridden out of their tents and were choosing their spears. He paced the tent through the further wait for the trumpet to start them riding at each other, and on through the now absolutely unreasonable wait before the final crash of their encounter—all these seemed amplified in Jim's mind. All of these were bad enough. But worse, even to his unpracticed ear, was the sound of them actually hitting each other, either louder or harsher than he had heard all day.

There was a moment's dead silence and then something like a roar trailing off into a groan from the crowd. Then silence again.

Jim started toward the entrance of the tent. To hell with his not being seen—if that was what Brian had told him to stay here for. But Theoluf came in through the flap before he could reach it and stopped him.

"It might indeed have been a third course with no victor, m'Lord," said Theoluf, "but something about Sir Harimore's saddle broke or gave way. They say it was his saddle girth, but that is what they usually say when some such thing happens. Sir Harimore did not fall; but he had to hold on to his horse's neck to stay upright, dropping his spear. But both spears had been broken as fairly as before. Nonetheless, Sir Brian wins the day!"

"Where is he?" said Jim.

"He rode back into the large tent," said Theoluf. "No doubt he will be with m'Lord soon. Perhaps I might pour a cup of wine ready for him?"

"Yes," said Jim, drumming his fingernails on his thigh impatiently, "yes, do that. And if you have a chance to say a word to him, Theoluf, tell him I'm impatient to see him again."

"Yes, m'Lord," said Theoluf.

He poured not only a full cup for Brian, but a small amount into Jim's cup. Jim woke to what he should have realized before—that of course he would have to congratulate Brian on winning the day, and that meant drinking a cup of wine with him. However, Brian would not insist on a full cup for him this time; and in any case,

Jim had intended merely to touch his lips to it. Theoluf, having finished filling the cups, went out.

But the next one to enter the tent was not Brian. It was Aargh; and he literally crawled in under the bottom edge of the tent at its rear.

It was startling to Jim that anyone of Aargh's unusual size could have managed to creep under the tight-pegged ground edge of a tent. Aargh stood up and shook himself, sending snow and a certain amount of dirt spraying around. He looked at Jim.

"The trolls have moved in closer," he said.

Jim stopped his pacing abruptly.

"How close?" he said.

Aargh laughed without a sound.

"Not too close," he said. "And they'll come no closer. They've already seen too many people with weapons here. Those two brothers may in time teach their kind to fight as a group against humans; but that time's not yet. There're still too many generations of trolls who've learned early to run at the sight of any armed two-legged person."

"But we've got Mnrogar and the boar just back in the woods a little ways," said Jim. "John Chester and some of Brian's men-at-arms are with him; but mightn't they take a chance against just a few such enemies to get at the boar, if not Mnrogar—Mnrogar's in a tent."

"I know he's in a tent," said Aargh. "Even if they knew he was there—though they'll have smelled him there, long since—I don't think that even the two brothers would attack him now, with weaponed people about him. And if they don't want to attack, they won't want even to be seen. There's no need to worry for the moment—at least."

Jim discovered he had been holding his breath, waiting for Aargh's answer. He breathed out, now.

"But," went on Aargh, "I'd suggest that when most of you out there go back into the castle, none are left behind to stagger in by themselves. Alone, or by twos or threes, with night falling and night-trolls making up most of those that are with the brothers, the chances are you would not see those laggards alive again."

Jim nodded.

"But if there's no immediate danger—" he began.

"I came to tell you this," said Aargh, "so that you'd guard Mnrogar, after he is through play-acting for you, back to his tunnel to his den under the castle. Some of those trolls may be braver than any others. But once Mnrogar's through the tunnel's mouth, none of them will follow."

"Why?"

"Why?" snapped Aargh annoyedly; but then his tone softened. "I keep forgetting all of you upright people are nose-blind. Because once in the tunnel, they would be as blind as you. Everything will reek of Mnrogar, and there will be places where he can step into a space off the tunnel and wait for them to pass and leap on them when they are unsuspecting. Nor will their numbers help; because some troll will have to go first—and no troll will. There's not one of them that would not fight to the death against any other trolls that tried to force them into the tunnel, rather than go down and die in the dark under Mnrogar's teeth and talons."

"Why guard him, then?" said Jim.

"To hide the opening of his tunnel from them as long as can be."

"Oh, I see. Well, we can do that—" Jim was beginning, when Brian entered the tent and stopped short on seeing Aargh.

"You here?" he said to Aargh.

"No," said Aargh, "I'm a half a day's travel away from this place, explaining something else to some other noseless two-legged person."

"Well, well," said Brian, "it's good to see you—"

"He came to tell us that the army of trolls have moved in closer," Jim said. "He says though, that Mnrogar and the boar are in no danger as long as John and our men-at-arms are with them."

"That is a good word," said Brian. "But come, there's no time to lose. People will be leaving the stands. We must hold them where they are and bring Mnrogar out on his horse as soon as possible. You said you would have a herald, James?"

"Yes," said Jim. "Ned Dunster—the kennel lad from my estate. You've seen him around the tents here. But I've brought the horn Carolinus magicked up, and I'll sound it by magic, and then speak by magic from him to the crowd, in a voice that's not mine, or his. I'll go get him, now."

"I will be close," said Aargh, and started back out under the edge of the tent in back. Meanwhile, Jim had already started out through the opening flap in the front of the tent, with Brian close behind him. He stepped out—and almost stumbled over Ned Dunster, who was standing there with an eager face.

"Forgive me, m'Lord," said Ned, "but I thought you might need me."

It was all too obvious he had been listening to the conversation in the tent; but there was no time to say anything about that now. Ned was already dressed in the hose and jerkin—considerably better than his ordinary clothes—that Jim had supplied him after they had gotten to the Earl's castle. He had also just put on his herald's tabard, which was simply a length of cloth with a hole for his head so that it draped before and behind him, with a green background showing a solidly black shield by way of arms, on both its front and back. And he was holding the magic horn.

"All right, Ned," said Jim, "out in front of the great tent quickly, and put the horn to your lips. Everyone has left the tent area, thinking the contests over. Pay no attention to anything that the regular herald says or does to you. I'll take everything from there. You just stand there, hold the horn until it sounds, then pull it down and stand facing those who watch and make movements with your lips as if you were shouting to them. I'll speak through you magically."

"Then I'll go get Mnrogar a-horse," said Brian, "and you'd best get ready whoever's to be his squire, to present him. I must not be seen helping, otherwise. Have you Mnrogar in armor and the boar in horse-shape?"

"No," said Jim. "Damn it, I forgot. But I can do that from here by magic while you're going back there, come to think of it. Go ahead, Brian."

Brian went; and Ned, after looking at Jim for final approval and getting Jim's nod, moved out beyond the large tent.

Watching around the curve of the tent, Jim saw the kennel lad put the horn to his lips and visualized the horn blasting forth three ascending notes, louder and more fierce than any that had been blown so far today. The regular herald had turned and stared at Ned, but had not yet decided to approach him. Ned dropped the horn to his side and turned to face the stands. He opened his mouth.

Jim, staying well behind the curve of the tent, where he could see Ned but was still out of sight of most of those in the stands—and not likely to attract attention in any case, since he was not in anything like jousting armor—raised his cupped hand and spoke into it barely above a whisper, concentrating on imagining the words that came booming forth, deep-toned and ominous, from the lips of Ned.

"*The jousting is not over!*" Ned seemed to thunder. "*A challenger comes!*"

There was obvious consternation in the stands. At least half the people had stood up to leave and were only waiting for those seated below them to get out of the way. A muted hubbub of query and baffled answer floated back across the distance separating the stands from the tents.

Jim stood there, warmed with the success of this first move—then suddenly remembered he had still not turned the boar into a horse and put magic armor on Mnrogar.

Hastily he closed his eyes and visualized first Mnrogar in armor, then the boar as a huge black horse, completely saddled, bridled and caparisoned with a black cloth with gold edges. The saddle and spear, sitting upright in its boot and tied to the saddle, were also black. The armor was uniformly black, from the massive tilting helm to the iron covering—and hiding—the troll's taloned feet.

He felt, like an actual physical movement inside his head, the magic take hold and the changes happen in troll and boar. Turning, he hurried to the place where Mnrogar and the boar had been kept.

When he got there Mnrogar was already in the saddle; looking unbelievable, like a black giant who might well have emerged this moment from a split in the riven earth and unknown reaches underground.

"All right," said Jim, "I'll take it from here—no, wait a minute. There's one thing missing."

He had worked up the scenario for the Black Knight's entrance in his mind, and one of the details had completely slipped out of memory. For the entrance he wished Mnrogar to make, another person was needed, and he had planned to take this part himself.

"A horse!" he said. "I'll be squire, it's just a matter of changing my face magically. But I'll need a horse. Do we have a horse? Where can we get a horse?"

"There's my palfrey," said Brian. "Those in the stands would instantly recognize Blanchard of Tours."

The truth of this was undeniable. Brian's war horse, on which he had spent all of his patrimony except the run-down Castle Smythe he had inherited, was almost as famous as he was.

"Someone get the palfrey—quick!" said Jim.

"He's right here, my Lord," said John Chester. He ran off and returned, bringing along the good-natured brown riding horse that Brian used for everyday purposes. It was a gelding, deceptively fast, but neither large nor especially strong; and almost too sweet-natured for its own good. It already had Brian's extra saddle and bridle on it.

"Good!" said Jim. "I'll have to change his color, though—"

Hurriedly he tried to visualize both horse and equipment as turning the same shade that Mnrogar and his steed showed.

"Zaap! You're black," he muttered to himself.

However, the palfrey only turned a sort of muddy gray for a moment and then faded back to brown again. Jim was uncomfortably faced with the fact that visualizations could not be made offhandedly. He took a deep breath, willed himself to calmness, shut his eyes and concentrated. The palfrey was suddenly black in every part, including its hooves. This time the color stayed.

Jim swung himself into its saddle. Then remembered Brian.

"Brian, is it all right—"

"Certainly," said Brian.

But just at that moment a strangely hoarse, almost falsetto voice spoke from about the level of Jim's knee.

"Did messire wish for a herald?" the voice said. Jim looked down and blinked at a slim, rather ridiculous-looking man, standing by his right knee. The fellow had a curiously pointed chin and exaggeratedly pointed ears; a corkscrew mustache, like that of the fictional detective Hercule Poirot, was under his nose.

"Angie?" said Jim disbelievingly.

"I showed up to help after all," said Angie. "Do you still need a herald?"

"No!" said Jim. "But I need a squire!"

He swung down from the saddle on the palfrey and helped Angie up into it.

"You're terrific! They might have recognized me," he said, "but they'll never recognize you. How did you do it—no, wait, don't tell me now. We've got to rush. Just sit this horse, and I'll speak through your mouth magically."

CHAPTER 36

"Papier mâché," said Angie, as he was leading the palfrey by its reins, Angie on it, out of the woods behind the tents that concealed their approach from the crowd in the stands.

"Papier mâché?" echoed Jim. The word brought up a vague image of strips of newspapers soaked in water with glue and then molded with the fingers into different shapes. That would account for how she had made her pointed ears. The fourteenth-century paper they had would probably work for that—but how had she colored the ears to make them look like flesh? Jim checked his mind from running off and hauled it back to more important matters. He reached the entrance of the large tent and halted; and as he did inspiration came to him.

He had not given much thought to how he would word Mnrogar's challenge. But Angie's homemade make-up had started his mind to perking.

"Hang on a moment," he said to Angie; and concentrated. The black cloth that he had magicked up to caparison the boar-horse suddenly developed a thicker band of cloth-of-gold added to its bottom. The studs on the face of Mnrogar's shield were replaced with bright gems—diamonds, rubies and sapphires; and around the top of the troll's tilting helm appeared a golden crown.

"What on earth—?" said Angie.

"You'll see, when I utter his challenge through you," said Jim. "Now, Angie, what I want you to do is simply ride out around the tent, to near Ned Dunster, ahead of Mnrogar. Mnrogar will say nothing whatsoever. Then Ned will put his horn to his lips, and I'll magically make it sound once. Wait until the last note has had a chance to linger on their ears for a few seconds. Then open your mouth and mime the motions of speaking. I'll speak through your mouth magically and issue Mnrogar's challenge. It'll end up with a question—does anyone here want to take up that challenge?"

"That other trumpet's going to answer yes within seconds, I bet," said Angie.

"I think so, too," said Jim. "However, you wait for it; and when it comes, turn back and ride past Mnrogar, taking hold of the bridle of his horse and leading him back around the large tent and into it. Both Mnrogar and you look like something the devil dreamed up, so I'm pretty sure by that time no regular attendants will be showing up to help. Brian, myself, and our men-at-arms will still be here. Mnrogar's all ready."

"Why take him back inside, then?" Angie asked. "It seems to me—"

"I want him out of sight except when he's actually jousting," said Jim. "He or the boar-horse might do something to make people too suspicious. Now, when you go out later for the jousts, you'll be carrying his spear. You get down and hand it up to him. Then Ned Dunster will play herald again; I'll make his trumpet sound, and Mnrogar will ride against the first knight chosen to ride against him. We may have to wait for some time in the tent first, though, while the knights who want to try taking on Mnrogar argue who's to be first."

"That's all right," said Angie. "Both Enna and the wet nurse are in our rooms, the men-at-arms are there—and that was a very good idea of yours to have Hob-One up the chimney."

"Oh, you know about that?" said Jim. "I haven't had time to tell—"

"Hob-One's beginning to trust me," said Angie. "When I was alone in the front room, he came down and really talked to me for the first time."

She stopped speaking, because Brian, Mnrogar on the boar-horse and the men had come up behind them. Jim turned his attention to them as they halted with the boar-horse just behind Brian's transformed palfrey.

"All right, Brian," Jim said to him. "Angie's ready to ride out as the squire, and Mnrogar should come out maybe ten feet behind her. Is he all ready?"

"He is," said Brian. "I'll leave you to say when he is to follow though, James, and how to act. He obeys all commands since Carolinus magicked him. But it is no doubt best he hear only your voice commanding him from here on. Now I must get back to the stands, myself, to be on hand there when knights start to call for their chance to ride against Mnrogar. As winner of the tourney I have pride of place."

"Brian!" said Jim. "You're not thinking of riding against Mnrogar, are you? You know what he's capable of doing, particularly with that boar-horse—"

"Oh it would pleasure me to ride against him. It's just possible I might—but, no," said Brian, "we want Mnrogar to win over all he rides against. After me, Sir Harimore has best claim to ride first against the Black Knight. He will defer to me, of course; but I will say that Blanchard has come up with a limp, and I do not want to risk him by riding him in the lists again today. All understand that no knight would want to joust unless he was properly horsed. Harimore will know the limp is only an excuse; but he will also know I am not saying this out of any lack of will to fight. He will take it as a courtesy to him, because of his saddle breaking and costing him in our last essay."

Angie unsuccessfully did her best to smother a chuckle. Brian glanced at her in a puzzled fashion for a moment, then went on.

"After that," he continued, "there will be whoever else wants to ride. I would warrant a half-dozen at least, for all Mnrogar's size and fearful appearance. Also, you remember we talked of someone in the stands who could suggest that Mnrogar might be other than human, against which it was the duty of a Christian gentleman to ride. I will be there to help that idea along, if any should be doubtful that a gentleman might be lowering himself to oppose this Black Knight from nowhere."

"I'd forgotten about that," said Jim. "All right, Brian. You can start right away if you want. Mnrogar, are you listening to me?"

"Yes," came the hollow and slightly distorted voice of Mnrogar from inside the enormous helm.

"You are to ride out peaceably after the squire, here, on the horse in front of yours, just now. You are to say nothing. The herald will sound his trumpet," Jim said, "and the squire will deliver his message. Then the squire will ride back past you, take the reins of your horse and lead it and you with him back into the tent, where you will wait until the time for the first spear-running. Remember, you're to say nothing. The squire will say all that's necessary for you. Do you understand me, Mnrogar?"

"Yes," said Mnrogar, again.

"Then here you go," said Jim. "Go ahead, Angie. Mnrogar, you follow. When the squire stops, you stop and stay stopped until he comes back for you."

"Yes," said Mnrogar.

Angie lifted the reins of the palfrey and rode out around the curve of the tent's side into view from the stands; and Mnrogar followed her. There was a strange sound, almost like a groan from the crowd—as if half in apprehension and half in delight—at the first glimpse of him, massive in his armor upon his massive black horse.

Angie reined the palfrey to a stop. Behind her, Mnrogar hauled back on the reins of his boar-horse and it stopped. Standing a little in front of them, Ned Dunster lifted the trumpet to his lips.

Jim, peering around the curve of the tent, concentrated on making the trumpet sound—a single note this time, rising, and ending in a sort of eerie wail; a sound he remembered he had heard once made by a bagpipe, back in the twentieth century.

The notes were effective, but entirely unnecessary. All attention was on Angie and Mnrogar in any case. Angie had been involved in amateur theatricals when she and Jim had been undergraduates, and Jim had the feeling that she was enjoying the role she was presently playing. Leisurely, she reined the palfrey around so that she faced the distant stands, although Mnrogar still sat facing down the lists.

She opened her mouth and Jim, still watching, created for her a booming voice and words that echoed across the distance to the stands, louder than a human voice should be able to sound.

"My master, the Black Knight, is of no man nor woman born. But he is a king in his own country and he is come here bidding me issue this challenge to all present. These are his words: *'I am come here to take part in no human tourney; but to see English knights go down before the end of my lance—if sobeit there are any brave enough to ride against me!'* "

There was a moment's dead silence from the stands, and then a welling uproar of vocal rage and excitement. The Earl could be seen leaning forward to shout down to his herald.

A trumpet blast answered immediately. A figure in monk's garb was leaning toward the Earl, out around a red-robed figure between them. Whoever it was, he seemed to be protesting. The Earl was not listening.

Angie turned her horse the rest of the way around and rode back, catching hold of the bridle next to the bit in the mouth of Mnrogar's horse, and leading it after her, back around the curve of the large tent and into it. Ned Dunster, holding the trumpet, followed them around behind the tent.

Even inside the tent, the hubbub across the way from the stands could still be heard. Angie dismounted from the palfrey and dropped its reins. It stood obediently. She looked at Jim.

"Shouldn't Mnrogar be allowed to get down too?" she said. "I'd guess they're going to be a while sorting out who rides first against him. It sounded as if everyone there were shouting at the top of their voices. I've never heard a crowd that worked up."

"Oh, yes," said Jim. "Mnrogar, you can dismount. John, Theoluf—one of you, or one of the men-at-arms probably—should hold the reins of his horse. We don't want it getting excited or moving around here in the tent. There's no room for that sort of thing."

Theoluf took the reins and passed them to a nearby man-at-arms, who shortened his grip on them until his fist was almost up against the lips of the boar-horse; and he stood holding them like a sentinel. Even Jim's household servants were normally nervous in the presence of magic; but everyone associated with this project seemed to be caught up in the play-acting aspect of it, Jim thought.

There was a bed in the tent, evidently intended for any hurt jouster who might need it, and five stools around the square table. Angie had already sat down on one of the stools.

"How are you going to watch the spear-runnings from in here?" she asked.

"I'll lift the back edge of the tent up from the ground, a little," he said. "It's easy. Aargh's been scouting around and he can get under them all right, so I ought to be able to lift the edge enough to see."

"I see what you mean," said Angie, who was seated facing the side away from the stands. "Here he comes through it now."

Jim turned around on his stool; and, sure enough, the edge of the tent was pushed up and Aargh was coming in underneath it, not really crawling this time but merely crouching. He came all the way in, stopped and looked at them with his noiseless laughter.

"The trolls have moved in closer," he said. "But not much closer. They're upset. They can't understand what Mnrogar's doing in armor, and why he's riding a horse that smells like a boar. You've puzzled them. They expect those who go on two legs to do strange things; but any of us who go on four should act the way we always do. When we don't, the world is turned upside down."

"Could they get upset enough so that they'll go away and not bother us and Mnrogar any more?" asked Angie.

"Not that," said Aargh. He lay down and began to lick one of his forepaws.

"Why, your paws are all cut up!" said Angie, getting up from her stool and squatting beside him to look at them. "What happened?"

"You don't dig through ice and frozen ground without a few scratches, Angie," said Aargh. "It's nothing. I'll keep them clean with my tongue, and in a day or so they'll be as they were."

Angie went back to her seat at the table.

"As a matter of fact, there are a couple more things you might find interesting," the wolf went on. "Brian's on his way back here."

"Already?" said Jim. "I thought he'd wait a while, then slip away when nobody was looking. If he comes back this fast, maybe something's gone wrong."

"I doubt it," said Angie. "Nobody there has their mind on anyone but Mnrogar, right now. But, come to think of it, did you know Carolinus is in the stands now? That red robe of his really stands out, on a day like this."

"Carolinus!" said Jim, sitting up straight on his stool. "I hope he stays there. I've been trying to get hold of him—"

"I know," said Angie. "That's why I mentioned it."

"I thought you both knew," said Aargh indifferently, still stropping a paw with his long tongue. "Otherwise I would have mentioned it too."

"He's sitting beside the Earl," said Angie, "with someone in a black monk's robe on his other side. I imagine that's the Bishop. Agatha Falon's on the other side of the Earl; with the Prince on *her* other side."

"Bound to be the Bishop," said Jim thoughtfully, "if he's allowed to sit that close to the Earl. But what do you suppose Carolinus is doing there?"

Aargh did not bother to answer.

"I wouldn't have any idea," said Angie, "but if you want a guess, I think he's there to help us."

"What makes you think that?" Jim stared at her.

"He's got to know what you've been up to all along, with Mnrogar," said Angie.

"Well, of course," said Jim. "He was told about it at the time I first came up with the idea, just as Aargh was; and he helped set it all up."

He looked over at Mnrogar, who had gotten down from the horse; and, somewhat to Jim's surprise, was now simply squatting, with every appearance of comfort, armor and all. It might be perfectly natural for a troll to squat if he wanted to adopt a resting position; but it was most disconcerting to see someone that large, particularly wearing full armor—and particularly armor that rich with gold chasing and the gold crown on top of the tilting helm, in that position. Knights did not squat—at least Jim had never seen one doing so, and particularly not in armor.

"Oh," said Jim, "you can take off your helm for now, Mnrogar." The troll did, exposing his grim countenance.

Jim turned his attention back to Angie.

"But what makes you think Carolinus is here to help us?" he said. "There's a lot of reasons besides that, that could bring him here at this time."

"It's just an idea," said Angie. "Maybe Brian will tell us more about Carolinus when he gets here."

"I hope so," said Jim glumly, peering out through the slightly open flaps of the front entrance to the tent. "I need to know what's going on down there."

But it was a good quarter of an hour before Brian actually walked into the tent—a time during which Angie sat calmly and Jim fretted.

"I did not have to speak out about a knight's duty to fight evil beings, after all," said Brian, as he passed through the front flap of the tent. "Carolinus had already put that idea into the heads of those there."

"You see, Jim," said Angie, "I told you he was here to help us."

"That must indeed be his purpose, Angela," said Brian. "He has been busy talking both to the Earl and to my Lord Bishop. The good Bishop believes no one should have to do with this unknown knight; and speaks darkly of commerce with the Evil One. Carolinus gave him the same answer you suggested, James, that it's a knight's duty to combat such ungodly things, as well as other evil-doers. The Earl, certes, had never a thought of doing anything else. He was talking of wanting to run a course with the Black Knight himself. Naturally, voices were raised immediately to beg him not to, reminding him of his noble station, his duty to his guests and other reasons."

"But there are some knights who definitely will fight the Black Knight, aren't there?" said Jim.

"No lack of them," said Brian. "However, the tourney has run late enough so that sext is already past. Cast a glance outside for yourself, James, and you will see the sun past full mid-day. Therefore it was decided there is only time for five knights to ride against the Black Knight; or else this last day's dinner—our last all together of this year—will be undone, counting the time that it will take all here to get back to the castle and dress before appearing in the Great Hall."

"Sir Harimore is going to go first, then?" Angie asked.

"Yes. He accepted my tale of Blanchard's lameness most courteously. But, no, Angela, I speak too quickly. He will ride, of course, but last rather than first. It was felt that if one of the other knights could unhorse the Black Knight, they should have their chance first. Indeed, I think none of them will have a chance. Harimore may, but it will depend on how he uses his lance. I believe he is not aware of somewhat that I have become aware of."

"What's that?" asked Angie.

"Oh, a mere trick of lance-work," said Brian lightly. "I will not tire you with the details, Lady."

"It wouldn't tire me, Brian," said Angie. "But if it's something you want to keep to yourself, by all means do so."

"Thank you, Angela," said Brian. "I believe I will. James, five knights have been chosen, as I say. I do not know who the first will be to joust with the Black Knight. John?"

John Chester, who had been peering outside, turned about.

"Yes, m'Lord?"

"Has any pennon been brought out for the first knight to meet the Black Knight?"

"Yes, m'Lord," said John Steward. "The arms upon it are of a sheaf of grain and a battle-ax."

"Sir Murdock Tremaine," said Brian cheerfully. "A good spear; but relies more on the speed of his horse, than skill, in placing his point. But, James, we should be getting Mnrogar ready to come out again. They will sound a trumpet from the other tent shortly; for the pennon would not be there unless Sir Murdock was already inside and making himself ready."

"Right!" said Jim.

They got the boar-horse turned around, Mnrogar put on its back—and were ready just in time when the trumpet pealed a single note from the far end of the list. Ned Dunster, tabard and all and walking behind Angie riding the palfrey, led out the huge black animal with its rider, and positioned him properly at the near end of the list. Angie dismounted from her palfrey, put the spear in Mnrogar's hands, and the troll took it, laying it down carefully as he had been trained, under Carolinus's magic and Brian's teaching, properly across his saddle, with its business end pointing out over the barrier toward his opponent. Angie remounted and rode back toward the tent.

"All right, Ned!" said Jim, through the tent flap.

Ned put the trumpet to his lips and Jim produced a single magical note from it.

Both knights sat their horses, waiting. Then the trumpet sounded again, and Sir Murdock on his horse hurtled forward. Mnrogar was a little slower getting started, but both he and the boar-horse were behaving properly when the two opponents came together.

Sir Murdock's spear snapped in two pieces as they passed each other; but in spite of Mnrogar's lance being awkwardly aimed, so that it struck high on Sir Murdock's shield, it had enough force to send the knight flying off his horse. Mnrogar's spear, of course, disintegrated in the process into a spray of splinters, but that was unimportant.

The boar-horse's momentum carried him on for about twenty yards. Then Mnrogar got him reined in, turned him about and rode him at a walk back to his own end of the list, completely ignoring Sir Murdock, lying unmoving on the ground, and Sir Murdock's horse, struggling back to its feet.

Happily, attendants were running out from the tent at the far end; and after a few moments, Sir Murdock sat up under his own power, and with their help got to his feet. They had brought forward another, smaller horse, which he mounted and rode slowly back to the tent.

"Clumsily, clumsily done!" said Brian, peering out a slit he had cut with his poniard in the back of the tent, where he and Jim had been looking out. "In the ordinary way, there would be questions among those in the stands who were experienced—that Sir Murdock should fly so lightly from his saddle, from a strike that high on his shield. But, with all this I will wager all those in the stands had their eye on Mnrogar, rather than poor Murdock. Probably no question will ever be made. Though, James, I myself wonder that so high and seemingly easy a touch should move a knight so strongly from his saddle."

"Well," said Jim, "the mass—I mean the weight of Mnrogar

and the boar-horse together may make a difference."

"There's that, of course," said Brian. "And certes, the heavier knight and horse will ride down the lighter in open field—"

Angie rode Brian's palfrey back into the tent, leading the boar-horse and Mnrogar upon it, perfectly silent and showing no sign of having been through any encounter at all; except that close up, the black paint of his shield showed some scratches. Not a gem there, however, was missing or loosened.

"*I must congratulate you, by the way,*" said Carolinus's voice unexpectedly inside Jim's head. "*The troll and steed did very well indeed. I see evidence that you have been handling your magic well. That third note of the trumpet that one time from your herald was a masterpiece. Some day you must tell me where you found it.*"

"Carolinus!" said Jim, out loud without thinking. Angie and Brian turned their faces inquiringly toward him.

"I was just wishing I could get in touch with him, that's all," said Jim hastily. "Pay no attention." They turned back to the matter of getting Mnrogar to dismount and getting the boar-horse turned around so that he would be ready to go out without delay when the next trumpet call sounded for a joust.

"*Tut-tut,*" said Carolinus. "*You should come up with better excuses than that, James. But, as I was about to say, while you've done very well with your magic, it's still somewhat rough around the edges. Definitely C-class—but rough. Practice, James, as I've always told you. Practice is the thing!*"

It was not practice, Jim thought rebelliously, that had brought him to this. It had been his own ideas and imagination. Unless simply using magic itself could be considered practice.

"*Anyway, I'm glad you got in touch with me, Carolinus,*" he thought. "*I've badly needed to talk to you—*"

"*Not now, my lad,*" interrupted Carolinus. "*I've just called you to give you a small warning. Both the troll and the boar are doing very well indeed; and they should continue doing well. But I should put you on guard that any kind of emotional shock, such as might follow if one or the other of them was actually pierced or otherwise hurt by an opponent's spear, could bring them out of whatever magic either you or I have put on them. I just thought I'd warn you.*"

"What can I do about it?" asked Jim.

But there was no answer. Carolinus evidently had disconnected for the moment.

CHAPTER 37

Sir Bartholomew de Grace was waiting to collide with Mnrogar at any moment now.

Brian had cheerfully lengthened the slit he had cut in the wall of the tent, and spread it apart so that he could look out at almost the full length of the list where the two contestants would come together. At the far end of the barrier Sir Bartholomew had just been handed his jousting spear; and right outside the large round tent at this end, Angie was performing the same office for Mnrogar.

Once more, the troll took his spear in completely indifferent, automatic fashion, laid it in position, and sat indifferently waiting for the trumpet that would start him on his way.

Jim abandoned the small opened seam through which he had been watching Mnrogar being readied, and went over to join Brian at the cut in the tent wall. Brian companionably spread the cut and gave Jim the left hand side of the cut cloth to pull even wider if he wished. Jim joined him at looking at the scene.

Sir Bartholomew was fully in view. Mnrogar was for the moment out of sight. But then the trumpet from the stands sounded once more, and he burst into view. The black boar-horse was already moving from a canter into a gallop, and Sir Bartholomew was approaching from the other end of the list; if not with the all-out speed displayed by the troll's previous opponent, at least clearly at the limits of what his war horse found best to do. He was still holding his lance loosely, so that the point would not waver up and down. He would grasp it firmly and tense up only at the moment immediately before the impact. But Mnrogar had gradually learned this skill, also.

"A steadier man and a more seasoned one than the last, Sir Bartholomew," observed Brian, without taking his eyes off the lists. "I had rather have him by my side in an advance across the open field than many another. Though not outstanding at jousts—"

He did not have time to finish, for at that moment the two charging knights met with the usual crash and breaking of spears.

For a wonder, Mnrogar's spear had taken Sir Bartholomew properly and squarely right in the center of his shield; and like the rider before him, Sir Bartholomew soared from his saddle and fell to earth, to lie still. As before, Mnrogar needed some twenty or thirty yards to pull the boar-horse to a stop and turn it. Then he rode back, again without so much as a glance for his fallen former opponent.

There had been a roar of anger from the crowd, when Sir Murdock had been so thrown down from his horse. It came again now, but mixed with a certain amount of groaning.

Whether these simply signaled dismay at Sir Bartholomew's downfall or at the force with which he had been driven from his saddle, Jim could not tell. In any case, Mnrogar rode back to his end of the list, and Angie led him and the boar-horse back into the tent—the boar-horse still panting and inclined to be a little excited, in spite of the magic Carolinus had used on it, but Mnrogar as indifferent as if he had merely been digging himself a new den. Once in the tent Mnrogar restrained the steed with brute force on the reins. He climbed off as before, squatted on the ground, took off his helm and sat staring at nothing.

"I am almost shamed," said Brian, in a thoughtful voice, "to have had a hand in so easy an overthrow of two such good knights, even though neither one could be called great spears. It is his weight and the weight of his mount, as you said, James, that gives this troll such an advantage. Indeed, if I were to stand aside and judge, knowing what I do, I would have to say that those were foul wins, achieved by unworthy ways."

Brian's tone was not markedly emotional; but Jim caught in his voice the clear signal of self-accusation.

"It's for a good end, Brian, remember," he said.

"Oh, yes. I tell myself that, too," said Brian. "But still I would there had been another way to achieve it—or a better end to strive for."

Jim glanced at Mnrogar, on the tent floor; but the troll seemed as indifferent to what they were saying as he had been to his fallen opponents.

Brian's glance had followed Jim's.

"But of course that means nothing to him," said Brian grimly. "To such as he, winning a joust is like a man chopping down a tree. A necessary labor, no more. He has no concept of honor and courage."

"It's kind of unfair to expect it of him, don't you think, Brian?" said Jim. He had not thought to find himself defending the troll. But ever since he had seen Mnrogar's wild display of emotion at the thought of losing what he had fought to keep for nearly two thousand years—his territory—and the humanlike tears where he would never have believed he would see them, he could not help but credit the troll with feelings. "He may respond in the same way—only to other things to which we would attach no importance."

Brian looked away from the troll.

"No doubt you are right, James," he said, "but I have been on the losing side too many times, during the years in which I was learning the art of the lance, to search for what those things might be."

A trumpet pealed once, suddenly, from the direction of the tent at the other end of the list.

"Why, here's something less than honorable from the other side, also," said Brian, raising his head sharply. "Another opponent so soon? They are of purpose following too quickly one on another, so that the next rider may take him when both he and his steed are winded, and weary from their last passage at arms. I advise you delay our return trumpet as long as you feel necessary, James. It will serve them right, those in the stands, to sit on their hands awhile and keep them warm while the troll and his horse get back to normal breath and strength."

"I don't think it's necessary, Brian," said Jim, looking from Mnrogar to the boar-horse. "Mnrogar acts as if he'd been out for a Sunday walk; and I think if that boar-horse was back in his normal shape and mind, he'd be tearing up not only us but the tent and everything within view, because he hasn't calmed down from the last charge down the list, let alone the one before. It's only magic that's keeping him quiet enough to be in the tent with us, at all."

"It just may be you're right," said Brian, staring at the black steed. "A normal horse would be sweating and snorting and wild-eyed after such a charge. This one is only a little fractious, and shivers a bit from time to time. Still, I would counsel that you wait a while before making any move. The next opponent must wait until the troll is out and ready, in any case."

"This is something that you understand well and I don't, Brian," Jim said. "But why wait at all? Judging from the way he handled his first two opponents, Mnrogar isn't going to have any trouble—"

"Never you think it, James!" said Brian. "The best lance in the world can be undone by some little small thing that is unexpected. An error, an oversight, an act of God—what will you?"

"Well, of course that makes sense," said Jim. "I was just thinking it would be impressive if Mnrogar went out there, even with this short notice, and had no trouble with the next knight at all."

"If he did," said Brian, "perhaps. But as I have said, the last two were not great lances and there are always those things I just mentioned, to change any certainty of victory into something else. But it is never wise to pass up any advantage you may honorably gain. Mischance is always the reason when some unknown is victorious over a champion. The first time after I had been jousting for only a year or so, it chanced that I won over a knight of renown in one bout; and thought immediately that I now knew all that was needed to be known. Fool that I was, I had overlooked the fact that some small mischance on his part might have given me an advantage. So the next time we met, I faced him with confidence and, certes, he swept me from my saddle as if I had been a feather. As for other, more solid reasons, if you wish I can give you two."

"What are they?" said Jim.

"First," said Brian, "if you send Mnrogar out, without waiting a due time, you will be playing the game the way they want it, rather than as we do. They may crowd yet the fourth knight upon your troll even more quickly, sure that they have him weakened by this tactic; and by next time he may be. And you dare not let him rest then, or they will be sure of it. But by not letting yourself be pushed now, in this manner, you send the message that you are aware of what they are trying and view it with contempt."

"I see," said Jim.

"Secondly," went on Brian, "by waiting you will also give the impression that our champion here and his horse needed the extra rest; and therefore may indeed now be weaker—which could lead to over-confidence in the upcoming jousters—and you will remember his last is to be Sir Harimore, the most dangerous, with whom the troll will need all the advantage he can get. Better you lead them into error where they intended to lead you into such. On both points do you gain. As I say, James, overlook no advantage, no matter how small. It may be needed."

"It's a good thought," said Jim. "All right, we'll wait."

"And meanwhile," said Brian, sitting down at the table, "you and I can have a pleasant cup of wine together with Lady Angela."

"Not for me, I'm afraid, Brian," said Angie, already seated at the table.

"It will warm you, Lady," said Brian.

"Thank you," said Angie. "But I'm quite warm already. I believe I will decline."

They sat and talked. But Jim estimated that it was no more than fifteen minutes before Brian emptied the last of what he had put in his cup and stood up from the table.

"I would judge now would be a good time for Mnrogar to ride out," he said. "Waiting is a good thing, but we don't want to overdo it."

Matters were set in hand accordingly. Jim and Brian watched through the slit in the tent side, while Mnrogar and his opponent waited for the trumpet that would set them in motion against other.

"Who is this now?" asked Jim, trying to peer at the coat of arms on the pennant that the cold breeze was rippling almost directly away from him.

"Sir Reginald Burgh," said Brian. "He is a Northumbrian knight, like Giles, though from the other end of the Border— what is this? Look, James! Did you notice that when his charger moved its rump to give us a little more of a side view, Sir Reginald's corselet showed itself half-unlaced on one side, at least. How could a mistake like that happen? I wonder if—"

A trumpet sounded from the stands. Sir Reginald's horse was instantly in motion; and a second later Mnrogar burst into view from right next to the tent. They came at each other at what seemed to be tremendous speeds.

"Hah!" shouted Brian suddenly. "Here's craft! I thought so! Watch his shield, James—"

That was all Brian had time to say before the two horsemen crashed together; but Jim did not need to be told any more. He saw.

Sir Reginald at the last moment had crouched down in his saddle—this was why his corselet had been half-untied to allow him to crouch even the small amount he did. He had also then tilted his shield sharply backward, so that Mnrogar's point would bounce off it. It was perhaps a not very honorable, but a perfectly legal trick in jousting to loosen corselet strings and tilt a shield. In any case, in jousts it very seldom mattered how the winner won, as long as he did win—unless the manner of his winning reflected a lack of honor upon either his audience or some important person in it.

It was a highly effective device; and certainly would have worked if Mnrogar himself had known anything about jousting. But, as luck would have it, Mnrogar's lance was once more very badly aimed, and it struck far lower on Sir Reginald's shield than it should have, with a result that he was pushed out of his saddle sideways. His fall was therefore not as spectacular as the falls of the first two knights had been. But it was a fall nonetheless. Mnrogar rode back past him to the tent with the same unmoved indifference.

The fourth knight to oppose Mnrogar came after only a reasonable pause following Sir Reginald Burgh. He was Sir Thomas Hampter, a tower of a man, who looked welded in his saddle.

The encounter between him and Mnrogar this time was apparently faultless on both sides. Even Mnrogar got his spear point in the area of the center of Sir Thomas's shield, and Sir Thomas was even more accurate. But Mnrogar was apparently unmoved by his opponent's weapon, while Sir Thomas, though he stayed in the saddle, leaned over to one side; and seemed unable to direct his horse back to the tent, until attendants came running to take its reins near the bit and lead it back, with him still leaning from the saddle, but supported by a footman on that side.

"And now," said Brian, turning away from the slit in the tent as Sir Thomas vanished into the other tent at the far end of the list, "for Sir Harimore."

Mnrogar was also just at this moment being led into his tent, still in the saddle. He dismounted, took off his helm and squatted again. There was no change as far as could be seen in him.

The boar-horse was another matter. In spite of the magic by which Carolinus had restrained it and made it teachable, it was beginning to show a very strong desire to break loose of all restraints and do something destructive. It stood, after it was brought all the way in; but it pawed the ground—the one natural boar-movement that, superficially, it had in common with the natural movements of the horse—and it made curious sounds from time to time, which were evidently an attempt to snuffle boar-style, with the result emerging as something like the snort a horse might make.

"Will he stay obedient to Mnrogar, James?" asked Brian, looking at the animal. "If there was one other knight with whom it would be not well to have him lose his head, it would be Sir Harimore."

"I'm afraid I can't tell you, Brian," said Jim. "I don't know what Carolinus did to him, or how Carolinus did it. I'm only sure it's something that's beyond my ability; and that means that I'd better not try to monkey with the commands that control him. Why don't we just let him stand? He may calm down." Brian looked bemused by the Americanism Jim had unthinkingly used, but he said nothing further.

They sat down at the table which Angie had returned to.

"What do you expect from Sir Harimore?" Jim asked Brian.

"I can make no guess, James," said Brian. "I know no more in this instance than if I was about to ride against him myself. We will simply have to wait and see."

They did wait, and it was not an abnormally long wait, but it was not a short wait either. Looking out through the tent-flap in front, Jim got the idea that the people in the stands were either becoming deeply annoyed over the fact that four of their warriors had gone down before Mnrogar's lance, or else impatient to see the final bout; particularly since it was with Sir Harimore, whose reputation was known to all.

But the time passed, and eventually the trumpet rang out from the other tent. Brian did not dally then. He got Mnrogar on the boar-horse, which might have calmed down somewhat, but still looked as if it might start foaming at the mouth and running wild at any moment. But the iron hand of Mnrogar was on its reins; and the horse walked out of the tent into the lists and stood while Mnrogar was handed his spear, without giving any unusual trouble.

This time the wait to hear the trumpet blast that would signal the beginning of the actual engagement was as hard on the nerves of those in Mnrogar's tent as it apparently was in the stands themselves. At the other end of the list, already holding his lance, was Sir Harimore, looking very motionless and capable in his saddle.

The trumpet finally spoke. The horses leaped forward and rushed down their separate sides of the barrier at each other. Sir Harimore looked as he did at all times and in all activities, as if he was perfection itself and completely in charge of the situation. He sat his horse with ease and authority, his lance balanced loosely in his grasp until the last moment, when he clamped his grip tight on it and pressed it hard against his armored side with his elbow. The sound of their meeting was if anything louder than the sound of the previous meetings Mnrogar had been involved in were concerned.

Both spears flew into splinters. Mnrogar was carried on by the boar-horse, seemingly unmoved. But Sir Harimore also was carried on by his, looking equally untouched.

They returned to their respective tents.

"Oh, pretty. Very pretty—I knew it!" exclaimed Brian, as soon as Mnrogar was inside. "Or rather, I should have known it. Of course, Harimore would want to ride two courses to make the most of the meeting. Also of course, as it must happen in these matters, Mnrogar handled his lance the best he has today. Now Harimore has him coming into a second meeting; and with our luck, the troll will miss horse and rider completely."

"Well, maybe not," said Jim. "Look on the bright side of things, Brian."

"Hah!" said Brian. "Bright side!"

"At any rate," said Jim, "the boar-horse looks like he'll be all right. Maybe he's getting used to these runs down the list against horses and riders he doesn't know."

"It may be," said Brian, "for all that his training was only against dummies and the creature conjured by the Mage."

"Well, tell me," said Jim, "is he at the top of his form today? Doing as well or better than he's done before? Or is he worse?"

"Yes to any and all of those questions, James," said Brian glumly. "There was never any predicting him. He would carry his spear almost in Christian fashion for as many as three or four runs in a row, and then miss his foe entirely."

"But he must have improved as he went along, didn't he?" Jim insisted.

"Oh, he got better," said Brian. "But only up to a point. Look at him now—"

Jim looked. Mnrogar was squatting on the floor with his helm off, as usual, and looking at nothing in particular.

"—He has no *feeling* for the jousting!"

"Yes," growled Mnrogar unexpectedly from the floor.

Both Jim and Brian stared at him. Mnrogar's face was no longer absent. A savage look had come over his unlovely features.

"That other with the stick said something to me as he passed," said Mnrogar.

"Said? What?" demanded Jim.

"I don't know," snarled Mnrogar, his voice a little louder in the tent. "I couldn't quite hear. Why should he say anything? He is on my land. And he says things to me!"

"Oh, that's just one of Harimore's little tricks," said Brian. "The other rider isn't supposed to make out what Harimore says when he does that. So the other man imagines something—and he usually imagines the worst possible thing that Harimore could say. That gets him angry; and an angry jouster is not a wise jouster."

"Well, it seems to have an worked with Mnrogar," said Jim.

"True," said Brian, suddenly thoughtful, looking down at the troll. "He only said it to make you angry, troll."

"I am angry!" said Mnrogar.

"Well, don't be, Mnrogar," said Jim hastily. "He just made a noise to anger you, so you'd make mistakes and he could win over you. You don't want him to do that, do you?"

"Win? No one can win over me!" growled Mnrogar.

"But he may if he gets you angry enough so that you can't concentrate on your jousting," said Jim.

"Jousting!" Evidently a troll's mouth, jaw and tongue were not built to allow spitting; but it certainly sounded very much as if Mnrogar would have spat the word out if he could. "I will smash him and eat his bones!"

"No you won't, troll!" snapped Brian. "You'll ride the best ride you can and use your lance the best you can; and that's all you'll do! Now just think on that, keep thinking on that until you are a-horse and going down the list!"

Mnrogar snarled wordlessly, looking past both Jim and Brian off in the direction of the other tent, as if he could see through the cloth side of this one to it.

CHAPTER 38

The trumpet sang at the far end of the list.

Mnrogar put on his helm and climbed on the back of the boar-horse without needing to be prompted. They were led out together from the tent, and a moment later Jim and Brian were in position, looking through the slit in the side of the tent, Jim stretching his as much as he could to get a look at Mnrogar and his steed.

"I just hope the boar-horse doesn't break loose and do something wrong," he said.

"Oh, it's not the horse that gives me concern," said Brian. "It's the troll."

"Mnrogar?" said Jim, taking his eyes off the list for a moment to glance at Brian. "But you know his limitations. He shouldn't behave any worse than usual, at any rate. On the other hand, the boar-horse is excited and looking for a fight—"

"So is the troll," said Brian. "And he wasn't before. It's that which is not good."

Jim would have said something more; but at that moment the trumpet sang and Mnrogar and Sir Harimore hurled themselves at each other.

Both were traveling faster than they had in the previous bout; and they came together with what was, even to Jim's untrained ear, a sound more loud and angry than any he had heard this day. The lances flew to pieces, and Sir Harimore was forced backward at an angle in his saddle, but not in any sense loosened from it. Mnrogar also seemed to be pushed back by the impact, though much less than Sir Harimore.

"Now, that was anything but pretty," said Brian with satisfaction. "But what's to do now? There were only supposed to be five encounters, and the rule has always been two rides to an engagement. Aha—I half expected it!"

Sir Harimore had called out to the footmen around his tent, and one of them was picking up a new lance while Harimore rode back for it. Mnrogar was already on his way back, at better than his usual speed, and the boar-horse was now clearly excited.

"What is it? What's going to happen?" said Jim.

"Sir Harimore is offering to encounter again immediately!" said Brian. "See, he takes a fresh lance and holds it up over his head. We must get a new lance to the troll, right away."

But Mnrogar was already back and reaching for the new lance that Angie was passing to him. It was only then that Jim realized that Angie had not come back into the tent. Brian's voice, of course, had carried clearly to both Angie and Mnrogar; but it was almost as if it had not been necessary. Angie was handing up the new lance and Mnrogar was taking it. He turned his horse around.

"The Earl's trumpeter must sound from the stand to give them permission, first—" began Brian, but broke off. Mnrogar had yanked the boar-horse's head around, so that the animal had turned with him. He put his lance in position. At the far end Sir Harimore was doing the same thing; and while the trumpet did indeed sound from the stand to give them permission, both horsed figures were already in motion by the time it echoed over the lists.

"Now," said Brian tensely, "is the time to watch Harimore, James. He will have some trick in mind, now that he has his opponent afire. Yes—look! He has realized he cannot force Mnrogar out of his saddle, but if he damages one of his legs, the troll may fall, from his plainly seen lack of skill in the saddle. There—"

Brian had no time to finish. Sir Harimore's lance did indeed dip toward the lower part of Mnrogar's shield, which was something that could happen as much by accident as on purpose; but Jim saw that in this case it pointed very close indeed to Mnrogar's left thigh. But that was all they had time to see, before the two reached each other.

Sir Harimore's lance point struck and the lance broke. Roaring inside his helm—Jim could hear Mnrogar from here—the troll's point struck directly at Sir Harimore's shield, hit it, and the lance snapped—only a little in front of the handguard by which he held it. Furiously, Mnrogar rode literally into the barrier, reaching out over it and straight-arming the broken butt of his lance and his closed fist against Sir Harimore's upper body.

Sir Harimore went out of his saddle to the ground.

But the boar-horse had now been led to shake off all control in an explosion of bottled rage and desire to be at war himself. The only thing he saw to fight was Sir Harimore's horse on the other side of the barrier. Instinctively, he tried to slash his way through the barrier with his nonexistent tusks, but only smashed his nose against it.

He screamed as only horses can scream, and his boar instincts lost out to the horse instincts. He raised himself on his hind hooves and attacked the barrier itself with his front hooves. The barrier disintegrated.

"Brian, help me!" cried Jim, running out of the tent and starting to go as fast as he could down the list to where the boar-horse was running wild. He heard the thud of Brian's feet behind.

But they were forestalled. Mnrogar himself, not thoroughly appeased with having knocked Sir Harimore off his horse, was now quite ready to fight his own mount. He was yanking the boar-horse's head around, and the beast, balanced on two legs, literally was forced to dance backward from the barrier and very nearly go over backward.

But it recovered its balance in time and got down on four legs, and stood there shaking and snorting as Jim and Brian approached. Mnrogar, however, was not content with having it on the ground, and he kicked it immediately into a gallop back down toward his tent. Jim and Brian had to throw themselves in two different directions to keep from being ridden down.

Meanwhile, a little ways up the list, Sir Harimore's attendants had picked him up and were carrying him back to the tent.

"Is Sir Harimore hurt?" Brian called to them.

Sir Harimore said something that neither Brian nor Jim could catch; and one of the attendants called back to Brian.

"My Lord says he is only winded, Sir!"

"Good," said Brian to Jim as they turned and began to walk, panting themselves. Once back, they found Angie trying to calm down the boar-horse, which was already somewhat subdued, but still had Mnrogar—though with his helm off—in his saddle and refusing to get down.

"Lance!" he was almost shouting. "Give me lance!"

"What is this nonsense, troll?" said Brian, stepping to the head of the boar-horse and confronting the furious troll above him. "You've already unhorsed your opponent. You get no more lances."

"Then I'll tear him with my hands!" roared Mnrogar.

The situation in the tent was becoming dangerous; and Angie was there with them. Jim suddenly decided that whether it would mix properly with Carolinus's magic on the troll and the boar-horse or not, he would have to do something to stop the situation from getting out of hand.

"Still!" he ordered, jabbing a pointed finger at Mnrogar and with a clear picture in his mind of the troll frozen in position.

And Mnrogar suddenly was.

Without his agitation, the boar-horse now began to quiet down, too.

"I hope I didn't overdo it," muttered Jim. "But now what? And where's Angie?"

"She went off around the back of the tents, m'Lord," said Ned Dunster, who was himself now back inside with them.

"What for?"

"I don't know, m'Lord."

"Whew! Whew!" said Brian, stepping back from Mnrogar, turning to the table and pouring himself half a cup of wine. He took a swallow from it with a great air of relief.

"Why, since you asked, James," he said, as if there had been no interruption in the conversation between Jim and himself at all, "Mnrogar has swept the field. He has unhorsed all who rode against him. Now, out of sheer courtesy, the Earl should invite him to ride up across the lists to the stand, so that the Earl can acknowledge his victory. We should hear a couple of trumpet notes at any minute now."

"Well, that'll be fine," said Jim. "Mnrogar—*unstill*. Now listen, when you get to the stands, that's going to be your chance to smell out this other troll among the guests."

"Yes!" snarled Mnrogar. "That other—almost I'd forgot!"

Without another word, and before they could stop him, he had pulled the head of the boar-horse around to face the flap in the tent, ridden it out and started down around the lists toward the far end of the stands. Jim and Brian burst out of the tent behind him, only in time to see him well on his way, kicking the sides of his mount futilely with his armored, heelless shoes—Brian had refused to trust him with spurs—and the boar-horse, now taking refuge in the stubbornness that was the other side of its wild character, was refusing to travel at any speed faster than a walk.

Balked of the fight it had wanted, it was still going to have something to say about what it would do; and as they stood there Angie walked up to them without her false mustache and nose and dressed once more in women's clothes, topped by the green travel cloak the wet nurse had borrowed to sneak down to Jim at dinner in the main hall.

"I wore my costume over all this," she said, "and then took the other off in one of these little tents." She stared at them. "What's the matter?"

Jim pointed at Mnrogar.

"The Earl has not invited him over!" said Brian. "This is irregular—"

"Irregular or not," said Jim, "I've got to get there before he does, or at least be there when he gets there, to hold him back by magic, if necessary in case he does something crazy. Carolinus should be taking care of that, but I don't know whether to count on him or not—"

Suddenly realizing he was going about this the wrong way, Jim raised his voice to a shout.

"Ned! Ned Dunster! Bring me that palfrey!"

"I've got to go, too," said Brian. "There may be some who recognized me when I ran down the list with you just now. I must get back, come into the stands from the opposite side and pretend I've been around all the time—or at least confuse things so that no one will know."

Ned Dunster showed up, leading the palfrey. Happily, it was still saddled and ready to go.

"You can ride behind me," said Brian, beating Jim to the saddle and swinging up behind him.

"I've got to go back, too!" said Angie.

"Angela," said Brian, with a touch of exasperation in his voice, "this palfrey cannot carry the three of us! Besides, you cannot be seen riding so. It is not seemly."

"The hell with that!" exploded Angie.

There was a sudden, momentary awkward moment of general paralysis around her. Brian looked shocked.

"What's the matter with you, Brian?" cried Angie. "Women swear around here all the time. Geronde swears. You've heard her often enough!"

"But," Brian said, "not you, Angela. You—you—you are—" He stammered into silence.

"That's right!" said Angie. "I'm not like the others, am I? I've got no children of my own. I haven't got a husband most of the time. I'm not even a female, as far as everybody around here is concerned—"

Tears were starting to roll down her cheeks. Brian looked demoralized and paralyzed. Jim put out a hand toward her, but she knocked it away.

"Don't comfort me!" she said. "I don't want comforting. I'm angry! I'm angry at all of you!"

"And well you might be," said Brian, returning with a snap to his ordinary decisive self. He leaped down from the saddle to the ground and raised his voice. "Ho! Siward! To me, with Blanchard, immediately—saddled and bridled!

"The hell with it, then—and I take the sin of your blasphemy upon my head along with mine, Angela," he said. "I will ride the war horse after all, go around left and you go around right, both of us through the trees; and I'll be there before you. In fact, Blanchard will even help. I can say I went to get him in hopes that the Earl would let me run a course with the Black Knight, after Sir Harimore had fallen."

He put out an arm to stop Angie, who—after staring at him for a moment as he spoke—was now stepping forward to mount.

"No, no, Angela," he said gently. "There are limits. James must take the saddle and you must ride behind him, holding to his waist; or the story of this will do you more harm than an army. I promise you that."

Angie stopped, and stood aside. Jim stepped forward and lifted himself into the saddle, then reached down an arm for Angie. He had left the stirrup free of his toe, and she put her own toe into it and he swung her up with one arm, astraddle the horse behind him. The sidesaddle for women riders was yet to be invented; and riding without a saddle of some kind while sitting sideways on the back of a moving horse was inviting a fall. He felt her arm go around his waist.

"Through the trees, then, and may you be in time," said Brian. He turned to look at one of the small tents farthest from the large one. "Siward!"

"Coming, m'Lord," and a short, blue-eyed, flaxen-haired man-at-arms burst from between the smaller tents, leading a saddled and bridled Blanchard behind him.

Brian ran lightly to the horse, vaulted into the saddle; and, at the touch of his hands on the reins, Blanchard rose on his hind hooves like a dancer, half pivoted in standing position to face the forest, and went off into it at a gallop, so that it almost seemed a single movement from the time Brian had started to run toward the war horse.

Jim turned the palfrey's head toward the forest in the other direction; and in a moment, both he and Angie were in among the trees.

This close to the Earl's castle, the space in among the larger trees had been cleared of fallen branches, bushes and brambles; the first, because dead wood on the ground was a perquisite of the serfs and tenants. Firewood could be cut only by order of the lord of the estate. The brambles and bushes had been cleared, partially by traffic in the normal course of events, and partially because the Earl and those of his household sometimes rode into the woods for some little distance simply on pleasure.

As a result, they were able not so much to gallop, as canter, the palfrey. They made swift progress, accordingly, but still Jim found himself counting the seconds until they were beyond the stands, and had brought the palfrey up behind them, tethered him there, and walked normally out to join the rest of the crowd.

They had made it in relatively short time, however, and as they turned the corner of the stands and walked down in front of it, they were in time to see that Mnrogar was now close to the far end of the stands. He had ceased kicking his mount and rode quietly while the boar-horse plodded along also quietly—ominously so, in both their cases, Jim thought. A troll two thousand years old would not be the sort to forget his fury once it had been kindled; and Jim had his doubts as to whether the boar would, either. But for the moment they looked silent and ominous, rather than potentially and actively dangerous.

Jim and Angie made it to the stands and climbed up to where Geronde was still sitting, still holding space for them. Angie had had time to recover from her emotion and wipe her face with a cloth crunched in the snow until it was wet; and Geronde saw no sign of emotion, evidently, as they climbed up and Angie sat down next to her.

Brian was already there, sitting on Geronde's other side, and his eyes met Jim's in a meaningful glance for a second, before Angie sat down next to Geronde. Geronde immediately began talking, telling her about how the jousting had looked from the stand. Geronde had, Jim inferred, been in on the fact that Angie was going to play helper to Jim in the matter of Mnrogar and the lists, for there was an air of conspiracy about her and she pointedly avoided asking Angie where she had been all this time.

In any case, it was not their talk that concerned him, Jim thought, but whatever Carolinus might be saying to either the Earl or the Bishop—if it was the Bishop in that monk's outfit, of which he was pretty sure. The three of them were only about ten feet over and one seat-row lower than Jim; for the Earl was always given a seat right in the middle of the stands not only measured from end to end but from the first plank level to the top plank level.

There was a steady chatter, low-voiced but continuous, throughout the crowd, as people there commented and speculated on the advance of the Black Knight toward the stands. As the boar-horse reached the corner of the stands at last, an inviting trumpet pealed out twice, belatedly, from below the Earl; and the voice of a herald boomed at him.

"You may approach the noble and gracious Earl of Somerset and the royal Prince of England. Approach!"

Mnrogar made no sound in reply, and as he began to pass the stands the chatter stopped, so that a line of silence moved through the crowd steadily but slowly.

Slowly—because Mnrogar had literally reined his steed back to a lesser pace even than the boar-horse had been insisting on, and was watching all those in the stands as he passed.

It would be more a careful search by nose to sniff out the troll among them, Jim reminded himself. Outdoors here, with the breeze blowing from behind Mnrogar, he was evidently not able to pick up the scent of those not close to him.

There was something strange and threatening about his slow progress, even though, with the helm over his head and his body immovably in the saddle, with only the eye slit facing toward all the people seated on the five ranks of seats in the stand. The expressionlessness of that armored body drew the silence along with him like an invisible veil of command over the crowd.

Sitting high in the saddle of the huge black boar-horse, his eyes were on a level with those in the third row of the stands. As he approached the Earl the silence passed him by and began to spread ahead of him; until even before he reached that nobleman, all the people there were silent.

"Smile at him, Hugo," said Carolinus, in barely above a whisper; but now, in the complete silence, Jim made out the words.

In fact, the troll had little farther to go. He moved on until he was level with the Earl, then reined in his horse abruptly, staring and searching with the helmet slit among those there until it stopped, staring directly at the stands, at the middle plank of the stands, where the Earl and those with him sat.

The Earl cleared his throat with a sound audible from one end of the stands to the other.

"Sir—er, Black Knight," he said. "Much as it has pained us to see our good knights go down before your lance, we must give you due acknowledgment and praise for having won against all who came against you. However, as you yourself said, you were coming to join no tourney; and as the tourney was over in any case, you cannot be considered to have won it in any sense of the word. Nonetheless it has been an honor and an instruction to us to watch you in the lists."

Mnrogar slowly reached up and took off his tilting helm. As his grim head and savage face were revealed, there was a strange change in the silence. It could not be any less without sound than it had been before; but in some indefinable way, it was as if everyone there had suddenly held their breath at once.

"You!" said the Earl.

But Mnrogar was not looking at him. Instead all his attention was directed to Agatha Falon sitting beside him.

"Why, granddaughter," he said, "how do you come to be here?"

"Seize him!" roared the Earl. And nearly seventy of his weaponed and armored men-at-arms ran to do his bidding.

CHAPTER 39

"Bring him in!" said the Earl.

The day was still bright outside, with a cloudless sky, but the tower chamber of the castle they were now in had nothing but arrow slits to let in light; and as a result the interior was gloomy, in spite of the fact that cressets had been set alight on all three interior walls, and a fire blazed in the room's fireplace.

But if the fire warmed anyone, it would have to be those few who sat directly in front of it, at what was—if unofficially so—a table of judges. The Earl sat at the table's exact center, with the young Prince to his right, looking uncomfortable. Beyond the Prince was the Bishop, in his customary dark academic robes, his gold pectoral cross glinting brightly against the black fabric; and his chaplain—the thin man in priest's clothing Jim had met at the high table the night the Bishop was absent.

On the Earl's left side was Carolinus. Jim, Angie and Brian were seated on stools a short distance in front of the table and against the wall on the table's left. Agatha Falon was in a comfortably padded barrel chair against the wall opposite them.

Agatha Falon looked entirely unconcerned. Jim and Angie sat close together, trying to put a good face on it, but secretly perturbed. Under the cover of her full skirt, Angie was holding Jim's hand. Brian, beside them, was looking grumpy.

This would not normally have been the case, since he had won not only the armor and horses of his opponents, but the tournament as well.

In fact, the tournament win had entitled him to a capful of gold pieces the King had sent down with the Prince for the winner. But he already had all these things; and what occupied his mind was what he had not had—a proper dinner. When it was time to eat, unless there was a crisis at hand, Brian needed to be fed.

From his point of view, the dinner was far more important than what was going on here now.

Of course, he had been allowed to start on something *called* a dinner. There had been wine and food in the fashion that had been set out during the previous eleven days of the Christmas season, but from Brian's point of view not enough of either; and not only that, but the ordinary conviviality of such a meal, particularly considering it was the last one of the Christmas season and they would all be parting, had been missing.

To top it off, he had hardly gotten a few mouthfuls before his chance to eat had been cut short by the Earl ordering all here to hold this . . . it would have to be called a gathering, for the Earl had refused to call it a court . . . since Agatha was involved. As Earl, he had the legal right to hold a court; but now he clearly wanted as few witnesses and as little fanfare as possible.

So Brian grumphed. Meanwhile, Jim suddenly had his mind on other things.

When Angie had first taken Jim's hand, there had been other people talking in the room and he had been able to speak to her quietly under the cover of these.

"What's the matter?" he had asked.

"I don't know," she said in a low voice. "I'm worried. After all, we did help Mnrogar pretend to be a Black Knight."

Curiously enough, this had not really been bothering Jim until then. But now he considered it. The only person there besides themselves who had known anything about the Black Knight was sitting at the table with the Earl.

"Don't worry," Jim had said then to Angie. "Carolinus is the only one who could bring that up, and he won't."

But can I be sure of that? Jim was asking himself.

Angie had squeezed his hand; and he thought he had reassured her. But he now found himself continuing to be concerned himself about the present situation.

It came back to him that he had been thinking sometimes lately that Carolinus was not necessarily whole-hearted; that the Master Magician might just be playing a game of his own and simply using them all. Jim had no doubt of Carolinus's very real affection for Angie and himself. But if Magickdom needed Carolinus, Carolinus must also need Magickdom. If there was a real danger of losing his own magical status, the Master Magician could almost not be blamed for throwing Jim and Angie to the wolves, to say nothing of tossing Brian as well; and this present situation might somehow make that necessary.

Now, it occurred to Jim that there had been almost too many things going wrong at once. Perhaps there was a larger, hidden problem behind all the visible ones.

But how to find it, if so? Clearly, at the moment, the Earl, in addition to not liking Mnrogar anyhow, wanted to clear Agatha Falon's name of any association with trolls. Yet the surface evidence was strong that she might well be the troll in disguise that Mnrogar had been smelling among the guests. Strange, it had never occurred to any of them that the disguised troll might be female rather than male.

Jim's mind was still searching for some cause, or root problem, from which all the others might have sprouted. "*Look for the missing witness!*" Sherlock Holmes had said . . .

—Just then, Mnrogar was led in, clanking, loaded down with what looked like about a hundred pounds of iron, in the shape of chains and fetters. His strength seemed equal to its weight, however. He appeared to pay no more attention to the restraints than if they had been made of cloth rather than metal.

He looked around at them all savagely, and the glitter in his eyes only softened for a moment when his gaze stopped briefly on Agatha. But then he looked back, straight ahead at the table and the Earl, and the two regarded each other with a concentration of enmity that ignored everybody else present.

"Shut the door. Now!" said the Earl, to the room at large. "In this room are the only people who know anything about this troll, except the fact that he pretended to be a knight at today's tourney. Necessarily, what else is to be known about him must be kept a secret, for the good of this Earldom, for the good of the realm, for the good of Christendom. Therefore I swear you all to silence—"

"Forgive me, my Lord Earl," said the thin priest next to the Bishop, leaning forward to speak to the nobleman, "but since this is not a court, you cannot swear us—"

"Hush, hush, James!" said the Bishop, without looking at the other man—who quickly drew back his head and said no more.

Jim was staring at the Bishop's priest with curiosity. Whatever or whoever changed the actual speech of this world into what sounded to him like modern English was, as he had noticed before, a very astute translator. Ordinary speech of all kinds came through as recognizably Modern English, only with a certain difference in emphasis and form, depending upon the speaker. But sometimes there were larger differences—as in the songs sung by the other guests at that earlier dinner when he had gotten drunk himself, and sung 'Good King Wenceslas.'

The other lyrics then had come to his ears like the four-teenth-century London English of his university studies. On other occasions, tags of Latin had come through. Also, he had noticed in Ned Dunster's speech a trace of a rural accent he had heard when he had been visiting Somersetshire one summer back in the twentieth century.

Now it seemed to him the priest with the Bishop was speaking in what came to Jim's ear very like a modern Oxbridge accent—that particular, academic, upper-class English accent which had gained its name from a combination of the names of the famous English universities—Oxford and Cambridge.

"—Swear you all to silence!" the Earl was repeating, with a baleful glance in the general direction of the chaplain.

There was a discreet murmur that could have meant anything, from everyone in the room except the Bishop, the chaplain, Carolinus and Jim. The Earl seemed not to notice.

"Now!" he said, turning his attention on Mnrogar. "At the tourney you spoke to Lady Falon as if you knew her. Do you?"

Mnrogar said nothing. His eyes only stared steadily and unblink-ingly into the eyes of the Earl.

"We can make you talk, if necessary!" snapped the Earl.

Mnrogar still said nothing, nor showed by any sign of face or body that the Earl's words had any meaning for him.

"I'm sorry to interrupt, Hugo," said Carolinus smoothly, "but as a matter of fact you can't, you know."

The Earl turned his head sharply to look at him.

"Can't? Can't?" he said. "I damn well can!"

"Well, you can try, Hugo," said Carolinus. Jim watched with interest. That soft tone of Carolinus's voice was something he was only too familiar with. It meant bad news for someone.

"Well, then, why do you say I can't?" said the Earl.

"As Richard's chaplain will undoubtedly confirm," said Carolinus, "the troll is one of what are ordinarily referred to as the Naturals—one of the '*longaevi*.' Humans may speak under torture and duress. The *longaevi* don't. They merely become silent and stay so. One's ability to force others to his will is restricted to men or women using such force against other men or women. It is a way that will not work with other kinds of life. For example, you could not torture a Holy Angel and make him speak."

The Earl blanched at the suggestion, his eyes popping noticeably.

"Just so," went on Carolinus, "the human use of torture is not effective against any other classes of Creatures, Shades, or natural Forces. Even some men and women have been sustained by faith, above and beyond their ordinary human frailties. They have ignored the worst that could be done to them. I'm sure the Lord Bishop or his chaplain would easily find examples for you if you wish. Even some knights, of whom you have certainly heard examples, have on occasion been able to ignore the worst pains that can be put on them for reasons of honor alone—"

"Hah!" said Brian quietly, deep in his throat, a distant part of his attention roused momentarily from contemplation of a Farsed Fesaunt—otherwise more mundanely known as a pheasant or chicken stuffed with spiced apples and oats. But only Jim heard him.

"A Natural," concluded Carolinus, "will only answer if the one questioning him is someone he wants to answer."

The Earl threw himself backward in his chair.

"All right, by Saint Anthony!" he said. "You question him, Carolinus. And find out what he means by calling himself a king!"

"Very well, Hugo," said Carolinus. He transferred his attention to Mnrogar. "Mnrogar, I don't believe we've met, but most Naturals have heard of Carolinus. In two thousand years, you must have heard of me yourself."

"Yes," growled Mnrogar.

"And am I correct in assuming that what you heard was that Carolinus was a friend to all Naturals—indeed to all creatures; and that they could safely be friendly with him? Is that right?"

"Yes," growled Mnrogar again.

"Well, then," said Carolinus, "the only question is whether you believe that and would trust me enough to talk to me yourself. Will you?"

Mnrogar gave him a long look.

"Yes."

"Very good, then," said Carolinus. "Then, to take a lesser matter first, some of us here are a little surprised that you should have announced yourself as a king."

"I am a king," snarled Mnrogar.

"King of what, Mnrogar?"

"King among the trolls," said Mnrogar. "For that I have held my land longer than any of them, and none has dared venture upon it. For two thousand years nearly I have been king and kept my land here."

"Your land—" The Earl choked himself off. He grumbled at Carolinus. "Go on, Mage."

"Well, then," said Carolinus lightly, "since you are so regarded among trolls, even if not among us who are human, then we cannot indeed say that you lied in announcing yourself as such."

"No troll lies," said Mnrogar. "We have no need to."

"Who made you a knight, then?" shouted the Earl. "You named yourself as the Black Knight. Knighthood is given, not assumed—ask him who made him a knight, Mage!"

"Who did make you a knight, Mnrogar?" asked Carolinus.

"I did," said Mnrogar.

The Earl's face went a dusky shade of red. Carolinus turned to him and smiled gently.

"I don't think we can quarrel with that, Hugo," he said. "Even by our own standards, a King can make a knight, I believe?"

"Yes, but he—he—"

The Earl gave up and threw himself backward once more in his seat, having been carried away enough to lean forward toward Mnrogar when the subject of knighthood had come up.

"Enough of this footling," he said. "Ask him why he spoke to Lady Agatha."

"Very well," said Carolinus. "Now, Mnrogar, you spoke to Lady Agatha as if you knew her. How did you recognize her?"

"I smelled her," said Mnrogar.

"I take it," said Carolinus, "you mean you recognized her by her scent. How does it happen that you would recognize her that way, instead of someone else?"

"I'd smelled her before," said Mnrogar.

"Can I ask where?"

"In the woods," said Mnrogar.

"Where? How? Why? When?" barked the Earl.

"Can you answer the questions that Hugo has just mentioned?" asked Carolinus.

"Yes," said Mnrogar.

There was a pause. But Mnrogar said nothing more.

"Let me ask, then," said Carolinus to him. "Will you answer them?"

"No," said Mnrogar.

"Can I ask why?" asked Carolinus.

"Yes."

"Why, then?"

Mnrogar was silent.

"Mnrogar," said Carolinus in a mildly reproving tone, "I thought you were going to answer me."

"I do," said Mnrogar. "What you ask. Not him."

"Well, then, if I asked the same questions now—" Carolinus hesitated and the second stretched out into another, newer, more stubborn silence from the troll.

"Ah, well," he said, at last. He turned to the Earl.

"I'm sorry, Hugo," he said. "Since the questions came from you to begin with, he will not answer. I'm afraid there's nothing to be done about it."

"But we've got to find out some way!" shouted the Earl. "Lady Falon's been sullied by this creature's pretending to know her. In truth—"

Jim half heard the words as if the Bishop was instead saying, "*Yn sooth*—" He seemed to hear more of the actual speech when he was not really paying attention, he told himself . . . "*Yn sooth*." It had a familiar ring.

"—It must be made clear, once and for all, he was lying!" The Earl was finishing his protest.

"As you heard him say," said Carolinus, "trolls don't lie. Most Naturals don't. In fact, those who do have lying as a necessary part of their individual character—you might say, as part of their purpose and reason for being. I'm afraid, Hugo, you're never going to be able to find out from Mnrogar why he spoke to Agatha."

"By Heaven, we've got to find out!" said the Earl, thumping the table with his fist. "A name must be cleared! A fair Lady has been sullied—yes, sullied—by some wild words said by what you call a Natural—*Unnatural*, I call him! She must be cleared; as I said in the beginning. That is why we are here!"

"That is to say," broke in the Bishop, equally loudly, "the truth must be established! Supposedly this troll wished to smell out another troll among your guests, my Lord Earl. But who does he choose to speak to, out of all there? Lady Falon. He addresses her as 'granddaughter.' If Lady Falon has even the slightest trace of troll blood in her, then it must be known. She has been close to our royal King, whom God defends; and whom it is our duty also to defend from all things, human and otherwise. The royal Son sits by you at this moment, Somerset! Certainly we are concerned with calumny against any human soul—if indeed it be wholly a human soul. But our duty to the King comes before all, even Lady Falon's reputation!"

The Bishop and the Earl were both on their feet, facing each other.

CHAPTER 40

"*Sit down*," said Carolinus in a voice that even Jim had never heard before.

The two men glared at each other; but they sat.

"Angie," said Jim softly, under the cover of a small competition of meaningfully angry throat clearings and coughings on the part of both Bishop and Earl that had broken out, "have you any idea where that '*soothing box*' is—the box the Sea Devil gave me for a Christmas present?"

"It's right in our second room," said Angie, "in a slot under the crib I had some of our men-at-arms make secretly for little Robert, after we got here. I brought it because Carolinus and Rrrnlf talked about you keeping your magic in it. I thought you might need the magic you had in it while you're here; so of course I packed it with the rest of the things we brought."

"Here? That's terrific!" said Jim. "Look, I'm going to keel over now in a dead faint. Don't worry. It'll just be an excuse to leave this room so I can get the box. You're sure it's under the crib and nowhere else?"

"Of course I'm sure," said Angie.

"All right," said Jim, "here I go—"

He closed his eyes and fell forward off his chair on to the floor, doing—he flattered himself—a very realistic job of it. Certainly he hit the floor a lot harder than he had expected.

His eyes were closed, but he heard Angie give a very realistic shriek.

"He has succumbed to a virus!" cried Angie. "My Lord Earl, Your Grace! I must take him down to our rooms immediately. It may be only a passing thing and he can be back in a moment; but he must be taken immediately!"

"Sir Brian," said the Earl, "see to it. You will find men-at-arms outside the door, who can carry him for the Lady Angela. Lady Angela, once he is down there and safe to be left, you come back, leaving word that he is to return the minute he is able to do so!"

Jim heard a thud near his head. Cautiously he opened the eyelid of his right eye, which was almost pressed against the floor.

He looked and saw Brian down on one knee by his left side. Brian's left hand took him by the belt; his other hand took his right wrist and lifted him into a sitting position as Brian's shoulder was tucked into his belly. Then Brian stood up, sliding Jim even farther back over his right shoulder until he hung balanced by his middle there. By that time Brian had let go of his right hand and his left hand came around to take both Jim's wrists, while Brian's right hand slid down to hold him by the knees.

Brian walked out. It was not so much what Brian had done, as the swift and practiced ease with which he had done it, that impressed Jim. Evidently, Brian had been a one-man rescue team before, for other individuals who had been unconscious on the ground—probably as a result of combat. But it was still a remarkable demonstration and a reminder of Brian's strength.

Jim would not have thought it possible to pick up and carry off an unconscious body single-handed that matter-of-factly—simply put it on your shoulder, get up and walk away with it. It was one more in a long string of surprising examples of how strong most of these medieval people had all been made by the necessities of their work, play and fighting.

Angie slipped ahead of Brian to open the door, and let them through. Jim heard the door close behind him and kept his eyes closed tightly.

"Here, fellows," said Brian's voice. "Lady Angela will show you where to go."

Jim found himself passed into a number of hands, at least two holding him by his legs, a couple of different arms holding his waist and another pair holding his shoulders and head. They made their uneven way off along what was obviously a corridor.

It was not the most comfortable way to travel, and the trip seemed unreasonably long. At last he found himself laid down more or less gently on the sleeping mattress on the floor of their first room. He stayed where he was until he heard the feet of his carriers go out the door and the door close behind them. Then he opened his eyes and sat up. Angie was not in the room with him.

In almost the same moment, though, she came through the leather door from the other room, holding the "soothing box."

"It's empty as usual, as far as I can see," Angie said. "I wondered about that when I decided to bring it. But then, I suppose your magic is invisible?"

"I hope so," said Jim. "But of course, Carolinus will know if I use any."

"He certainly knew I was faking with that 'virus' excuse," said Angie. "All the rest swallowed it with no question. But anyway, what good is the box going to do you, since the Bishop already blessed the castle? Isn't it true no magic can be made inside since then, until he's left?"

"No *new* magic," said Jim. "That's what I'm counting on. Whatever magic is in this may still work. But then there's Carolinus—well, I'll cross that bridge when I come to it."

"How are you going to take the box into the room without everyone wondering what it is?" asked Angie.

Jim stared at her. He had simply not thought that far ahead.

"Well, there's something I can do," said Angie, "if it'll help. I can hang it from a cord around my waist and tie it to the outside of one leg. These wide skirts can hide anything. It's light enough."

"Angie," said Jim, "you're a genius!"

"Oh, you say that to all the geniuses," said Angie. "I'll get some cord."

She went back into the other room and did not come back right away. When she did, she twirled about in front of Jim.

"Can you see any sign of it under my skirt?" she asked.

"No," said Jim. "Will you have any trouble untying it and passing it to me once we're in the room? You could pass it behind my chair and I could hold it there until I was ready to use it."

"There's no problem to that," said Angie. "But we'd probably better head back, shouldn't we?"

"Yes!" said Jim. It suddenly struck him that things might already have gotten into a situation—during even this short absence—in which even the soothing box wouldn't be able to be of help. He climbed to his feet, and they started to hike back toward the room out of which Jim had recently been carried.

"What are you going to do with it?" asked Angie as they went.

"Use it as a lie detector, if I'm lucky. You know how, when we hear people, the dragons, Aargh and everybody else seem to say things in ordinary modern English—you know it isn't really what they're saying? If you listen, you get little echoes now and then of the real sounds they're making?"

"I know it," said Angie.

"Well, it just suddenly struck me," said Jim. "The Earl had just said 'in truth—' and when he did that I heard just sort of a ghost of the sounds 'yn sooth.' In other words, he was saying exactly the same thing, only in archaic language. Then I suddenly realized that when the Sea Devil gave me this box as a Christmas present Carolinus called it a 'soothing box.' I'd been thinking of 'soothing' in the modern form of the word— meaning comforting, easing. But what I think now it really is, is a *sooth-box*—a truth-box; or maybe just a box that separates the truth from anything false. It could be the answer to how to find out the true relationship between Agatha Falon and Mnrogar."

By the time they had finished talking, they were almost back to the room where the Earl, the Bishop and the others were. The men-at-arms standing and squatting about the hall outside the door of the room stood up and came to the medieval equivalent of attention. Without having to be asked, one of them scratched at the door, then opened it without waiting for an answer and put his head in. They could hear his voice.

"Sir James and Lady Angela are back, m'Lord!"

"Send them in!" boomed the voice of the Earl.

Now, with the door open, and the two of them approaching it, they could hear the Earl and the Bishop still in hot argument. The man-at-arms closed the door behind them, and they found everything almost without change from the way it had been when they had left it some minutes earlier.

The only difference was that Brian was sitting in the first of the three seats on their side of the room, with the other two vacant beside him. Jim sat down next to him, so that there would be two bodies to hide Angie when she passed the box to him.

Except for Carolinus and the chaplain, no one paid any attention to them. The Earl and the Bishop were still arguing. The Prince was frankly asleep, undisturbed by the loud voices right next to him. Mnrogar stood in the middle of the room; as if he had not only stood there for a century already, but was able to stand another century if necessary.

"—My castle is my castle!" the Earl was saying. "Here I have sovereignty—"

"—Not over matters of Church or Realm!" roared the Bishop. "And I speak for the Church—"

"My Lords, my Lords," said Carolinus, "this disagreement between you could go on forever. Let us make one more effort to determine from Mnrogar whether he will tell us if there is indeed any relationship between himself and Lady Falon; or whether the matter is impossible to resolve. If it is impossible to resolve, then I can only suggest that nothing is to be gained by questioning Mnrogar any further; and we must seek by other means to find whatever other troll was in this castle—if indeed there was one."

His argument clearly offered a welcome excuse to both men to stop their verbal fighting. But both had to sputter, grumble and protest a bit before they agreed to it. Meanwhile, Jim took the opportunity to whisper to Angie.

"Can you pass me the box now?" he asked.

"Just a minute," said Angie.

With her arm that was between her and Jim, she reached back behind her and sat, looking forward at the room with an innocent face for a few minutes. Then Jim felt something hard pressed against the small of his back. He reached back with the arm next to Brian, and his fingers closed on the box.

"Thanks," he whispered.

"A pleasure," said Angie.

Meanwhile, up at the long table, the Earl and the Bishop had settled down to listen while Carolinus resumed his questioning of the troll.

"Ah, Mnrogar," said Carolinus affably, "is Lady Agatha Falon your granddaughter?"

"No," said Mnrogar.

"But you called her granddaughter when you spoke to her there in the stands," said Carolinus.

Mnrogar said nothing.

"Why did you call her your granddaughter?" Carolinus said gently.

"She is young," Mnrogar said.

"And you, of course," said Carolinus, "are very old by comparison. I see. It was just a natural thing to speak of someone born just recently by your standards as granddaughter or grandson—am I correct?"

Mnrogar did not answer.

"There!" exploded the Earl. "More of his stubbornness—"

"If you please, Hugo," said Carolinus. "I believe we can take Mnrogar's silence in answer to my question as evidence that he does so speak when addressing someone younger than himself. Otherwise he would have answered 'No.' "

He turned back to Mnrogar.

"But you had told us all that you were interested in finding another troll disguised as a human among the guests of my Lord Earl," he said to Mnrogar. "Yet, when you are given a chance to examine all the guests there, the one you choose to speak to is Lady Falon. If there had truly been another troll among the guests, and you knew that other troll was there, we would have expected you to put your attention on whatever person that was. Or will you tell us that there never was a troll among the guests to begin with, and your saying there was one was only a lie?"

"Trolls do not lie," said Mnrogar.

"Hah!" said the Earl derisively.

"No, Hugo," said Carolinus. "He's telling the truth in that. This is something that because of my rank and knowledge I happen to know is a fact. I think we can take it for granted that he does have some knowledge of Lady Falon. Whether there ever was another troll in the stands, or what connection all that has with Agatha, I don't think we're ever going to be able to find out."

Jim cleared his throat.

"My Lord Earl—Carolinus," he said in his politest voice, "might I suggest something?"

"Anything! Anything!" said the Earl.

Jim produced the box from where he had been holding it out of sight between Angie and himself.

"It happens I have a magic box—" he began.

"Magick!" roared the Bishop. "There can be no Magick here! I have put the blessing of the Almighty upon this place and the Magick your box contains is useless here and now!"

"I'm afraid, Richard," said Carolinus, turning to him, "that you may not be exactly right. No new Magick can be made here, of course. But that box is very old Magick indeed; and all it is concerned with is old Magick. It is therefore a part of the Everything; and since it has been a part, cannot be made to disappear by what in this case is an *ex post facto* blessing. Also, it is a box which was given by another personage to my apprentice; and therefore I cannot gainsay its use—although it concerns me that his use of it might possibly put him in some danger. I have an idea of how he intends to use it; and I must warn him—I must warn you very strongly, Jim—that what you evoke from that box must have an effect on your own future, either for Weal or for Woe."

"Hah!" said Brian in Jim's left ear; and Jim turned to see his friend, thoughts of food left far behind and a martial glitter in his eyes.

He turned to look at Angie, and read very clearly in her eyes and face that she was telling him it was up to him.

"Whatever effect it has, I'll use it now; and maybe we can get some of the answers Mnrogar won't give us," said Jim. Mentally he crossed his fingers that what he was going to try would work. He was holding the box in his lap. He opened its lid and spoke into its apparently empty interior.

"Is the father of Agatha Falon there?" he asked.

"I am here," replied a hollow, but deep-toned voice from the box. It was a voice such as might have been heard above ground by someone speaking, far out of sight below, in an opened grave. The fire in the fireplace and in the cressets suddenly burned lower and the room dimmed. A chill and an earthy smell seemed to come into the whole room.

"Tell us," said Jim, "anything you know about your daughter and any connection she might have had with a troll."

"That I will tell," said the voice. "I am Sir Blandys de Falon. I was born nearly a century ago and she was the child of my second wife. I had only one son, who is now dead as I am dead. I had only the one daughter, my Agatha, late in life. I loved her dearly for that my son had turned out to be a bookworm, and showed no desire to live as a man should and wear the golden spurs of knighthood."

The voice broke as if it was too painful to go on, and ceased. Indeed, in spite of its hollow, forbidding quality, as if it was speaking from a distant, vast and empty tomb, there was a pain to be heard in it that visibly touched everybody listening in the room. It was as if the voice would weep, but could not.

"Go on," commanded Jim, after some seconds.

"I loved her dearly," the voice went on, "until her age was of barely six years. Then, one day when her nurse had taken her walking in the woods near to our home, that same nurse came back without her, distraught, torn and bleeding from deep cuts and slashes.

"It was then she told me she had lost my daughter. That a female troll had sprung out from behind some bushes and snatched my daughter away, though the nurse fought to hold her. But the troll was too strong, and she disappeared carrying my little girl; and that was the last I saw of her."

The voice ceased again.

"Who then—?" said the Bishop, but in a muted voice, looking at the adult Agatha Falon, expressionless, and motionless in her barrel chair against the far wall.

"Can that nurse hear me now?" Jim asked the box. "If so, answer."

"I am here," came a thin and wailing voice like a small breeze lost among dark trees in the distance.

"Then tell us how you came to lose young Agatha Falon to the troll," said Jim.

"I will tell," said the thin voice. "I am Winifred Hustings, the daughter of a poor knight, who on his death, my mother being dead, found a place and work with Sir Blandys de Falon as nurse to his daughter. I died but two years agone—an old, old woman. But well I remember the day I took the child Agatha walking in the near woods, the safe woods not far from the stout walls of the home of the Falons. But in those woods, as we were passing some bushes, barely in leaf—for it was but the first of spring— there leaped a female troll, as large as I was, and tried to snatch Agatha from me. Agatha clung to my hand and I tried to protect her. But the troll was stronger than I and her claws and teeth were cruel. Before I knew it, she had gotten Agatha from me and was gone; and I had only strength enough to get back with word of what had happened to Sir Falon. Then I fell and was unconscious for some days.

"For a long time after that I lay abed, for the wounds made by the troll festered, and I was too weak to rise and do anything. When at last I was recovered, I was put to some small duties having to do with ordering the housekeeping of the castle— for Sir Blandys's second wife, Agatha's mother, had died in childbirth."

The nurse's voice died as if all the strength had gone out of it.

"And you never saw Agatha Falon again, either?" asked Jim.

"Oh, yes," said the thin voice of the nurse, "she came back two years later. One morning as we opened the great gates in the main wall, there she was, with hardly a rag of clothing on her, dirty, scratched, and hardly recognizable by anyone but me. But I knew her. So we took her in, and cleaned her and cared for her; but she could not or would not tell us where she had been all that time, or what had happened to her."

"She couldn't even tell you?" said Jim. "Would she talk to her father about it?"

"Sir Blandys would have nothing to do with her," said the voice of the nurse, hopelessly. "He believed she was a changeling—"

There was an indrawn breath from all in the room except Jim, Angie and Carolinus.

"—Not the girl we had lost two years before," the voice of the nurse went on. "But he gave directions she was to be kept and cared for and brought up exactly as if she had never left us; and all were forbidden on pain of death from mentioning the fact that she had been missing those years—though it was known on his lands and possibly even further. But, with time, I think most forgot. Sir Blandys died only four years after that, and everything fell into the hands of the Lady Agatha's older brother; and she was all but ignored and forgotten, and her story with her."

"Sir Blandys!" said Jim.

"I am here," said the voice of Sir Blandys.

"Why would you have nothing to do with your daughter after she came back?" said Jim. "You said you loved her dearly."

"I loved her dearly—but was this that came back to my gate my daughter? I did not believe so. Two years had gone by. She was not the same. She was a changeling, sent back by the troll that took her—"

"And you actually had no more to do with her after she came back?" said Jim.

"After that," said the hollow voice of Sir Blandys, "I could not bear the sight of what had been sent back to me. All that I had loved was gone. I did not find it in this new creature that wore her shape. But, for the good of the family name, I kept the fact of what she was secret. I gave orders that it be kept secret. And secret it was kept from then on."

Sir Blandys's voice stopped.

"A changeling," said the Bishop in a low voice, looking at Agatha. "Lady Agatha, on peril to your immortal soul, tell us the truth about what happened after the troll took you!"

Agatha did not answer. In fact, she did not even seem to hear what the Bishop was saying.

"If you will not answer, Lady Agatha," said the Bishop, "I must conclude that you are indeed a changeling. That—"

Agatha woke suddenly and stared at him.

"I am no changeling!" she cried. "These are only voices that mean nothing from an empty box. Magick, where no Magick should be, if the Church had had the power it pretends to have. It's true that my father would have nothing to do with me. But he never liked me, even when I was very young. Find anyone to tell you different. You cannot convict me of being anything but what I am, the true daughter of Sir Blandys de Falon, not on the basis of Magick alone. That is the law; I have heard it said so many times. Is it not the law?"

"In fact, my Lord Bishop," said the Bishop's chaplain, "what the Lady Agatha says is true in the legal sense. The Church in its infinite mercy does not judge or condemn on the basis of Magick, alone. That is a principle long established and invariably respected."

The Bishop brushed his words aside with an angry flip of his large hand.

"We seek to find out if she is a changeling and a troll, not to punish her in law," he snapped. "Here are witnesses from beyond the grave who cannot lie, also a troll who was to find another troll by scent and picked her out of all else there."

The Earl was looking aghast. Suddenly, he was looking old and crumpled.

"My Lord Bishop!" said Angie, unexpectedly and in a carrying, cutting voice. "You are making some assumptions, aren't you? Who says these people from beyond the grave can't be wrong simply because that's where they're speaking from? Also what makes you sure that Mnrogar 'picked her out'?"

"Lady Angela," thundered the Bishop, "you are not here to give us your opinion. Furthermore—"

"Hold it!" said Jim—and, remarkably, the Bishop did.

Jim had been startled at the note of angry command in his own voice almost as much as by its success. In fact, in the following split second he recognized that everybody else around the room was looking at him with startled faces too, with the exception of Mnrogar, who was expressionless, and Carolinus, whose expression gave the impression of a cat licking his whiskers after finishing a bowl of particularly thick cream. Jim hurried to take advantage of the transient opportunity.

"Two of the witnesses from my box," he said, "have given us conflicting answers. I will ask again—'Winifred Hustings, do you believe that the girl found outside the gate and taken back into the family was the same girl that had been lost when you had been with her two years before?'"

"I believe so," said Winifred's thin voice. "She was changed,

it was true. She had something like a round rock she trea-
sured and kept always with her; and she seemed to have forgotten somewhat of the manners of eating and dressing that she
had known before she was taken away. But they came back to
her quickly; and in every movement and in every tone of her
voice, I heard the little Agatha I had cared for before she was
taken."

"A knight's word, against that of a mere servant," said the
Bishop. "The nurse could well be working off some ancient
resentment against Sir Blandys by lying to us."

"I do not lie!" wailed the voice from the box.

"She does lie!" It was the voice of Sir Blandys.

"Carolinus," said Jim quickly. "Could you ask Mnrogar if he's
willing to tell us anything more he knows about Agatha Falon,
now that we've heard what her father and her nurse had to say
about her being taken away by a troll early in life?"

"Mnrogar," said Carolinus, "have you any more to tell us now
about Agatha Falon?"

Mnrogar said nothing.

"Oh, leave him alone!" burst out Agatha Falon. "You all know
nothing. You can prove nothing. It matters not to me, in any case,
what you think or say!"

There was a moment of silence in the chamber—baffled silence
on the part of the Bishop, thoughtful silence on the part of his
chaplain, and a still, stunned silence on the part of the Earl. Jim
felt nagging at him Sherlock Holmes's words about the missing
witness. There was somebody somewhere who had not been heard
from. Well, there was one last thing to try.

"Soothing box," he said, "is there someone else there who saw
and knew Agatha Falon during the two years of her childhood she
was missing from her home? If so, I call on whoever that is to
speak."

There was a short pause in which it seemed that everybody
in the room was suddenly tense, and then a voice came strongly
from the box.

"I am Mnrogar and I still live!" said the voice—and it was the
voice of the troll.

A clanking noise was Jim's only warning. He looked up from
the box to see Mnrogar hurling himself, a hundred pounds of iron
and all, at Jim and the box.

CHAPTER 41

"Still!" cried Carolinus, pointing a finger at the troll.

Mnrogar, suddenly motionless, but unable to halt his momentum, crashed forward to the floor at Jim's feet, still glaring up at him in awful silence.

"All right, Mnrogar," said Carolinus sternly. "You can move now, but only to get up and come back and stand where you were. And don't try that again!"

Mnrogar did so, his eyes still implacably on Jim, but swiveling toward Carolinus as he reached his former place in the middle of the room and stood still. It had all happened so quickly, that nobody else had had a chance to move or make a sound. Now the voice, Mnrogar's voice from the box, went on.

"—I am Mnrogar, and I go where I will. None wait to face me. Sometimes I have gone far afield to see if there was not another troll who would not run at sight or scent of me—"

"Still the thing!" said the chain-bound Mnrogar himself, suddenly and harshly. "I will speak!"

Jim hastily shut the lid of the box, which was still talking, clipping off the voice from it in mid-syllable.

"I was far from here once," said Mnrogar. "I smelled a female, her scent mixed with that of a human. I went to it, found her den, at least two days empty. But lying just outside it, almost dead but not moving, was a small human. A young human.

"I was not hungry. I watched it a little while and it tried to crawl to me. I was not hungry. I picked it up and brought it back here with me. Here to my own den—"

He stared at the Earl.

"—And you know where that den is."

The Earl said nothing.

"On my own land here there are deer, swine, rabbits, many things. Here I have never been hungry. I offered food to the little human, but it could not eat as I eat. But living here, I have come to know humans. I went upstairs at night when all were asleep and brought down their kind of food, and water. This she ate. In time she became strong. The female had not known how to feed her. She had taken the small one to replace a pup of her own which had died—but it had been no use. This human pup could not eat the fresh meat she threw to it. It would not follow her when she went out of the den to hunt. It was weak and useless. She left it.

"I was wiser. I fed it and kept it. The little her grew. She would hide a small piece of rock, then tug and pull at me to look for it until I found it. Then, she would give it to me to hide, so she could find it. It came to me I liked finding her there when I came back from hunting.

"But in time she ceased eating, and grew thin again. I took her back to her own human place, not far from that female's den and left her there before sunrise. Then I came back here."

He stopped speaking so abruptly that it was a moment before those in the room realized that he was actually done.

"This is all very well," said the Bishop. But he spoke in a somewhat less loud and angry tone of voice. "The fact remains that this troll before us said he smelled another troll among those who would have been in the stands this morning; but the only one he smelled out was Lady Agatha. If Lady Agatha is not a troll, or has no troll blood, how does she come to smell like a troll?"

The question hung on the air of the room, it seemed to Jim, like the single strand of hair that had been tied to the hilt of the sword hanging directly above the head of Damocles as that unhappy courtier at the court of King Dionysius sat in his chair at a banquet. He looked at Carolinus for help; but Carolinus's face was expressionless and unhelpful. Then the memory of the suspended sword gave Jim a sudden inspiration.

"Lady Agatha," he said, "your nurse has told us that you were very attached to a piece of stone after you had returned to your family home and carried it with you constantly. Would you happen to have it with you now?"

Agatha Falon glared at him.

"What matter to you whether I have or not?" she snapped.

"Don't be a fool!" said Angie. "He's trying to help you and this troll."

"If you've got it," said Jim, "may I see it?"

Agatha did nothing for a moment and said nothing. Then she reached into the purse at her belt, and brought out something that appeared to be somewhat smaller than a tennis ball. For a moment it seemed as if she would throw it overhand with some force directly at Jim; then her arm dropped and she merely tossed it to him.

He caught it in one hand, holding the box safely on his knees with the other—but still it stung the skin of his palm. It was heavy and hard; and this in spite of the fact that it seemed to be completely covered by a thick matting of some fine finely tangled material.

Jim put it close to his nose and sniffed at it. Then he passed it to Brian.

"Don't say anything out loud just yet, Sir Brian," he said, "but would you smell that?"

Brian took the object, his eyebrows raising. He put it to his nose, and then lowered it and looked at Jim.

"Did you ever remember running into that odor before?" asked Jim.

"I do," said Brian. "It was the stink we ran into in the den of this troll here, below the castle, when we went down to remonstrate with him at Mage Carolinus's command."

"Yes," said Jim, taking the rounded, heavy ball back from him. "That was what came to my mind when I smelled it, too. By its weight I would judge it indeed to be rock; and it has become completely covered with something that smells strongly of troll. As everyone can see, though I think all here knew it before, trolls have a sort of fine hair or fur all over them; and no doubt they shed this either at certain seasons or regularly, like other furred creatures. I remember noticing this hair clinging to all the lower surfaces in the den; and eighteen hundred years of shedding by Mnrogar could account for it. If this rock came from there, it would be covered and smell of troll so strongly—this is only a guess on my part—"

"You are right, however, Jim," said Carolinus. "Trolls do shed; and in nearly two thousand years that den of Mnrogar's would be thick with it. Also, any small piece of stone down there would acquire a coating too."

"Mage!" said the Bishop. "What was the command you gave these two knights to send them down to the troll's den? What specific orders did you give?"

Carolinus turned and smiled benignly at him.

"With all respect to your high office in the Church, my Lord Bishop," he said affably, "I must plead the privilege of confidentiality where matters of Magick are concerned."

The Bishop's jaw clamped shut, but he said nothing further. Carolinus turned back to Jim.

"I take it you were about to suggest something, Jim," he said.

"Only that with this on her person, the Lady Agatha could not fail to smell like a troll to another troll from a distance. I believe that, limited as my own human nose is, I can smell this ball at arm's length myself." He looked across at Agatha.

"I don't suppose you'll deny, Lady Agatha," he said, "that this was the piece of rock with which you played games with Mnrogar during the time you were with him?"

"No. I don't," said Agatha.

"So," said Jim, looking at the table. "With due respect, my Lord Bishop, I submit that there is no longer any doubt that the Agatha Falon here in this room is the same child that was stolen away from her father in the first place; and that her father was ill self-advised in never seeing her after she had returned, nor having anything to do with her. So that he fell into the error of assuming that she was a changeling when she was not."

"A pert knight, this apprentice of yours, Mage," said the Bishop grimly to Carolinus.

"Nonetheless, my Lord," said Carolinus, "I find myself very much of his opinion. Do not you?"

"I am considering it," said the Bishop. "In any case, we still have the troll in our hands. Let us at least dispose of him properly."

The Earl had been regaining his upright posture, and even something of the years he had appeared to lose a little earlier. He was once more upright and bristling.

"Men-at-arms!" he shouted.

The door opened and five of his armed men poured into the room, their swords either all the way out or half out of their sheaths.

"M'Lord?" asked the first one, who was not only oldest but in the lead of the others.

The Earl pointed at Mnrogar.

"Take him out," he said. "Slay him! Make sure he is dead!"

"No!" shrieked Agatha Falon.

She jumped up, ran across, and fell on her knees in front of the table before the Earl, her hands clasped on the table before him.

"My Lord, I beg you," she said, "in the name of Heaven's mercy—"

"Get out! Get out!" snapped the Earl at the men-at-arms, his face turning pink and looking suddenly very flustered. The men-at-arms hastened to do so.

"In the name of the pity enjoined upon us by the Lord Jesus!" said Agatha. "Let him live! You and your family have owed more to him over many centuries than any of you ever realized! You have grown so used to having your woods fat with game, and free of other night dangers, that you may have forgotten what it is like when trolls come and go through those same woods, killing the finest bucks and other breeds, fighting each other and sometimes even preying on humans. He has never preyed on humans. Spare him, my Lord. I, Agatha Falon on my knees to you, beg you to spare him. Let him live and you will not regret it. Your land will stay clear of other trolls that might ever prey on humans— night-trolls, and other grim creatures. All stay away now for fear of him. You would be doing yourself a disservice to slay him, m'Lord; and you would break my heart!"

"Lady—Lady Agatha, this—this is not seemly—"

Sputtering, the Earl got up suddenly, knocking his chair over backward. He hurried around the end of the table and took both her hands in his, raising her to her feet.

"You must not kneel to me like that," he said. "You must not. Perhaps—perhaps you are right. Perhaps he has been of more benefit than trouble. Still, there are matters of which you do not know that have to do with the very fabric of this castle—"

"Whatever these other matters are, perhaps Mnrogar will be willing now, to see them as you see them, m'Lord," she said. Her voice softened, became husky and she moved a little closer to him. "If you would endure my presence as a guest for some more little time, perhaps all things between him and your Lordship could be arranged. He is lonely and unhappy, I know; and if I was here, at least for a little while, I could go down and visit him from time to time—"

She turned to Mnrogar.

"Would you like me to come down and spend part of an hour or so with you occasionally, grandfather?" she said to him.

Mnrogar stared at her.

"Yes," he said.

She turned back to the Earl.

"Will you show mercy and charity then, m'Lord?" she said. "And at the same time solve whatever problems you may have in which friendship with Mnrogar could give you? And I—I myself—"

Her voice became even more low and husky.

"—would be loath to leave you as well as him and this castle, m'Lord."

"Harrumph!" The Earl cleared his throat. "Reasonable suggestion! Why not? There's a question of his good behavior, though, if we take him out of those irons—"

"Oh, m'Lord," said Agatha, "I am sure, so sure he will give you no more cause for worry if you release him. Would you, grandfather?"

Mnrogar noticeably hesitated before answering.

"No," he said at last. But Agatha looked over to the Prince at the table; he had woken up somewhere along the line and had been watching everything that was happening and being said with interest.

"My Royal Lord," she said, "of course if I stay here, this means I would not be returning to London with you. Sad I am not to go back there now to all my friends at the Royal Court. But I feel I have a duty here. Perhaps you will remember me to your Royal father; and say that while I would like to see him again someday, that whether I do or not is in the hands of God."

"Indeed," said the Prince quite cheerfully, "I will be most happy to carry your message."

"And you, my Lord Bishop," said Agatha. She still had hold of the Earl's hands. "Are you satisfied now that I am no evil creature, that I have nothing but pure human, Christian blood in my veins?"

"Daughter," said the Bishop sternly. "Can you say the Lord's Prayer?"

"If your Lordship wishes," said Agatha. "*Pater noster qui es in caelis, sanctifietur nomen . . .*"

She continued through all the Latin words of the prayer the Bishop had asked for.

"Well, well," said the Bishop gruffly, "there is no smoke coming from your ears and nostrils. Perhaps you are indeed innocent in this matter, my child. Nonetheless, you are proposing to visit what is surely an unclean creature from time to time here. Are you sure that your visits will not be involved in anything that would put your immortal soul in danger?"

"Certainly not, my Lord Bishop," said Agatha seraphically. "Upon my immortal soul, I go only to speak to him from time to time, so that he does not become lonely. For it is the lonely who cause much of the trouble in the world; and often only a little conversation can mend things for them."

"If it is as you say," said the Bishop, "then I see no reason—in other words, I can hardly bless such endeavors where a creature like this is concerned; but I gather you believe what you intend is an act of charity and that, of course, is always commendable."

At this moment there was a frantic scratching on the door, followed by an actual knock.

"Come in!" roared the Earl.

The older man-at-arms who had led the rest into the room before stepped through the barely opened door just enough to make himself visible.

"Crave pardon for disturbing you, m'Lord," he said, "but word has just come. The castle is surrounded by trolls in the nearby woods. More than a few of them have been seen from the lookout in his post on top of the high tower."

"Trolls!" said the Earl, the Bishop and the Bishop's chaplain, all at once. Mnrogar said nothing, but his eyes glittered.

"Also, m'Lord," said the man-at-arms with a gulp, "the lookout says he is almost sure he has seen one or more dragons landing out there—"

"Dragons!" snarled Mnrogar. Everybody else stared at him. "On *my* land?"

"If there're any dragons," said Jim hastily, "I can handle them. Tell me, lad—"

Jim had a dislike for using the word "fellow." Though perfectly correct if used by a superior to an inferior whose name he did not know, it also had a contemptuous implication. On the other hand, "lad" implied that you knew the underling you were talking to; and the man-at-arms was at least in his thirties. It was something of a toss-up, therefore, but Jim invariably took the second choice.

"—how close are these trolls supposed to be to the castle?"

"They were only seen for moments, m'Lord, as they passed cleared spaces among the trees, one at a time or sometimes two," answered the man-at-arms, "a half-mile off or perhaps a little further."

"I thought as much," said Jim. "They won't be too anxious to get any closer than that." He looked over at Angie. "However, Lady Angela, perhaps we had best put off the entertainment we had planned while the daylight lasted?"

"Take off these," snarled Mnrogar, lifting the chains. "Let me go out with you. There are two there that want me—and they can have their chance. The rest are only come to see what happens, in spite of what the pair that seeks me may believe."

"Hah!" said the Earl, his mustache bristling. "Do you think that such as we have to hide behind a troll against other trolls? No! Any trolls approach us at their peril—I care not what the numbers."

"And I will go with whoever goes out!" said the Bishop. "Bearing a mace—"

"My Lord," interrupted the chaplain in a low reproachful tone, "the days of Bishop Odo are long over."

"Well then, bearing a cross," said the Bishop, "a good, heavy, metal cross. We must have such around the castle here some place!"

Angie looked at Jim.

"It was to be put on right close to the castle," she said.

"And as for that," said Brian, "there are a few of we gentlemen of coat armor among the guests, who would like nothing better than to find a troll who would stand before us. As for the dragons—"

"Never mind the dragons," said Jim firmly. "The lookout was excited by seeing trolls, and probably mistook some large birds for them. Forget the dragons. Actually, I would second Mnrogar. I believe that most of the trolls are no threat. They have long since learned to run from armed humans; and also there are only two to seek Mnrogar and battle with him for this land."

"What gives them the audacity to think they'll win land here by slaying this troll—well, well, dammit, leave all that aside for now," said the Earl.

He made an obvious effort and lowered his voice.

"The fact is," he said, "I have no lack of men-at-arms; and, even if there were no other people guesting here at this time, I would go forth on my own earth wherever I want, no matter how many trolls be sighted from the tower."

"Good!" said Angie quickly, before Jim could say anything more. "Well, I guess that settles it, then, doesn't it, my Lord James?"

Jim looked at her and around at the other faces, all but the chaplain's animated with martial fervor.

"I guess it does," he said.

CHAPTER 42

"But how did you get the stand moved from the tourney ground to here?" asked Jim.

They were in the spot where Angie's planned entertainment was going to be put on. Trees seemed to surround them completely; though of course those between them and the castle—which could be seen faintly between the tree trunks—were only an illusion created by Jim's magic. The set for the play to be put on, which Jim had envisioned and created also by magic, already set up.

It consisted of the framework of part of a barn, including a small section of roof over the stall which was to hold the crib in which the Christ child was supposed to be sleeping. On the other side of the low walls on either side of the crib manger was another stall with walls and part of the wall of the structure; with an ox on one side, and on the other a creature that Jim suspected to be a mule, rather than an actual ass or donkey.

Angie was already dressed in a white flowing robe—Jim wondered where she had gotten the material—which made her look rather heavy, since it was necessarily over a lot of other clothes, in spite of the fact that the area around the manger was magically heated. Robert Falon was happily asleep under covers in the warm manger.

A short distance from where he and Angie stood, in the open snow between them and the stands, squatted Mnrogar, facing the actual forest itself rather than the magical trees between them and the castle. He was not moving. He was doing nothing but waiting—but the very motionlessness of his posture conveyed an ominous sense of latent threat.

"Carolinus moved it for me," said Angie.

"Carolinus?" said Jim. "You've been talking to him, then?" He felt a sudden burst of anger. "I've been trying to get a word with him, ever since we met in that room where Mnrogar and Agatha were put on sort of an unofficial trial."

"Oh, yes," said Angie. "He showed up as soon as I was out here, and asked if he could do anything to help; so I said it would be nice to have the stands and he just sort of waved his hands and here they were, instead of back down where they had been."

"I don't know what he's up to," said Jim. "But I'm willing to bet it's something. And I don't like it."

He hitched up the waist of his own brown robe, which he was wearing over his own heavy clothing and light armor, as a costume for his role of Joseph. It was actually more like the friar's robe it had started life as, than something worn in Biblical times. But the audience could be counted on to be very tolerant as far as both costume and staging went.

Jim had just gotten here, after having let Angie go out ahead with a small contingent of men-at-arms, who were now posted around the clearing—and looking not at all pleased about it; since by now the word that there were trolls all around the castle had penetrated everywhere. Depending upon how they felt, people were either feeling timorous, or breathing fire and eagerly looking forward to the chance of combat with something unhuman.

Jim looked at the stands; for now, happily, they were still empty. There had been some discussion among the male guests as to whether the ladies should go outside at all.

It had been settled by the ladies determining that they would be going out, and managing to impress this point of view upon their male opposite numbers. They were not going to be done out of watching an entertainment, simply because the gentlemen might consider it some trouble to keep them safe. They would keep themselves safe, thank you—and there was not one of them who was not herself armed and ready—decorously so, of course, with the poignard or other long dagger, strapped to the waist, but either covered by something like a sash, or hidden between two folds of a skirt.

Geronde, in the forefront of the women who were determined to go watch the play, had caused something more than a usual disturbance by insisting that she was going to carry a boar-spear. It was her favorite weapon and the one with which she had actually tried to face Jim in his dragon body, when Jim had first landed in her castle as part of an effort to save her from being held prisoner there. Still, there were those who thought that she carried her ideas of freedom a little too far, particularly for an unmarried woman.

On the other hand, she had never been known to pay attention to anyone but Brian; so gossip had nothing specific to chew on.

It had all been settled by a compromise, whereby a man-at-arms would attend her, carrying the boar-spear himself, but under strict orders to hand it to her in case of danger. She also, of course, had a very wicked-looking knife in a sheath at her waist. But her fondness was for the boar-spear. It was light, useful, and the crosspiece that was designed to keep the boar from charging up at whoever was using it against him, would also hold off any troll or anything else trying to get within arm's length of her.

In fact, she had almost convinced a number of other ladies to use the same weapon. But not quite. There was enough opinion of the unladylike quality to doing so, that held back some others who longed for larger weapons themselves. It would be a little indelicate to do so in public, where the story of their activities could be spread around. Geronde, herself, was famous for not giving a hoot about what people said about her.

"We're going to have to make up the dialogue as we go along, of course," Jim said now to Angie. "Happily, it's just you and I."

"That's the good part," said Angie. "But what I want to do is start out and tell them the story ahead of time, so they'll know what to expect. They'll still have the surprises later on when we let the Earl and a few others to come up and find out there's an actual living babe in the manger."

"Also when they see real dragons coming out of the woods and making Joseph afraid," said Jim. "I'm looking forward to that. And, of course, I'll do young Robert's voice for him. It may sound a bit falsetto and odd; but it'll come from inside the manger where they can't see him, and nobody should question. They'll just think it's all magic until the dragons show up.

"Which reminds me," he went on, "I'd better go talk to Secoh now and make sure that he and the others know which ones are to come, and exactly what they're going to do when they get here.

Now remember, Angie, it'll be up to you to talk fast and keep knights like Sir Harimore and others in the stands from rushing down with drawn weapons when they see the actual dragons. You'll have to make sure they understand that the dragons aren't here to hurt anyone, and so forth."

"I've got that figured out," said Angie. "I'm going to tell them that there's an invisible wall between them and the stage area; and that nothing on the other side of that wall that they can see is going to be able to come through at them and they won't be able to get through to it, unless they're invited."

"Fine idea," said Jim. "Why not make it real?" He concentrated. "There, I've just set up the wall by magic."

"I didn't know you could do that," said Angie, looking at him. "You're doing an awful lot of magic lately—rather important magic, aren't you?"

"I do seem to have got a grasp on it lately," said Jim. "It started with this visualization business, but I really think I'm beginning to get the feel of it otherwise, too. But I've got to go talk to Secoh and the other dragons now."

"All right. I'll wait till you get back to send the man-at-arms to tell the people in the castle they can come. Go on to the dragons, then. Go!"

Jim turned and headed off, stopped and turned back.

"What?" he called.

"Watch out for those trolls, now!" said Angie.

"Oh, for Lord's sake!" said Jim. "Don't go worrying about that now. I can take care of any troll, or any number of trolls, that pop up around me. Anyway, they're not going to try it!"

"Well, take care," said Angie, waving him off.

He went.

He had not been exactly specific about where the dragons should land, except that it was away from the place where the play was to be given, so they would not be seen ahead of time. But his own experience in being a dragon part of the time had given him something of the way dragons thought. The prevailing breeze at the moment was from the southwest—and doing a nice job of clearing the last few clouds from the sky; although he had forgotten, in spite of several years here, how England was at a more northern latitude than Michigan; and how early sunset came in wintertime here.

They would only have a little over an hour or so of good light in which to put on the play. Of course, he could light the scene magically. But in spite of the bravery of the knights, none of the guests would really feel comfortable outdoors after dark. This was still the last night of the Christmas season, which meant the Wild Hunt would still be riding the sky overhead, with the legendary danger of it reaching down to snatch one of them up from the ground and carry them off to the devil's dominion.

In any case, he had been thinking about where the dragons were to be found. Or rather, he had been simply heading toward where they would be found, without actually having to think about it; and he had unconsciously headed into the woods in the proper direction.

With a wind out of the southwest, they would be landing from the northwest, which was what had probably made a few of the latecomers noticeable to the lookout in the tower. The majority of them really should have been on the ground here long before this. No more than the trolls were they bothered by the temperature and snow underfoot. When he thought of it, Jim found he could almost sense dragons, a little distance ahead of him through the trees in the direction in which he was going now.

But it was not dragons he came across first, but another old friend. Aargh was standing in a little open space as he entered it, very obviously waiting for him.

"Aargh!" said Jim. "I rather thought you'd be around; but I didn't think I'd stumble across you this early."

"You didn't stumble across me," said Aargh. "I came to meet you."

"Well, well," said Jim, "either way. How do things look to you?"

"Things look the way they always have," said Aargh. "If you're asking about the trolls, they're all around. They're waiting for the twins to get up the courage to challenge Mnrogar; and both they and the twins are wishing that you and Angie and the men-at-arms you've got there weren't with him."

"They're afraid of us?" said Jim. "That's good."

"I wouldn't exactly say they're afraid of you," said Aargh. "But you're an extra part of the situation that shouldn't be there, and they haven't yet figured out just how you fit in; or how you might be involved when the twins challenge Mnrogar. In fact, that's what's holding the twins back from attacking him right now, in my opinion—and my opinion about this, Jim, is something you should well listen to."

"I know that," said Jim. "But what I mean is, if they're hesitant about doing anything because there's just a few of us here, they'll be even more hesitant once all the people come out from the castle—don't you think?"

"Maybe," said Aargh, sitting down in the snow and scratching under his chin with a hind leg. "Cold weather like this, these fleas should all be asleep!"

"Would you like me to try to use magic to get them off you?" said Jim. "I don't think I can just make them vanish; but I might be able to transport them some place else."

"Never you mind," growled Aargh. "They're my fleas. If anything's done about them, I'll do it. If it was summer I could wade into water slowly until only my nose was above water and then stick my nose on the edge of a log or a lily pad and let them escape onto that as I gradually go down under the water completely. But the ice is too thick on the lakes now, and the running water in streams under the ice is too cold. Never mind fleas, Jim. Your dragons are just a moment away, even at the pace you move at. I'll let you talk to them alone. Gorbash is an old friend, but other dragons and I have nothing to say."

"Will I see you later—" Jim started to ask; but Aargh, in his customary elusive way, had already disappeared.

Jim went on through the woods and came out into a clearing where the air was perceptibly warmer. The reason was obvious. The clearing was full of the large bodies of dragons, not indeed breathing fire as legend had it about them, but great clouds of warm breath white into the air. Like all very large animals they gave off body heat, particularly when clustered together.

"Secoh?" Jim asked. But Secoh had already emerged from among the larger dragons and was doing his best to bow in a courtly, human fashion before him.

"Yes, m'Lord," he said happily. "Here I am. With all the Cliffside dragons too—well, almost all. Old Garnoch stayed back at the cliff because his rheumatism was bothering him; and Tanjara was about to lay her egg. Everybody here wants to know how soon we can see the young Prince."

"I can't tell you yet," said Jim. "That's not a simple question to answer. First you must understand—can everybody here hear me? Are all the Cliffside dragons close enough to hear me?"

There was a chorus of "yes" from the crowd around him; with a touch of asperity in some of the basso profundo voices.

"M'Lord," said Secoh reproachfully, "you know how well all we dragons can hear."

"Of course. Forgive me," said Jim.

He remembered how, once when he had been in his dragon body, flying on a dark night, his own hearing had worked remarkably over a considerable distance. But then, with being that sensitive, he asked himself, didn't they all go deaf, shouting into each other's muzzles during the arguments that were their form of ordinary conversation?

"Anyway," he said, "here's how things are going to go. You'll be able to hear what will be going on with Angie and myself and all the people watching the play."

"Play? Play?" said a number of voices in a multitude of different tones, but all of inquiry.

"Yes," said Jim. "In fact, this is going to be something of a treat for all of you. Angie, or somebody, is going to start out by telling all the people there a story; and I'd like you to listen to it. I think you'll like it. It's the story you heard about the young Prince and the dragons, only it'll be the way it was told in the beginning. The way it was when it was first told, so everything is told right. You'd like that, wouldn't you?"

There was a general deep murmur of approval.

"If you like," said Jim, "and if you can do it without being seen by the people sitting in the wooden thing there—'stands,' we call them—you could even come closer and see what's happening. Because we're going to do something more than tell the story. Using magic, and people actually doing what the people in the story did, we do what's called 'acting it out.' It makes what we call a 'play'; and it's like seeing the story actually happen for the first time before your eyes."

This time the murmur of approval rose to a volume that made Jim wince. He could imagine it being heard by Angie and the men-at-arms back in the woods'-edge clearing.

"But be very quiet, and be sure you're not seen," said Jim.

They all told him in a jumble of voices that they wouldn't be seen and that they would be as quiet as ferrets/mice/snakes/shadows . . . and a number of other examples of creatures particularly known for their quietness.

"Good!" said Jim.

"But what about these trolls, m'Lord?" said Secoh. "Should we do something about these trolls? Like tear a few apart and chase the others away?"

"No, I don't think so, Secoh," said Jim. "They've got their own ways, after all; and it's only right they be left to them. Besides, they aren't troubling us right now; and I don't really think they will. It's just a matter of the troll who lives underneath the Earl's castle here possibly being challenged by a pair of twin trolls."

"Ah, a fight!" said Secoh happily, and there was an added buzz of pleased excitement that went back through the dragon ranks. Much as dragons detested trolls, given a choice, they would ordinarily rather watch any kind of a fight any day than be in it—that is, unless the instinctive fighting fury that slumbered in the breast of every mature dragon was triggered; in which case there was essentially no question of anything but action. Jim in his Gorbash-dragon body had experienced this himself. In fact, he had gotten both Gorbash and himself almost killed by letting it take him over.

"Well then, Secoh," he said. "If Angie hasn't sent word to the guests to come already, she will as soon as I'm back in the clearing, so things will begin to happen pretty quickly now. I'd say before the sun has moved much more in the heavens, you'll be able to move in and watch the proceedings."

"Thank you, m'Lord," said Secoh.

Jim left, and behind him the dragons burst into low-voiced, interested discussion of what watching a play might be like, what to watch for in observing a troll-fight, and other related subjects. Jim strode back through the forest; and, going around a rather thick-bodied oak that was in his path, he almost bumped into Carolinus.

"Carolinus!" he said, staring at the magician. "You're almost as bad as Aargh."

"That is something not to be said by an apprentice to his Master!" retorted Carolinus severely. "I am not someone that others are almost as bad as, Jim. I am someone that others might hope to be almost as good as—but with little or no opportunity, probably."

"Of course," said Jim. "By the way, thank you for magicking up those stands for Angie."

"Oh, that," said Carolinus, with a wave of his hand. "I'd almost forgotten that. Nothing at all, really. You've been using a lot of Magick yourself, lately."

"Well, yes," said Jim cautiously. "Necessarily so—"

He felt like an ordinary chess player who somehow (probably in a dream) had found himself in a match with a grandmaster of the game; and who had built up an apparently innocent but actually very strong arrangement of pieces to put his opponent's most powerful piece, the queen, in danger.

He had until this moment just been waiting for the grandmaster to make one more incautious move; and it seemed to him that now, Carolinus had just committed his final error by moving an unimportant pawn. A harmless and uninteresting move that merely cleared the way for his opponent's bishop to threaten Jim's queen. But actually that bishop could simply be taken by one of Jim's own, humble pawns; thereby ensuring Jim's total, crushing victory. The grandmaster had really been asleep on this move.

"Good!" said Carolinus, interrupting him before he could finish what he had been just about to say.

"Good?" echoed Jim, thrown off stride temporarily, "I'd thought you'd want me to lie low at this time, by using as little magic as possible."

"Not at all, not at all," said Carolinus cheerfully. "You remember what I've always said to you, Jim. Practice! Practice! Practice! Every time you use your Magick you're practicing. That pleases me."

"Yes, but with this difficulty building up against me in Magickdom—" said Jim.

"—Oh, that. What will be, will be," said Carolinus. "If you're going to survive here, the more practice you put in, the better. If you're not, then it doesn't matter, does it?"

"I suppose not," said Jim. "I'm just a little surprised that you're taking the matter so lightly. I thought you were concerned on my behalf."

"Why, of course I am!" said Carolinus. "But while I can do many things, Jim, there have to be a few things that I cannot do. Saving you from the concerted opinion of the majority of other magickians of Magickdom is, I'm afraid, one of them."

That statement did it. Jim found the suspicion he had been nursing inside him for some time now becoming a certainty. Mentally, he reviewed his own position on the imaginary chessboard. No, his position was invincible. With one clear accusation he would now crush Carolinus with the truth.

"Carolinus," he said, accordingly, "you've simply been using me in a game of your own, haven't you; from the moment you arranged to have all our friends delayed from coming to our help at Malencontri when the castle was attacked by Sir Peter Carley and his gang of raiders?"

"Why, of course!" said Carolinus.

CHAPTER 43

"Tut-tut, my boy," Carolinus was saying. "Don't tell me you were under any other impression. Why, that's what an apprentice is for. I believe you told me when you first came here from where you used to be that you were a 'Master of the Arts'—hah! Or, at least, what they considered a 'Master of Arts' in that place you came from. But even under those conditions, you must have been familiar with the relationship of the student to his Master. What you mention is a natural part of an apprentice's job, Jim! To do the troublesome small things. To take care of all the time-consuming details that his Master can't be bothered with—while, of course, being educated in those things that an apprentice needs to learn if he is to have any future in a professional sense—"

Jim thought bitterly of Professor Dr. Thibault Shorles, the head of the History Department of Riveroak College, who had been Jim's own particular taskmaster there.

"The apprentice is to sweep up, so to speak," Carolinus was going on cheerfully, "polish something perhaps roughed out by the Master. Perhaps even to do some independent work, for which his Master can afterwards take the credit. These are always the terms of an apprenticeship, Jim; and you must have known that from experience. I find it hard to believe you've forgotten it already. For shame, my boy!"

Jim's head whirled. By his rash taking of the bishop with

his king's pawn he suddenly realized he had removed the only protection his king had; opening a clear path, so that his own king was now in an uncovered check from the grandmaster's well-protected knight; and, with no way to rescue the situation—since all his forces had been concentrated on attack rather than defense—Carolinus had, in effect, won the game.

He could, of course, reproach Carolinus for his hypocrisy in pretending to be such a close friend that he would never make such callous use of their association. Then it suddenly came to Jim that, after all, this was the way it was here in the fourteenth century. People of lesser rank were routinely expended for the benefit of their superiors. If they escaped being so, it was only because they were too valuable at the moment to be used up in such a way.

To say anything like "I thought you liked Angie and me better than to throw us to the wolves just for some use of your own!" however, would probably convey no sense to Carolinus at all. He was just doing what was always done. Besides, saying anything like that would sound like whining. It would not mend the situation at all; and in any case Jim could not whine. It was simply not in him. He drew himself up.

"Well, let me tell you something, Carolinus!" he said, his anger breaking out in spite of himself. "You can do what you want; and I may not be able to do anything about it; but I'm not going to pretend I'm happy about it."

"Jim!" said Carolinus, looking shocked.

"But I'll tell you one thing," Jim went on. "I've done a pretty good job of handling every problem that's come up since you first rigged things so Angie and I would have to visit this damnable twelve-day Christmas party; and I can finish it without any help from you!"

"I sincerely hope so, my boy," said Carolinus; and vanished.

Jim was left staring at the snow, the leafless trees and the rapidly reddening sky as the sun slowly descended toward the horizon on this northern winter day.

He shook off the emotion that had held him and began to plod back through the trees toward Angie and the play that was to come.

"I've already sent one of the men-at-arms to tell the guests to start coming; and if you'll look at the stands, a few of them are here already," said Angie, when Jim finally got back to her. "Some of the knights like Sir Harimore didn't even wait to be told they should come. Do you notice how dark it's getting? Is there some way we could light things up if it gets too dim?"

"Oh, that," said Jim dully. "Yes, I can take care of that."

Using his new way with magic, he envisioned something like the troll-light he and Brian had encountered the first time they had gone down into Mnrogar's den at Carolinus's orders. Only in this case, the light was emanating from all the trees and branches—including the magical ones that were not really there—around the clearing. It was not a particularly noticeable illumination now, because there was still too much daylight coming from the sky; but as the early winter afternoon dimmed, this other light would become more apparent.

Rather neatly done, he told himself. The stands were now filling, and none of them seemed to see anything unusual in the extra light that was coming feebly at the moment from the trees around them. The tension of his talk with Carolinus began to ease.

"Oh, by the way," Angie said. They were talking behind the wall that held the manger, out of sight of the audience, just so that the audience shouldn't see their costumes until the performance actually started. "Carolinus took down your wall between the people in the stands and us here. He said I was right; it wasn't really necessary. If the people in the stands are told to stay where they are, they will; and if we should need the men-at-arms and the knights to come down to defend us, then they'd be able to."

"And he just took it down? Like that?" said Jim. "Why, that—"

He choked on his own words; then, suddenly, all the anger in him drained away, leaving him feeling briefly exhausted. It was no use. Carolinus was as he was; everybody here in this time in this world were like they were. You lived with them or else—there was really no choice in the matter.

"Jim!" said Angie. "What's wrong?"

"Nothing, really," said Jim. He looked through a crack between two planks, above the manger, and saw that the stands were close to being filled. Not only that, but Carolinus's red robe was conspicuous in the middle of them; and the Earl, Agatha Falon and the Prince were also there to the magician's right. Jim came back to Angie.

"The Earl's here already," he said. "He's used to things starting the moment he arrives. It's almost twilight. We better not delay. Do you want to go out and start now?"

"Any time," said Angie cheerfully. "But Jim, there is something wrong!"

"No. No, actually there isn't," said Jim. "I get a little worn down by being here in the fourteenth century, sometimes, that's all. Pay no attention."

Angie hugged him, kissed him and went around the corner of the wall out in front of the audience.

Feeling better, and thoroughly angry with himself for feeling better after being consoled, Jim went back to the crack between the two planks he had located before.

I'm not four years old, he growled to himself . . . but perhaps in some corner of him he was. The crack gave him a view out over the manger from which he could see Angie and nearly all the audience in the stands. He had told Angie to speak just in an ordinary voice; and he would make sure everybody could hear her.

Now he concentrated on visualizing her voice being—not so much amplified—as simply reaching out to everyone in the stands; as if she was speaking just a few feet in front of each one of them. Hastily, at the last minute, he remembered to also have her voice come to his ears in the same way, so he could check on whether the magic was working or not.

He was reassured it had been wise to make things work that way, once she began to speak. Her voice came as easily and clearly to his own ears as if she was standing beside him.

"My Lord Prince of England, my Lord Earl, my Lord Bishop, and all other lords, gentlemen and ladies here assembled," she said.

She was doing a marvelous job of it, Jim thought admiringly, peering between the two planks. That stage training of hers was standing her in good stead. Angie went on.

"—On this last eve of our gathering this Christmas, by the gracious permission of our Lord Prince, my Lord Earl, and my Lord Bishop, I wish to present to you all a famous legend of our Lord Jesus Christ, fitting to this holy time and place. After I have told what took place, you will see it acted, taking place again here, before your eyes."

She paused.

"I will now begin," she said.

She paused again.

"As the writings of a holy man tell us, there came a time in the early life of Christ, our Lord, when word came to Herod, King over all the land at that time, that there was a child born who would himself come to be King.

"At this Herod was suddenly fearful that the child so spoken of would rise to take his place as King. Therefore, he, Herod, made an order that all the children under four years of age should be slain forthwith, that none should survive and whoever among them was the child who might be King would also be slain."

She paused—but this time because of the angry growl from the stands. Once it had died away, she went on.

"Word of this came to Mary and Joseph, and they resolved to take our young Lord Christ to Egypt, where he would be safely out of the way of the men sent forth by Herod to kill all the children.

"So they went forth; and with them went representatives of all the animals; the lion, the ox, the ass, the horse, the camel, all the many animals went with them to guard them along the way; and after they had been traveling some days, it happened that they were out without shelter when night fell. So Joseph built a fire, and set up a shelter for Mary and the Child; and the animals lay all around to guard.

"And so they slept the night."

She paused.

"But when the morning came, and the sun rose, they awoke, they and the beasts that had lain about to guard them, they all— Mary, Joseph and the Lord Christ, himself—saw, by the early light of the sun, a little ways away to their right, a place of rocks with trees thick among them. And from those trees in that same light they saw all at once huge dragons coming toward them.

"The animals and the beasts were afraid and drew away. Joseph was afraid.

"But Christ spoke from the place where he lay to his father, saying:

" 'Fear not, Joseph, for remember what the Prophet David hath said: "*Praise the Lord from the earth, Ye dragons, and all deeps.*" These dragons have only come to be blessed. Let them approach, that I may bless them.' "

She waited a moment to let the words linger in the minds of the audience; and then went on.

"Then Joseph was no longer afraid. He stood aside, and the dragons came forward quietly and meekly to the place where the Holy Child lay. And the Lord Christ blessed them and they were glad and went forth, harming nothing."

There was a drawn-out murmur of general pleasure and awe from the stands.

"Watch now, therefore," said Angie, "and you will see all this happen, from its very beginning."

She turned and went back around the corner of the set to where Jim was, out of sight with him behind it.

"Ready?" she said to him. He nodded. "Have you any idea of what you're going to say?" Angie went on.

"Oh, yes," said Jim, taking his eyes from the crack, "I don't worry about that. You and I can follow each other, ad-lib, without any trouble."

"I think so, too," said Angie. "Now I'll go back out, around the corner I came back around just now; and you go around the other corner so we meet in front. And let me speak first, all right?"

Jim nodded.

"Then you can start your dialogue by answering me," said Angie.

"Right," said Jim.

They turned their backs on each other and went out around different ends of the set and came forward in front of it to meet with perhaps ten feet between them. They both turned to face the audience.

"I am Mary!" Angie announced. She turned and pointed to Jim. "And he is Joseph."

The audience acknowledged this with another pleased murmur.

"And in the manger there," said Angie, turning and pointing at it, "lies the little Christ child."

Hastily, Jim projected at the audience a snatch of the sound of a very young child's pleased cooing.

The response from the audience this time was considerably more vocal, with some near-shrieks mixed in with it, whether of pleasure or astonishment Jim could not tell. He hurried to project his own voice to the audience.

"Mary," he said, peering into the sunset-red western sky under the palm of his hand, "night draws near, and there is no shelter in sight. I fear me we must spend until morning in this wild place. But fear not, I will build a shelter, for you and the babe, and I shall lie outside it all night on watch; while the good beasts lie around me and all of us on guard; for there are some trees and rocks and dark places that I mislike greatly. However, with the Lord's protection we will be safe."

"I do not doubt it, my husband," said Angie clearly; and, turning, went to the manger and apparently began talking to the happily still-sleeping Robert. The audience voiced their entire approval of this last statement of hers.

Jim realized that now was the time in which he was supposed to go through the motions of lying down and going to sleep. He had forgotten that it meant putting the side of his face into about four inches of snow. However, there was nothing too much to be done about it, so, turning his back to the audience, he lay down, watching Angie who was still going through the motions of Mary paying attention to her child. This was his chance, it suddenly occurred to him. It offered him a golden opportunity to check on the dragons and their entrance on the scene.

He puzzled for a little while, with his left check uncomfortably in the snow, figuring out exactly how what he wanted to do might be accomplished magically. Then, without anything in the way of visible movement the audience could see, he substituted an image of himself to occupy his place in the snow in front of the set, and his actual self was projected off into the trees to appear wherever the dragons might be gathered, listening to the story, waiting for the play itself and some of them—not more than the original five he had specified—planning to come out.

He had aimed at appearing before Secoh, and so he did. Used to him as the dragon was, and to the magic things that happened around Jim, Secoh was still considerably startled and half spread his wings involuntarily when Jim appeared before him.

"M'Lord," he gasped. "I didn't expect to see you—"

"Quiet!" said Jim hastily, cutting him off in mid-syllable; for the dragons were now just barely out of sight behind the trees close to the manger and Secoh had spoken in something very close to a normal dragon voice, volume and tones—which could have been heard by the audience.

"All of you," said Jim to the hushed Secoh and the other dragons. "Be very quiet—particularly those to be blessed. Secoh, now tell me, are the five of you who are to come out, ready?"

"Yes, m'Lord," said Secoh. "Me, and Gorbash, Tigatal, Norganosh and Arghnach."

"Good. You first, Secoh, then the other four. Now," said Jim, raising his voice to speak past Secoh and the dragons just before him, "the young Prince will actually bless all of you dragons here, even the ones still back in the woods—so no one should feel left out. Just listen carefully to what he says."

A deep-voiced murmur of satisfaction came from the surrounding forest.

"Now, I've got to get back to the play," said Jim. "When I look into the woods and say, '*The dragons come*—' then the five of you come out and up to the manger; but stop about ten feet from it, a little to one side, possibly in front of the ox; because the ass is liable to get excited and start plunging around if it sees dragons coming close—on second thought, forget about that. I can take care of that matter with magic. But anyway, don't come any closer than the ox's stall. That's so the audience can still see the manger holding the Christ child. Otherwise they're likely to get excited and think the Christ child is going to come to some harm."

"Oh, we won't, m'Lord," said Secoh.

"Excellent!" said Jim. "I'll leave you, then."

He turned and hurried off through the woods. Just before he came out behind the set, however, he found his way barred by Aargh.

"Aargh!" he said. "I'm glad to see you here—"

"You may be more glad later on," said Aargh. "The twins have finally got up their nerve to attack Mnrogar; and the other trolls will be coming in to watch. But you'd better tell all those two-legged ones in the stands that the rest of the trolls are only watching."

"Are they coming right away?" asked Jim. "I mean, will they interrupt the play?"

"No," said Aargh. He laughed his silent laugh. "The trolls are enjoying your performance too—believe it or not. They don't know what's going on, but it's something they've never seen before and they want to see it through. That is, all but the twins. They might decide to attack Mnrogar at any time; but I think they need to work themselves up some more to, yet."

"Thanks for telling me," said Jim. "Now I really have to get back. Is Mnrogar still where he was sitting before?"

"He is," said Aargh. "And puzzling your people in the stands, very much indeed. Since he hasn't moved at all, they're not as worried about him as they might be if he'd been prowling up and down. But if he moves, every eye there is going to be on him."

"Thanks. Fine," said Jim. "You'll stick close yourself?"

"I'll be here," said Aargh, "if only to see what happens."

"Good," said Jim, and ran off toward the set.

He did not stop at the back of the set, even to peer through the crack. He simply paused for a moment at the corner of it to get his breath back, then went through the visualization in his mind that would substitute himself for the simulacrum he had made, and returned to the snow where he had been to begin with.

He found himself with his cheek once more pressed down into iciness; and got up more quickly than he had intended.

He stretched, glancing at Angie. She was standing up from the seat he had made her next to the manger, with a relieved look on her face.

"Ah," said Jim to the audience, "it is morning. How glad I am to see the daylight. To think that I was worried about what might come out of those rocks and trees last night. Why, I can look at them now and see—"

He had turned his head and body dramatically toward the forest and was just about to extend his arm to announce the dragons, when there was a shriek from someone in the stands.

"Trolls!" cried a voice—high-pitched, but whether male and excited, or female, could not be told at this distance.

"Trolls all around us! They're coming to kill us!"

The people in the stands rose as one body; and at the same time Jim, looking around the clearing, saw trolls appearing everywhere between the trees. They might not be attacking, as the voice in the stands had assumed, but they had certainly moved into a position to attack, if the twins' success over Mnrogar should show them the way.

He searched his mind frantically for some word that would calm the audience; but at this moment, Mnrogar changed from a statue to a living troll. He stood up abruptly—erect and suddenly massive like a giant sprung from the earth; and the setting sun red between the lower tree trunks behind him cast his black shadow long, long, to the far end of the clearing; where a clump of visible trolls drew back from it, revealing the two challengers among them.

"Mnrogar!" cried the twin voices in perfect unison. "I come for you now!"

And, still in perfect unison, screaming as they went, they raced across the open snow toward the waiting Mnrogar.

CHAPTER 44

M nrogar did not move.
   The twins continued their screaming, their arms held high,
their talons arched toward him; but as they reached the mid-point
of the distance between the woods and Mnrogar, they began to
slow, and their slowing became rapidly greater until they came
to a halt.

They stared a moment at Mnrogar, who was still impassive,
then turned abruptly and yelled at the trolls directly behind them,
clustered at the edge of the woods.

"What are you waiting for?" cried the wild, paired voices. "I
told you I'd take care of Mnrogar; you can have all the others.
That was the agreement. There are more of you than there are of
them. Why do you wait?"

The twins pointed at the Crèche scene.

"There are even two there without sharp things and a pup you
can have for no trouble at all; and still you hang back. Now,
follow me!"

The trolls at the edge of the wood moved out, into the clearing
but not with any great speed.

There was a sudden bellow from the stands and the equally
sudden glitter of swords, as men-at-arms and gentlemen poured
down from the stands and onto the open space. But then both
they and the trolls checked abruptly, as there was a different
sound of anger from the forest close to the western side of the

set and behind it—a swelling roar such as only dragons could make. Dragons about to be deprived of their blessing.

The twins had already started another rush toward Mnrogar again and had already covered half the distance. But they stopped at that sound, also, and turned toward it. For a moment, everything on the field was motionless.

It had only been a warning roar, as Jim had recognized. The reaction that produced that sound from dragons was instinctive. But the trolls already knew the dragons were there; and this intrusion by them on top of the failure of the twins to carry through their initial rush confused them; while the people in the stands had been literally stunned by the sound, which they had recognized as quickly as the trolls.

For a moment the silence lasted; then a single voice almost wailed from the stands.

"Get Sir Dragon!" it cried. "Where is Sir Dragon?"

It was Jim's turn to be, if not stunned, startled. Then he remembered from his medieval studies how, after plays had been put on in the Middle Ages, the actors would come forward and remind the audience that they were not the characters they had been portraying.

The man who had played the part of the devil—for most of the plays were religious plays—would come forth and say, "Look, it's just me, your old neighbor. I'm not really the devil—" And, turning to whatever principal holy figure was among the characters, he would start to chat with him about their ordinary, everyday affairs in life; just to reassure the audience that there was no touch of devilishness still clinging to him. He was really not the figure that had sent chills down the backbones of imaginative watchers.

The moment of uncertainty, with everything in the balance and nothing moving, held for a second longer; and in that moment Jim's urgent mind leaped to an idea like a spark from the end of a wire to its ground. Something was needed to shake the nerves of the other trolls just a little more; and he had suddenly remembered the aurora borealis, the northern lights, which on these frosty nights would sometimes display their colors over half or more of the sky.

It was not quite close enough to night for the lights ordinarily to show. But Jim made an effort with his magic to visualize them painting the sky anyhow.

It worked.

From behind the westward trees and out of the red sunset sky sprang great streamers and waves of color—yellow, green and a finer, lighter red than that of the sunset, arching across the heavens. Heads turned upward, human and troll alike.

Jim made his voice huge, and spoke as if from some point high above the clearing.

"Mnrogar's den fights for Mnrogar!"

As if they had been activated by a single impulse, all the trolls around the clearing turned and plunged back toward and into the forest. The twins stared—then ran after them, calling to the other trolls to come back.

But none returned, and the twins slowed and stopped at the forest edge. For a long moment they stared into the darkness between the trees, then turned about and looked at Mnrogar.

Mnrogar was still and unmoving as a statue.

"You!" screamed the twins; and, arms aloft, talons arching, teeth bared, they charged toward him, this time without hesitation crossing the middle distance between them, then three-quarters of the way—finally almost to collision with Mnrogar. Only just out of Mnrogar's reach, at last, did they slow abruptly and come to a halt. They and Mnrogar faced each other, their eyes glittering.

For a long moment they stood; and the whole clearing held its breath. Nothing moved, nothing made a sound. Only, overhead, the northern lights moved ceaselessly, now painting three-quarters of a sky in which a few stars were beginning to be seen in the east.

Mnrogar had not moved and he did not move now.

Suddenly, the twins took a step backward. Then another, then another—then two more. Abruptly they whirled as one and ran from the field, to the edge of the forest and into it. A chorus of jeers and boos went up from the stands, and a voice spoke from behind Jim.

"The others are gone; and now those two are gone as well," said the voice of Aargh. "It is over."

Jim jerked out of the near-trance into memory of the unfinished play; also the last thought he had thought, that those in the stands might be thinking of Angie and him not as Lady Angela and Lord James, but as Mary and Joseph.

"Mary!" he said to Angie; and Angie turned her eyes sharply from the forest to meet his—and he saw she understood and was back in the play, herself.

"Mary," said Jim again, "I have heard the voices of dragons. And I am looking into the trees now. I fear me that dragons come!"

"Is this so, Joseph?" said Angie.

"I fear so," said Jim—and, indeed, he could see Secoh and the other four beginning to move from between the nearer trees on their way to the manger right now, Secoh leading. "Mary, the faithful beasts who came with us to guard us this far, cannot guard us now. I am afraid!"

Secoh and the four dragons with him solemnly emerged from the trees, waddling on their hind legs. Under other circumstances, it might have been a somewhat comic sight. But, caught up in the play as Jim was, he actually felt a thrill of the fear that any single human might feel, facing so much lethal tonnage coming toward him. Hastily, he made his voice come from the manger in the best approximations he could manage of the high tones of a child.

"Fear not, Joseph," he said in that voice, directing it across the field to those in the stands, "for remember what the Prophet David hath said: '*Praise the Lord from the earth, Ye dragons, and all deeps.*' These dragons have only come to be blessed. Let them approach, that I may bless them."

"Our Son has spoken!" Jim cried in his own voice to the audience. "Let us do what he says, Mary, for he is no common son!"

"Yes, let us, Joseph!" echoed Angie.

Jim turned toward Secoh, who was now quite close, and the four behind him.

"Dragons, our Son, who is more than ordinary sons, has told us you have only come to be blessed. Is this true?"

The four dragons behind Secoh looked thoroughly confused. They had not been prepared for this. But Secoh had the wit to nod.

"Yes, m'Lord," he said.

Oops, thought Jim. That "m'Lord" could have spoiled everything. He sneaked a glance at the audience in the stands; but they were all still silent as if hypnotized. Maybe nobody noticed, then. I'll talk fast, he told himself.

"Approach, then," he said—unnecessarily, as it turned out, since Secoh and the dragons were already doing this. "*Still!*" he added, hastily directing the command toward the ox and the ass, for these two were already beginning to strain at their tethers and roll the whites of their eyes on the approach of these huge and dangerous-looking predators. But he immediately remembered that the command would not work on such animals.

Before he could think what else to try, the two domestic beasts seemed to calm by themselves; and the dragons came on.

"But no closer than the stall of the ox," commanded Jim. The dragons stopped. "Now, if you will stand reverently silent, our Son will bless you."

He hastily changed his voice back to the squeaky, childish version. To his own ear it sounded completely unbelievable; but those in the stands seemed to be accepting it. It came to Jim that they would probably accept anything. The magic that lent reality to this scene was in them, not in him.

"May you be blessed from this moment forward, all ye dragons," he said from the manger. "Go forth to be better and wiser dragons, to play your part in this earth that we all share and that my Father in Heaven hath made."

It was hard to believe, Jim thought, but the dragons actually seemed to do something very much like glowing, once the blessing was said. In an entirely different way, they drew deep breaths and appeared to inflate, but with happiness and pride.

"And let this blessing be for all dragons, henceforth!" said Jim, in his manger voice. "Return now to your own kind and live in harmony together!"

Privately, Jim had as little hope of the dragons ever living in harmony as any species of creature on earth. He was sure that within a matter of hours they would be back to their regular wrangling and disputing, arguing and counterarguing and disagreeing with each other's account of the blessing. But that did not matter; because now Secoh had turned around, the other dragons had turned around, and they were heading back into the woods.

A cheer rose from the stands. Jim turned to look, and saw Mnrogar was loping without undue haste off the field toward the woods. The Middle Ages loved a winner; and among those standing up and cheering, Jim was interested to see, was the Earl himself.

Jim turned back to Angie.

"Mary!" he said, pitching his voice to the audience. "Now the dragons have been blessed and left, doing us no harm. All has ended well."

Mary picked up the cue immediately.

"You are right, Joseph," she said, and faced the audience. "Our play is over."

She turned to face the stands squarely.

"Would our gracious Lord Prince, our Lord Earl and our Lord Bishop wish to honor us by coming forward and looking closely at the place where this story has been told, and this play has been performed?"

An invitation like that, thought Jim, was something of a two-edged sword. It was a gracious way of asking the most important people there if they wanted to be favored with a close look at the stage area; at the same time it was something of a challenge—in that the three people invited were being asked to come forward into an area where wondrous and magical things had been taking place.

Naturally, none of the three could turn it down.

The Earl was already on his feet. The Prince stood up. The Bishop did the same. They made their way down from the stands and across the snow to the scene, approaching firmly enough, but not in any particular rush to get there.

Jim glanced again to the ox and the ass—or mule, or whatever it was. They were as calm as he had ever seen such animals. He also glanced at the sky; and the northern lights were still doing remarkable things up there, even more impressive and brighter now that the sun was all but below the horizon.

Jim sidled over until he was standing closely side by side with Angie, and spoke to her out of the corner of his mouth.

"They'll be thinking we're still Joseph and Mary—the characters in the play," he said, without taking his eyes off the three approaching figures. "You go on being Mary and I'll go on being Joseph until we have a chance, and then we'll duck around behind, take off these outer robes and come back as ourselves. I'll give you some kind of a signal to let you know."

"All right," said Angie.

It was only another moment or so before the Earl, the Bishop and the Prince came up to them. Jim risked a glance off toward that part of the forest where the dragons had been waiting. Happily, he saw, they were waiting to take to the air until the audience was gone, evidently; for he saw no winged figures mounting from among the trees.

This was, in its own way, a remarkable tribute from the dragons to their recent experience; for with the exception of Gorbash and himself and Secoh, now, most of the local dragons disliked flying by night—even on bright nights—for fear they might lose sight of the ground, or make a bad landing. This, however, was going to be a very bright night.

The moon was just beginning to rise; but it could be seen clearly over the clearing, in spite of the magic light Jim had arranged to be shed from the surrounding trees. The light coming from them, of course, did not glow the way an electric light bulb would, but illumination simply emanated from them. So far, none of the audience seemed to have recognized how they were illuminating the clearing.

The Earl, Bishop and Prince came up to them. Their approach was so diffident that Jim felt confirmed in his idea that they were completely lost in the play and were approaching not Lord and Lady Eckert, but Joseph and Mary.

This was not so noticeable with the Prince, who, being a Prince, was not used to being diffident; but it was remarkable to see two burly, normally commanding individuals like the Earl and the Bishop almost shuffling as they got close.

"Welcome, my Lord Prince, my Lord Bishop and my Lord Earl!" said Jim in his normal Jim Eckert voice. He had hoped the sound of it would build a sort of bridge between the character of Joseph and himself. But apparently it did not work. The three still looked at him rather like altar boys approaching the Bishop, himself. "Willingly, we'd have invited all here to come and see our scene up close, but there's not much room. In any case you, my Lords and Prince, would be invited first."

They still looked at him as if tongue-tied.

"This way, my Lords," said Angie crisply. "Let me show you the manger and the Christ child."

They followed her within the mockup of the manger, their feet crunching on the snow that had drifted within since Jim had set the stable in place.

"But it is warm here!" exclaimed the Bishop in surprise, as they entered.

Jim thought quickly.

"Here," he said in his Joseph's voice, "in these lands, it warms quickly, when the sun rises as it has just done. Am I not right, Mary?"

"You are right, my husband," answered Angie in the words and tone that suited her character. She turned her attention back to the three men, who had stopped, still about ten feet from the manger itself. "Come forward, your Grace and my Lords. Come!"

Almost reluctantly they came right up to the edge of the manger and looked within.

"It is He!" exclaimed the Bishop in a tone of wonder.

"Actually not, my Lord," said Angie in her normal best no-nonsense voice as Lady Eckert. "It's just young Robert Falon, who's being honored by being allowed to play the part of the Christ Child."

The three visitors looked at her with a strange doubt.

"Nonetheless," said the Bishop, and sank on his knees with his hands clasped in prayer on the edge of the manger above the sleeping infant. The other two followed his example.

Angie looked at Jim and Jim looked at Angie. There was evidently nothing to be done. At the very least, the roles of the actors and their actual selves were being hopelessly confused by the three, even up close. Jim beckoned Angie silently to him, and she stepped a couple of long steps back as quietly as she could on the crunchy snow to stand close to him.

"Look," said Jim in a whisper in her ear, "unless the Bishop has had some miraculous change of his own, he's going to be praying for more than just a minute or two. Besides, they aren't paying any attention to us. I don't think they even heard you step back here. Let's go around behind the set now, take off these Joseph and Mary robes, and come back to be here in our normal clothes—me, with sword belt and sword, even—when they finally get up and turn around and see us."

She nodded. They turned and went.

It did not take them more than a minute or two to strip off the robes covering their ordinary clothes. Angie took both costumes and stuffed them into a cloth sack she had waiting there. She smoothed out her own dress and tweaked Jim's clothes a little. They started back around to the front of the set again—and stopped.

Carolinus, red-robed and beaming, had appeared in front of them.

"*Callooh! Callay!*" he shouted. "Don't worry, those others in there can't hear me—*Come to my arms, my beamish boy!*"

And he embraced Jim, which was absolutely unlike Carolinus. Jim had never seen him even touch another person. But then, Carolinus also turned and embraced Angie, who accepted it more naturally. Nonetheless, when he had stepped back, she spoke to him in a sharp voice.

"How do you happen to know that?" she demanded.

"It's part of *Jabberwocky*, a poem from Lewis Carroll's *Through the Looking-Glass*."

"I know it's part of *Jabberwocky!*" snapped Angie. "I asked you how *you* came to know it!"

"I'm a AAA+ magickian, my dear," said Carolinus. He turned to Jim. "Jim, my boy! You've done it. Created new Magick!"

"New magic?" asked Jim. "What new magic?"

"No time now to explain," said Carolinus. "I'll tell you later! Farewell!"

And he vanished, leaving only a momentary faint echo of another "*Callooh! Callay!*" lingering on the air behind him.

Jim and Angie looked at each other.

"We'd better get back out front to the Prince, the Bishop and the Earl," said Angie.

Jim nodded, and they hurried off around to the front of the set. No one had left the stands. Apparently as far as the audience was concerned, what was going on now was as important as the play itself. Jim and Angie stood with their backs to the audience, and still had to wait several minutes before the Bishop slowly stood up, and the Earl and the Prince—who had been clearly waiting for him to lead—stood up with him and also turned.

"Sir James?" said the Bishop on a questioning note.

"Yes, my Lord," said Jim.

The Bishop's face fell, and so did the Earl's and the Prince's.

"I had been hoping—" said the Bishop hesitantly. "I had been hoping He might bless me as He blessed the dragons."

This was clearly more a hopeful question than a statement.

"I'm sure he would, my Lord Bishop," Jim said quickly, "but as you saw, he's now asleep. But I feel sure he'd have given you his blessing, if he could. He'd undoubtedly have blessed all three of you. I'd guess you could consider yourself as good as blessed by him."

The three faces before him still looked disappointed, but they had lightened somewhat.

"My Lord," said the Bishop, with some of his old force of voice, turning to the Earl, "I suggest we return as soon as possible, to inform those others here of our glad tidings."

"Yes. Yes, of course!" said the Earl; and the Prince made an affirmative noise. The Bishop turned back to Jim.

"Have we your leave to depart, Saint Jo—" He broke off. "That is to say, Sir James, we must leave you now."

"Of course, my Lord," said Jim. "As my Lord wishes."

Without another word the three turned and started back across the field considerably faster than they had approached the set.

"That's one of the wonderful things about little Robert," said Angie. "Not only does he fuss very little when he's awake; but he sleeps like an angel when he's asleep—" She was interrupted by a small, fretful noise from the manger.

"I shouldn't have said anything," she said. She turned and went hastily back to the manger and examined its occupant. "Jim, we'd better get Robert back up to our rooms as quickly as possible—by magic, if you can do it. I've got a cloth doll up there that Enna made for me to use in the manger, before we thought of using Robert. I can send that back to you, and if anyone else comes looking, that's what they'll see. It was more than enough, the Bishop, the Earl and the Prince seeing a live child there."

"You're right," said Jim. "You pick Robert up, and I'll stand in front of you as if we were talking, then I'll send you back by magic, both of you, to the castle gate. You'll have to walk up from there. When you get there, find the doll and throw it out the window and say, 'Excelsior!' "

"Then what'll happen?" asked Angie.

"I'll have it set up so magic will catch that doll and bring it to the manger, just in case anybody else comes by before I've got the set taken down. Meanwhile, I'll have Theoluf take the ox and the ass off to wherever they came from in the first place."

He moved with Angie to the manger, Angie picked up Robert, Jim visualized them back at the castle; and they disappeared. Jim visualized a magic net to catch the thrown doll and bring it to the manger; then he turned about, went back out in front of the set and shouted to the nearest man-at-arms.

"Oh! Edgar! Fetch another lad with you, and the two of you can take the ox and the ass away. Find my squire and ask him where they must go."

His shout was clearly heard in the stands, because some people began to trickle off; although there was quite a knot of those who were still there, clustered about the Bishop, who seemed to be lecturing, or possibly preaching to them all. The faint sound of his voice floated back, but it was impossible to make out his words, except that they were impassioned.

The men-at-arms had not shown up to take the ass and ox away yet, either.

Jim looked once more at the woods where the dragons had been and possibly still were. There was still no sign of any of them taking off, mounting into the night sky and flying together, in a group for company toward Cliffside. Secoh would lead them, if it came to that, he told himself.

He stood looking again across the clearing and watching for some little time; and then suddenly Angie was back beside him, clutching a cloth doll to her breast.

"Angie," he said, "you weren't supposed to come back."

"I wanted to," said Angie. "That's why I held on so tight to the doll. I'll put it in the manger now."

She took it over, and as he turned to look, she put it in the manger, then came back and slid her arm through his.

"Has anything remarkable happened?" she asked.

"No," said Jim, "unless you count the fact the dragons still haven't left and the Bishop is preaching or something to the people in the stands. None of them have gone—"

He stopped abruptly. The Bishop was no longer talking. Suddenly the people across the field were beginning to flood toward the stage set, and them.

"I was right," said Jim. "I don't like this, Angie. I'm going to send you back to the castle. Get Robert, Enna and the wet nurse or whatever you want and our men-at-arms—Brian, although Brian's here, but at any rate you and Robert; get the horses and any of our men-at-arms you can find and leave for home right away."

"No," said Angie. "I'm going to stay here with you."

The people flooded across the field and stopped in front of them. Then they all knelt, some yards in front of the set, while the Bishop prayed over them, including the Earl and the Prince. Then they stood up again. Jim and Angie waited.

Then, without warning, one strong bass voice began to sing "Good King Wenceslas" and they all took it up.

"Jim!" said Angie. "There's nothing wrong, everything's fine. They're just thanking us. They're just showing how happy they are! Now that everything's all right!"

All of the audience was now singing "Good King Wenceslas"— and from the woods off to their right the dragons chimed in.

The dragons had no idea of tone, and could not sing, although their voices had considerable range. But they were now trying to sing, trying to join in with "Good King Wenceslas" with a sort of sub-sub-bass echo of it . . . and, curiously, it did not clash with the human singing but matched it.

"See, Jim," breathed Angie, "I told you everything was all right. Look! Look up!"

Jim stared at her for a moment and then raised his eyes to the sky. The northern lights were still there, but going across them, causing them to fade into nothingness with its own light, like a comet with a many-colored tail—there was the Phoenix, awake and crossing the sky . . . with his multicolored tail blazing across the heavens and—better late than never—promising great new things to come in a new millennium.

EPILOGUE

"So, you see," said Carolinus to Jim and Angie as they sat in the solar room of the tower at Malencontri—Jim and Angie after a two-day ride home through the snow, with their men-at-arms and the wet nurse; and Carolinus after appearing just a few minutes before in his usual unexpected way—"Magick is both a Craft and an Art."

"I'd come to that conclusion," said Jim warily.

"Good," said Carolinus. "You must never forget that, my boy. Craft and Art, yes. Now, the Craft part can be taught; and it is, as you know, to apprentices and those in the lower ranks. But Art, which earns promotion to the higher ranks, can never be *taught*, it can only be *learned*. This is because Art can be learned only after Craft has been mastered. As a result no two magickians, once they become competent—which is approximately and ordinarily not until they reach A level—work Magick the same way."

He said this last with particular emphasis.

"It is only then," he went on, "that they begin to use their own unique way of doing Magick to explore new frontiers, to blaze new territory. It is so, actually, with all the Arts; but of course Magick is far and away the most important of them."

He paused, took a sip of wine from the glass beside him and looked piercingly at Jim and Angie.

"You follow me?" he said.

"Of course," said Jim. "As far as the Arts go, everybody knows—"

"If you please, Jim," said Carolinus solemnly. "I am trying to instruct you in something."

"Sorry," said Jim.

Carolinus took another sip of wine.

"This experimentation," he went on, "finally begins either with the magickian stumbling across the usefulness of combining two different bits of magical knowledge in a new and different fashion to get a specific result; or finding himself faced with a problem, or a set of problems, that do not seem to have either any solution, or a solution that he finds palatable. By palatable, I mean, the kind of conclusion he would like it to have. As a result he reaches out into the unknown, as it were—into creativity—to produce a different means of solving it than anything in the Necromantick—"

Jim winced, remembering the huge volume of magical lore Carolinus had made him swallow on the occasion of his becoming Carolinus's apprentice. True, Carolinus had shrunk it down until it was hardly bigger than a very tiny pill. But it had felt just as heavy and uncomfortable in his stomach as if it had retained its original size and shape.

"You are not attending, Jim," said Carolinus. "I will go on. He reaches—or she reaches—out into Creativity, as I say; and what does he or she come up with?"

He paused. Jim was tempted to say something, but decided that this was a moment in which he was supposed to sit and merely look expectant. So he did. Angie had evidently already come to that conclusion; she was sitting back and waiting quite pleasantly and patiently.

"He or she," said Carolinus emphatically, "then procures *New Magick*. Magick that no one else has ever accomplished before; but which, now that other magickians know it exists, they in turn can search their own abilities and knowledge for a parallel type of Creativity so they can achieve something like the same end. In other words, New Magick can not be counterfeitable and is priceless."

"I can understand that," said Jim. "But—"

"Jim, you absolutely must get over this habit of interrupting every other word I say," said Carolinus. "Now, where was I? Oh yes. In your case you were faced with a multiplicity of problems. Not only that; but they were a multiplicity of problems that, taken together, threatened to disrupt History for our whole human race, and by implication every living thing in the world."

He stopped and frowned at Jim.

"Quite frankly," he continued, "if there had been someone else in your unusually fitting position to deal with it, some other magickian of the very top rank like myself would have been expected to take care of the matter—and there was no certainty that anyone could take care of it."

"So," said Jim grimly, "you knew from the start it was a tangle!"

"Oh, yes," said Carolinus. "Knew it well before, of course. But there was no stopping it, then. Nothing but Natural forces were involved. The twins had been born Naturally, even if they were something in the way of freaks, even as far as trolls go. Mnrogar had already been in the castle for nearly two thousand years. Agatha Falon had been worming her way into the King of England's attention for some time—all these things were coming together at the Earl's Christmas Party—you understand?"

He looked hard at both Jim and Angie.

"We understand," said Angie.

"I knew you would," said Carolinus. "Now you, Jim, encountered the situation, and the problems, one by one; and to your credit, my boy, you found that taking the easy way out of each particular problem was one that did not suit your taste. For example, it would have solved the destruction, alone—the eventual destruction—of the Earl's castle if the twins had simply been allowed to destroy Mnrogar. They would have never had the courage to take over Mnrogar's den; and somewhere along the line they would have been attacked by a group of trolls fighting together, now that they had set the example of several on one. They would have been killed, eaten, and there would be anarchy in trolldom. Likewise, it would have been simple, merely to lead Agatha Falon to her own destruction."

"I didn't think of any such things," said Jim.

"No, you didn't," said Carolinus, leaning forward. "And it's to your credit, Jim. You have something that I cannot put my tongue to at the moment—a feeling for other people and other creatures that is seldom found in this time and place. At any rate, your way of solving matters not only made Mnrogar's life happier, and incidentally made Agatha Falon more admirable; but dealt with the Earl, the gathering of trolls, the fact that the dragons had completely misread the whole matter of Christmas; and that the general misunderstanding caused by all this could have caused real trouble between them and the human race."

"Thank you," said Jim.

"I'm glad to hear you say that," said Carolinus. "Since now you know why I left you on your own so much to handle things. But it paid to do it—why, you even deserve all the credit for rousing the Phoenix. That much happiness and the prospect of a bright future you ensured, welling up from the earth below, would rouse several Phoenixes, let alone a slugabed like our current one. Would you be interested to know that our present Phoenix was very happy, once he got up and moving?"

"It's about time," said Angie.

"I agree with you, Angie," said Carolinus. But then he paused and his face lost its cheerfulness.

"But," he said, "now we come to an unfortunate matter, Jim. While you did excellently with all the problems that were wished upon you, in an entirely separate other small area you made an unforgivable mistake. You must set that right at once. I'm sorry to tell you so, but this is the case."

There was silence in the solar. Jim and Angie stared at Carolinus.

"Well," said Jim after a moment, "tell me what I'm supposed to have done, then."

Carolinus did.

"Hob-One?" asked Jim, peering as far as he could see into the chimney above the low fire that was barely alit in the serving room fireplace.

There was a pause; and then a familiar little voice answered.

"Yes, m'Lord?"

"Hob—no, you needn't come down," said Jim hastily, as a small face peered, upside down, from under the top edge of the fireplace.

"Very well, m'Lord." The face vanished.

"The fact of the matter is, I have some rather unhappy news for you," Jim said. "I'm afraid an authority higher than mine has corrected me on a certain point; and it affects you. Otherwise, believe me, nothing would be changed for you."

"Changed, m'Lord?"

"I'm afraid so, yes," said Jim. "It seems—in short, I've been told that when I renamed you Hob-One of Malencontri, I violated a certain law that applies to magicians and their dealings with beings belonging to another kingdom. You hobgoblins belong to a different kingdom, of course; and therefore—I'm sorry—I had no right to rename you."

There was a moment's pause, then a little choked sound.

"Wrong, m'Lord?"

"Yes," said Jim grimly. "To make a long story short, you're going to have to be known to all the world, even here in the castle, not as Hob-One de Malencontri, but simply as Hob. Also, I'm afraid, you're going to have to tell any other hobgoblins you spoke to, including the one at the Earl's castle, that you were mistaken about being named something else."

There was a long pause this time.

"Not—Hob-One de Malencontri?" choked the little voice.

"No," said Jim. "I'm sorry, but that's how it has to be."

There was a definite sob from the chimney.

"Now, Lady Angela and myself will go on calling you Hob-One," said Jim hastily. "That's our privilege; and as individuals nobody can take it from us. But it will be just between us and you, unfortunately. It will not be an official name for the world at large."

Another sob.

"If there was any way of avoiding this, Hob-One," said Jim, "believe me, I'd have done it. But there are some times you have to go by the rules. I broke one, and now I must mend it."

"I—I understand, m'Lord."

"I—I'm glad you do," said Jim. "And again, I'm very, very sorry."

"That's all right—m'Lord."

"Maybe some time in the future things can be changed. Anything's possible in the long run."

"Yes—yes, I suppose so, m'Lord. Don't—don't you give it another thought, m'Lord."

"I most certainly will, Hob-One," said Jim. "I will never cease thinking of ways to get you your name back."

"That's good of you, m'Lord."

Jim waited to see if Hob would say anything more, but no other sound came out of the chimney.

"Well then, good night, Hob-One," he said.

"Good night, m'Lord."

"Sleep tight!" said Jim, strongly attempting to get a note of cheerfulness in his voice.

But there was no answer from inside the chimney.